JASON FLEURY

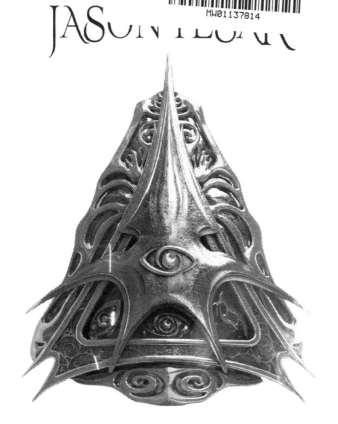

REGENERATION

WANDERING STARS VOLUME FOUR

fourshadow publishing

Quotations from the *Authorized King James Version*, Public Domain, 1611

Quotations from the *Book of Enoch*, Not in Copyright, Translation by R. H. Charles, 1917

Cover design and artwork by Mike Heath | Magnus Creative
www.magnus-creative.com

Maps, diagrams, and page layout by Jason Tesar
www.jasontesar.com

Published by
4shadow, LLC

ISBN-13: 978-1514275276
ISBN-10: 1514275279

ADDITIONAL CONTENTS

... the angels which kept not their first estate, but left their own habitation, he hath reserved in everlasting chains under darkness unto the judgment of the great day ... **wandering stars**, *to whom is reserved the blackness of darkness forever.*[1]

SA 1657

(One year after the Fracturing)

1

Baraquijal's flesh was gone. The fires that came up through the bowels of the earth had turned the floodwaters to vapor, and there was nothing left but his skeleton, gleaming white against the gray soil. The water of the bubbling pool had evaporated months ago, but Ezekiyel could still feel the sweltering air coming up against his face as it left tunnels at the bottom of the crater. He stood at the rim and looked down on the remains of his former master, noting how the hollow eye sockets of the skull were facing up toward the sky.

"He didn't fall in by accident, if that's what you're thinking," said the demon next to him.

Ezekiyel turned, shifting his perspective into the Eternal Realm.

The Seraph's face was a swirling cauldron of shadows, and when he spoke, the darkness parted to allow the light of the red sky to shine through. "He was thrown in."

"How can you be sure?"

"He's lying parallel to the rim," the Seraph explained. "Someone set him here on the edge and rolled him in."

"So he was already dead?"

"Baraquijal wouldn't have permitted his body to be handled in such a way if he had been alive."

Ezekiyel grinned at the absurdity of someone laying their hands on his former master.

"Besides, we had many witnesses at the Fracturing. The seed from Galah was used as a weapon."

"Where is it now?"

"We don't know, but we're searching."

Ezekiyel turned his attention back to the bottom of the crater and let his perspective overlap both realms. "It had to have been Sariel. He stole the seed just before Rameel and Arakiba arrived at the human city. Did anyone see him at the Tree?"

"No," the Seraph replied. "But we reached the same conclusion. No one else would have dared to get so close."

"Well, he obviously survived the flood. It was his proximity to the Tree that saved him; he must have been pulled inside with the rest of us. Though I don't know how he managed to escape our notice."

"Yes, and before that he also killed Vand-ra's handler. The Idnan would very much like to see him suffer for it. If you would like, I can have more resources applied to their tracking effort."

Ezekiyel didn't answer right away. With Baraquijal's death, he was finally free from Marotru authority and control, and any agreements with them from this point forward required careful consideration and planning. Baraquijal's superior had been quick to step in after the murder, sending another Seraph to convey his proposal. Leading Ezekiyel to Baraquijal's body was the Seraph's way of proving how valuable their continued cooperation could be.

"You should know," the Seraph added, filling up the silence with more incentive, "there are survivors—both human and animal. There aren't many, but if you're careful, their numbers can be multiplied. We can lead you to them and help you rebuild. After all, what is the use of being the god of your own world if there is nothing to rule over?"

The earth trembled beneath his feet and Ezekiyel turned from the crater to look out across the landscape, desolate in both realms. In the Temporal, patches of green were beginning to sprout up in the crevices of the lower elevations where the water had flowed. At the higher elevation where he stood, black rock and gray soil had been pushed up from the depths of the earth to form a mountain range. It was a new world, bleak, yet regenerating itself from the corpse of the previous one. How long would the process take? Hundreds of years? Thousands? If humans were out there somewhere, Ezekiyel and the others would eventually find them. But is that what they really wanted—another world full of humans? It was certainly what the Marotru wanted, for humans were critical to their strategy for invading the Temporal Realm. But the Myndarym were no longer required to obey the Marotru. They were free.

A new world, indeed! Ezekiyel mused. The Myndarym were in a unique position, one with leverage. He considered the offer, along with everything else the Seraph had told him, and came to a conclusion.

"I'll speak with the others about what you're proposing."

The Seraph's passive gaze became direct. "I can have their spirits assigned under your authority."

Ezekiyel smiled. Such was the first instinct of the Marotru. "No, the Myndarym will choose for themselves."

"As you wish."

* * * *

THE IN-BETWEEN

"Baraquijal admitted to us in Sedekiyr that he had experimented with human inhabitation," Satarel pointed out.

"Yes. And now we know that those experiments have become the hope of the Marotru," Ezekiyel explained.

The Myndarym were gathered around him, not in their bodily forms or even in their spirits, but in some other, purer form that only existed here between worlds. As they had learned to do in those long moments while the Temporal Realm reached a state of equilibrium, they now projected their thoughts to one another. They did so freely, without fear of being overheard by the Marotru. The In-Between was a place separated from the other existences they had known—which made it the perfect meeting place. After learning that Pardeya and the other cities had been destroyed, each of the Myndarym had returned to the Tree of Wisdom. It was a common reference point among the worlds, the only *known* within each of the *unknowns*, drawing them toward each other as steadily as gravity. Their return brought them all in contact with one another, making it apparent that there were only three worlds instead of the ten they had intended to create.

Now that the sharing of observations had passed, Ezekiyel could see that the In-Between was becoming a crutch for their fears. In the last year, no one had ventured back out into their worlds more than a few days away from the stump. Until now, there had been nowhere else to go and no purpose in leaving. The information from the Seraph would change that, and was already doing so.

"The former Nephiylim were too stubborn and powerful for their wills to be dominated," Ezekiyel continued. "And we all know what miserable failures the latter Nephiylim turned out to be. Humans have apparently survived the flooding, and the Marotru desire our cooperation in reestablishing the Temporal Realm with humans at the center of it."

"The way I see it, we have three options," Danel replied. "We can defy the Marotru and go our own way."

"We don't need their assistance, or their interference," Satarel agreed.

"But part of us exists where they rule," Rameel argued, turning his attention back to Ezekiyel for confirmation.

"That's correct. The consequence is that the Marotru will most certainly try to exert their authority over our demonic spirits to influence and control us. Though we are no longer under their direct authority, I think life for us would become nothing more than a battle of wills. We would likely be drained of all motivation and creativity. We would lose our focus for anything else we might want to achieve."

"That is ... if the Marotru made such an operation their priority," Satarel replied. "Which I doubt."

A short lull in the conversation allowed Danel to continue with her reasoning. "The other extreme is to submit ourselves to their authority."

"I don't like that," Rameel answered quickly.

"None of us do," Kokabiel added. "To submit ourselves is to lose control of the very thing that drew us to this realm—freedom."

Zaquel's pride swelled up before her projected thoughts even made their way to everyone gathered. "We've already suffered under Semjaza's leadership, and it was hardly any different with Baraquijal. Both of them were obstructions to our common goal."

Ezekiyel smiled inwardly at this. Though he was clearly leading the Myndarym, they didn't interpret it as such. By bringing this decision to them, it provided the opportunity for everyone to approach it as equals. Whatever resolution came from this meeting would have the backing of all the Myndarym from the start.

"The third option is to find something between defiance and submission," Danel concluded.

Ezekiyel waited for someone else to jump in, and when no one did, he decided it was time to begin making his case. "The position in which we find ourselves is more agreeable than any in the past. Other than what the Evil One did to the first humans, the Marotru hold no rightful claim over the Temporal Realm. Therefore, it is we who have the leverage in this negotiation. I propose that we consider what all of us would like to achieve and compare that with what the Marotru want to achieve. Perhaps there are some overlapping areas of cooperation?"

"What are their goals for us again?" Armaros asked.

"To oversee the replenishment of the human population in each world. Then we are to subjugate that human population with multiple types of control. Physically, of course, but also their mental development as well as their spiritual inclinations. There can be nothing left for the Amatru to get hold of. And then we are to develop and advance their culture and technology. Again, this involves multiple levels of control. Militarily. Economically. But whether we take an active or passive role is up to us."

"How do these pursuits help the Marotru?" Armaros wondered.

Ezekiyel appreciated Armaros' direct way of thinking. "Ultimately, what do the Marotru want? They want to destroy the Holy One and His Amatru. The fact that humans have survived the flooding is proof that the Holy One is up to something, and humans are obviously at the center of it. We all know that He has favored them from the beginning. The Temporal Realm and humans are both critical to the Amatru, so controlling them will become pivotal at some point in time. Now, we have access to these humans and thereby a way to inflict pain upon the Holy One. That is what we have to offer."

"But is that what we want ... to help the Marotru?" Arakiba asked.

"Only because it helps us achieve what we want," Kokabiel replied.

Ezekiyel smiled; his former protégé was seeing the connection.

"Do all of you realize what has happened here?" Kokabiel continued. "Until now, there have only ever been two sides— Amatru and Marotru. We have ascended to become a third side in this conflict."

"I care not about sides," Arakiba replied. "I only want to rule as a god."

"Yes, but is that goal even attainable while the Holy One and the Evil One are alive?" Armaros asked.

The question hung in the space between realms while each considered it carefully. Finally, Zaquel was the one to answer, "No, it's not. Each one seeks total victory."

"So what are you proposing?" Armaros asked.

But Ezekiyel didn't have to answer. Others were already recognizing what had to be done.

"That we help the weaker of the two," Danel replied. "Bring this conflict to a swift end."

"Let them destroy each other," Satarel realized.

"And we will be the only ones left when it's done," Rameel added, projecting a great deal of pleasure with this strategy.

Ezekiyel allowed the conversation to go quiet for a moment before he led their thoughts toward his conclusion. "Then, and only then, will we truly be gods. Free to remake the Temporal Realm as we see fit. And the other realm, if we so desire."

A long moment of silence passed as each Myndar considered the magnitude of what they were agreeing to.

Finally, Danel broke the silence. "In the meantime, what do the Marotru have to offer us?"

"They are steadily gaining control of the Borderlands," Ezekiyel replied. "Because part of our existence is there, the information and power they possess can be accessible to us. Just as they could become a hindrance if we don't comply, they could also help us if we are allies. And they also know where the surviving humans and animals ended up, so we can begin rebuilding our worlds immediately. I, for one, am eager to get started."

"Is there anything else that they expect of us?" Armaros wondered.

"Nothing that hasn't already been implied. Of course, we are not to produce any more Nephiylim; they would only threaten the human civilizations that we will build. And they would like us to agree not to cross over into each other's worlds. They want each one to grow without the influence of the others, in order that we might all develop unique resources and achieve the broadest realization of success. I believe that at some point they will want us to pool our resources in the fight against the Amatru. But for now, such an agreement will provide stability. However, this is one area where I would like to assert our leverage over the Marotru for a time."

The collective interest of the group was piqued at this statement.

"Baraquijal's death has emphasized two weaknesses that might later affect us. The first is that Sariel is out there somewhere, and he is clearly capable of doing us harm. The

Marotru will help us find him, but at the moment, passage between realms is unrestricted. The search area is just too large, and we lack the ability to even contain him to a single world. It would be wise to change this, and I believe I have a way to do it. It will require all of us to cooperate with each other in searching for the fractured pieces of the Tree of Wisdom ... which brings me to the next of our weaknesses. Sariel used the seed from Galah to kill Baraquijal. As we all know from the size and scope of the *naming* required to fracture the Tree, it has no physical equal in this realm. The seed and all remaining pieces of the Tree would be just as strong. They could be used against us as weapons, and there would be nothing we could do to defend against them. Therefore, it is critical that we locate everything that came from the Tree."

"This would be easier if we spread evenly among the worlds," Arakiba pointed out. It was something that he had brought up several times in the past year, and he was clearly not done arguing about it. "Rameel and Zaquel could use some assistance."

It was true that their world only had two Myndarym, while the others had at least three. But Ezekiyel suspected that Arakiba also wanted to remain close to Rameel, as they had been for centuries while serving under Baraquijal. This had to be his motivation, because he wasn't insisting that Ezekiyel relocate to that world, as some of the others had previously suggested. Every time this argument came up, it always ended with frustration all around.

Ezekiyel decided to end it once and for all. "Have you forgotten that it was I who realized Baraquijal was gone? I was the one who discovered that there are only three worlds. I am the one who has been travelling among them to figure out what went wrong. Because of this, I have not had a home or time to do anything except what is in all our best interests."

He wanted to add that it was he to whom the Marotru came with their proposal, but such a comment would only make him seem more like Semjaza, a prideful oppressor, which he wanted to avoid. "You all made your choices. You should take responsibility for them."

There was an awkward silence until Kokabiel asked, "Have you made your choice, then?"

Turel, who had been silent throughout the meeting, suddenly projected his thoughts. "Danel and I believe that Ezekiyel's goals align quite well with ours. We have invited him to join us, and he has accepted."

Arakiba's anger was palpable, but he didn't direct it toward any specific thoughts that the group could interpret. The relief from Zaquel and Rameel was equally felt, providing a balance to the emotional state of the meeting. But it was still painfully clear to Ezekiyel that there was a great deal of potential for conflict among the Myndarym. He had a double motive for wanting to find the seed from the Tree of Wisdom. Not only was it critical to controlling passage between the realms—if his suspicions were correct—but it also held the possibility of creating new realms. Realms that were altogether outside of Amatru or Marotru jurisdiction and influence. In the end, when the Evil One and the Holy One destroy each other, the seed is what would allow everything to begin anew. Perhaps that new creation would give the needed separation between the Myndarym, or perhaps Ezekiyel would have all realms to himself.

"Shall I accept the Marotru proposal?" he asked.

Danel and Turel were the first to agree, and the rest began adding their approvals until only Arakiba was left. "So be it," he replied.

"Very well. I will inform them," Ezekiyel said. "Let us each go now to our worlds and begin working toward our future success. I will check in with each of you from time to time."

SA 2169

2

The rain was slow and steady. A gray sky loosed its burden upon the land, easing it down as gently as it could. The land drank up the moisture, absorbing it before it had the chance to collect and flood. It felt as though the earth were cautious, as one healing from a great wound. And indeed it was—a wound greater than any since this realm had separated from the Eternal. The earth had already made much progress. The trembling of the ground that was nearly constant in the early days had finally calmed. Whatever need it had been crying out for had eventually been pacified. There was still the occasional mountain of fire, belching its dark smoke into the air while rivers of molten rock slid down its sides. But sightings of those were becoming fewer and farther between.

Sariel reclined beneath a large tree, taking refuge under the shelter of its foliage. The dry patch of soft grass cushioned his body, and the sound of the rain lulled him into a peaceful trance. There were others all around him, towering spectacles of plant life, drinking up the nutrients that the falling moisture brought to their roots. In the absence of company, the plants and trees had become his companions. Sariel watched through the haze of gray as the grasses of the meadow dipped and bowed with each droplet that landed upon them. He couldn't help but smile. It was as if they were speaking with the sky—a conversation without words.

Sariel lay back upon the grass and closed his eyes. It was midday, but this body was tired and in need of rest. Whether the sun was above or below the horizon didn't matter; the age of following such practices had almost passed from his memory. Besides, resting one body would give more strength and attention to the others who were still exploring. Sariel now had one self in each of the worlds, and none of them had found so much as a footprint after that first day to indicate where any of the Myndarym had gone. It would happen eventually, he was sure. But there was no telling how long it would take.

First Earth. First self. Southeast of the Tree.

Repeating what little he knew helped keep his thinking oriented. He thought of this Earth as the first, since it was the one he had come into after the Fracturing. From that point of reference, the Second Earth was the next one downstream in the flow of the In-Between. He thought of his selves in this manner also, in order to distinguish between them, as one might do in thinking about his right arm as separate from his left. And then there was direction. The stump that remained of the Tree of Wisdom was the only physical landmark common to all worlds. There wasn't much use in paying attention to distances, for he could spend all day getting across a narrow river or just a few moments to cross a wide meadow. The direction from the Tree was primary, helping him know where he had searched and where he hadn't. Though there was still far more of the latter than the former. Each Earth was impossibly large.

For quite some time after the Fracturing, Sariel had attempted to record the cycles of the moon and sun. But such an undertaking required him to stay in one place in order to mark the passage of time on the trunk of a tree or some other object. This interfered with his desire to find the Myndarym, and so he gave up on it. However, what he had managed to learn in that time was that the annual movements of the sun had become more drastic. Instead of rising and setting in the same relative places along the east and west horizons, the sun now moved farther north and south throughout the year. Before the Fracturing, there had been only slight differences in the temperature between the summer and winter months, or between higher and lower elevations. Now, there was a great deal of variation between these things, the Fracturing having caused extremes. Along with the moisture that now collected in the air, this produced all manner of weather conditions that had never existed in the past.[2] And where there was no moisture, vast expanses of dry and hot land had come into being. The opposite of this was displayed by the oceans, seemingly infinite stretches of water that made the seas of the old world small by comparison. These new reservoirs gave their moisture to the sky, and in turn received the moisture back again through the collection of rain into rivers. It was an endless cycle that still managed to feed the trees and plants. Though it was very different from the mist that used to come up from the ground, this new method had now become just as familiar to Sariel. It was like seeing the oldest of friends change dramatically, only to learn that she was really the same person you always thought her to be.

A strange noise stood out against the rain, causing Sariel's eyes to suddenly open. He listened carefully to the drizzle, wondering if he had imagined it. Then it happened again, a soft whistle that lasted only a brief moment.

Sariel sat up and looked out across the field of grass. His eyes searched but failed to find anything to account for this new sound. And yet, it wasn't entirely new. There was something familiar about it, as if he had once heard it in a dream.

Am I dreaming it now?

It came again, sounding from the branches above him.

Sariel climbed slowly to his feet, feeling an overwhelming need for caution. Not because he feared anything, but because the moment might pass if he was reckless. He wasn't sure where this feeling came from; it was nothing he understood on a conscious level. It seemed as if his body realized something that his mind didn't yet comprehend.

He crawled out from beneath the lower branches and stood, letting the rain soak his clothing of woven grasses. Whatever produced this new sound was worth the cold that his skin would experience later in the day. He looked up, carefully inspecting the shadows beneath each leafy bough. He stepped quietly to one side and continued the search, hoping for the sound to repeat.

It happened again, and his eyes went instantly to it, recognizing a small brown body sitting atop a branch, with green leaves behind it. The bird's head pivoted suddenly. Then the creature noticed Sariel and took to the air with a rapid flurry of wings. It flew north, and after only a few seconds, it was gone. It was only a small bird, something that would have gone unnoticed in the old world, but this encounter felt to Sariel as one of the most important in all his life. As he stood in the field, looking north, his tears mingled with the rain spilling down his face. The bird was more majestic and beautiful than any other he could remember. The only living creatures he'd seen since the Fracturing were insects, and even those were somewhat rare.

How could it have survived?

SA 3718

3

Sariel pulled at the edges of his cloak and tied it around himself. The wind was picking up, and the fluttering cloth was making it difficult to see the ground below him. Loose rock and patches of snow created many obstacles to navigate. Though he was making good progress in coming down from the heights above, finding safe footing still required concentration. The cold wind brought white flurries that beat against the side of his face, clinging to his long beard or melting if they were able to touch the warmth of his skin. The temperature was dropping quickly, but wasn't cold enough to warrant using the hood of his cloak. For now he left it down, letting the long strands of his white hair flail about his head and neck.

As Sariel descended, the terrain underfoot slowly transitioned to soft grass that was not yet pale. This became the dominant feature of the land, running in wide paths down the mountain with ridges of gray rock on both sides like the old walls of a city. The wind grew calm, and Sariel was able to look out upon the lower elevations. Though the skies were gray, the view reminded him of being in Aleydiyr where he could see above the mist, all the way to the horizon. But he dared not allow his memories to go beyond that; there was no cure for the pain that waited for him there.

Sariel stopped walking and breathed deeply of the cold air, letting it refresh his skin and lungs. The flakes of snow were smaller than before, and there were fewer of them. It was still early in the fall season, but he could imagine how cold it would be in the dead of winter. The grass around him would be covered in white, filling up the areas between the ridges of rock.

Sariel turned and looked at the wall of stone beside him, imagining how far up the snow might pile. The wall was more than three times his height, and as soon as his eyes met the rock, he realized that this was no natural formation. Along the sloped bank, bands of a lighter color stretched up to the top like columns. In some areas, these bands stuck out from the wall, denser than the darker, eroded stone around them. Sariel glanced up and down the slope, realizing that the columns were arranged at regular intervals. They looked like the ribcage of a deceased animal, but one that was far larger than any he had seen before.

Downslope, the wall of stone grew shorter and eventually disappeared into the ground. Sariel followed it in that direction, heading for a rise on the other side of the wall. He wanted to view this unusual sight from a different perspective and hopefully make sense of it. But when he reached the end of the wall and turned, he saw another in the distance, which mirrored the first. As he walked across the rise between them, he turned to look upslope.

These are not the remains of a creature!

The walls paralleled each other, widening to where they intersected another that was perpendicular to them. This other wall was the highest point of the whole structure. Beyond that, the walls narrowed until they converged at a point. Sariel quickly turned around and looked at the other end of the walls, noticing again how they did not meet, but simply ended. One end was blunt, the other sharp.

This is the stern, and that is the bow, he thought, turning again to look upslope. "It's a boat!"

The words sounded awkward in his ears; it had been so long since they had heard anything beyond the sounds of nature. But the realization was one that couldn't be confined to just his thoughts. The intermediate walls that ran perpendicular he now recognized as the internal supports. The outer walls were the petrified remains of the hull. It appeared that the whole structure had been under the earth and only recently exposed to the open air. A boat implied humans. Possibly even survivors. And this boat was many times larger than the ones he had seen in the old world—those that Ezekiyel had built in Senvidar. If there had indeed been survivors, this boat could have held hundreds, perhaps even a thousand.[3]

As the wind began picking up again, bringing more snowflakes along with it, Sariel lifted his eyes to the peak of the mountain and then turned to let his gaze sweep from horizon to horizon.

Perhaps I am not alone after all.

SA 4224

4

The sun shone brightly through a clear sky, the heat reflecting off the dirt in waves that distorted the horizon. A simple hat of loosely woven strands of grass kept the sunlight off Sariel's face and shoulders, but it couldn't prevent the sweat that clung to his skin. The heat wouldn't relent until the evening came, and his body would continue to lose moisture.

There were still areas where water collected below the soil. The sparse vegetation that seemed to grow in clusters all around this area was evidence of that. When the sun dropped below the horizon, he would find a place to stop for the night and begin digging for water, as he had done countless times before.

Topping a rise in the terrain, the ocean came into view once again on his left. Sariel stopped to admire the shimmering spectacle. He'd been paralleling the coastline for months now, occasionally wandering away from it when the terrain required or when he noticed a grove of fruit trees. But the water was always a welcome sight when he returned. The vastness of the ocean was remarkable; the thought that most of it used to be found throughout the earth in subterranean chambers and caverns only made this world feel even more mysterious. What else had changed? What other secrets waited to be discovered?

Sariel's eyes followed the stretch of sand near the waterline and came upon something to the north that made his heart lurch inside his chest—dozens of white cubes dotted the landscape. He immediately dropped to the ground and hid himself. His breath came out in quick puffs as if he had just exerted himself. Through long blades of grass in front of his face, Sariel inspected the cubes in the distance and noted that their sides fluttered in the breeze.

Tents!

Farther to the north, something floated in the shallows. It was long and pale, looking like a giant insect, with numerous wings that rose gracefully into the air. Others stuck out from its sides, gently touching the water as it swelled and abated. The translucent wings also caught the light of the sun and reflected it, flashing white one moment and a rainbow of colors the next.

Now that Sariel was looking in that direction, he realized that there were more of these floating objects gathered in deeper water. The glare of the sun from the ocean surface made it difficult to see them, but when he shielded his eyes and looked between his fingers, he could make out several more arranged in a floating circle. And then he noted dozens of tiny silhouettes moving across the body of the insect.

They're boats ... and people!

Sariel was at once fascinated and terrified. He wanted to believe that he had happened upon human survivors. But there was something about the vessels that told him this couldn't be the case. They didn't look like anything humans would build. There was a sophistication to their form that hinted at some other origin.

Are they Myndarym?

It couldn't be. There were far too many of them, though he wasn't close enough to be sure. This led him to the obvious conclusion that he would have to move closer. Sariel slowly turned his head and began studying the terrain around him. There was a high plateau to the northeast that would provide a better vantage point. He would need to keep low between the clumps of grass and mounds of sand in order to reach it without being spotted. And it was a long way off for what would need to be a crawl. There would be no quick solution to this dilemma.

Sariel's heart was still pounding. His body had evidently forgotten who he was and the things he'd done in his former lives. But his mind had quickly adapted to this strange new situation. It was the most exciting thing that had occurred since the Fracturing, and he wasn't about to ruin it by panicking or rushing to find his answer.

Surely you've learned patience by now! Go slowly. Go carefully. They don't look to be leaving anytime soon.

* * * *

FAR SOUTH OF THE TREE
FIRST EARTH

The tall grass was bent over in multiple places beneath the shelter of the trees. It might have been a weather-related occurrence except for the fact that Sariel had been following a trail through the fields for almost a week, and had already found several prints from a cloven hoof. The sight of animal droppings around the area confirmed that this location had served as a bedding place for a small herd of mammals.

The chirping that he heard in the surrounding forest was now a common part of the landscape. Animals had most certainly survived the flooding, though he wasn't sure how. Perhaps a few had managed to cling to floating debris, or had fled to a mountain taller than the water had reached—though the height and violence of the waves that Sariel had seen coming into Aden made such an idea seem impossible. Perhaps they had been aboard a boat, like the one he had found on the mountain slope in Second Earth. If that had been the case, it would make their survival an intentional action by someone. And not only an intentional action, but one that was planned in advance. Sariel could think of no human other than Enoch who had ever been allowed a glimpse into future events, which indicated that if there were indeed human survivors, Enoch's descendants might possibly be among them.

Of course, a boat could have been constructed by the Myndarym, but all of them were present in Aden for the Fracturing. And Sariel doubted that the Myndarym even realized what would happen to the earth as a result of dividing the Tree of Wisdom. Nephiylim might have constructed a vessel to escape the coming floods, but they weren't the creations of the Holy One, so it seemed unlikely that any of them would have heard His voice. Which only led back to the question—who else but the Holy One would have known the floods were coming?[4]

All of these thoughts were nothing more than speculations. But the fact that birds could now be found flitting from one tree to the next, and a herd of mammals could be found bedding down for the night beneath the shelter of a tree, was very encouraging, to say the least. Sariel had been alone for so many years now that just the thought of having a conversation with someone brought him to tears.

* * * *

IDORANA (EYE OF THE SUN)
THE CAPITAL CITY OF THE RANA EMPIRE
EAST OF THE TREE
FIRST EARTH

"Describe it to me," Zaquel said quietly, looking down from the raised platform where she sat. She didn't have to raise her voice; her throne room was silent but for the distant trickling of water. The stone walls behind her were angled in such a way that her voice was projected forward.

Zaquel's chief priestess stood at the bottom of the steps. Her skin was the color of the darkest earth, like her goddess, stark against the pure white fabric of her robes. But she was merely human—an imitation of *Mwangu Rana*, the Goddess of the Sun, whom she worshipped and served. The priestess whispered the words of the goddess in a foreign tongue, translating it for the explorer who knelt beside her.

The pale-skinned man was trembling. His long, blond hair hung in clumps from his bowed head. When he turned to reply to the priestess, it clung to the sweat on his face. His words were barely above a whisper, indicating that he understood what was expected of him. He kept his head downward, forbidden to look directly upon the goddess.

The priestess waited patiently as the explorer's description came out in a long series of harsh, clipped sounds. Then she turned and translated the words for Zaquel. "My goddess, he says it was dark. It sparkled like the moonlight upon the ocean."

"How big was it?"

The priestess translated the question, and the explorer answered quickly. The priestess was apparently unsatisfied with what she heard and asked the question in a different way. When the man replied, the priestess was silent for a moment.

"My goddess, I believe he is trying to compare it to the size of a ship, but not the one he uses to sail upon the ocean."

Zaquel inhaled deeply, feeling the cool air of the temple calm her frustration. Had she been outside, under the oppressive heat of the sun, she might have done something rash. But her temple was set deep into the sands of the earth, where the soil was cool. She lifted her gaze to the ceiling and stared at the brilliant shafts of light that streamed down from the ventilation holes. The sunlight was so intense compared to the darkness inside the throne room that the shafts of light looked almost as substantial as the wide columns that upheld the ceiling.

"Can he draw it?" Zaquel asked.

The priestess relayed the message and received a quick answer. "Yes, my goddess."

"Bring a drawing table," Zaquel commanded, louder than before.

All around the perimeter of the room, men stood at attention with spears upright. Her guards were barefoot, wearing only white loincloths and no adornments of any kind. The one closest to the door, opposite from Zaquel's throne, turned and ran out of the room. When he returned, it was with two more guards who were struggling to carry a wooden box filled with sand.

They sidestepped the long, rectangular pool at the center of the room and carried their burden between the water and the engraved columns.

As they neared, the chief priestess motioned with her hand to indicate where the guards should set the table. The golden bracelets around her wrists jingled like instruments in the quiet room. The guards placed the sand table before the kneeling man and backed away with their heads down. As they retreated, the priestess whispered some instructions to the explorer.

The man brushed aside his lank hair and picked up the golden writing implement from the smooth sand, his finger and thumb leaving dimples upon the surface of white grains. With one hand, he pulled back the loose sleeve of his leather tunic while the other began dragging the golden stick through the sand. At first, he made long, wavy strokes that ran the length of the table. Then he began making short, rapid marks at one end.

Zaquel stood from her throne to get a better view.

The guards around the room, as well as the priestess, went to their knees. If the room had been quiet before, it was silent now. Even the water in the long pool seemed to calm itself at the movement of its goddess.

The explorer finished his rendering and laid the golden stick upon the sand, backing away on hands and knees as he lowered his forehead to the floor.

On the stone platform of her throne and wearing her Myndar form, Zaquel towered above her subjects. Their posture showed obedience, but Zaquel could also feel the fear in their hearts. Their minds lay open to her, thoughts as transparent as water. And she was pleased with what she found.

She descended the cold steps, moving so gracefully upon bare feet that she appeared to float downward. On either side of the stairs were two men, held by metal collars and chains. They went everywhere the goddess went, as a reminder of who held the power in this empire. They had already been kneeling, but now they turned outward and faced the walls to ensure that their eyes never fell upon their goddess. Zaquel floated between them and came before the drawing table. When she looked down, she saw the likeness of a tree. Its long trunk was without foliage, twisted as though it had been wound together with something else that was now missing. Near the top, branches extended outward in only one direction—a lopsided canopy of leafless limbs.

Zaquel smiled. *At last, I have found it!*

"You will go with my soldiers," she told the explorer in his own language, now too impatient to bother with a translator. "They will sail at your direction. You will take them to the place where you found this tree, and if they do not find what you have described, you will pay with your life."

5

Sariel laid down his walking stick and lowered his exhausted body to the ground. The small cave wasn't as comfortable as some places he'd slept, but it offered a break from the wind. He'd been traveling across a rugged landscape of wide, treeless valleys. The mountains that could be seen along the horizon in every direction were so far away that it was difficult to tell if he was making any progress at all. The cold wind that howled constantly in his ears had swept the land clean of anything but the shortest and most stubborn of grasses. When the rains came, charging across the valleys like an army of mystical creatures, the wind became frigid and unbearable. Fortunately, the weather had been tolerable for a few months now.

Sariel was grateful to have somewhere quiet, away from the incessant howling, to lay his head. It was more of a hollow than a cave, a place where the river had eroded the bank during its higher season when the snows were melting. Now the river was only a small stream, and the soft trickle of water was a welcome sound, despite its constancy.

Outside the hollow, the opposite bank of the river was bathed in the pale light of a declining sun. There were still a few hours of sunlight left in the day, but Sariel had gone as far as he wanted to. His feet were aching, and they needed a long night of rest if they were going to serve him again tomorrow. With his back against an earthen incline, he pulled his foot closer and began probing the tender skin beneath the wrappings of grass. The bottom of his foot was likely blistered, but he couldn't tell if there was any blood. He didn't want to unwrap his makeshift sandals because he wouldn't be able to put them together again, and there wasn't anything in these lands to use as a replacement. Tree bark made for an uncomfortable sole, but the thought of using animal hide now seemed like such a waste of precious life. That is, it would have been if there were any animals at all to use. He hadn't seen any signs of life since he'd found the remains of the boat. And even that discovery now seemed like something from a dream, a relic of a different age. He'd found no birds, no migrating mammals in this earth. Only the occasional fish swimming up a stream.

It was possible that the survivors in this world had died shortly after the floodwaters abated. Or perhaps they had perished while still inside their floating refuge. Whatever subtle differences had existed between the worlds following the moment of fracturing had become exaggerated since then. Each Earth had taken its own course, and Sariel was aware that he might never find anything worth discovering in this one.

Worth discovering, or worth killing? he asked himself.

When he had made the decision to split up his selves among the three worlds, he had been motivated by revenge. He wanted the Myndarym to pay for what they had done—to pay with their lives. He had wanted to seek them out wherever they could be found, but finding them had proven to be quite a challenge. Over the years, Sariel's thirst for revenge had dissipated. And then years turned to decades, and decades to centuries. He wasn't exactly sure how much time had passed since the Fracturing, but he felt certain that it had been longer than his time in the Temporal Realm before the Fracturing. Somewhere along the way, he had begun looking not for the Myndarym as much as the regeneration of the earth. He wanted to see its waters teeming with life and its forests sheltering creatures of every imaginable sort. The chirp of a bird in First Earth had brought him such joy and relief that it seemed to have overshadowed any thoughts of revenge. Now, what he wanted above all else was simply to know that humankind had not perished.

And if they haven't, what then?

"Then ... I'll know that all of my wandering will not have been in vain," he whispered. It had been so long since he'd spoken aloud that the movement of his lips felt awkward.

So you seek them to regain a sense of purpose?

"No," he argued. "I already have a purpose."

Which is what?

"To protect them."

From the Myndarym? Are you even capable of that anymore?

Though his demon had been conquered long ago—so long that he had forgotten its name and lacked the desire to recall it—Sariel still felt as though he had another being living inside him. Whatever negative associations there were with that feeling, they weren't strong enough to dismiss the question. If he ever did find human survivors, the inevitable conclusion was that their interests were still opposed to those of the Myndarym. Eventually, he would find himself in conflict again.

Are you prepared?

Sariel considered the question very carefully. He allowed his thoughts to wander back through the ages of conflict he'd survived in the Eternal Realm. Friends lost. Enemies defeated. Tactics refined. Over and over again. Then there was the Temporal Realm. Fellow soldiers of the old realm had become the enemies of the new. Alliances were redefined. New enemies arose. More friends were lost. And on it went until the oldest of all enemies had become part of him, had saved him.

Semjaza, Azael, Yendarmal ... Baraquijal. Sariel's thoughts finally settled on his last confrontation, which had ended many centuries ago. The Myndar, inhabited by a Seraph, had been able to exert force upon the Temporal Realm without the aid of demonic underlings. And from the information he had gathered about the other Myndarym before that confrontation, it seemed that Baraquijal's servants also had the same ability.

How?

If Sariel ever hoped to defeat the remaining Myndarym, he would have to find the answer to this question. The orange light illuminating the opposite bank of the river was now a red glow. With the sun touching the western horizon, Sariel stretched out his body on the dirt floor of the cave and set his mind to the task. But sleep pulled at him, begging him to give in. Other thoughts distracted him so that he didn't make any progress until after the sky had grown completely dark. Only then did he remember that Shapers possessed the ability to affect the Temporal Realm by using their *songs*. If that was possible, which he knew to be a fact, then there had to be some sort of a connection between the realms. Some way of affecting one with the other.

But Baraquijal wasn't singing!

At least, not at first. Before the clawed weapons had taken shape at the end of Baraquijal's fingers, the Seraph had come at Sariel with nothing more than a beating of his wings. The result had been a wave of sand that had thrown Sariel across the tunnel.

Movement!

Was it possible to affect the Temporal Realm with movement instead of sound? Could Vinlagid—a Song of Force—be generated with a gesture? Or better yet ... a Song of Unmaking?

* * * *

SOUTH OF THE TREE
SECOND EARTH

Armaros pushed the dense foliage aside and stepped down onto the muddy riverbank, his bare feet squishing into the soil. The rain that had been falling for days without end felt cool against his sweating body. He lifted his face to the gray skies and let the shower wash him clean. Voices and movement behind him indicated that the rest of his tribesmen had caught up, but he paid them no attention. He accepted the moment of refreshment before turning his attention to the river. The shallow waters below were clouded with the ruddy earth that was constantly being washed to the lowest places of the terrain. Scanning the length of the river, what was visible between the thick foliage of the jungle on both sides, Armaros located a tangle of debris restricting the flow only a few hundred paces downstream.

Without waiting for his fellow hunters, he bounded down the riverbank, leaping from place to place like a creature of the forest. Then he paralleled the flow, following the water's edge until he reached the pile of brush and timbers that had caught upon something in the middle of the river. He set out into the flow, using his spear as an upstream support. The water climbed up his calves and then past his knees. By the time he reached the pile of debris, he was thigh-deep in the muddy river. Driving his spear into the riverbed so it wouldn't be lost, he proceeded to pull away long strands of rotting vines that had collected.

Upriver, dozens of his tribesmen were exiting the forest and coming down the bank. They wore loincloths of thin animal hide and various parts of their bodies were pierced with animal bones. Their hair was black. And their skin was the color of the red soil beneath their feet—a natural camouflage against their surroundings. Though Armaros' tanned skin was many shades lighter than theirs, setting him apart, he had earned the respect of the tribe by his ferocity and wisdom. He taught them not to fear the beasts of the forest, but to hunt them and steal their power. Their flesh was food. Their skin was clothing. Their bones and teeth—weapons to hunt yet more beasts. The jungle people followed him out of respect, which was a very different motivator from any he'd used in the past. In his view, humans were far better subjects than the Nephiylim of the old world had ever been.

The debris was removed in layers of increasing weight. First the vines and brush were set loose to drift downriver. This was followed by branches with rotting leaves still attached. Then came thicker tree trunks. Piece by piece, Armaros worked at the pile until the human hunters caught up with him and lent their hands to the task. In less than an hour, the pile had been cleared enough to see what had caused it to collect in the first place.

"Wait," he announced, noticing something that sparkled in the shadows. He climbed farther into the debris and heaved a log away from the pile, exposing a thin branch sticking up above the surface. It was only as thick as his pinky finger, and should have been snapped easily by the weight of the logs resting upon it. But this branch was from a different sort of tree. It was as dark as the night sky and glittered as if the stars were contained within it.

Armaros reached out and set his hand upon the smooth, glassy surface. It was colder than the water. He let his fingers trace its shape, following the thin branch down under the water where it converged with another that was just a bit thicker. At last, he'd found the Tree fragment just where the Marotru had said it would be. They had all been looking for so many centuries, but when Ezekiyel had found the one in his world, it had helped the search effort. Then Zaquel had located the one in her world, which made the last piece that much easier to find.

"Its beauty has no equal!" one of the hunters exclaimed.

"We have found it!" another yelled.

The rest of the tribesmen cheered.

Armaros let go of the branch and backed away into the water. His people moved forward to fill the void, swarming over the pile of debris with renewed vigor. Their voices became a chatter of excited conversation, and Armaros let them have their fun. His own excitement would have to wait. Already, his mind was focused on the logistics of how they would accomplish the unearthing of the fractured piece.

The river will have to be diverted, he realized immediately. Without an abundance of rocks in the area, this task would likely be quite difficult. *And then the tribe will have to acquaint themselves with digging.*

* * * *

Sariel's new vantage point was higher than the last and much closer to the sea. He had the peak of a sand dune behind him, which would keep his silhouette from being noticed against the blue sky. He lay on the sand, watching the ocean from inside a thicket of pale brush. The prickly vegetation offered shade for most of the day except when the sun was directly overhead. And when the sun went down, he would be able to leave his hiding place to find food and water.

Now that he was able to conduct proper surveillance, he counted twenty-one tents of cubical shape, made from pure white fabric that had been stretched over a rigid framework. It was a camp, and judging by the sophistication of the boats, it was only a temporary one.

The people walking the decks of the ships were clothed only from the waist down, with pants of flowing white fabric that swayed in the breeze just like their tents. They were tall—not as large as Nephiylim, but certainly much taller than humans. All were male, and each of them had a muscular physique. They had pale skin, though all were tanned by the sun. And their hair was a pale blond that bordered on being white. If he didn't know better, Sariel would have thought they were ...

Myndarym?

They were not the enemies he was searching for. Perhaps these were others from the Eternal Realm. But that didn't make any sense; there was no variation in their coloring. And the Myndarym were unique in the types of colors displayed with their bodies. If these were the temporal manifestations of additional Shapers, it would be obvious.

And what would the Amatru be doing in this realm anyway?

These beings certainly weren't *shaping* anything. They were working. A circle of six boats was anchored a short distance out into the ocean, though their translucent sails remained fully extended in various horizontal and vertical positions. Perhaps the sails were catching something other than wind. Another boat went back and forth between the circle and the camp at regular intervals. When it came ashore near the tents, Sariel noted that its segmented hull appeared to be made of polished metal, though this made no sense, as metal was far too heavy to be used for a floating vessel. The boat was loaded with long poles of metal, and these were transported back to the circle where the tall beings would fit them together and lower them into the water.

Sariel didn't understand what he was witnessing, but he knew it was important to stay hidden and pay close attention. He had the feeling that whatever he learned would be of great value in the future.

SA4226

6

A deer stood with its front legs in the water. It lowered its head and drank from the slow-moving stream in short, cautious intervals. Whenever its head came up, its eyes were moving, looking for signs of danger. Long ears pivoted to capture the sounds of the forest, then twitched to disturb the insects that hovered around them.

Sariel watched from upstream, hiding behind the trunk of a tree. One group of migrating mammals had led him to another, drawing him northward away from fields of grass and forests of tall trees. He'd climbed in elevation, passing through rugged and desolate mountains, much like the terrain he'd experienced in Second Earth. But as he began descending again, the air had grown warmer. Rain had become more frequent, and the forests transitioned to jungles. Where dense brush and tall, pale grasses used to inhibit his passage, now he contended with vines and broad-leafed plants. Insects were no longer an occasional sight but a constant nuisance. Although, Sariel was grateful to have found them, for when they dipped toward the water to drink, fish would rise to the surface of the stream to eat them. One enabled the other to survive.

In this place, the earth had come back to life, not as it was before but in a new way. The recovery was pleasing to witness, and every day Sariel discovered something new. He was right in the middle of Earth's regeneration, and he could feel it bringing him back to life as well. How long had he wandered the earth alone?

Too long.

The waiting was over; he wasn't alone after all.

The deer lifted its head suddenly, ears turning. Then it sprang across the stream in a single bound and disappeared into the jungle.

Sariel shifted his perspective toward the Eternal and immediately received the answer for the deer's abrupt departure. From the side of the river where the deer had been drinking, two spirits were approaching. They weren't the ethereal shadows of demonic spirits crawling along the ground, or the dull conglomerations of the Nephiylim. These swirling tapestries of brilliant color came forward in an upright posture— something he hadn't seen since before the Fracturing. His heart was already beating fast, surging with hope. He wanted to believe that he wasn't imagining it. He wanted to scream from excitement. But instead, he shifted his perspective back to the Temporal and crouched to the ground, watching the tree line across the stream.

Please let this be real!

Almost a minute passed before something became visible through the trees. It moved through alternating patches of light and shadow, revealing something both dark and substantial.

Yes!

Two women came out from the tree line and began walking along the sandy bank of the stream.

Sariel felt his throat tighten, and tears came instantly to his eyes. These weren't figments of his imagination, nor were they creatures who simply moved in an upright posture. They were actual humans, and he was staring right at them with his own eyes. Their skin was dark, like Adam and his son, Kahyin. Though Kahyin's descendants had always been the enemies of the Shayeth, Sariel didn't care one way or another. They were people, and they were alive. Both women wore long, sleeveless tunics and hair cut close to their scalps. Each had a bundle of fruit slung over her shoulder, and they were moving at a casual pace, speaking softly to one another. Sariel wasn't close enough to hear them clearly over the gurgle of the stream, so he couldn't tell if they spoke in a language he understood. But one of them laughed, and the sound transcended all languages, conveying an expression of joy.

Oh my!

Sariel put his hand over his mouth to keep from startling the women with his crying. Tears rolled down his face, and he couldn't control the shaking of his body. He sat on the ground and just watched them for as long as the women were visible. When they finally disappeared into the trees, Sariel stood and tried to compose himself.

They survived!

* * * *

NORTHEAST OF THE TREE
FIRST EARTH

The fire of the torches in the distance reflected off the water, two strips of light amidst a sea of darkness. They appeared as the smoldering eyes of a gigantic demon, waiting for its foolish victims to come just a bit closer. The undulating reflections hinted of a long, flat snout, with skin twitching in anticipation of the impending attack. At least, that's what Zaquel imagined her servants were thinking as she tasted the fear emanating from them. And they had good reason to fear; they were approaching the shores of a land where demons were said to live. They haunted the forests looking for men to devour. The night was eerily quiet, with only the sound of gentle waves lapping at the hull of Zaquel's ship to break the silence. If not for such a tangible, earthly reminder, it might have felt as though they had already passed into the underworld of spirits and shadows.

As the royal vessel of the Sun Goddess neared the torchlight, the demonic illusion dissipated with the appearance of a wooden dock lit beneath the soft glow. The female captain standing at the prow gave the order to drop the sails, and the men of her crew worked quickly to fulfill her orders. When the sails were secured and the ship was no longer driven by the power of the breeze, the men took up their oars and began rowing. They kept their eyes on the foredeck, intently watching their captain's hand motions so that the ship did exactly as she wanted at the precise moment she wanted it.

Zaquel reclined upon a bed at the aft deck, beneath a canopy of ornately carved wood with gold accents. Just as in her throne room, the only subjects in the immediate area around her were her two slaves. The men knelt on either side of the stairs leading up to the aft deck, and both kept their eyes forward, forbidden to look directly upon their Mwangu Rana.

When the captain had guided the ship to a safe and gentle stop beside the dock, she closed her fingers into a fist. Her crew took in their oars and immediately went to work securing the boat to the landing with ropes.

Zaquel watched the men, feeling how the urgency of their movements was motivated just as much by fear as it was by obedience. Though it couldn't be seen from here, they knew that the other end of the long wooden dock led into a place of mystery and unspeakable horrors. They knew that something waited in the darkness, and they were terrified of what that might be.

When the crew had secured the ship, and there was nothing else to distract their minds from what lay ahead, they gathered around a massive object that lay along the deck. It was nearly as long as the ship itself, covered in cloths and bound by rope. It had been recovered from lands far away and brought to Zaquel. She, in turn, had brought it here. Though it seemed that there weren't enough men to lift an object so large, the crew was able to pick it up from the deck and carry it toward the dock. One end of the precious cargo was larger than the other, and the men struggled to transfer the awkward shape to the landing and get it pointed in the right direction. When all the men were off the ship and positioned evenly along the length of the cargo, the captain left the ship and walked to the head of the procession. Slowly, they began moving forward.

Zaquel rose from her place of rest and descended the stairs to the main deck. Her slaves, hearing her movement, went ahead of her to keep their eyes from violating their goddess. At nearly twice the height of her human servants, Zaquel covered distances quickly despite her casual pace. She crossed the main deck and stepped onto the dock, while her slaves ran to stay in front.

Beyond the illuminated area, toward the unseen shore, the darkness began to move. A crowd of shadows was gathering, approaching. Individual shapes bobbed up and down and the dock began to vibrate in response.

The crew came to an abrupt stop. Several of them tripped, and their cargo slipped from their hands. The others began to panic, trying desperately to keep the wrapped bundle from hitting the docks while keeping their eyes pointed toward the shore.

The darkness was swarming now, black and gray shapes crawling along the wooden surface. Pale, dead faces hovered in the night air, staring out with eyes that wept blood. Wings of skin stretched out and clawed at one another, competing for space along the dock.

The crew of Zaquel's boat began to scream. They dropped the cargo and stumbled backward. The creatures of their nightmares were real, and the men weren't prepared to die. The fact that their goddess stood behind them was no consolation; no amount of loyalty would give them the courage to endure their flesh being torn from their bodies and consumed while they watched. Some fell to the deck and began crawling backward, crying as though they were children. Others were more practical; they simply turned and fled.

Zaquel remained in the middle of the dock and watched her servants come toward her at a run. They shielded their eyes and fell at her feet in supplication. The captain watched her crew with disgust, yelling curses at the retreating cowards. But she was just as scared as the men. The huddled mass at Zaquel's feet cried out, begging for her protection. Hands stretched toward her, careful not to touch her for fear of death.

"Part," she commanded.

The crew slid across the wooden planks, dividing into two groups to make way for their goddess.

"Stay," Zaquel ordered her slaves, feeling their immediate relief. Then she stepped past her crew and walked away from the lighted end of the dock.

The Tree fragment was supposed to be taken to the dark end of the dock and left for Rameel's servants, who didn't usually come into the light or allow men to see them. Zaquel's crew had only managed to transport it half of the way. The cargo was now sitting too close to the illuminated end of the dock, and Rameel's servants wouldn't come out of the darkness any farther to retrieve it.

Zaquel had always planned on escorting the cargo all the way to its destination, but she had anticipated this transfer going smoother. *No matter,* she thought. What had taken place only served to reinforce the natural order to which the humans were accustomed.

"Wait here. I will return," she told them all. Then she proceeded down the dock and came alongside the wrapped bundle. Passing her hand through the air above it, she took control of its physical presence.

The enormous object rose from the dock as if it were nothing but a feather drifting on the wind.

The crew behind her gasped.

Zaquel began walking forward, and the fragment from the Tree followed her like an obedient slave. She walked confidently into the darkness and the demons waiting there to receive her.

* * * *

FAR NORTHWEST OF THE TREE
SECOND EARTH

Fog hung thick in the air. The early morning light came through in a diffused haze, shining from all directions as if the Holy One were hovering above the earth. The only areas of subtle shadow were those cast by great columns of wood that seemed to uphold the sky. If Sariel had fifteen selves joined hand in hand, he still wouldn't be able to reach around the diameter of these massive trunks of red bark.

The air was warmer in this part of the world than what Sariel had passed through in the last several years. But there was more moisture in it, making it difficult to endure throughout the night. There were a few hot coals hiding beneath the damp ashes near his makeshift shelter, and Sariel's first task of the morning was to gather dry pine needles and downed wood from the surrounding forest. After coaxing the glowing coals into a proper fire, he sat down beside the flames and warmed himself as he ate a breakfast of gathered berries and nuts.

There had been no signs of human or animal survival on this earth since finding the remains of the boat. Sariel had searched the northern and central lands without success, and now he planned to move south toward the Tree. He hadn't laid eyes on the stump since coming into this world, but perhaps there might be some activity near it as with Third Earth and the mysterious beings working upon the ocean in their boats.

In-between bites of food, Sariel extended his cold, stiff hands toward the fire. The dancing flames, the gathered meal, the cool, damp air clinging to his back—he suddenly remembered the morning after Sheyir's death. He wondered how long it would be until he forgot about that horrific scene below the waterfall. Sometimes he'd make it a few weeks without seeing her body— and that black hand, slick with blood—but it always returned. He wished the good times they'd shared would be the things that came easily to his mind, but those took a conscious effort to bring back. It was the opposite of how it should be. Tearing

Azael open from the inside out and shattering his bones upon the ground hadn't been enough.

He deserved worse.

Sariel suddenly realized that the fire was roaring louder than normal. The flames were bent away from him, as if being blown by the wind. Embers were shooting outward into the forest, but the air was perfectly calm.

He pulled his hands back from the heat and curled his fingers into fists.

The fire relaxed, flames licking upward once again.

They all deserve worse!

The Myndarym had inadvertently killed almost every living creature upon the face of the earth. And for what—so they could take this realm for themselves? It wasn't theirs to possess. The beings who had died—*that's* who deserved to be here. This was *their* world. Though Semjaza had led the rebellion, it was the Myndarym who had turned out to be mankind's greatest enemies. Satarel. Armaros. Kokabiel. Unless they had died or had decided to leave for another world, they were here ... somewhere. Perhaps they were wandering just like Sariel. Perhaps they had already built kingdoms in which to live; there had certainly been enough time for that. Sooner or later, Sariel would find their trail. The question was—what then?

It's going to take more than bending flames to get rid of them, he told himself.

Sariel extended his hands toward the fire again. The waves of heat were detected by his palms first, felt on his fingertips a moment later. But there was another sensation moving in the opposite direction, one that Sariel had been cultivating and strengthening ever since he discovered it while crossing those windswept plains a couple years back. He could feel the form and weight of the logs in the fire, though he wasn't touching them with either his physical or his spiritual body.

Then, with no visible cause, the logs in the fire began to move.

7

Gathering information about Baraquijal's kingdom and supplying it to the Viytur had been difficult, to say the least. Sariel had been forced to use Vand-ra's demonic underlings to accomplish the task. Seeing through another being's eyes presented its own challenges. But the problems multiplied exponentially when trying to combine those observations to understand the broad scope of Baraquijal's operations. All the while, he'd had to avoid the conventional forces of both the Amatru and Marotru, as well as keep away from the Idnan's operatives and spies. It had required patience, focus, and precision.

Compared with that reconnaissance mission, this one was simple. The pale beings he'd been watching for two years now had no enemies and, therefore, no need to worry about their surroundings. They simply performed their work, unaware that they were being watched. Sariel continued his routine of observing during the day and gathering food and water during the cool hours after the setting of the sun. He occasionally changed his position in order to get a better look at something, but most of the time he kept to his primary observation point, directly inland from where these beings were working.

Their circle of boats had provided a platform from which they'd eventually built a semi-circular wall extending all the way to the shore. When the ocean water had been removed from inside the wall, it became apparent that it was actually a dam. The arrangement of metallic panels held back the ocean, providing them with a dry seabed upon which to work. When several carts were brought out from tents, Sariel learned why there were more structures on the beach than people to sleep in them. These carts appeared like the boats, with segmented metallic bodies that reflected the bright sunlight, but there weren't any creatures being used to pull them. These moved on their own, and not by any force in the Eternal Realm that Sariel could see, leaving him to ponder who these beings were and what they were doing here.

When the carts broke themselves into pieces and began digging into the seabed with dozens of appendages, Sariel received the answer to his ponderings. He was reminded of the weapons used by the latter Nephiylim—blades and other instruments of war that extended from the arms and legs of those abominable creatures. They had hunted the former Nephiylim to the ends of the earth, using Ezekiyel's machines to assist their efforts.

The digging machines had the same look, though much more sophisticated. And once Sariel realized that Ezekiyel was behind this operation, the appearance of the pale beings also began to make sense. Turel and Danel had both ended up here in Third Earth, and there had always seemed to be a special connection between them. Sariel had even reported this to the Viytur, though nothing had ever come of it as far as he knew.

If these beings were indeed the offspring of Turel and Danel, then they were in fact Myndarym. However, this was a new breed of angel, one that had not been brought from the Eternal Realm but had been born here in the Temporal. The very idea of temporal angels seemed a contradiction in terms, but here they were.

The digging machines had created a trench that ran all the way from the seabed back to the shore in a steady incline. Other carts had been moving back and forth along the trench, carrying sand away from the dig site and depositing it on the beach. The temporal angels interacted with the machines on occasion, inspecting and redirecting them as the citizens of El-Betakh had done with their animals in the old world. But otherwise, the tireless machines worked on their own and had done so continuously until they unearthed their objective.

Several days ago, Sariel recognized the dark, shimmering material that had been hidden beneath the ocean and sand. It was a large piece of the Tree of Wisdom—a third of what had been severed at the Fracturing. Since then, the machines had managed to remove all of the sand from around it. Earlier this morning, Sariel had watched the temporal angels tie the crystalline object to a small, sturdy cart with ropes. It dragged the tree fragment up the trench and onto the beach where it was loaded onto another, longer cart and fastened in place.

And now, after observing this bizarre operation for two years, Sariel watched the temporal angels take down their tents and load everything onto carts. It appeared that they were leaving, and if Sariel's assumptions were correct, he would be able to follow them back to their parents and the one who had created their machines.

*   *   *   *

SOUTH OF THE TREE
SECOND EARTH

Satarel stepped out of the jungle into a field of mud and tree stumps. The loss of a protective canopy had allowed the rains to ravage the land, washing away the undergrowth and leaving a maze of eroded valleys and water-filled depressions. It was an indication that he and his men had come to the right location, and also that Armaros was hard at work nearby.

Satarel's army spread out behind him as they left the trees. The archers came first, fingers resting upon their bowstrings, ready to act on a moment's notice. They were followed by foot soldiers carrying stone-tipped wooden clubs. Some of the men had been able to employ their weapons for hunting along the way to feed the army, but the tools of warfare were really just a precaution. There would be no battles here; Satarel was coming to help.

"This way," he instructed, turning north to follow the path of cleared vegetation.

Another hour of ascending the terrain brought them to the top of a ridge overlooking a bend in a river. The course of the water had been altered, evidenced by large walls of timber and mud that diverted the flow around a low point where hundreds of men were working. They were organized into small groups, with some men using wooden tools for digging while others transported the removed soil to a pile farther down the riverbed. The trunk of the fractured Tree had been exposed, but the branches on the opposite end were still beneath the earth. Ropes had been attached to various parts of the Tree and secured to nearby branches and boulders in case the river decided to resume its former course. It appeared that Armaros was already doing everything that needed to be done; a few hundred additional hands would simply make the work proceed faster.

"What took you so long?" Armaros asked, walking up the steep embankment.

"Our passage across the mouth of the sea was without incident, but I'm afraid we are not accustomed to the density of your ... jungles."

Armaros came up the last few paces and clasped Satarel's hand. "Thank you for coming. I assume Kokabiel won't be joining us?"

"He didn't want to be distracted from his work, but he'll be here when everything is ready for Ezekiyel."

Armaros shook his head before looking back over the excavation site. "I can think of one of Kokabiel's forms in particular that would have made this task far easier."

Satarel remembered the sharp claws of Kokabiel's favorite reptilian body, but it was the gigantic wings that would have been the most useful in this situation. "Yes. Flying this thing over the treetops seems preferable to what we will be forced to endure."

Armaros smiled.

"How can we help?" Satarel asked.

"I've already informed my men on how we will use your assistance. If you send your men down, my general will give them instructions."

Satarel turned and shouted to the group of soldiers gathered behind him. They started moving down the steep bank immediately. He watched them go, noting when they reached Armaros' group that there was little difference between the two except for the style of their clothing. Satarel's group wore long tunics that fell to their upper legs, while Armaros' men only wore loincloths. Both groups had ruddy, earthen skin and dark hair, having ultimately descended from common ancestry.

"I see you're taking it slow as well," Armaros said.

Satarel was offended by the comment until he realized that Armaros was looking at the weapons left behind and was not referring to the pace of Satarel's men. "Ah, yes. I figure we've already tried a heavy-handed approach. The old world was proof enough of that."

"Indeed. I suspect Ezekiyel will push things as quickly as possible, but I'm in agreement with you. We haven't seen yet what might come from allowing humans to believe that they're in control."

"I suspect they will rise up and become quite strong in the absence of ... more obvious gods."

Armaros smiled and shook his head slowly. "Rameel."

Satarel was already thinking the same thing. "There is only so much one can do with a form that inspires fear."

"Yes. It was short-sighted of him, although he couldn't have anticipated being stuck with it."

Satarel looked down at his own body. "I'm relieved that we ended up in this world together."

"As am I. Had we not, our chosen forms might have become our weakness instead of our strength."

* * * *

The caravan of temporal angels and their machines moved east across a wide, flat valley. Since leaving the ocean, Sariel had stayed well behind them to ensure that he wasn't spotted. Now he watched from a closer distance as they approached a vast city without walls. Stone buildings formed several interlocking crescents, with covered walkways radiating from their intersections. The same translucent material that had formed the sails of their ships had been employed here to create shaded areas within the city. Beneath the shade, groves of trees and shrubs formed sections of green that stood out against the tan and red colors of the surrounding terrain. And the unmistakable shimmer of water could be seen where the trees were gathered. It was an oasis amid a parched landscape, sitting directly atop the location of the Tree.

When Sariel had come into this world from the In-Between, he had been forced to climb out of a long canyon etched into the soil by the flow of water that had been pulled into the Tree. Once he reached higher ground, he had noted the strange pattern of crescent shapes left behind on the valley floor. The equalization process between worlds had caused a continual push and pull of water that resulted in not just a single canyon, but several.

Sariel hadn't been back to the Tree since then, but it was obvious that this city had been built upon the natural formations of the landscape. What had been added to it bore the look of Ezekiyel's creations—a sophisticated mechanical expression of things found in nature.

The caravan of angels came to a stop outside the pointed end of the closest building. The pale beings gathered at the front, while their carts moved into a wide formation without any assistance. When the whole caravan was standing at attention, a door opened outward from the building and a human, dressed in tight-fitting white clothing, stepped out into the bright sunlight.

Sariel shielded his eyes and squinted to get a better look.

*   *   *   *

Ezekiyel walked straight past the soldiers without a word. Stopping beside the interlocked cargo vehicles, he climbed a series of handholds and footholds that led to the flat bed above. He lifted the corner of the tarp to find the third piece of the Tree of Wisdom. Even in bright sunlight and the intense shadows that it created, the sparkle within the glassy surface was unmistakable.

"Did you encounter any difficulties?" Ezekiyel asked, turning to look down upon the statuesque forms of the Myndar soldiers.

"None but what we expected, my lord," replied the squad leader at the front of the assembly.

Ezekiyel climbed down and walked back among the ranks of these truly magnificent creatures—Myndarym born into the Temporal Realm. These soldiers had been bred from the strongest of Turel and Danel's first generations. They were nearly twice as tall as humans and almost as powerful as the Nephiylim. But it was their intelligence that made them such valuable assets. In fact, all of the lines, whether soldier or otherwise, exhibited mental capabilities that exceeded any creatures of the old world. They represented the future, and not a day went by without Ezekiyel being reminded that he had made the right choice in aligning himself with Danel and Turel.

"Cargo bay six," he instructed.

"Yes, my lord," the leader replied.

At once, the entire squad crossed their arms in front of their chests in salute. Then they turned on their heels and headed toward the cargo bay entrance, moving with a fluid precision that only other lines within their race could match. The cargo vehicles followed obediently, as they were designed to do.

When the dust stirred up by the vehicles had been carried away on the breeze, Ezekiyel paused to admire the city he'd built. Panels of light-sensitive material absorbed the power of the sun even as they provided shade for the city beneath. The fountains of the deep still rose to the surface in this place; the flow and the heat were both additional sources of power that fed the city. After cooling, the water was diverted and channeled to a multitude of tasks, the most visible being the liquid streets upon which boats traveled. Beneath the dry and dusty surface was a vast civilization that had already exceeded the technology and resources of Senvidar.

There had never been anything like it in the old world, because such a thing wasn't possible under the rule of Semjaza or Baraquijal. Both had been oppressive in their own ways, and Ezekiyel had limited himself in response. His inventions were dealt out in a slow, paced manner—just fast enough and frequent enough to keep his superiors happy. But they had no idea what Ezekiyel was truly capable of. Despite the slow and cautious beginnings required by this new world, the master Shaper was now making unprecedented strides toward his goal.

8

Sariel opened his eyes to see a shaft of gray light shining against the wall of his hut. For a moment, he felt as though he were still in Bahyith among Sheyir's people, and everything that had transpired since then had only been a terrible dream. But the illusion vanished, and he was left with his sorrow as proof of what was reality. Particles of dust drifted through the air. He watched how brilliantly they shone against their shadowed backdrop. Each one was like a star in the night sky. The dirt floor was uncomfortable beneath his body, but he dared not move or even acknowledge it for fear of reminding himself how closely this resembled the first months of his time in the Temporal Realm.

When the dust particles ceased to be a sufficient distraction, Sariel became aware of his hunger and thirst. From the angle of the sunlight, it seemed to be midmorning. He would have to gather some fruit on the way to his observation point above the human village. But first he needed to get a drink from the nearby stream.

Climbing to his feet, Sariel ducked beneath the overhanging branches and stepped out into a misty morning. Dark clouds hung thick overhead, and it appeared that the rain would not wait until the afternoon as it had done for the past few weeks. A yawn suddenly came to his mouth, and he accompanied it with a long and satisfying stretch of his arms and back. When it passed, Sariel turned downhill and began walking toward the stream. All of a sudden, his body tensed.

A short, dark-skinned man stood within the trees by the stream. He was dressed in a loincloth and sleeveless tunic, like others Sariel had observed in the nearby village. The man's eyes went wide as he realized he'd been spotted, and he quickly held out both hands.

Sariel found himself in a crouched position, ready to fight. Several seconds passed before he realized that the intruder was attempting to present himself in a nonthreatening way.

The man stepped carefully out from the trees, hands still held outward. "I'm sorry," he said quietly. "I was waiting for you to wake."

The language was Shayeth, and Sariel was suddenly overwhelmed by a mix of emotions. The familiar language washed away centuries' worth of silence and held the promise of filling the void of his indescribable loneliness. It felt as though he had come home to El-Betakh. And yet, he was angry with himself for being found—for making contact. Humankind needed to be left alone more than anything. To be free of the corruption that was inevitable with his and the other angels' presence. But Sariel had been living in contradiction to that. He couldn't stay away. The best he'd been able to do was to watch them from afar.

"I don't mean you any harm," the man said.

Sariel realized that he hadn't moved since he first spotted the man.

"Can you understand me?" the man asked.

Sariel just stared into his eyes, large and full of wisdom. There was something mesmerizing about him that made Sariel want to draw near. *But I can't!* he told himself.

"Du Syvaku?" the man asked in another language.

I shouldn't!

"Du eru fra Nijambu?"

Sariel recognized the angelic language and wondered how this man had come to learn it. But as soon as his curiosity rose within him, he feared what it might bring about.

The man looked down at the ground and breathed deeply, obviously wondering how he could break through the stranger's ignorance. "Who doesn't speak Common?" he mumbled to himself.

Sariel couldn't take it anymore. "Is that what you call your language?"

The man suddenly looked up from the ground. "You understand me?"

"Yes."

He smiled larger than what seemed possible for his miniature face. Then his eyes grew more serious. "You speak Common, but you call it by another name?"

"Yes," Sariel replied. And now that he was speaking, his curiosity couldn't be restrained. He had to know what connection this man had to the old world. "Shayeth."

The man's face suddenly went slack, and he glanced over his shoulder before replying, "Where did you hear that word?"

"Have I offended you?"

"No, but ..."

Sariel was intrigued by the man's response as well as his sudden hesitation. "What was the other language you spoke a moment ago?"

"Syvak. I thought because of your white hair and pale skin ..."

Sariel waited for him to finish, but the man seemed lost in his thoughts. "What is your name?"

"Ebnisha," he replied.

"Well, Ebnisha. What are you doing outside my dwelling?"

"That's the same question I came to ask you," he answered with a smile.

"I don't understand."

"You've been watching my village for weeks. We heard you on the mountainside. Some people in my tribe believe you mean us harm. I told them that dangerous things eventually come near when their fears become weak. You haven't come near; you've just been waiting."

All of the tension was gone now from Sariel's body. It was disappointing to realize that he'd been discovered by humans after managing to evade enemies in both realms for so long. Perhaps his isolation from other intelligent creatures was to blame for his carelessness.

"I don't mean you any harm," Sariel confirmed.

"Then what have you been doing outside my dwelling?" Ebnisha asked, smiling at the clever way he'd turned Sariel's question back on him.

Sariel couldn't help but smile in return. Amusement was something he'd forgotten about. "It has been a long time since I've seen other people."

"So, *you* were afraid of *us*?"

Sariel tilted his head. "Not exactly."

"Your answers are very confusing," Ebnisha replied with a frown. "What is your name?"

The question came as a shock, and Sariel quickly tried to think of a lie. His own name seemed like a liability—something that should be kept a secret. But as he struggled with his response, Ebnisha's expression calmed his fears. There was something honest and safe about the man. Or perhaps it was Sariel's own loneliness that caused him to trust. Whichever was true, Sariel felt the need to be honest.

"Sariel," he admitted.

Ebnisha's eyes grew wide again for a moment as they suddenly looked Sariel up and down. Then the intensity drained from his face and a smile replaced it. He began nodding as if he understood something important.

"Today is a good day," Ebnisha finally replied.

*   *   *   *

Curling wisps of steam rose from the lake, glowing like apparitions from the Eternal Realm as they passed through columns of light spilling down from the high ceiling. Water surged upward from the depths of the earth, bringing heat with it as it flowed out of the cavern through passages in the walls. When it returned from the city, the cool water entered through other passages and was collected in different segments of the lake, where it was used for a variety of purposes before returning to the earth. The continual cycle kept the underground lake at a constant level and temperature. But the sense of anticipation in the cavern was even more tangible than the moisture in the air. The portal that led to the In-Between and the worlds beyond sat at the center of the water, appearing as a low platform instead of the tree stump that it was. It shimmered beneath its glassy surface, more pronounced even than the reflected sunlight from the waters of the lake.

Thousands of temporal Myndarym were gathered—artisans who had been bred to reinforce their natural capacity for understanding the form and functionality of created things. They were here to assist Ezekiyel by receiving and holding ideas during the *shaping* process. They would become extensions of his mind and would thereby serve to amplify what he was capable of achieving.

Their forefather and foremother, Turel and Danel, were also present. They stood on the perimeter of the cavern and watched in silence. Arakiba stood next to them, a few heads shorter, his dark, demonic appearance looking out of place among the crowd of pale angelic beings.

The artisans filled the walkway around the cavern as well as the bridge that led to the stone platform beside the portal where Ezekiyel stood. All eyes were intently fixed upon him, all minds open. The master Shaper bent down and laid his hand upon the piece that had been severed from the Tree of Wisdom. It was lying on the platform beside him. Its trunk—one third of what had existed in old Aden—had been split down its length. Leafless branches spread upward, and only in that direction. In this world, the gigantic object of hidden power had been buried under sand and ocean for over two thousand years. And now that the other two pieces in their worlds were being brought near the portal, the time had finally come.

Ezekiyel stood and removed an elongated sphere from his pocket—one that he had been searching for since the Fracturing. Like the portal itself, this object shimmered with a silver radiance and cast a rainbow of colors in all directions. When it had been the centerpiece of a human crown, it had been bathed in shadows. But now it was in the presence of the Tree from which it had come. It seemed to vibrate in the palm of his hand as though it were coming to life. And the fractured piece of the Tree was doing the same. Creatures of lesser knowledge might have dropped to their knees in fear, even worshipped the objects. But Ezekiyel understood what was happening. It was what Shapers first tried to achieve with a Song of Naming—a state in which every atom within the object resonates with some thread of the *song*. The state in which the entire object was known ... *named*. Only then was it pliable. Only then could it be *shaped*.

The portal and its fragment were being *named* just by their proximity to the seed. They wanted to come back to each other. They pleaded to be made whole again. But Ezekiyel had something different in mind. He was grateful that their *naming* was happening naturally, for it would take all of his talent, experience, and concentration to do what was required. Shifting Semjaza and his soldiers into the Temporal Realm had been challenging, but he'd found a way for his fellow Myndarym to perform the more basic translations. Dividing the Temporal Realm itself had required even greater understanding and resources. The Atah from the Eternal Realm and the Myndarym from the Temporal had both been given tasks to perform, and though only three worlds had been produced, Ezekiyel had still ultimately accomplished his goal. But that had been just a fracturing, a division—the equivalent of splitting wood with an ax. What he wanted to achieve now was to take that split wood and craft it into something. Such a thing was more intricate and complex than anything he'd yet attempted. For *shaping* these objects couldn't be done in stages. It was not like wood or stone, where one could carve a section here and then smooth out another section there. This *shaping* had to be done all at once. The end goal had to be a firm concept, fixed within the mind of the Shaper. But in this case, the end goal was too vast a concept to be held by a single mind.

This was where the temporal Myndarym would become useful. They were perfectly obedient, and though their intelligence was broad, these artisans had a capacity for this specific type of intelligence. They would be given pieces of the final concept, leaving Ezekiyel free to hold in his mind how the pieces should fit together.

In the Eternal Realm, the higher orders of angelic beings were capable of speaking and understanding more complex, layered arrangements of the language used by the Holy One to bring matter into existence out of nothing. They were more complex beings themselves, and so were able to hold greater complexities within their minds. In being, in thought, and in communication, they lived on a higher plane. The lower orders were simpler creatures, and had been given individual threads of the same language in keeping with their capacity to understand and speak it. Each order with its unique thread was powerful in its own right, but that power became exponentially greater among the higher orders.

Ezekiyel was only a Myndar, and he no longer lived in the Eternal Realm. But he had found a way to achieve through numbers what the higher orders could do by design. Turel and Danel had brought forth a new race of angel, and these creatures possessed raw materials that could be reconfigured in a multitude of ways. Through breeding, Ezekiyel was able to build the individual pieces of a collective mind—the temporal equivalent of a higher order being. And now it was time to put the pieces together and see what they might achieve.

The temporal Myndarym were ready, waiting to receive concepts that Ezekiyel would give them. Turel, Danel, and Arakiba were also ready, holding ideas in their minds that were either useful or meaningful to their reign as gods of the Temporal.

"Let us begin," he said to everyone gathered.

* * * *

Something significant was taking place, of that Sariel was sure. He'd watched from the Eternal Realm as the temporal Myndarym had taken the piece of the Tree into one of the interconnected buildings. The colors of their spirits were brighter than humans, but just as varied. And the cargo they transported was made all the more visible when surrounded by them. A while later, another group of Myndarym came and moved the cargo to the center of the city. Though there were many structures and objects blocking his temporal view, Sariel was able to see that the fractured piece had been returned to the stump.

The one who had inspected the cargo as it came into the city was Ezekiyel. Sariel had learned to interpret the appearance of all the Myndarym's spirits while spying on Baraquijal's kingdom. And it was no surprise that the master Shaper was involved in this effort. He'd assumed as much after seeing the machines that had been used to unearth the Tree. What was unexpected was the realization that Arakiba, Turel, and Danel were also inside the city. At first, Sariel had been excited at the prospect of finding all four of his enemies in this world gathered in one location; it made his task of killing them that much more efficient. But when the spirits of the temporal Myndarym, which had been spread throughout the city, began concentrating at its center, Sariel knew there would be no way to even reach his enemies without becoming entangled in a secondary conflict.

In the old world, when demonic underlings were his to command, Sariel might have flown straight into the city and accepted whatever battles presented themselves. But he no longer had such power. Losing this self while killing four of his enemies would have been an acceptable sacrifice. But to die before even reaching them made no sense at all.

Now the Myndarym and thousands of their temporal counterparts were gathered around the stump of the Tree of Wisdom. Clearly, they were not just meeting for conversation. But from his vantage, Sariel couldn't draw any conclusions.

I need to get a better view.

Sariel kept low to the sand and crawled backward away from the thicket that had been obscuring his outline. When he was safely hidden behind a dune, he rose to a crouch and stepped quickly to the south, using the natural features of the landscape to hide him as he moved closer to the city.

9

"There are many people throughout the world, not just mine," Ebnisha explained.

Sariel could hardly believe it; he'd been searching for so long and had only found animals until he happened upon two women from Ebnisha's tribe. "Are you sure?"

Ebnisha smiled before scooping up a handful of stream water and raising it to his lips. When he was finished, he wiped his mouth with the back of his hand and scooted back from the water's edge. "You don't believe me?"

"I have searched for … a very long time."

Ebnisha squinted. "Do you not know how long it has been since the waters came?"

"I tried keeping track of the years, but … it was important that I kept moving." Then Sariel realized there was a sad look in Ebnisha's eyes. "Why? Do *you* know?"

"Two thousand, five hundred and seventy years."

"No," Sariel replied, almost laughing as he did so. "That can't be right."

"It is."

Sariel shook his head, "That's too much time. And how could you know that anyway?"

"The stories of my people have been passed down from generation to generation. Each father tells his sons and makes them remember every word. Then they tell their sons, and so on."

"But everything changed," Sariel protested. "Your forefathers would have been struggling to survive, not counting days and years. And who knows how long the waters—"

"A year and ten days from the time the floods came until my ancestors were able to leave their boat.[5] Most of that time was spent telling stories. When the families of Shem, Kham, and Yefeth began to grow numerous, they ventured out from their settlement seeking new places to live. New resources and opportunities. My people are descended from Kham, and there are now thousands of tribes all throughout these lands. Many of them have forgotten the stories of our ancestors, but not my tribe."

Sariel vaguely remembered how he felt in the In-Between. Time had seemed such an unknowable thing there, as if every moment lasted an eternity and the blink of an eye all at once. And since then, he had wandered. He knew instinctively that it had been a long time, even centuries. But millennia?

"Two thousand, five hundred and seventy years," he said aloud, as if that would make it easier to accept.

"A long time to be alone," Ebnisha pointed out.

Sariel felt his eyes begin to water, but he choked down his emotions. "Yes."

A moment of quietness passed, filled only by the melodic sound of the stream and the breeze moving through the trees. Ebnisha had been coming to Sariel's camp each day. The man had an insatiable thirst for knowledge, and when he had learned that the visitor spying on his village shared the name and physical appearance with one of his people's legends, he acted as though he had found a fountain of wisdom.

Sariel plucked a long blade of grass from the ground in front of his crossed legs and began to roll the stalk between his fingers. It had become a habit over the years, a way of occupying his attention with something physical.

Ebnisha turned his head and looked into the forest behind them. "In that time, you must have seen the whole world."

"Much of it, or so I thought."

"But recently, you came from the south. Yes?"

Sariel looked up from the grass in his hand. "That's right."

"Most of the people are north of here. Well ... they have spread to the east and west also, but in this part of the world, there is only one group farther south than my tribe."

"And these people all live as you do?"

"Oh no," Ebnisha replied with a smile. "We are a simple people. Others travel the land on horses. Some sail the ocean in their boats. There are cities so great that one end cannot be seen from the other. There are people with skin and hair almost as white as yours. Others are dark like me, and still others in between. The children of Noah have spread all over the earth ... except, it seems, the places where you have walked."

Sariel smiled at the irony, but if this was true, he had to ask the most obvious question. "How do you know all this?"

"The city of Nijambu is only a few days' journey to the northwest. It is a port on the coast where boats bring goods from all over the world. The sailors trade with each other and take their new treasures back to their own lands. Many stories are told in Nijambu ... and some of them are even true."

Sariel laughed for the first time in as long as he could remember.

"You like this? I shall take you there someday so you can see it for yourself."

"I would like that," Sariel replied, stretching his legs out on the grass. "So you hear these stories, but how do you know which ones are true and which are false?"

"As I said before, my people remember what was handed down to us from our fathers. We had to memorize the words. Of course, we didn't like this as children. My brothers and I would much rather have spent our time climbing trees and catching fish. But as we got older, we learned that there was plenty of time for those other things. And the words we were forced to memorize became important to us."

"You compared the stories from Nijambu to what you had already learned?" Sariel guessed.

Ebnisha smiled again, and each time he did, his mouth and teeth looked far too large for the rest of his face. But Sariel didn't find it strange. In fact, there was a perfect symmetry between this physical expression and the man's personality. It was as if Ebnisha were filled to the brim with joy and couldn't help the ways in which it spilled out.

"This helped my people to understand where Noah's other children had gone and what they had accomplished."

"And did you memorize these new stories also?" Sariel wondered, still astonished that he had somehow managed to miss all of these humans and their cities during his time of wandering.

"Yes, we tried. But there were too many things to remember. I found that even the stories that seemed too strange held something valuable. They helped me learn the ways in which the truths of the old world had become something new. And this was important for me to understand how other tribes view the world and make decisions. My brothers didn't care much for this, but I wanted to learn all of it."

"You must have an incredible capacity for memory," Sariel replied.

Ebnisha smiled again before reaching beside him to pick up a satchel, one that he carried with him each time he came from his own village. "I have a gift for you, my friend."

"A gift? You don't have to give me anything."

"I wish it could be more," Ebnisha replied. "If you had not come to the aid of Lemek and saved his family from the Nephiylim at El-Betakh, his son Noah would have perished. His grandson Kham would not have been born. My people and I would not even exist."

Sariel hadn't admitted yet that he was the same person as the one in Ebnisha's stories, but he hadn't exactly denied it either. Part of him wanted to forget about the old world, but hearing the names of his friends and the places he'd lived brought back enough good memories that he couldn't bring himself to lie about it.

Ebnisha pulled something cylindrical from his bag and began to unroll it.

"What is it?" The material looked like cloth, but its fibers were much finer, mashed together at random instead of woven in a logical pattern.

"This is where I keep my memories now that there are too many for my mind."

Sariel took the cloth, as wide as his forearm and three times as long. He held it in both hands and stared at the dark markings upon it. At once, he was reminded of the symbols he had scratched into the dirt so long ago in Bahyith. The Chatsiyram tribe helped him make the sounds of a *song* that had forced several demons to relinquish their hold upon one of their men. Sariel had used the symbols to represent the sounds that each of them needed to make. "This is your language," he realized.

"Yes," Ebnisha replied excitedly. "I knew the defender of my forefathers would understand."

Sariel ignored the comment and scratched at the cloth with his thumbnail.

"You are obviously familiar with making clothes," Ebnisha added, pointing to Sariel's own tunic. "I'm sure you know that separating the fibers of plants is easier when you soak them in water."

This had been practiced by the Chatsiyram as far back as Sariel could remember, though he hadn't stayed in one place long enough since the Fracturing to bother setting up such an operation. He simply gathered what he needed along the way and spent his evenings repairing his clothing or making new items by firelight.

"One day, I found that my younger brother had neglected to clean out the trough. The water had dried, leaving many small fibers stuck together at the bottom. I made him scrape out the mess and clean the trough so that he would remember not to neglect his duties in the future. The next morning, I found the clumps of fibers that he had cleaned lying in a pile in the sun. They had dried into sheets like a thick cloth. This gave me an idea. I tried many types of plants until I found one whose fibers were very fine."

"This is amazing," Sariel remarked, running his fingers over the smooth surface. "And these markings are made with ...?"

"Ashes from a fire. I grind them between stones until there is a fine dust. Then I add it to plant milk that has been boiled down. It becomes a very dark liquid that can be applied with anything. I prefer to use a stalk of grass."

"Remarkable! Tell me about these symbols. How did you think of them?"

Ebnisha's teeth were gleaming in the morning sunlight. It was obvious that he was enjoying himself. "Well, I began by drawing pictures. For *bird*, I drew the shape of a bird. For *rain*, I drew many lines like this," he replied, scratching short lines in the dirt with his finger. "I did this for several months until I found that many words could not be drawn. Some were ideas and not things. How would I draw happiness? I could make a picture of the sun, but then it would be confused with the sun itself."

Sariel smiled and nodded, but kept silent.

"I tried to make the pictures more elaborate and then I tried making them very simple. No matter what I did, I was frustrated that I could not draw everything that my language could describe. For over a year I wrestled with this before realizing that my spoken language already contained all the things and ideas that needed to be described. All I had to do was find a way to draw the sounds of my language."

Sariel had been nodding his head for the last several seconds. Not only was it fascinating to hear Ebnisha's reasoning process, it was wonderful to be sitting in the grass before a stream, speaking with a human being. The sound of the wind and the rustle of leaves used to be the only sounds of conversation at one point of his life.

"I tried to separate every sound we use and make a symbol for it. Some were smooth and others harsh, so I drew symbols that looked smooth or harsh. It was easy to remember that way."

Sariel looked over the symbols on the cloth and could tell at a glance that none of them were repeated. "This isn't a story, is it?"

"No. It is all the symbols of my language. You already know how to speak it, but I would like to teach you how to draw it."

Sariel looked up from the cloth into Ebnisha's eyes, large and bright. "This is a remarkable gift. I can't think of anything better."

Ebnisha clapped his hand against his own leg, his excitement evidently needing some other way out besides his smile. "Are you ready now?"

Sariel laughed. "Yes, but ... how about something to eat first? Are you hungry?"

"Very much. I forgot to eat breakfast in my haste to come this morning," Ebnisha replied with a lopsided grin.

SA 4227

10

Of all the worlds, Second Earth seemed to best resemble the original, at least around the Tree. Aden had been a wide, flat valley, surrounded by cliffs of gray rock. Waterfalls spilled down from the heights and fed thousands of streams flowing through the forest and meadows. In First Earth, Aden had been covered by molten rock that had hardened into conical mountains. In Third Earth, the wide valley was present, but the cliffs and forest had been replaced by sand dunes and sparse shrubbery.

Here in Second Earth, the valley was not as wide, but mountains still rose up on all sides. The sheer cliffs had been replaced by steep faces of rock and soil held in place by dense vegetation. The jungle was almost so thick as to be impassible. Rain fell every afternoon and sometimes into the evenings. The moisture returned to the sky the following day with the rising of the sun. Mist drifted upward in great swirls of white and gray, searching for its home among the clouds where it would find a temporary resting place. And by the afternoon, the cycle would repeat. The valley was a secluded, forgotten place.

It still felt like Aden ... most of the time.

At the moment, the sun was standing at its peak. The oppressive heat was made even more suffocating by the moisture in the air. Sariel was standing on the valley floor, using his tunic to wipe the sweat from his face. He had removed it to let his skin breathe, but it didn't seem to help much. The grass, which was taller than his head in most places, had been cut down in a path that led from the southern mountain pass across the valley floor and around the rim of the crater at its lowest point.

The shortened grass wasn't the only indication of a foreign presence. Sariel stood at the edge of the crater, looking down its steep mud faces. The soil was being retained by a lattice of branches tied together with long strands of grass. On the southern slope, the lattice was denser, forming a staircase that led up from the stump of the Tree of Wisdom at the bottom of the hole. It looked like the walls of Sedekiyr, and Sariel felt the same sense of impending doom as he stood above it. Nephiyl armies may not have been camped around him now, but he had finally found the first evidence of the Myndarym here in this world. How strange to think that they had once been allies, taking shelter from a common enemy.

* * * *

EAST-SOUTHEAST OF THE TREE
FIRST EARTH

The fire crackled and hissed as the moisture was driven out of the wood by the heat. It had been raining for several days, and dry leaves or branches weren't easy to find. Sariel had built a slanted shelter above his fire pit and was now tending to a fish roasting over the open flame. He had intended to wait until midday, to share the meal with Ebnisha just before the man went back to his village. But Ebnisha hadn't yet arrived. It was now midmorning, and Sariel split his time between rotating the fish above the fire and watching the swollen stream that had risen almost five paces higher than normal.

"Good morning, my friend!"

Sariel turned to see Ebnisha coming down through the trees beside the bank of the stream. He waved before rotating the fish, then stepped out from the shelter to meet his guest. "Is everything alright?"

"Yes, of course," he replied, but there was a strange look on his face.

"Come out of the rain," Sariel replied.

Ebnisha jogged across a short expanse of meadow and joined Sariel, ducking beneath the slanted roof. "I apologize for being late. It has been a ... troubling morning."

"Why? Did something happen?" Sariel replied, taking his usual seat beside the fire.

Ebnisha set down his satchel and lowered himself to the dry grass, crossing his legs. "When I got back to the village yesterday, I found that the holy men had come to visit."

"Who are they?"

Ebnisha brushed the water from the top of his head before responding. "They are from many different tribes. They've always been superstitious, listening to the priestesses of the east and adopting their ways. They believe it is their duty to protect the tribes from evil spirits, so they travel from place to place with their rituals. They have protected these lands for generations now, and most of the tribes look up to them, even seeking them out for their wisdom. Others do not find it easy when it comes time to provide the sacrifice."

Sariel's eyebrows shot upward.

"Every year, the holy men accept a virgin girl from a different tribe."

"A *human* sacrifice? For what purpose?"

"To appease the demons across the sea."

"Did you refuse them?"

"It is not my place. I am not the elder," Ebnisha replied. "Of course, my people do not believe the superstitions of the holy men, but if we refused, the other tribes would kill us. The demons have kept to their own lands, and the tribes will not do anything to upset this balance."

"So they took a girl from your village?" The thought disgusted Sariel and made him angry on the girl's behalf. Now he understood why the joy that was usually present in Ebnisha's face was absent.

"This morning," Ebnisha replied with a nod. "I stayed for the ceremony, which is why I'm late."

"Why do they need a ceremony to take someone?" The irritation in Sariel's voice was stronger than he intended, and he hoped Ebnisha didn't interpret it as an attack.

"They brand the girl's skin with the symbol of the Kaliel. It is something they have done since the beginning."

Sariel suddenly realized that he had forgotten about his meal. He grabbed the stick and pulled the burnt fish from the flames, suddenly disgusted by the thought of eating another creature. "What is the Kaliel?"

"Not *what* but *who*. It is what the demons are called."

"Alright. What is this symbol, and why do they brand the girl's skin with it?"

Ebnisha removed a twig from the pile of firewood and began drawing in a patch of bare soil beside him.

It was obvious that he was used to drawing symbols, for within just a few seconds, an image began to take shape. Nine men stood in a circle, legs together and arms outstretched. When Ebnisha finished drawing the outlines of their bodies, he began making longer strokes between them. Several confusing seconds passed before Sariel realized that they were wings—one pair larger and another smaller. The men were not men at all, but angels.

Ebnisha finished drawing and looked up. "The mark is not this large, of course. I've just drawn it so that you can see it clearly."

"Those are Iryllurym," Sariel said aloud.

Ebnisha frowned and looked down at the symbol again. "From the stories of Enoch?"

"Yes. Wait ... you know the stories of Enoch?"

Ebnisha smiled, though not as large as usual. "I have many scrolls filled with the things that he saw in this realm and the other. He told them to his son, Methushelak. Methushelak told them to Lemek, and Lemek told his son Noah."

Sariel put his hand over his mouth. There were too many thoughts running through his mind all at once.

"Yes, that's right! You lived with him in El-Betakh. I almost forgot. You actually knew Enoch."

Sariel just nodded.

"Yes. Iryllurym. And there were others. Anduarym and ..."

"Vidirym," Sariel added.

Ebnisha looked down again. "Enoch described them as winged creatures, but there were others in the White City with wings also. Why do you think these are Iryllurym?"

Sariel pointed at the symbol in the dirt. "The fore and aft wings. When I first came into this realm, *that* is the form I wore."

Ebnisha nodded slowly. "That was before Enoch pronounced the judgment and the forms of the Myndarym were made permanent."

"That's right," Sariel replied, amazed that Ebnisha could recall such detailed information. "But why is that one larger than the rest? And why are the wings different?"

"That is the demon god of the Kaliel. He has wings of skin, like a bat. The others are lesser gods, with wings of feathers like birds ... or so it is said. No one has ever seen such things."

All of a sudden, Sariel realized the meaning behind the symbol. "Rameel."

"I know this name ... from the stories of Methushelak."

"Yes. He was with us in Sedekiyr when the armies of the Nephiylim attacked. He is neither a demon, nor a god. But he is certainly real."

"It is strange for me to be speaking with one who was there. I have always believed these things to be true, but ..."

"But they were just stories until now?" Sariel offered.

Ebnisha nodded.

"Tell me more about the Kaliel. How did these human sacrifices begin?"

"Well, this was generations ago," Ebnisha began. "Other tribes don't remember the way we were taught, so their stories aren't as reliable. But somehow the knowledge of the demons across the sea came to these lands. The holy men were already practicing their other rituals by this time, and they came to believe that something had to be done to keep the demons from leaving the underworld across the sea. They had their own stories about the early days of man; they remembered that demons ate the flesh of mankind and preferred virgin women above all else. The holy men decided to appease the demons, to give them what they desired so they wouldn't have to come seeking it. During this time, several of the holy men were from the same tribe and they had the authority to do as they wanted. They took a virgin, tied her to the mast of a ship, and three of the holy men sailed with her across the sea. Only one man came back from the underworld. His eyes had been put out with fire, and this symbol had been carved into the flesh of his forehead. It was several months before he spoke again, and when he did, he talked of dark creatures with wings and claws, pale faces and eyes of blood. They had gathered within the dark forest along the shore, drawn by the light of the holy men's torches. The girl was untied, and when the ship reached the shallows, they threw her overboard. But she began swimming back out to sea. The men tried to turn the boat around to chase her, but during the confusion, the demons attacked. Two of the men were captured and dragged away into the trees. The third man wouldn't speak of what had been done to him other than to say that he was only allowed to live as a warning."

"What happened to the girl?"

"She was still swimming when the third man was captured. No one knows for sure. Some believe that she still wanders the forests of the underworld, doomed to run from the demons for all eternity. Most assume that the Kaliel caught her and feasted upon her flesh. But from that day until now, the holy men choose one virgin from a different tribe. They mark her forehead with the symbol of the Kaliel. She is tied up in a small boat of her own, and when they reach the shallows of the underworld, they place her boat into the water and set her adrift. No one sets foot on those lands, nor does anyone sail within sight of their shores except the holy men ... and only once a year. To this day, no demon has ever crossed over into our lands."

* * * *

HRIDIAM (CLIFFS OF DARKNESS)
THE CITY OF RAMEEL
FIRST EARTH
NORTH OF THE TREE

The girl lay on her side on the floor of her cell, facing away from the barred entrance. The plate of food beside her remained untouched. Her body rose and fell in a steady rhythm. When she had first been brought to Rameel, she used to pace the floor. She used to call out to anyone who might be near enough to hear. She used to cry. Every day that passed stole a bit more of her will. And now, all she did was sleep.

The rips in her tunic had become gaping holes, exposing large areas of her bare skin to the moonlight. Rameel traced her outline with his eyes, rising with the gentle slope of her legs, pausing at the curve of her hips, then falling into the valley of her abdomen. The silver light reflected off the skin of her face, carving out the features of her chin and cheekbone. She almost looked like a statue—someone's idea of perfect beauty—if not for the slight movement of her breathing.

In the old world, Rameel could have taken any woman he wanted. Indeed, most of his colleagues had done just that. But no woman had ever interested him. Humans always seemed so weak, so inferior. They lacked the aesthetic gracefulness of angelic beings and had failed to capture his attention in any way except for his disdain.

This girl might have thought of herself as the one enduring suffering, but it was Rameel who felt tortured. Finally, someone had captured his attention. But taking her would ultimately end her life. And this was the new world; Nephiylim were forbidden here. He couldn't let her go, of course; there were appearances to uphold. All he could do was watch, and she would die anyway ... slowly.

The rhythm of her breathing changed. Her graceful body stopped its seductive movement.

"If you're going to kill me, just get it over with," she said softly, without turning.

The pace of Rameel's heart quickened. His mind suddenly fought against itself—at once believing that her words had been imagined and also arguing that they were real and required a response. But these weren't words yelled into a vacant silence, a desperate plea to anyone who would listen. No, she had spoken to him ... directly. She knew he was there. Had she always known? How long? Had she known during all the other times?

The girl turned her head, pausing as if to listen. Then she slowly rolled over and faced the bars of her cell.

The sight of her—not from the back as when she slept, or the side as when she paced, but the front—felt intimate. Confrontational in a way. Was it a challenge? Rameel suddenly felt ashamed of his appearance. He had always watched from behind the protrusions of rock that were plentiful among these caves and tunnels. He'd never revealed himself in any way. How would she react to see his height, his wings, his body chosen for the fear that it would inspire?

She lay still with her eyes open. Her breathing was faster than when she had slept, but it was still calm and steady.

Rameel stepped out from behind the rock and into the dull moonlight coming from the window.

She didn't even blink.

Rameel took a few steps forward.

Her eyes rotated slowly, inspecting, assessing. Her expressionless face remained still, graceful lines carved in stone.

Rameel waved a hand through the air. The lock opened, and the gate swung outward with a squeal.

She stayed on the floor, eyes locked on his.

"I know you like to look out the window. This one in the hall is bigger," he said, the words coming out as a growl.

She just stared at him without replying.

Rameel wondered if she was too scared to move. Was it the sound of his voice? His appearance? He stepped forward and reached up to one of the iron bars, wrapping his long black fingers around the rusted metal. He watched her carefully as he moved, looking for tensing muscles or dilating eyes. There were no signs of fear. If she wasn't afraid, what was it that she felt?

"Thou, who art most powerful," came a voice from behind.

The memory vanished from Rameel's mind, and all he saw was an empty cell and his fingers curled around the metal bar. The light inside was still dull, but daylight instead of moonlight. Rameel turned, seeing a cloaked man on the floor of the hall, bowed so low that his face was pressed against the stone. "What is it?"

"The goddess of the south has arrived at the temple. She has brought you a gift to prove her allegiance."

"Anything else?"

"No, most powerful," the man replied, backing away immediately.

When the priest was gone, Rameel let his eyes linger on the cell a while longer. Then he walked down the hall and turned into a cavern whose mouth was open to the eastern sky. Forested hills rolled into the distance beneath a cloudy sky. Though the temple was a full day's travel by foot to the south, it would only take him a moment to cover the distance by air. But he didn't delay, for it was not wise to keep Zaquel waiting. She was Rameel's equal—not his subject as the messenger had been led to believe—and it was a courtesy that he would expect of her if the situation had been reversed.

Rameel walked to the ledge and jumped, spreading his great membranous wings to catch the air. A few thrusts sent him into the sky and moving forward with blinding speed.

11

Sariel swam against the current and into the shadows. Above him, the water still rippled as it did in the light areas, indicating that there was room to surface. He rose slowly, craning his neck. His nose and lips broke through first into the air, and he sucked in a desperate breath. Then he took another and went under once more. Seconds later, his lungs were no longer starving and he was able to let the rest of his face and head out of the water without causing a commotion.

The shadow was cast by a metal bridge suspended a few feet above the water. It connected the platform on the right with a walkway on the edge of the cavern to the left. The lighter areas were produced by windows in the ceiling hundreds of feet above the water. But the ceiling wasn't natural stone, as with the cavern in First Earth. This one had been constructed of metal and glass panels.

The air was thick with moisture, fed by the steam rising from various locations across the lake. In fact, there was more water in this cavern than hard surfaces, if one didn't count the walls and ceiling. And all was quiet except for the sound of running water.

The gathering of Myndarym that Sariel had witnessed weeks ago from the outskirts of the city had involved thousands. But most of those spirits disappeared suddenly. Only three of them had left this chamber in a normal manner, walking back through the building passages and into the city. Those had been Turel, Danel, and Arakiba. And afterwards, whenever Sariel had caught glimpses of them in the Temporal, they were carrying dark objects that sparkled like the Tree of Wisdom.

Sariel looked around the chamber now but found no evidence of the Tree fragment, Ezekiyel, or the temporal Myndarym. They had to have gone through the In-Between and into another world, but why such a large group? For what purpose? And how could they have taken the fractured piece of the Tree? The branches spread out far too wide to fit through the diameter of the stump.

Unless they divided it further, Sariel realized. *That would explain the objects the others were carrying.*

He reached up and grabbed hold of a support pole, lifting his body out of the water. He pulled, adding his legs to the effort until he was climbing the structure like a ladder. Water dripped from his clothing and skin, but the noise of it was lost to the other sounds of water inside the chamber. Climbing around an overhang, Sariel came to his feet on a metal walkway. From this raised perspective, he could see all the way across the chamber. Beyond the platform that he had seen from the water, the stump shimmered. It was the only object in the room that appeared different from everything else, which ruled out the possibility that Ezekiyel had been using the Tree fragment to build something, or had left it behind. There was no evidence for Sariel to discover.

What were you doing in here? he wondered.

Sariel turned and began walking across the bridge, heading for the perimeter of the cavern. When he reached the outer walkway, he circled the water in methodical steps, eyes searching the walls, the ceiling, and the depths of the water. There hadn't been any Marotru Unshapers at the gathering, but whatever had taken place had been on a similar scale to the Fracturing in Aden. And anything that critical had to have left signs.

"Stop right there!" a voice yelled from across the room.

Sariel turned to see one of the temporal Myndarym standing in an open doorway. He was clothed from his neck to his feet in a white fabric, coarsely textured, that clung to his muscled body. He looked enormously tall, but when two others came up behind him, Sariel realized it was just a matter of perspective—he'd never seen them up close until now. Their pale appearance made them seem otherworldly against the dull surroundings.

"How did you get out?" the first one asked in an angelic tongue. He stepped out from the doorway and pulled a white staff from the belt at his waist. The two Myndarym behind him came out and began jogging in opposite directions along the perimeter walkway. Even at their casual pace, their strides covered much distance quickly. It would only be a moment before Sariel was flanked by enemies.

He spun around and ran toward a passage only a few paces away.

"Stop!" the first Myndar yelled.

Sariel reached the passage and found it blocked by a door with no handle. He scanned the area for some sign of a latch or a lock, but there were no features, only smooth metal. When he turned back to the walkway, the two Myndarym were already halfway around the room. Sariel's only way out was the stump in the middle of the cavern, and the shortest path to the bridge was along the perimeter walkway to the right.

He started into a run, knowing immediately that he would meet the Myndar coming from that direction before he reached the bridge. His only choice was to go through the temporal angel.

As soon as Sariel chose a direction, the first Myndar on the opposite side of the room began running that way as well.

Sariel's strides lengthened. His speed increased, driven by the power of his spiritual body in the Eternal.

The bridge was getting closer, but the Myndar on the right had already passed it. With every stride, he seemed taller and taller. The angel was at a full run now. The white staff from his belt was in his hand, and its tip was glowing with blue light.

Sariel didn't understand what it was, but he knew by instinct that it was something to be avoided.

As the two enemies closed the distance between them, the angel raised his staff, implying that it was an impact weapon.

Sariel waited until the last moment before separating his physical and spiritual bodies. His temporal self leaped to the right side and began running up the wall, while his eternal self veered left.

The Myndar—seeing only what was temporal, and being shocked by it—swung his staff in a desperate motion. It hit the stone wall below Sariel with a shower of blue sparks and the crackle of fire. The motion left his right side exposed.

Sariel's eternal self clawed through the Myndar's spiritual body as he passed him by.

For reasons invisible to everyone else in the room, the angel's right side split open from his abdomen to his ribcage. The unseen force twisted his body, and he spun in mid-stride and hit the walkway in a tumble.

Sariel leapt from the wall and flipped, bringing his selves together again before his feet touched the walkway. The bridge was now only a few paces away, and he turned along it, heading for the stump.

"Stop right there!" a voice yelled.

Sariel ignored it and kept running, his only exit just a few seconds away.

Pulses of blue light from the left were accompanied by splashes of water that rose up like fountains beside the bridge.

Sariel ran through the spray, ignoring whatever was taking place and focusing only on reaching his goal. At this speed, one misstep could mean the difference between success and failure. Suddenly, he reached the stump and dropped, sliding across its glossy surface. When his momentum halted, he was just beyond the center of it.

The first Myndar had reached the edge of the bridge and was raising his staff. The other one was still coming at a run from the other side of the room.

Sariel rolled onto his hands and knees, readying himself for the sensation of enormous pressure that would soon close around him. He looked back to the first Myndar, who now had one end of his staff against his shoulder and the glowing blue end pointed straight at Sariel. But instead of the blue light wavering, distorting sideways along with everything else—as it should have done when the vortex of the In-Between pulled at him—the blue light pulsed brighter.

Every nerve in Sariel's body suddenly felt as though it were on fire. He dropped to his face, unable to control himself. His body convulsed, and the pain was excruciating. Even his lungs were paralyzed; he felt as though he were being choked to death. The moment seemed to stretch out into minutes, agony that refused to end. But it eventually subsided.

When Sariel's eyes began to take in information once more, he saw the Myndar lower his staff and begin walking forward along the bridge. The other one was still running along the perimeter, as if the pain had only lasted the blink of an eye. Sariel rolled onto his back and groaned. It seemed the only expression of which his body was now capable of producing.

The glass panels and the sunlight above now seemed so far away.

The gurgle of water was louder than it should have been.

Suddenly, two majestic faces were looking down at him. Their eyes were turquoise in color, almost glowing with a light of their own. Their white hair was cropped short, and their pale skin was smooth and without blemish. The coarseness of their clothing, Sariel now understood, came from the miniature designs woven into them. The edge of their tunics rose up along their necks on one side, giving them an even more dignified appearance. These were of a higher rank than the ones Sariel had observed working on the ocean. One of them spoke, and Sariel was almost surprised to learn that his mind was still capable of deriving meaning from sounds.

"Who are you?"

Sariel couldn't have responded even if he wanted to.

"He's not one of ours. Just look at him," the other stated.

"How did you learn to move like that?"

Sariel just lay still, unable to do anything but stare.

The first Myndar leaned down and wrapped his fingers around Sariel's throat. Then he stood and raised the limp human body into the air. Without the slightest appearance of straining, he pulled Sariel's face toward his own.

"Who are you?"

The weight of Sariel's body was being mostly supported by his jaw, leaving him unable to breathe or speak if his muscles ever decided to obey. Sariel attempted to reply, but he only managed to grunt.

The angel slowly moved his hand to one side, then the other, inspecting Sariel's helpless, dangling body.

The other Myndar glanced across the room at the bloody mess of his fellow soldier. "He's dead." The statement sounded as though such a thing were impossible. "What should we do?"

"Lock him up until Ezekiyel returns. He'll want to study this one."

"Which habitat?"

"The pale ones."

Sariel's arms twitched with a flicker of returning feeling.

"And before that," the angel added, "make sure there's no fight left in him."

"Gladly," the other replied, raising his staff.

From the corner of his vision, Sariel detected blue light just before his body began to spasm in pain again.

*   *   *   *

EAST OF THE TREE
SECOND EARTH

Sariel hid among the vines of the jungle. The vegetation was so thick that nothing in the Temporal Realm could ever hope to find him. In the Eternal, he'd darkened his spirit to match the landscape so he would be concealed there as well. With his perspective straddling both realms, he watched a large group of men moving through the valley below. Several dozen of them were carrying the fractured piece of the Tree on their shoulders. The branches of the dark, crystalline cargo stuck up into the air behind them. Every so often, the leafless twigs would become entangled in the canopy of the jungle, and the group would have to stop to cut it free.

Most of the men walked in front of the cargo, clearing a path through the tall grass and brush with their spears. In all, there were several hundred humans, regularly rotating their responsibilities in order to make the fastest progress. At the rear of the procession, Armaros and Satarel walked at a casual pace. On occasions where the Tree began to tilt or move in a dangerous way, one of them would extend his hand and rebalance the cargo with an unseen strength.

Though he was hidden and safe from harm in this earth, Sariel's heart was racing. One of his other selves had just been discovered inside a large chamber at the center of Ezekiyel's city in Third Earth. Three temporal Myndarym were now aware of his presence there.

Even if I escape, Ezekiyel and the rest will know that I survived the flood!

But he couldn't stay in that chamber and allow himself to be caught. He could kill the temporal Myndarym, but that would leave behind evidence proving his survival as well. There was no way out of the predicament without losing something.

Go for the stump! he told himself.

The men transporting their cargo through the valley below now seemed like a distraction. Sariel backed deeper into the foliage and let his attention be diverted to his other self. All of a sudden, the nerves of his body twitched with dull pain. Whatever was happening in Third Earth was strong enough to reach him here. He wished it were possible to reach out the other way, across the void between worlds, and help his other self. But he'd never been able to coordinate anything more than thoughts.

Down in the valley, Armaros and Satarel were still moving in a relaxed manner and talking to each other. Kokabiel was not with this group, but if the Myndarym were intending to gather at the Tree as they had done in Third Earth, it was only a matter of time before he arrived as well.

Another jolt of pain washed over Sariel, suddenly rearranging his priorities. His third self needed physical help, and he needed it as soon as possible. The ambushing of his enemies in this world would have to wait. Sariel turned and crawled back through the vines, keeping low to the ground so that his movements wouldn't be spotted. When he crested the hill and started down the other side, he stood and began to run as fast as the terrain would allow.

12

Rameel glided slowly in a downward spiral, dropping through the cylindrical void that ran all the way through the center of the volcano. The smooth, black stone had formed rapidly around the stump after the Fracturing, when it flowed upward in molten form from the depths of the earth. But as the outer shell of the volcano was cooling and hardening, the portal was drawing the liquid interior through the In-Between and sharing it with the other worlds. The flow had created this smooth-sided shaft, as well as the spherical chamber around the stump.

As he descended, Rameel noted that his masons had completed the staircase carved in a spiral along the inside of the shaft. This vertical entry point was in addition to the four horizontal ones carved into the sloped sides of the mountain— one for each primary direction. Eventually, this volcano of black stone would become a temple, a place of worship for his Kaliel. They would come from the north, south, east, and west. Their pilgrimage would be an act of worship in itself. And when they arrived, Rameel's subjects would find their god ready to receive them. His Kaliel already feared him as a king, and they called him a god, but Rameel's home among the cliffs to the north wasn't as majestic as his reputation required. If he was truly to become their god in every sense of the word, he would need to elevate himself in their understanding.

The spherical chamber opened up below him, and Rameel flared his wings to slow his descent. He touched down gently upon one of the wooden bridges that connected the stump to the tunnel leading into the wall of the cavern. The bridge on the opposite side of the stump was occupied by the severed fragment of the Tree; Zaquel's cargo had already been received by Rameel's servants and set into place for the ceremony. All was ready for Ezekiyel's arrival.

Rameel pulled his wings around himself and inspected the inside of the cavern. Along the perimeter, an elaborate system of wooden scaffolds crawled up the walls in various locations. Large sails of cloth had been stretched over the framework to cover the masons' latest project—nine images that would encourage the proper mindset among his worshippers when the temple was finally opened. It would be a three-dimensional depiction of the Kaliel symbol. Eight of the statues had been made to look like Iryllurym without their battle armor. Their feathered wings and shorter stature would make them seem kinder and less powerful than the ninth. The largest of the statues had been made to emphasize Rameel's fear-inducing appearance. If he was to be the god of these lands and its people, Rameel's power over the other gods had to be reinforced at every opportunity. These carvings were his way of acknowledging the other eight gods of the Temporal Realm, while confining them to a visual representation that worked in his favor.

Rameel had always envied the Iryllurym during his service to the Amatru. When Semjaza had given him the opportunity to come to this realm, he quickly chose a winged form. But among so many other angels with forms that were majestic and awe-inspiring to the human inhabitants, Rameel needed something that would set him apart. He had found his inspiration among the creatures of the earth that humans naturally feared. A serpent was too restrictive a form, and a spider might have made him something for the Kahyin to hunt instead of worship.

In the end, Rameel had settled on the form of a bat, with just enough of his angelic features to make him seem otherworldly.

As important as these statues were to the purpose of this temple, Rameel didn't want any of the other Myndarym to look upon them. There was far too much of his private thinking represented there. It was one thing to display the carvings for humans, but quite another to reveal them to fellow angels who would immediately understand the deeper meaning behind them ... hence the scaffolding and the large cloths hiding them from view.

"Well, this is quite an improvement," came a startling voice from behind.

Rameel turned to see Zaquel coming across the bridge. She moved quietly on bare feet. Her skin, the color of fertile soil, was draped in loose white linen that billowed behind her as she walked. She wore a headdress of gold and onyx stone that spilled down to her neck and shoulders, enveloping her in the wealth of the earth. Her arms were bare, except for bracelets that jangled as she swept her hand to the side in a grand gesture.

"When I came out of the In-Between, I had to climb my way out of this place."

Rameel found his eyes following hers up to the cylindrical hole in the ceiling. "Yes, well ... my human worshippers lack your considerable abilities."

"Careful. Flattery only reveals one's weakness," Zaquel replied with a smile as she came to a stop before Rameel.

Both were equal in height, but she had chosen beauty over fear as her primary method of rule. Perhaps that was why Ezekiyel had suggested the portal to the In-Between be protected by Rameel—the more aggressive of the two. It had been a source of irritation to her ever since.

Zaquel's gaze wandered from place to place, appearing casual even though she was noting every detail in order to assess Rameel's strength. "Human worshippers ..." she repeated. "Tell me—are any of them soldiers? Or do you keep them all busy carving complimentary images of yourself?"

Rameel kept his eyes on her, refusing to confirm her speculation by looking at the scaffolding. "You traveled all the way here from the coast with my soldiers."

Zaquel laughed quickly and quietly as her gaze continued sweeping over the cavern. "Someday, you really must come visit me in the south. I would be happy to show you what real soldiers are. And true worship. There are many things you could learn from the Empire of Rana."

Rameel didn't bother to smile. The sight of his sharp teeth would only encourage more of her biting remarks. "Someday ... perhaps."

The air above the stump began to glow with a blue aura, and both Myndarym turned to watch. Long seconds passed without any perceptible change. The silence was awkward, and Rameel tried to think of anything that would bring an end to it. "It seems to be taking a long time."

Zaquel nodded.

"Have you chosen your object?"

She nodded again.

The blue aura seemed to be growing more substantial, but Rameel couldn't be sure.

"A scepter," she finally answered.

"Ah ... appropriate."

Striations were forming within the aura.

"There is a particular tree that is considered sacred among the tribes."

Rameel nodded. "A wise choice to use what is already revered."

The striations were becoming defined.

"And you?" she asked.

"A sword."

Zaquel turned away from the portal and looked into Rameel's eyes.

He couldn't be sure, but he thought there might be a trace of compassion there. "Well ... a dagger, really. It will have a blade that curves just slightly."

Zaquel's smile was one of sadness. "Like a vaepkir?"

Rameel's lungs suddenly felt as if the air had been stolen from them. The object that he had in mind was indeed very similar to the primary blade of a vaepkir. His obsession with the Iryllurym apparently went so deep that it was even below his own level of detection. He hadn't realized the connection until she looked into his soul and pulled it out.

Blue shafts of light were stabbing upward from the portal to the ceiling of the cavern. Wherever they touched, random shapes appeared and disappeared from the dark stone as though it were rippling water.

Rameel was grateful for the sudden distraction. "He's almost here."

Zaquel mercifully turned her penetrating gaze toward the stump.

The shafts of light began as a bundled column. Then they split apart at the top, fraying outward until they were shooting sideways. The illuminated outline of a human appeared to hover above the surface of the stump. As it began walking forward, its shape became more defined and it began to take on substance as well. By the time it stepped onto the bridge, dozens of other shapes, much taller, were beginning to appear.

Rameel and Zaquel backed away from the portal to make room for the unexpected quantity of visitors.

"Is everything prepared?" Ezekiyel asked, his human body now fully present in this world.

"Yes," Rameel answered quickly, looking down from his form which towered above the other.

Zaquel's attention was still focused on the portal. "Who are they?" she asked with a suspicious tone.

"The children of Danel and Turel."

Rameel watched as pale beings began walking from the stump and onto the bridge, filling the space behind Ezekiyel. When their bodies were fully present, Rameel could tell just by their clothing that the master Shaper's world was already far more advanced than this one.

"Children?" Zaquel asked. Her tone sounded like a mixture of jealousy and disgust.

"They are not Nephiylim," Ezekiyel explained. "I would never permit any of us to violate the agreement. These are pure Myndarym ... temporal angels. I've brought them to assist with the *shaping*."

For once, Zaquel was speechless.

"How was your journey?" Rameel asked, hoping to change the subject.

"Much longer than expected, but we can discuss that later."

Rameel just nodded in response.

"I see the fragment is in place," Ezekiyel added. "And you both have clear ideas of the objects that you want?"

"Yes," Rameel replied.

Ezekiyel turned to Zaquel and waited for her to stop staring at the temporal Myndarym still materializing above the portal and walking onto the bridge. The silence must have finally broken through her thoughts. She turned. "Yes."

Ezekiyel nodded. "Now ... let me reiterate that the purpose of this *shaping* is to prevent uncontrolled passage between the worlds. It is critical that we each respect the separation and keep to our own worlds until the Marotru indicate that they are ready for us. Is this understood?"

Rameel and Zaquel nodded their agreement.

"Very good. Let us proceed."

* * * *

NYADEN
THIRD EARTH

A painful impact brought Sariel out of a half-conscious state. He opened his eyes to find that his face was against a surface of cold, white segments. The perfect squares and their boundaries defined a flat plane that stretched away to a blurry, vertical horizon, but something about it seemed unreal. He blinked his eyes a few times, trying to clear away the feeling of disorientation. Seconds passed before his sense of proportion returned. The segments were tiles, and they didn't blur at a vertical horizon; they spread a few paces across the floor until they were obscured by mist. Beyond the tile floor, Sariel could make out the tall forms of two temporal Myndarym in white clothing glaring down at him. He made eye contact with them for just a brief moment before they descended a staircase leading through the circular hole in the middle of the tiles. As soon as their heads were below the level of the tiles, a panel of glass slid sideways to fill the void.

Sariel realized that the guards had just thrown him where he was now lying. The abrupt landing must have been the impact he felt earlier. The glass panel was a door. The white tiles were the threshold.

This is a holding cell.

It was a simple observation, and one that he should have arrived at more quickly. But it seemed profound to his addled mind. Though he couldn't remember exactly what had been done to him, he knew enough to understand that all of it had been painful.

Sariel heard movement behind him. On instinct, he tried to roll over, but his body was still not fully obedient to his wishes. The movement only resulted in his head turning. Now he was looking up at an expanse of diffused light, shifting in layers like clouds, instead of the ceiling that he was expecting.

"Are you hurt?" came a timid voice.

Sariel tried to roll over again, but all he could manage was a twitch of his shoulder.

"Help him," another said. The voices were speaking Shayeth.

Someone placed their hand on Sariel's arm and pulled. The sight of the clouds passed before him, quickly replaced by that of trees. Sariel was now lying on his opposite side, facing into his prison cell. But what he saw didn't help him make sense of the situation. The white tiles under his face merged with soil and grass. In the distance, mist swirled in and around a dark forest of pines. Two human-like creatures were kneeling in front of Sariel. The male who had rolled him over had green eyes that were full of compassion. But the rest of his appearance was nothing like Sariel had ever seen before—hair as golden as a sunset, skin that was as pale as beach sand. The other, a female, also had pale coloring, but her skin was speckled with a slightly darker color. She had eyes of blue, like the ocean.

"We've never seen one like you before," the man said.

"He looks almost like a demon," the woman replied, fingering a strand of Sariel's white hair.

"Do you speak?" the man asked.

Beyond him, at the edge of the forest, dozens of these creatures were gathered. All were staring intently at Sariel, as though his arrival was the most intriguing part of their day. But it was Sariel who was intrigued. All of them were quite short, with lighter coloring than any he'd ever observed. Their eyes bulged, and the protruding areas of their facial features—cheekbones, eyebrows, and chins—appeared exaggerated. Their limbs were longer than normal, and their joints looked swollen. They had short torsos, and all of them were completely naked.

"What is this place?" he asked.

Both of the kneeling ones smiled.

"What do you mean?" the woman replied.

"Are you prisoners?"

The man tilted his head to the side. "What is ... prisoner?"

13

Ebnisha dipped a stalk of grass into a small gourd, and when he pulled it out, the tip was black with writing fluid. He laid it against the parchment and continued making his marks to record Sariel's story. He was only summarizing; there were far too many details to capture everything upon the page. But that didn't stop Sariel from sharing the full experience. Ebnisha seemed to enjoy every bit of it. When the writing instrument came to a stop, Ebnisha looked up.

"The next morning, I was awakened by something touching my arm," Sariel continued. "My fever was quite strong by this time, and I couldn't look up because of my injuries. But I'd heard the footsteps upon the rocks and I knew enough to assume that it was human. I tried asking for food and water, but all that came out was a moan. That's when Enoch turned me over. He thought I needed help getting up. Of course, this caused me a great deal of pain, and I'm sure I yelled out. It was the pain that brought me out of my stupor, at first. Then I saw who had woken me."

Ebnisha's eyes were wide, as if he were there meeting Enoch face to face. Then he looked down and began writing again.

Sariel watched him for a moment, before his gaze began to wander around the hut. He'd been steadily enlarging and improving his shelter in the afternoons, when Ebnisha went back to his own village. The roof and walls now enclosed the fire pit, and there was a table upon which Ebnisha could lay his writing tools and his scrolls. The table was flanked by two chairs that were occupied for the majority of their time spent together.

"How fortunate it was that he found you in that place," Ebnisha said without looking up from the parchment.

Sariel smiled. This was the part he enjoyed most about telling stories; he hadn't yet revealed to Ebnisha the events that had led Enoch to that particular location. He'd found that life rarely made sense until after you were looking back on it. Only then could you see how each person's story was being woven together with others. The Holy One had brought Enoch to Sariel's rescue, and during his healing, Sariel had begun to think that he had also been brought to Enoch for a purpose. Suddenly, Sariel realized that the same thing was happening now.

After wandering alone in this world for over two thousand years ... the first human being I meet knows who I am!

Not only did Ebnisha know about Sariel, he knew about the Myndarym and Nephiylim as well. He had the cumulative history of his people either memorized or committed to parchment, the scrolls of which he brought with him for reference when his memory was too vague for his liking. Their meeting was no accident, and yet, Sariel had received no messages from the Holy One. There had been no strange feelings during his travels that led him to this place. He had simply walked, searching for any signs of life after the waters had ravaged the earth.

It was comforting to imagine that the Holy One might, even now, be working in this realm. *A relief, really,* Sariel thought. *Perhaps I'm* not *corrupting humans through my contact with them after all.*

Sariel realized that he'd been silent for quite some time, lost in thought. Ebnisha had finished writing and was waiting patiently for the next part of the story. The look in his eyes said that he understood the reason why.

"I would have died there, on the shores of the Great Waters, if Enoch hadn't found me. You see, he had been living in a meadow nearby. The Holy One had led him to it, and even Enoch didn't realize what was happening at the time. But he listened. He obeyed. And it turned out that he had plenty of food and fresh water for both of us. It was a safe place, protected by a forest all around. There was soft grass for me to lie upon as I healed. There was even a stream that connected it to the Great Waters so that Enoch could transport me all the way there without having to lift me."

"Marvelous!" Ebnisha exclaimed. "So, it was really the Holy One who rescued you."

"Yes," Sariel answered. "And Enoch was His method of accomplishing it."

Ebnisha dipped his writing tool and began marking the parchment. His symbols had been getting smaller over the last few days as he realized how much information there was to record and how little parchment there was on which to capture it.

As the stalk of grass scratched against the page, Sariel's mind began to wander once more. He wondered if the Holy One's intervention would come again, or if that time with Enoch had been a special occasion. He wondered if his third self would escape from Ezekiyel's soldiers. He wondered if his second self would even be able to enter the In-Between or if the stump had been changed there too. And if he was able to enter and cross the In-Between to the vortex of Third Earth, would it allow him to pass through?

* * * *

HRIDIAM
FIRST EARTH

The firelight of Rameel's city was only visible from the air. It glowed beneath the forests to the north like a subtle beacon for creatures of the sky. But Rameel was the only winged being in this world capable of seeing it as such. He banked to the west and descended into a break in the trees where the glow was strongest. The mountain chain, of which the temple was a part, had been eroded here in the north by the floodwaters. The eastern side of the valley rose gradually in elevation as one went inland, but the western side was a sheer cliff of black stone, with hundreds of caves. Most of the tunnels were dark, like the eye sockets of a skull. Ladders spilled out of them and ran down the face of the cliff like tears. A few tunnels flickered with orange light, just enough to illuminate the entrance into Rameel's city.

He touched down on the sand below the cliffs and retracted his wings, walking toward the largest of the tunnels. It sat level with the ground, and the stone around it was carved with many images depicting the human interpretation of what was inside. The Kaliel were stoneworkers by nature, descended from the nomadic tribes of the cold northeast lands who had learned to seek shelter from winter by tunneling beneath the earth. Rameel had given these southern tribes a more dignified purpose for their expert masonry skills. The God of the Underworld had made them his own people, giving them his strength and his knowledge of the stone and soil. In return, they sought to honor him with the perfection of their greatest skill.

Rameel had never witnessed their equal among any human builders of this or the old world. And yet, even the Kaliel weren't capable of understanding the complexity of what Ezekiyel had just done. The crystalline dagger that Rameel now carried was a marvel of *shaping* skill, elegant in both its form and function. The method of its crafting was simply unattainable by humans, because no other material in this world was strong enough to alter its shape. This was why Rameel carried it instead of wearing it like any other weapon. It had no scabbard, and until he found a way to create one that didn't make contact with the edge of the blade, it would not be safe to wear his key to the portal. For now, it would have to be hidden within Hridiam.

Rameel came to a stop just before entering the primary tunnel. His mind suddenly contained more than his own thoughts, which was something he hadn't experienced since his service to Baraquijal. Zaquel possessed this ability, but Rameel's own talents had taken a different course during their maturation. He turned slowly and shifted his perspective toward the Eternal.

The darkness to the east slowly lightened, gaining definition. The sky shifted from black to red, carving out the silhouettes of trees as the forest became visible. The spirits of tiny forest creatures could be seen glowing against the dull backdrop. Birds rested high in the branches. Nocturnal animals prowled the forest floor. But there was another spirit, large and swirling with a multitude of dull colors. Rameel hadn't seen such a thing since he and Arakiba had left Galah for Aden in the old world.

It was a Nephiyl.

It stood perfectly still, like a statue, while a breeze moved through the forest, swaying branches and some thin tree trunks. The thoughts running through the creature's mind had to do with Rameel's appearance. It recognized him, though it had never seen him before.

"Step into the light," Rameel said to it.

The Nephiyl shifted its weight, but remained where it was.

"Come to me, my son. Let me look upon you," Rameel added.

The Nephiyl glanced behind and then to either side, as if he expected a trap. Many seconds passed before he finally left the trees and came out into the open. Even though he was two times larger than Rameel, there was no sound to his movements. It seemed that he had inherited the natural stealth of his ancestors. But it was his other inherited features which made Rameel's throat constrict. The Nephiyl's face looked exactly like his mother's—high cheekbones, prominent mouth and chin, large, round eyes. Unlike his mother, whose skin was the deepest of browns, this child was as dark as the forest behind him. His hair was black, falling long and straight below his shoulders. He had a thin, yet muscular build that was only covered by a loincloth and short tunic of leather. He was barefoot and carried no weapons.

"How did you know I was here?" the child asked.

"I see and hear things that are beyond this world," Rameel answered.

The Nephiyl continued walking forward, firelight revealing more of his appearance with every step. "Then you must be able to see that I'm not well."

No sooner had the words left the child's mouth than Rameel noticed the green undertones to his skin. "Is this why you've returned to the place of your birth?"

"We're dying," the Nephiyl replied. "My older brothers and sisters taught me that our ancestors used to be great hunters of men. They showed me how to live in the forest and how to stalk the human tribes of the northlands without revealing myself. They told me about our winged father who gave them this wisdom before sending our people to live among the trees. Then their skin began to turn green and they died ... one after another. I am now the elder of my tribe, and though I have become a great hunter of men, I cannot protect my people from this sickness. I cannot even protect myself."

"And the younger ones?"

"Only one is showing signs."

Rameel was now looking up at the Nephiyl who had come to a stop just a few paces away. He was unsure of what to say; the Nephiylim of the old world had never died of sickness or anything besides war that he could remember. There were reports of humans becoming ill before the Fracturing, but the healthy ones typically lived many hundreds of years. Since then, the lifespan of humans had been reduced to a tenth of what it used to be.[6] Perhaps there was some unseen defect among the human mothers that resulted in this illness. Such things were beyond Rameel's expertise. Whatever the cause, this child was dying far sooner than he should—he was only a few decades old.

"What do they call you among your tribe?" he asked the Nephiyl.

"Akuji."

Dead but awake, Rameel translated to himself. *It seems a cruel name.*

"It wasn't meant to be cruel. I was called Akuji because I never cried as an infant. Now it is true for another reason."

Rameel raised his eyebrows; it seemed that they shared more than just a simple connection. "Take me to your siblings."

*   *   *   *

SARIEL'S CAMP
FIRST EARTH

Sariel reclined by the fire with Ebnisha's most recent work-in-progress lying across his lap. The scribe had gone back to his village hours ago, and now that Sariel's afternoon work had been completed and the sun had set, he found himself in a reminiscent mood. He unrolled the scroll, and the first words upon it brought a smile to his lips.

The words of Sariel, entrusted to his faithful servant Ebnisha.

He had no idea that this was how Ebnisha viewed himself. Sariel certainly hadn't said or done anything to suggest the nature of their relationship was anything different from a friendship. Sariel would have to discuss the matter with Ebnisha tomorrow to clarify that there was no hierarchy here. This was simply two people telling stories and learning from one another.

In the year SA 4226, the Angel Sariel revealed himself to my people ...

Sariel began reading, enjoying the surprising formality of Ebnisha's writing in light of his informal manner of relating in person. As he continued down the page, rolling and unrolling the parchment to reveal more of what they had discussed, Sariel was amazed at how the man had been able to condense their discussions into a concise story, without losing the important details. The quality of it took Sariel back to Aleydiyr, when he and Sheyir used to sit before a fire in the cool mountain air, listening to the tribespeople tell of their daily activities. The Aleydam would have been proud to see that their talents had survived, expressing themselves in a new way through another generation of humans in a radically different world.

Sariel continued reading, fascinated to see his own stories through another person's eyes. Ebnisha often made connections to the stories handed down by his own people, displaying a depth of thought and consideration that would have rivaled any elder of the old world.

Farther down the page, the symbol of the Kaliel drew his attention. Sariel skimmed the words below it, finding that Ebnisha described it in detail as well as its connection to the Myndarym. It was clear that he was writing to his own people. Sariel imagined Ebnisha speaking to a group of children who had gathered around the scribe, forced by their parents to memorize the stories of their history. He couldn't help but smile as he remembered the way the children in El-Betakh squirmed when Enoch's stories became boring.

Besides Sariel, there are nine other Myndarym who have survived. They are not friends or defenders of us, as Sariel has proven to be. They are in fact our greatest enemies. But we shall not fear them, for Enoch, the seventh Firstborn of Adam, prophesied their destruction when he told his son, Methushelak, of The Awakened.

Sariel scratched his chin. *The Awakened? What does that mean?* He read on, but Ebnisha didn't record anything more on the matter. It was simply a passing comment. Sariel looked up from the parchment to the handful of scrolls on the table. Ebnisha's pile of references grew as the topics changed. He would take scrolls back to his village when they weren't needed any longer, and then he would bring others to replace them.

Sariel rolled up Ebnisha's current work and climbed to his feet before going through the other scrolls. One detailed the life of Methushelak during his adult years in Sedekiyr. Another described the time when Lemek, his wife, Elah, and their son, Noah, wandered alone through the wilderness without a place to call home. Methu's years in El-Betakh, after the destruction of Sedekiyr, almost distracted Sariel from his goal. And Noah's story immediately following the receding of the floodwaters was particularly interesting. But finally, Sariel found a scroll that told of Enoch's return to Sedekiyr after his very first experience with the Wandering Stars.

Sariel skimmed through a story of Enoch being captured by the Kahyin and his rescue by Ananel in his wolf form. He unrolled another long section of the parchment and skipped down.

The corpses of slain angels surrounded me on every side. The Myndarym had each gone their own way, leaving me alone in the field. But they had opened my ears to their language. I was the first human to speak with the tongue of angels. And from that day, henceforward, the place where Semjaza attacked the Speaker was known to me as Haragdeh—the killing fields.

Sariel unrolled the parchment almost to the end of the scroll.

My son did not understand how the Holy One could love them and speak of punishing them at the same time.

This was from when Enoch had just returned to Sedekiyr. He had been close with Methu during those times, before the tribe shunned him. This was when Methu had learned the majority of Enoch's stories. But Sariel had gone too far. He backed up a few sections, finally locating a recounting of Enoch's visit to the White City. He skimmed over the visions that Enoch had already told him about, then settled upon a section at the end of the visit that he'd never heard before. He read of the Holy One's sadness over the rebellion of the Myndarym, and the judgment that would come upon their children.

Because they were born of the flesh, the abominations of the Nephiylim will be a curse to the Temporal Realm. And because they were also born of the spirit, their eternal bodies will be a curse to the Eternal Realm. I see what is to come and the sin of the Nephiylim is always before me. They will afflict, oppress, destroy, make war, and work destruction upon my creation.

They will rise up against the children of men and women, because they have proceeded from them. The Nephiylim will destroy each other before your eyes and by your hands. You will witness the death of your own children.

It was the Holy One, speaking to the Myndarym through Enoch about what was to come ... thousands of years before it took place. During the reign of Azael, his Nephiylim made war against the children of the Myndarym. And just as the Holy One had said, the angels watched their children die as they traveled toward Sedekiyr.

Though they claim to have revealed all things to you, I see their hearts and the things they keep hidden, even from each other. I see the things they have done and the things which they have yet to do. They have asked for peace, but will make war and teach the children of men to do likewise. Tell them, 'You will have no peace.'

Sariel thought of the Aytsam who attacked and killed Sheyir's people. He remembered the Kahyin who had been sent out from Khanok to round up the descendants of the Shayeth. He remembered the people of Galah with their swords and their walls of stone. It was the influence of the Wandering Stars that brought such things to the world of men, or at the very least, accelerated their arrival.

Now, Enoch, son of righteousness, I have another message that you will not speak to the Myndarym. You will teach it to your children and they will teach it to their children. Thus, it will remain with your household for generations to come. At the appointed time, it will be revealed to my Wandering Stars and they will hear and understand.

Sariel leaned closer to the table where he had the scroll laid out.

You will see your destruction from afar and will know it is coming. Because of your unfaithfulness, this judgment must come to pass. Therefore, I will raise up one from among those you despise. And I will awaken his eyes to the mysteries which I have hidden from men since the foundations of the world. His feet will I make to tread upon the paths of destruction and his hands to make war. He will uproot the seeds of corruption which you have sown throughout the earth. And then you will know that I am the Lord and my justice is everlasting.

Sariel skimmed the following words to see that it continued with Enoch telling Methu of how he delivered the judgments, all except this one, to the Myndarym in Aragatsiyr. Then Sariel went back up to the prophecy and read it again, paying close attention to each and every word.

Ebnisha was right. The other judgments had already come to pass, just as the Holy One had spoken. But this one had yet to take place. It said that the Myndarym would see their destruction from afar, but how were they to know it was coming unless someone told them? Perhaps it was this awakened being who would deliver the message. But why would he announce it if the judgments were going to take place regardless?

Sariel carefully rolled up the scroll and set it next to the others. He didn't need to look at it any longer; it was already committed to memory. He left the table and returned to the ground beside the fire, which had burned down to a single weak flame rising from a bed of coals.

"Those you despise," he said aloud. Who did the Myndarym despise?

Nephiylim?

They regretted producing most of the Nephiylim, perhaps, but that wasn't the same thing.

Humans?

In Gongur, under Baraquijal's rule, the fields to the west of the city had been turned into corrals. Humans had been kept like animals, bred as food for the inhabited Nephiylim. Such treatment reflected a deep feeling of superiority over another being. Superiority that considered the their kind undeserving of this realm—to be used and then thrown away. Jealousy turned to hatred.

Yes. They despise humans.

Sariel stretched his legs out and laid his head back upon the soft earth. Though his body was tired from the day's work, he knew that sleep would not come for many hours. This prophecy was the most important thing Enoch had ever told his son.

"I will raise up one from among those you despise."

Was this one a human ... or someone wearing a human form?

"I will awaken his eyes to the mysteries which I have hidden from men since the foundations of the world."

What mystery has been hidden from men since the foundations of the world? Sariel immediately thought of the Reshaping, when the Temporal Realm had become separated from the Eternal and required changes to prevent it from dying altogether. Before that time, there was only the Eternal, and the first humans used to live within it. They experienced the fullness of what it meant to be alive. Afterward, their experience was limited to the Temporal Realm just as the Temporal was a limited expression of the Eternal. *And this very moment, I can shift my perspective between both.*

"His feet will I make to tread upon the paths of destruction and his hands to make war."

I have certainly walked many paths of destruction. My hands have made war for ages in the other realm and thousands of years in this one.

"He will uproot the seeds of corruption which you have sown throughout the earth. And then you will know that I am the Lord and my justice is everlasting."

That day, on the shores of the Great Waters, I told Enoch that I didn't consider myself to be outside of the Holy One's plans—that I might actually be fulfilling them in some way. Could this be the way? Am I this Awakened One?

14

"What do you call this place?" Sariel asked.

Some of the human creatures who were gathered around began to snicker.

"He doesn't know?"

"He comes from the underworld," someone explained.

"Some of them don't know."

"But he should know. He ascended."

"Earth," one of them finally replied, looking at Sariel with a lopsided grin.

"This place?" Sariel asked again, motioning around them with his hands. They were sitting in a clearing within a pine forest, and though the air was dense with mist, the temperature was moderate. Sariel had already located the walls of this habitat, but these creatures didn't seem to understand that the boundaries were any different from the trees and the grass. It was all one environment to them.

"Yes, Earth," the male replied, eyes bulging to emphasize his words.

Sariel nodded, trying his best to understand how these creatures interpreted their existence. "Someone said *underworld*?"

"Yes ... the place you came from," a female replied.

"So the tall creatures that brought me here—you believe they're demons?"

"Everyone knows that," a male replied. "Demons are tall, with white skin and white hair. They live in the underworld ... below us," he said, patting the ground as if he were talking to a child. "Your hair is still white, but your skin is darker. You are shorter than the demons of the underworld, but not as short as us. And you wear something over your skin, but not as much as them. You must not remember these things because you are ascending."

"What do you mean, I'm *ascending*?"

All of the human creatures looked up to the misty sky.

"One day," the male explained, "we will all live in the overworld."

Sariel followed their gaze, knowing there must be a ceiling up there somewhere, but it was beyond sight. He slowly brought his attention back to the group gathered around him. "When I ascend to the overworld ... how will I change? How will I look?"

"You will be short like us. You will not be ashamed of your skin. And all of us will be as dark as the night."

"Like the god of the overworld," a female added.

Sariel wanted to shake his head, but he didn't want to offend these creatures. They were definitely descended from humans, but something was very wrong with them. And not just in their appearance; it was even in the way they carried themselves. Their thinking was limited to very simple things. When they weren't explaining their beliefs to Sariel in a patronizing manner, they were quite submissive. It wasn't as if their wills had been broken, but more as though they didn't have any to start with. Sariel couldn't help but think of what he had just read in First Earth.

I see their hearts and the things they keep hidden, even from each other. I see the things they have done and the things which they have yet to do.

The Myndarym were doing something strange in this world, but so far Sariel couldn't figure it out. From what he had observed of the city while sneaking into the portal chamber, it was clear that Ezekiyel preferred mechanical things to organic things. But if that was the case, how did these humans fit into his goals? And why were the children of Danel and Turel given such status in this civilization? Perhaps Ezekiyel only cared about angelic beings and not humans. But why go through all the effort to create a fake environment for these human creatures? Why not just kill all of them if they didn't matter? None of it made any sense at the moment, but Sariel knew there was definitely a strategy behind what his enemies were doing.

He tried going back to a line of questioning that he'd abandoned earlier in the day. He'd asked some of these creatures what their names were, and no one seemed to understand his question. "If I wanted to talk about you," Sariel began, pointing at the female closest to him, "what would I call you?"

"I am ... me," she replied with a laugh.

"Yes, I know. But how can I distinguish you from her?" he asked, pointing at another female.

"Because I am not the same as her," she answered.

"I know that, but if I'm talking to someone else about you, what do I call you?"

She frowned and looked at her fellow creatures for help.

"She looks different," a male answered. "She smells different. But she is still human."

Sariel rubbed his forehead. "So none of you have names?"

"This *names* is the word you used earlier?" the male asked with a tilted head.

"Yes," Sariel replied. "Names are how we know the difference between you and you."

"Oh," the female said, jumping back into the conversation. "I am me and you are you."

"Right," Sariel agreed. "So if you were talking about me, what would you call me?"

"Him," she replied with a smile.

"And what if you were not with me when you were speaking?"

She frowned. "We only speak to others when they are near. If they are not with us, how can we speak with them?"

Sariel opened his mouth to reply, but was interrupted by a metallic sound that rang out through the air.

The entire group looked up to the sky. "He brings us food and water," they mumbled in unison. Then they rose from their crouched positions and began to walk, moving like a herd of animals.

Sariel followed them, wondering how they knew which direction to go.

The herd walked for a few minutes, becoming denser as straggling ones joined and pushed toward the center. Without any perceptible reason, everyone suddenly came to a stop and looked up.

Sariel followed their stares, seeing now that the clouds above were becoming agitated, swirling upward in great, curling fingers of white. These swirls became more visible by the second as a circular darkness seemed to be gathering in the sky above them. Before Sariel could figure out what was happening, a dark figure appeared within the clouds, descending slowly.

Sariel immediately ducked and pushed his way through the crowd to the nearest tree. When he was hidden behind the wide trunk, he peered out around its rough bark.

The dark figure hovering over the crowd, two dozen paces in the air, was Arakiba. He was unclothed, with arms outstretched in a benevolent manner. "I bring you food and water," he announced in a gentle, but commanding voice.

Thin streams of water began pouring through the clouds.

The human creatures jostled each other to be the first to reach the streams, opening their mouths to drink their fill. This lasted for several minutes as each one took their turn behind the first. Then the streams disappeared, and small objects began to fall from the clouds. As they hit and bounced along the ground, Sariel could see that they were brown spheres, just thicker than one's thumb. The humans scrambled to scoop the food from the ground and shove it into their mouths. They lunged from place to place, crouching and springing like animals, knocking into each other. This lasted for several more minutes before the food stopped falling. The humans picked up the remaining pieces from the ground, and it appeared that the whole event had been timed just right for everyone to have eaten their fill.

Arakiba crossed his arms over his chest and ascended into the clouds.

When the darkness was gone and the swirling mists calmed, Sariel stepped out from behind the tree. "The god of the overworld?" he asked.

A male crouching nearby turned his head, slowly. "Someday we will ascend to join him."

There was something familiar about his eyes and the way this male moved. All of a sudden, the sight of this human creature brought a memory from Sariel's distant past.

The moaning and screeching was loud now as Sariel approached the pit. Inching cautiously forward, he could see that the hole was roughly four paces deep and double that in diameter. The latticed lid was constructed of tree branches as thick as a man's forearm, lashed together at their intersections with long strands of grass.

A hand shot out from the edge and swiped at the air in front of Sariel's feet. On instinct, he jumped backward. The skin of the arm and hand was a sickly yellow hue, covered in dirt. The fingernails were long and jagged, nearly black. Beneath the gaunt skin, bone and sinew could be seen in great detail. Then the arm retracted and gripped the cage. Something else pressed against the wood and the sound of sniffing could be heard.

Sariel closed his eyes for a moment to compose himself. When he was ready, he circled around to the south side of the hole to get a better look at the man. As soon as he found a good vantage point, the screaming stopped.

There, clinging to the lid and the earthen wall on the side of the pit, was a creature that only vaguely looked human. Its long, thin limbs stuck out at odd angles, clinging like a spider to the boundary of its confines.

As Sariel moved slowly around the perimeter, dark and lifeless eyes tracked his every movement from a bulbous head that swiveled in a cocked position, like a poisonous insect.

There was a striking similarity to the man in the village of Bahyith who had been possessed by demons. And the more he watched this animalistic human crouching on the ground, the surer Sariel became of the implications that were now coursing through his mind.

*   *   *   *

NORTH-NORTHEAST OF THE TREE
FIRST EARTH

Though Akuji was limited to movement along the ground, Rameel watched him overcome one obstacle after another without slowing. Mountainous terrain seemed to have no effect on his muscles. He leaped across narrow ravines and scaled cliff walls. When he reached open fields, he would burst into a sprint that was nearly as fast as flight. And when he encountered dense forests, he darted through them like a deer. He was faster than any land creature Rameel had ever seen.

Rameel followed from the air, letting his son set the pace. If not for the benefit of his Eternal perspective, there were several occasions where Rameel might have lost Akuji within the terrain. By the time they reached the Nephiyl encampment, Rameel was thoroughly impressed with his son. He came to a landing and followed Akuji on foot. The clouds were thick and hung low overhead. The air was cooler here than in the southwest—humid, with the occasional fleck of moisture landing on Rameel's face.

The trees opened into a wide clearing with dozens of wooden sleeping structures around the perimeter. They were long and rectangular in shape, constructed of saplings and covered on their roofs with pine boughs. As Akuji's massive form stepped silently to one side, Rameel could see a fire pit at the center, ringed with stones. A younger Nephiyl sat on the stones, turning a hand crank attached to a long iron rod suspended over the fire. A gutted and skinned human lay stretched out along the metal spit, being roasted for the evening meal. The smoke of the fire was clean and white, rising to the sky in a thin column. The Nephiyl looked bored, watching the rising smoke, until he noticed Rameel walking into the camp.

"This is where we live," Akuji said, turning to face his father.

Rameel looked around the camp, noting an area where several human hides had been staked to the soil and scraped clean. The handful of other Nephiylim that had been moving through the camp had come to a stop and were staring. "How many of you are left?"

"Twenty-eight, besides me. The rest will be back at sundown."

Among the ones present, there was a wide range of ages. The Nephiyl turning the spit was only six or seven years old. "Which other one is sick?"

"Gebhuza," Akuji called out, beckoning with his hand.

A large Nephiyl sitting at the mouth of a sleeping shelter handed an infant to another Nephiyl before standing up. Then he came across the camp in a steady and noiseless gait. It was obvious that he was a skilled hunter like Akuji.

"This is my brother, Gebhuza."

Rameel looked up at Gebhuza, who was roughly a year younger than Akuji. Though his skin was also black like Rameel, there was a green tinge beneath his eyes. The pale flesh beneath his fingernails was where the odd color was most prominent.

"You are our father?"

Rameel turned his attention back to Gebhuza's face. He was ugly by comparison to Akuji, having inherited the look of his unfortunate mother—another of the human sacrifices brought by the priests of the south. "I am."

Gebhuza looked like he wanted to ask another question, but he kept silent.

Rameel turned to Akuji. "And your older brothers?"

"After they died, we burned their flesh to purify them. I will take you to where we rested their bones."

Akuji began walking north across the camp. Rameel followed, looking back when they reached the perimeter. Gebhuza still hadn't moved. His eyes remained fixed on Rameel for a long and awkward moment. Rameel finally had to turn around and catch up with Akuji.

The burial grounds were just a few minutes' walk from the camp. Among the trees was an area where the soil was free of pine needles. An orderly array of spears had been stuck in the ground, presumably marking the grave locations. Some had feathers tied to them with leather cords, waving and twisting in the breeze. Others had human finger bones and other hunting tokens, clanking against the shafts with an eerie, hollow sound. The ground before Akuji's feet was loosely packed, having recently been turned over.

"Next year, Gebhuza will rest my bones here. And then he will become the elder."

Rameel closed his eyes and let his head drop against his chest. The weight of Akuji's sorrow was powerful, stirring up emotions within Rameel that he had never experienced before. The other Myndarym had produced children in the old world, and Rameel had watched the way those connections, however distant, pulled at the angels' emotions like gravity. He'd never understood it until now.

He felt the need to do something about this tragedy, but it was far beyond him. If anyone was capable of understanding this sickness, it was Ezekiyel. He knew things about this world and its creatures that none of the others understood. Perhaps Kokabiel might also be able to help. He still retained the ability to *shape*, and that in itself required an intimate knowledge of how a being was meant to function. But Nephiylim were forbidden to exist in any of the new worlds; they were too much of a liability. Neither of these Shapers would help save someone who could later pose a risk to them, not unless they were brought slowly to a point of understanding. But that possibility was remote. The portal was now forbidden to use; each of the Myndarym were expected to keep to their own worlds until the appointed time. The opportunity to influence the other

Myndarym had passed. Perhaps this would change again in the future, but certainly not for quite some time.

"They're asleep for the night," she said, laying her hand on Rameel's forearm as she looked down the hall.

The warmth of her touch sent waves of pleasure up the skin of his arm. Rameel looked down at her, studying the side of her face. She was a woman now, but there was still a childish innocence about her. She exuded beauty without being conscious of it. Even in the way she stood there.

Finally, she looked up and caught him staring.

Rameel didn't turn away this time. He couldn't. He was lost in her eyes.

She lowered her gaze, realizing suddenly that she had touched him. She pulled her hand away, then hesitated before putting it back against his arm. When her eyes came up again, there was a different look behind them. A fearlessness. A hunger. She stepped closer, laying her other hand against the bare skin of his abdomen. Then she leaned forward and kissed his body.

"Your mother was the only woman I ever loved," Rameel said, as much to shake off the memory as to break the silence.

Akuji turned his head. "Why do you say this to me ... now?"

"I want you to know that I didn't send you away because I was ashamed of you."

Akuji's gaze went to the ground, searching.

"I am proud of the leader you've become," Rameel quickly added, hoping to prevent the inevitable question of why he sent Akuji away at all. "You've become a mighty hunter, like your ancestors of old."

Akuji grinned, opening his mouth slightly.

"I do not have the ability to heal your sickness yet. But I will ... soon."

"How long will this take?" Akuji asked, his dull eyes suddenly brightening.

"The weight of that worry is for me to bear," Rameel answered, reaching out. "For now, my son, you must rest." As soon as his hand touched Akuji's arm, the Nephiyl collapsed to the ground.

Rameel quickly knelt, feeling along Akuji's neck for a pulse. Beside his windpipe, the skin throbbed with a steady heartbeat. Rameel placed the back of his hand in front of Akuji's nose and could feel his son's warm breath coming out in a calm, regular cadence.

"Akuji! Akuji!" yelled a young Nephiyl. This one was female and looked to be only ten years of age. She must have been spying on them and was now running through the trees toward her brother. "What's wrong? What happened?"

"He's very sick," Rameel answered, looking up from the ground with all the compassion that he could muster. "Go and fetch your brothers to help me move him."

*   *   *   *

AT THE TREE
SECOND EARTH

Sariel's speed picked up dramatically as he left the tall grass and began running along the path that had been cleared of vegetation. Instead of the swishing sound he'd become accustomed to, now there was only the soft padding of his running feet. Sweat was thick on his skin, unable to evaporate in the humidity. His breathing was becoming ragged, but there was no time for delay.

All of a sudden, the path opened up into a circular clearing, revealing the lowest point of the valley floor. The crater lay just ahead, the timbers of the staircase sticking up over the rim like claws. Sariel slowed his pace to a walk as he scanned the mountainsides in every direction. If Ezekiyel and his temporal Myndarym had arrived, there were no signs to indicate it.

With his heart still thumping loudly in his chest, Sariel stopped at the edge of the rim and looked down into the crater. It appeared just as he had left it. Armaros and Satarel were still in the process of bringing the fragment here to the stump, which hopefully meant that the portal to the In-Between would still work as it used to. But after what happened while running from the guards in Third Earth, Sariel was hesitant. Old assumptions were apparently dangerous now.

Sariel took one last look around the valley to ensure that he was alone. But when his gaze swung to the south, he noted something in the sky above the horizon. At first, it appeared to be nothing more than a dark spot—a bird perhaps. But as he watched it, he realized that it was quite far away and very large. The wings were angular, and there was a long tail hanging below them.

Kokabiel!

The remaining Myndar of this world hovered in his reptilian form, presumably over the location of the Tree fragment. If he was adding his abilities to the transport effort, their task would be accomplished in less than a day's time.

Sariel needed to find out whether or not this stump would take him to Third Earth, because if it didn't work, he needed to flee this area as quickly as possible. While he had hoped to ambush the Myndarym, he planned to do it carefully and individually. Three at once was an unrealistic goal, and Kokabiel would need to be in a less dangerous form when his turn arrived.

Sariel took the first step cautiously, testing the packed soil to ensure that it was stable. Then he began running down the steps. He reached the bottom in less than a minute and didn't hesitate to cross the plank bridge and walk onto the surface of the stump.

Stopping at its center, he looked down into the depths of its fragmented rings and held out his hands. His heart was racing, but not from exertion. He was hoping for the heaviness that he had experienced a few times in the past.

The sight of the Tree's rings began to distort inward.

Yes!

The earthen walls of the crater began to swirl.

It still works!

The air around Sariel began to glow with blue light. Gravity fell in upon his chest, forcing the air from his lungs. His bones began to ache from the pressure. Darkness closed in around him as consciousness threatened to slip away. Sariel lost all sense of direction. He was moving at a blinding speed as though he were wearing his Iryllur form, diving at the ranks of the Marotru with his vaepkir ready. But then he felt as though he weren't moving at all; he was perfectly still, and the universe was passing over his head like the crushing waves of the ocean. The water roared past his ears, and the silence was deafening. Darkness stretched out before him in an endless void, constantly swallowing him even as light flashed before his vision. Movement and stillness. Darkness and light. All of it at once. Sariel wanted to scream, but there was no sound here, and he had no mouth with which to produce it.

And then there was silence ... true silence.

Not the trick that had been played upon his senses before, but a simple, restful quiet. It was accompanied by darkness, but not the overwhelming and frightening darkness that he had just felt. This was peaceful, as if eternity held him in a gentle embrace. Sariel wondered if he had finally lost consciousness, but his thoughts seemed too clear, too lucid for that.

This was the In-Between.

Sariel had no body here, no eyes with which to see, but memory told him that he should be swimming in a river of light. He remembered the undulating ripples, like long ribbons of rainbows moving as if they were a school of fish. He remembered being pulled along, caught in the grip of a vortex, but these things weren't happening. Something was very different.

Sariel turned to look behind him, if there was such a thing as *behind* or even a body to turn. The vortex that he'd left was a shrinking point of light amidst the darkness. He was moving away from it, but as he watched, the light disappeared. There was no river, no object, nothing to use as a reference point. He might have been drifting or not moving at all.

He was alone, and in his desperation, he reached out to his other selves. Even from the In-Between, he could feel them. His thoughts were their thoughts. Their experiences were his experiences. Through their existence, he could feel the passage of time. In one world, Ebnisha arrived and then left again, visiting over and over again. In another world, the humans poked his skin and fondled his hair, trying to figure out what he was. Then he was sleeping among the trees. Then the humans were trying to give him food. All of it came and went at a distance, and the only part of it that seemed to matter to this self was how much of it passed by.

By the time this sensation occurred to Sariel, he was already surrounded by a vortex of shadows, less dark than the darkness in the distance. He had reached the entrance to Third Earth, but it was not the same as when his third self had gone through it. This time, it didn't pull him in as much as it swung him endlessly around its nucleus. It was as if ...

It's closed!

He tried to force his way in, separating the vortex and pushing himself into it by the power of his mind, as he might have done in the Temporal Realm. But nothing here obeyed his will. He simply kept drifting around the outside of the vortex.

I can't get through it. I cannot rescue my third self!

This disturbing realization was quickly followed by the knowledge that it had taken weeks to get here. The vortices were much farther apart than before.

Are they drifting? Are the worlds moving away from each other?

These questions evaporated from his mind as more pressing ones solidified.

What has Ezekiyel done? What about First Earth?

As Sariel had learned to do just after the Fracturing, he willed his consciousness to move out of the endlessly spinning shadows. He felt for the flow that had brought him here and the one that must also still exist between here and the next world. The difference between the vortex and the nothingness was the distinction from which he started. Then he felt other shadows entering the vortex. Finally, he located an outgoing flow. It was almost imperceptible, but it was there. And now that Sariel knew how to feel it, he willed himself to move along it, adding his motion to that of the flow. The vortex of shadows was quickly swallowed by complete darkness, and once again, Sariel was drifting alone through nothingness.

15

Ten robed men struggled to lift a long wooden box and slide it onto the deck of a wagon. The box was more than three times the length and width of a man, yet no one asked any questions about what they were hauling. Their arms and legs shook from the strain, but their devotion gave them strength. They persevered until their cargo was in place. Then they set about fastening it to the deck of the wagon with ropes. The lighter end, almost a third of its length, hung off the back; wagons weren't made for cargo of this size.

At the front, the driver offered continuous noises of consolation to his team of horses; they were always nervous when Rameel was near. The priests might have benefitted from the same treatment, but there was no one to comfort them. They served their god in fear and reverence, without anyone to act as a mediator. And so they kept their heads down, covered by the hood of their cloaks, and they worked in silence.

There was nothing to be said anyway, for no one but Rameel understood what was happening here. He turned away from the wagon and looked back upon the forest camp. The sleeping shelters had been torn down and piled at the center of the clearing. The stones that had ringed the fire pit had been scattered among the trees. Even the spears that marked the graves of the older Nephiylim had been taken down. Now there was only a great fire that blazed hot with the smell of pine and roasting flesh, sending black smoke into the sky. Tomorrow, when the flames were finally out and the tall pile of debris had collapsed into a smoldering ash heap, Rameel would have several more of his priests bury it right where it was.

"Ride for the port along the northern coast," Rameel instructed. "I'll catch up with you tomorrow."

"Thou, who art most powerful," the priests replied, bowing their cloaked heads.

The driver flicked his reins, and the team of horses lurched into motion, eager to be away from this place and the tall, winged creature. They leaned into their harnesses, hindered at first by the weight of their load. But momentum began to build, and soon they were moving through the forest where the land was mostly flat and free of obstructions.

Rameel turned back to the fire and crossed his arms. The orange and yellow flames danced, purifying the pile of Nephiyl bodies and their sickness. As the smoke rose into the clouded sky, Rameel imagined that his sadness was being taken with it. He would only allow himself this brief moment of mourning, and when it was done he would think no more about it. For these Nephiyl children were the evidence of his crime against Zaquel and the other Myndarym. His lie. The evidence of his lack of self-control.

Perhaps it would have been justified in his own eyes if it had been motivated by love. But he never loved the women who had given birth to these Nephiylim. Those unfortunate human sacrifices from the south had simply been an outlet for his true passion—an outlet that proved insufficient, as it turned out. For his true passion, suppressed and even denied for so long, had finally won the battle.

The air felt cool against the sweat on Rameel's face. His chest rose and fell with each labored breath, but the frequency was slowing. His heart, which had been racing a moment ago, was almost back to its normal rhythm. Things that seemed insignificant before now came to his attention, such as the uncomfortable stone floor beneath his wings. Rameel turned his gaze away from the cavernous ceiling and looked at the woman lying beside him.

She was on her side. Her arms were crossed over her chest, which was also still rising and falling in an exaggerated way from the exertion. Her face, glistening in the moonlight, rested gracefully against the back of her hand. Her eyes were closed, but she wasn't asleep; she was simply at peace.

Rameel watched her for a long moment, studying the lines of her face and the way her mouth was turned up slightly at the corner.

A muffled sound suddenly came from the hallway, and the woman's eyes popped open. She immediately climbed to her feet and shuffled out of the room.

"It's alright," Rameel heard her say.

A deeper voice responded, but the words couldn't be made out.

"There's nothing to be afraid of. Just lie down and go back to sleep."

Rameel climbed to his feet and stepped to the open doorway. When he looked down the hall, he saw a young Nephiyl, just barely shorter than his human caretaker, walking back into one of the side rooms.

The woman's hand was outstretched, having just let go of the child.

Several more Nephiyl faces were peeking out from other doorways. They were whispering their questions to her.

Suddenly, Rameel was struck with a realization. Seeing the object of his passion standing there in her motherly role, comforting the Nephiyl children who had been put under her care, brought an abrupt clarity to what had transpired. The brush of her fingertips against his skin, the gentle touch of her lips—these weren't expressions of her love; they were tactics.

Amidst her comforting words to the children, the woman realized she was being watched. When she turned her head, Rameel caught something in her eyes that had been there until now—guilt. The kind that comes when one's secret is discovered.

A cold emptiness stole Rameel's breath away, and his stomach turned sour. He backed away from the door and closed his eyes. That look of peacefulness on her face, the mouth turned up at the corner—they were the unconscious expressions of a woman who has achieved her goal. She hadn't come to appreciate her new life as she had led Rameel to believe. She still despised it, had despised it ever since she had been brought here against her will. With no way to escape, she had done the only thing that would ensure her life would reach its end soon. The suffering involved with a birth must have been considered less important than all her years of imprisonment. She had never loved him, had never desired him.

What has she done? What have I done?

When Rameel opened his eyes again, the woman was standing alone in the middle of the hallway. The children had all gone back to their rooms.

"Go wash yourself," he said, louder than intended. "The priests will be along soon, and they will make sure that you are thorough!"

The fire was raging now, hotter than what could be accounted for by the pile of wood beneath the bodies. Rameel's hands were outstretched. By the power of his will, the mound of debris and the air above it were being forced into an excited state. Objects that weren't even flammable were igniting, unable to resist his anger.

*   *   *   *

THE IN-BETWEEN

Considering the information from Ebnisha, it seemed likely that the stump in First Earth was located somewhere among the lands of the Kaliel. If Sariel was able to go through the vortex for that world, he might find himself immediately confronted by

Rameel and his followers. At several points during his life, Sariel would not have considered such a confrontation worth much thought. But he had no idea what his fellow Myndarym were now capable of. They had not been divided into three like Sariel, and since the reign of Baraquijal, the nature of their connection with the Marotru had been unknown.

But what choice did Sariel have? He had not been able to enter Third Earth, and the Myndarym were arriving at the stump in Second Earth when he left. At least First Earth still held the *possibility* of being deserted in the area around the stump. If it wasn't, perhaps a confrontation wasn't necessary. If the stump wasn't being actively watched, he might get a few uninterrupted seconds after entering that world, in which case he might be able to escape. He had managed to evade Rameel and Arakiba for hundreds of years in the old world. Perhaps he could evade Rameel again, if he had a sufficient head start.

Ahead, the darkness was becoming less dark. Instead of the points of light that he had hoped for, a vortex of dull shadow swirled within the nothingness. It grew so large that it blocked out all else. Sariel had arrived, but First Earth was also inaccessible.

Ezekiyel has already been here!

There was now only one choice left. Sariel moved himself along the inside edge of the vortex and entered the flow leading toward Second Earth. Armaros, Satarel, and Kokabiel had been less than a day out from the stump, and weeks had already transpired since then. Ezekiyel had likely already visited that world and had done whatever he planned to do with the Tree fragment and his temporal Myndarym. But Sariel wouldn't give up.

He pushed himself faster and faster, feeling out the subtle flow between worlds. Days continued to pass by, detectable through the existence of his other selves. But time felt different in the In-Between, both longer and shorter at once. When he finally reached the vortex of Second Earth, it was no longer the swirling cauldron of light that he had left.

He was trapped.

Ezekiyel must have gone from world to world, closing each vortex!

Refusing to give up, Sariel tried to think of any possibility that might lead him to freedom.

If Ezekiyel started with Third Earth, how did he get back? Or did he confine himself to Second Earth?

If Ezekiyel had some way of getting back into his own world, he might still be in transit. Sariel might catch up to him and go into Third Earth along with his enemy. Even the fight that would ensue from such a scenario was preferable to being stuck between worlds. He had to try.

Sariel moved into the flow leading to Third Earth and willed himself to move faster and faster with each moment. Temporal days flew by at a rapid pace. His first self walked along the stream with Ebnisha, talking of the old world and sharing insights. His third self tried to figure out what had happened to the humans of Third Earth, asking questions that no one understood.

Ahead, a shimmering light began to emerge. It wasn't a vortex, but it was there. He pushed harder, concentrating every bit of his attention on swimming faster through the flow—the only thing that wasn't emptiness. But it wasn't substantial. Every effort seemed wasted.

The light in the distance was growing, but it seemed to take longer than it should have. The light was moving away from him. As soon as he realized this, he knew that the light was Ezekiyel and his temporal Myndarym on their way to Third Earth. But they were so far away, and he couldn't catch up.

Suddenly, the point of light expanded, opening into hundreds of rays that swirled outward into a multitude of colors.

Sariel reached out for it, but the blossom of hope in the distance began to wither. The petals of the flower wilted, pulling inward. The vortex shrank. And just as Sariel reached it, the light disappeared.

* * * *

The jungle floor had become worn in areas by Ebnisha's passage. He'd been coming to Sariel's camp almost every day since their first meeting. This morning's trip was taking much longer than usual, because of the children. They didn't move as fast as the adults, and the delay only added to his heightened anticipation. Sariel would be surprised to meet all four of Ebnisha's brothers, and two of his sisters, as well as their spouses and children. The whole tribe knew about Ebnisha's daily trips, and his family had begun asking very specific questions lately. He could tell they were very interested in learning from this pale man who wouldn't come into their village. Ebnisha had been telling them that the old man also kept the stories of their people in his memory, and even knew details that had not been passed down through Kham and their forefathers. Ebnisha had been careful to refrain from using Sariel's name, because he wasn't sure if Sariel wanted his identity to be known. But the family didn't seem to care. They just wanted to finally meet this old man who was stealing so much of Ebnisha's time.

Ebnisha had finally given in last night, deciding it would be best to honor their persistence and curiosity before one of the younger children tried to follow him. It was preferable to make introductions before someone heard something they weren't supposed to.

"Almost there," he said, looking back over his shoulder.

Ebnisha's siblings smiled; they were used to walking. And though they didn't usually have all of their children with them during their journeys, they seemed to be in good spirits. The children were also enjoying themselves, either running in circles around the adults, or being carried on their uncles' shoulders.

The stream led them through the trees, which opened into a small meadow. Sariel was outside of his hut, standing beside a pile of saplings that had been stripped of their twigs. He was looking up at the sky and appeared to be lost in thought.

"Good morning, my friend."

Sariel turned, a look of surprise on his face.

Ebnisha jogged across the meadow, wanting to have just a few seconds to explain before his family arrived. "My brothers and sisters wanted to meet the old man who has been ..." Ebnisha trailed off as he came to a stop in front of Sariel.

The white-haired man had a distant look in his eyes. He didn't even seem to notice the additional guests coming across the meadow.

"Is everything well?"

"I'm afraid not," Sariel replied.

"Have I offended you by bringing my family?"

Sariel looked over Ebnisha's shoulder, finally noticing the others. "Oh, not at all." His eyebrows lowered. "It's just that I ... I've lost something valuable."

Ebnisha began looking around at the grass. "Can I help you find it? Where was the last place you saw it?" As far as he could tell, everything looked as it did yesterday when he left. Of course, if this valuable thing was small, perhaps it wouldn't be noticeable without a thorough search on hands and knees. When his eyes came up again to Sariel, the old man was smiling. "What?"

Sariel's smile widened. Then his mouth opened and he began laughing. Within seconds, his whole body was shaking with joy.

Ebnisha joined in, not knowing what was so funny, but unable to keep a straight face in the midst of such merriment.

When Sariel's laughter subsided, he looked exhausted. He grabbed hold of Ebnisha's shoulder to steady himself. "Oh ... it's not something that can be found, but you have helped me more than you could possibly know."

"Something lost that cannot be found," Ebnisha mused. "Have our discussions become so boring that you must resort to riddles?"

Sariel began laughing again, doubling over with his hands on his knees.

Ebnisha had never seen the old man like this. It was strange, but he had to admit that it was entertaining.

Sariel stood up and gained control of himself, finally extending both of his hands to the group that had gathered a few paces away. "I'm sorry if I've alarmed you with my strange behavior. Welcome. Ebnisha ... introduce us, please?"

"Yes. Come, come," he said to his family, waving them forward.

The adults stepped closer to Sariel, pulling their shy children along with them.

"Everyone, this is ..." Ebnisha began, suddenly panicking as he realized he didn't know what to call him besides Sariel. "Saba," he finally blurted out. It meant *old man* in Shayeth.

Sariel glanced briefly at Ebnisha, but otherwise he didn't let on that anything was wrong. He seemed to understand the situation.

"Saba, this is Mosi, my oldest brother. His wife, Ekua."

"And these are your children, I assume?" Sariel added.

Mosi smiled and bowed his head.

Ebnisha went on to introduce the other siblings in the order of their birth along with their spouses and children. The males had small bones running sideways through the flesh between their nostrils, and Sariel realized that Ebnisha was the only one without these decorations. At last, the scribe came to his youngest brother, who was just sixteen years old. "And this is Wekesa. He has not yet found a wife," Ebnisha said, rubbing the boy's head.

The group laughed, and Wekesa tried to move his head out from under his brother's irritating touch. "Neither have you," he shot back.

Sariel raised his eyebrows and looked at Ebnisha with a grin.

"Wekesa ... has a quick tongue," Ebnisha added. "But he's right most of the time."

The comment seemed to smooth over the ruffled emotions, and Wekesa stood up tall and smiled.

"Again, welcome," Sariel offered. "I was not expecting all of you, but I am glad you are here. Please come and sit down in the shade. It feels like this day will become hot before long. Are any of you hungry?"

The group followed Sariel toward his shelter, and Ebnisha hung back for a moment, relieved that the introductions had gone so well.

16

A ringing sound woke Sariel from his sleep. He was sitting on the ground, his back propped against a tree. When he opened his eyes, he could see that the sky was still dark, but the ever-present mist made it just light enough to see his surroundings. The visibility was aided by a dull light coming from one side of the habitat.

The human creatures around him climbed to their feet. "One will be chosen," they mumbled in unison.

Sariel stayed where he was, curious and nervous at the same time. Something clamped down on his wrist and pulled. Sariel looked up through the darkness into the face of a female.

"One will be chosen," she said.

"No, thank you," Sariel replied, trying to remove his arm.

The female pulled harder, nearly dragging Sariel across the ground before he got his feet under him. "One will be chosen," she said again, pleading. There was no anger in her expression; she appeared to be acting out of a sense of duty or perhaps compassion.

"Alright," Sariel agreed, walking along with her in hopes that she would let go when he started moving.

She kept her hand clasped firmly around his wrist and continued pulling as they walked. With her long, sinewy arms and thick fingers, she was much stronger than she appeared to be. If these creatures weren't so docile, they would be extremely dangerous. Sariel could have fought his way loose, but he would have had to injure her, and there was no telling how the others might respond.

"I'm coming," he assured her.

They walked through the trees toward the light, coming together with others as they moved. After several minutes, the herd stepped out of the trees and into a clearing at the side of the habitat. The light was coming from high up on the wall, near a panel of opaque glass. Sariel had noted five of these panels evenly spaced around the perimeter, and he had assumed that they were windows allowing the temporal Myndarym to observe the humans.

"One will be chosen," the crowd mumbled, keeping back from the wall.

Suddenly, the panel of glass slid sideways. A staircase of mechanical steps unfolded to the ground. The creatures who walked down the steps were very different from the ones Sariel was expecting. They were shorter than the temporal Myndarym, but still much taller than humans. Their facial features looked demonic, like Arakiba, but their skin was gray. Their bodies were thin and muscular, and they wore only black loincloths around their waists. They weren't Nephiyl, but neither were they human. Sariel shifted his perspective toward the Eternal and saw a brilliant coagulation of colors.

A different race of temporal Myndarym?

There were five of them who came down the steps, but one seemed to be leading the others. When he set foot upon the soil of the habitat, he began searching the faces of those gathered. It only took a few seconds before his eyes settled on Sariel.

"You," he said, pointing.

Sariel tried to turn away, but the female still had control of his arm. She smiled and tugged him forward. "You have been chosen."

"Bring him here," the guard commanded.

"No," Sariel replied, digging his heels into the soil.

Her grip tightened and she cheerfully pulled Sariel toward the front of the crowd. "Don't worry. You have been chosen."

"For what?" he whispered.

She looked back with a large smile. "You will mate with another. You will like it."

"He has been chosen," the crowd whispered, one statement coming right after another, overlapping into a murmur.

The female stepped out of the crowd and dragged Sariel before the guards. "He is nervous," she told them before letting go and stepping back.

The guard, almost twice Sariel's own height, pulled two metal rings from the belt around his waist. "Put out your hands."

"Where are you taking me?" Sariel replied, stepping back.

"Let's not make a scene," the guard whispered.

Sariel turned to look at the crowd, seeing a mixture of excitement and confusion on their faces. Given their mumbled chanting, this sort of thing must have happened many times before, but something was different about this occasion.

Clank!

A cold pressure was suddenly around both of Sariel's wrists. He looked down to see that the metal rings had somehow fastened themselves to his skin.

"Let's go," the guard said, casually.

Sariel looked up into his eyes, calculating the actions he would have to take to kill this one and the other four on his way up the stairs. Suddenly, an itching sensation crawled up the skin of his arms and made his neck twitch. "What is this?" he grunted.

The lead guard smiled for the benefit of the crowd. Then his eyes lowered to Sariel's. "Something to ensure your compliance. Now, come willingly or I'll be forced to do something that would scare these innocent people."

Sariel took one last look at the crowd. Most of them were smiling, and some were clearly jealous.

"You have been chosen," the guard announced, waving his hand toward the staircase.

Sariel took a deep breath and began walking toward the stairs.

Two of the guards stepped in front of him and two more came behind, while the leader walked beside him. As a group, they moved unhurried up the stairs and into a small, cube-shaped room built of the same material as the walls of the habitat. The staircase retracted into the room, folding upon itself as the weapons of Ezekiyel had done in the old world. Then the glass panel slid sideways into place.

Sariel was waiting for the movement of the glass door as his distraction. As soon as it covered the entrance, he spun around, his eternal body already separating from his temporal body. But a jolt of electricity shot through him, starting at the wrists. By the time it forced his consciousness away from him, his body was already limp and falling to the floor.

~

Sariel opened his eyes as soon as he became aware that it was something he could do. The first thing he saw was his own chest, then his legs and the chair beneath him. The floor under the chair was polished stone. Sariel's arms were fastened behind him, and a tingling sensation at his wrists indicated that it was pointless to try and escape. When he lifted his head, he saw a large, rectangular room with a ceiling hundreds of feet above. A few paces in front of his chair were stairs that led to a raised platform.

Turel and Danel sat upon dual thrones beside each other. Both wore long gowns of pale blue, stitched with silver thread. Their clothing stuck out in several places—around the neck, above the shoulders—as if their bodies had been *shaped* into creatures of the sea. Sariel didn't understand the function of what they wore, but it looked regal and difficult to construct. Danel's turquoise eyes almost glowed in contrast to her milky white skin. And Turel's sapphire eyes were filled with more hatred than Sariel remembered seeing in the past. Both of them wore their pale hair long and straight, flowing down the front of their gowns as if it were part of their clothing. There was a noticeable bump where Danel's white tresses rested against her abdomen. But it was the shimmering crowns of darkness resting upon both their heads that drew Sariel's focused attention.

"Welcome to Nyaden," Danel said in a condescending tone.

Turel smiled. "I trust you have enjoyed your stay thus far?"

Sariel now noticed two of the tall, pale Myndar guards flanking the bottom of the stairs. They were standing at attention, dressed in white and holding short staffs like those from the portal chamber. He looked back to Turel and coughed to clear his throat. "At the risk of offending you, I must admit your hospitality is lacking."

Someone on the left side of the room snickered.

Sariel looked over his shoulder, realizing now that a handful of the shorter, gray-skinned Myndarym were standing behind him. Unlike the guards who took him from the habitat, these were dressed in black and armed with spears. Arakiba was the one who seemed to appreciate the humor in Sariel's reply. He had a smile on his ghoulish face, but Sariel's eyes quickly followed the Myndar's crossed arms down to the long, curved blade of the crystalline weapon he held in his hand. It arced forward from the handle and came to a point like a single talon. The sharpened edge was on the inside of the curve, and it looked like something the Marotru would use.

"You'll have to forgive them," said a voice from directly behind.

Sariel flinched.

"They were waiting for me to return," Ezekiyel explained, walking slowly as he came from behind the chair and circled around in front of Sariel. "And we don't typically have visitors."

The master Shaper wasn't holding an object made from the Tree, but Sariel knew he must have one hidden somewhere. The fact that Ezekiyel was here and not trapped in Second Earth proved that he could still move through the In-Between and among the worlds. Sariel suspected that the objects crafted for these Myndarym were their keys to the portal.

"Now that I have you here," Ezekiyel continued, "I'd like you to explain a few things for me."

Sariel waited, thinking through what he knew about each of his enemies and whether there was any bargain that could be struck to get himself released.

"Why did you interfere in Aden?"

"My intention was not to interfere. My intention was to attack Baraquijal, which I did."

Ezekiyel raised his eyebrows. "You killed him."

"Yes."

"You followed him into his world and killed him. And then you dumped his body into a crater of boiling water."

"You're free now because of it," Sariel pointed out.

"Are you expecting gratitude?"

Sariel grinned. "It wouldn't be uncalled for."

Arakiba laughed openly this time, and Turel smiled. If Danel found any amusement in Sariel's reply, she didn't let on.

"I know it has been a long time," Sariel quickly added, "but let us not forget who freed you from Semjaza's rule. It was I who secured the forces of Amatru to make war on your behalf. I removed the sentries and led the initial assault on the land gate—"

"Walking the Amatru straight into Semjaza's trap," Ezekiyel countered. "And they did not make war on our behalf. They used our knowledge of his city to execute an assault that they were already planning."

Sariel shook his head slowly. "If I hadn't chased him down in those fields, you'd still be serving him now. I ended his life in this realm with my own hands."

Ezekiyel raised his head slightly before looking down his nose. "As I recall, you told us all in Senvidar before it began that you had your own motivations for opposing Semjaza. Now you would have us believe it was for our benefit?"

"No, but that was the result. And it was the same with Azael. You cowards fled from his Nephiyl armies and left the people of Sedekiyr to be slaughtered. I stayed. I killed the Iryllurym, and I fought against your enemies in a war that *you* started."

"We didn't start that war; Baraquijal did," Danel pointed out.

"Which brings us back to yet another oppressive leader who is no longer in authority over you because of something *I* did."

"Is there a point to all of this?" Turel asked.

"My point is ... I have done more for all of you than you're willing to admit. Being held as a prisoner is no way to repay my efforts."

"You're asking to be set free?" Ezekiyel asked, as if the idea were preposterous.

"So that you can turn around and work against us?" Danel added.

Sariel shook his head. "What have I ever done in any of the worlds to oppose your efforts?"

The room went silent for a few seconds.

"Did it ever occur to you that, if I wanted to work against you, you would all be dead right now?"

Ezekiyel, who had been pacing in front of Sariel's chair, suddenly turned with eyes narrowed. "So you wish to join us?"

Sariel shrugged and let the question hang in the air.

Footsteps sounded from the left. Arakiba came into view, moving at a casual pace. "I see two problems. You're the only one capable of ruining what we're building. And none of us believe you anyway," he said, raising his curved blade. The silver facets beneath its surface caught the light and scattered it into rainbows.

"NO! Wait!"

Arakiba's arm paused at the limit of his backswing.

Sariel looked from his would-be executioner to the master Shaper. "Alright ... look. I didn't come here to join you. I only hoped to speak with you as a fellow Myndar, and I assumed that you would listen to me because of the mutual respect we have for one another. I believe I have at least earned that."

"Granted," Ezekiyel replied with a nod.

"What did you come to say?" Danel asked from her throne.

Sariel took a deep breath and tried to sit up as straight as he could under the circumstances. "I killed Baraquijal to free all of you from the authority of the Marotru. The reason I did this was because I wanted you to reach a decision without their influence hanging over you."

"What decision?" Arakiba asked.

"The decision to leave this realm."

Ezekiyel's eyes narrowed.

Danel sat forward on her throne.

"All of us, myself included, need to leave this realm and stop interfering in the lives of humans," Sariel pleaded. "Look what we've done to the earth. We've broken it into three pieces."

"We've multiplied it," Ezekiyel corrected.

"And now the lifespan of humans is a tenth of what it used to be. We don't understand the full implications of what we've done."

"You may speak for yourself, but do not presume to speak for me," Ezekiyel replied.

"The humans of this world ..." Sariel added, "they're not even recognizable as human anymore."

"And why should this concern us?" Danel asked.

"Because it is their realm, not ours. All we are doing is corrupting it ... and we need to leave."

Turel stood up from his throne and walked down the steps. "The Holy One never cared for this realm. He had already abandoned it by the time we finished *shaping* it. We are the ones who have invested the time and energy to make it into something useful. This is our realm."

"No," Sariel replied softly. "He hasn't abandoned anything. Don't you see? If He had abandoned it, the humans would have perished. The animals would not have been saved. He has a plan for this realm, and we must stop impeding that plan or we will be destroyed."

"Why do you speak as you do?" Danel asked, now rising from her throne as well. Lines of concern were etched across her otherwise perfect face.

Ezekiyel nodded. "There is something you're not telling us. What drives this plea?"

Sariel looked from one Myndar to another, more sure than ever that they had to hear the judgment against them if they were ever going to turn back from their evil. "When Enoch was in the White City, the Holy One spoke a judgment against us."

"Yes, we know," Arakiba replied. "All of us remember that day in Senvidar."

"No. Enoch didn't share one of the judgments because the Holy One told him to keep it a secret."

Ezekiyel frowned. "Why?"

"So that our true motives would be revealed by our actions. Now this prophecy has come to me, and I share it with you because I believe that if we do not leave this realm, it will come to pass."

"Tell us the prophecy," Turel said.

Sariel took another deep breath before continuing. "The Holy One spoke to us through Enoch, saying, 'You will see your destruction from afar and will know it is coming. Because of your unfaithfulness, this judgment must come to pass. Therefore, I will raise up one from among those you despise. And I will awaken his eyes to the mysteries which I have hidden from men since the foundations of the world. His feet will I make to tread upon the paths of destruction and his hands to make war. He will uproot the seeds of corruption which you have sown throughout the earth. And then you will know that I am the Lord and my justice is everlasting.'"

Arakiba's gaze steadily lowered to the ground as he heard the prophecy. Turel began pacing. Ezekiyel suddenly looked very concerned, turning to look at Danel, whose face was slack.

"I felt the same way as soon as I read it," Sariel admitted. "You see? Nothing goes unseen from the eyes of the Holy One. If we don't leave this realm, He will destroy us by the hand of this … Awakened One."

All of the Myndarym nodded. Finally, it was Danel who replied. "If this indeed came from Enoch, then I would be most gravely concerned. No one heard His voice clearer than The Prophet. But how can we know for sure? Where did you hear this?"

"This prophecy was recorded along with all the other visions and teachings of Enoch. It was handed down from generation to generation among his descendants."

Danel nodded before glancing at Ezekiyel.

The master Shaper stroked his smooth chin as he turned back around to face Sariel. "I am grateful that you have brought this to us. It demonstrates your concern for us as well as your loyalty to the Holy One ... and it's also been quite informative. Arakiba?"

The dark Myndar raised his weapon.

"Wait! What are you—?"

* * * *

The Myndar's blade went through Sariel's neck without the slightest resistance. The severed head tumbled through the air, spattering blood across the guards' uniforms until it hit the ground and bounced across the floor of the throne room. The body slumped forward in the chair, still held in place by the restraints around the wrists.

Arakiba shook the blood from his curved blade and looked up with a grin. It was obvious that he was impressed with the new weapon Ezekiyel had crafted for him.

"Do you think the prophecy is actually true?" Turel asked.

Ezekiyel turned away from the execution and looked up at the Myndar. "Perhaps ... but we should remember that the details of Enoch's other prophecies were only the potential for things that *could* happen. That knowledge allowed us to alter events, such as when Ananel heard The Prophet's first warning to Semjaza. He told us what was spoken and we were able to escape the judgment that was coming upon our leader."

"Yes, but we would be wise to limit their potential for coming true," Danel added. "We need to erase these ideas from the collective memory of humanity so they don't fulfill themselves."

Ezekiyel nodded. "There are no humans in *this* world who remember Enoch or the old ways."

"He must have found it in one of the other worlds, which proves he was using the portal."

Ezekiyel crossed his arms. "Our fellow Shapers have not all chosen to be as aggressive in stamping out the memories of the old world. Who was it that kept the ways of the Holy One?"

Danel turned and sat down on her throne before replying. "In one world, I believe it was the descendants of Kham, which would be Zaquel's responsibility. In the other, it was Shem's descendants."

"They are under Satarel's rule," Turel pointed out.

"Very well," Ezekiyel replied. "I will have the Marotru inform the others that suppression of the old ways is not sufficient. They will need to openly punish it wherever they find evidence. Sariel said the prophecy was *recorded*, which should help narrow down the search."

Danel and Turel nodded.

Ezekiyel turned and walked across the throne room, passing the severed head on his way out. As he exited the doorway, he heard Arakiba say, "Well, that liability has finally been addressed."

17

The bay had been cleared of all other boat traffic in preparation for the arrival of Mwangu Rana. Zaquel's narrow boat sailed across the calm waters under the expert guidance of her captain, while the goddess reclined upon her bed at the aft deck. The fabric of the sunshade flapped in the same breeze that filled the sails, shielding the goddess from the intensity of the noon sun. To the west, the sand-colored wall of Idorana paralleled the shoreline, dominating the landscape. Only a few structures could be seen above it, but none higher than the sharp apex of Zaquel's temple. The only visual break in the wall was the ocean channel that ran from the bay, straight through the city and into the temple.

Zaquel had designed all of these features, and she had sailed into them hundreds of times since her subjects had built them. What dominated her vision at the moment were things that the eyes of her subjects couldn't see—the red sky of the Borderlands and the Seraph hovering before her.

"Sariel is dead, but knowledge of the Holy One is still very much alive."

"Why do you assume that he learned it in my world?" she asked.

"Nothing is being assumed. Ezekiyel is sure that this knowledge has been eradicated from his world; he is requesting that the same assurance be achieved in the other worlds."

Zaquel shifted her perspective toward the Temporal for a moment and surveyed her progress across the bay. This request wasn't as easy as it sounded. In this part of the world, worship of Mwangu Rana was widespread and thoroughly implemented, having pushed out all other beliefs and practices. But such a heavy-handed approach was not conducive to trade. When other nations feared her reputation, they were reluctant to come near, which was the whole reason for establishing Nijambu—the largest port city in the empire, situated on the far western coast of Zaquel's lands. It was as distant as possible from her temple here on the eastern coast. That separation, in addition to the lax enforcement of the goddess's customs and standards, created an environment that was essential to her imports and exports. Even though some human civilizations were being left to themselves, she was still able to benefit from their achievements in this way. She couldn't just recklessly destroy other cultures without damaging her own, but perhaps she could take a more direct approach.

"Tell Ezekiyel that it will be done," she replied, shifting her perspective back toward the Eternal.

The Seraph nodded, and the rapid beating of his six wings morphed into a slower and longer stroke. The abrupt transition sent him speeding away in the blink of an eye.

Zaquel watched him go, taking a great deal of satisfaction in having such a high-ranking demon act as her messenger. Among the Amatru, the Myndarym had never been given this level of status. But now that they had conquered the Temporal Realm, the Myndarym had made themselves valuable, drawing the Marotru into their wake like debris behind a boat. Eventually, the Amatru would come as well, begging for a favorable relationship with the newest power to enter the conflict.

The royal vessel of the Sun Goddess had reached the shallows and was now entering the channel. The citizens of her empire were gathered along the docks of stone and sand. They were on their knees with heads bowed to the earth. Up ahead, a contingent of soldiers waited on either side of the channel to greet their goddess and report any pressing issues.

Zaquel stood, and lifted her dark scepter from its resting place. As far as her people knew, their goddess had gone alone into the underworld, taking only an earthly treasure with her. When she emerged, unscathed, she held a branch from the sacred tree, a dark object of great power that proved her sovereignty over this world. Zaquel wouldn't have to craft the story or tell it to anyone; these things would arise naturally, whispered from person to person the moment her boat reached the temple. And they would be mostly true, except that no human could possibly know how powerful the scepter really was.

She carried her new treasure as she walked down the steps to the lower deck where her chief priestess waited. "Which of your priestesses in the west is the most knowledgeable of foreign beliefs?"

"None, my goddess," the woman replied quickly. "They worship you and you alone."

"Of course they do, but some people in the west who do not worship me are teaching their blasphemous ideas to others. I have been merciful and patient so long as these thoughts are kept hidden, but I will not tolerate them to spread."

"Yes, my goddess. Perhaps the ... holy men could help in this matter?"

Zaquel smiled at her priestess' reluctance to use the contradictory term. "Go on."

"They still offer the annual sacrifice. This detestable practice takes them from tribe to tribe, so they would be the most knowledgeable about such things."

The annual sacrifice was something that Zaquel had agreed to in order to keep her people from mingling with Rameel's. Fear had been an effective tool in this regard. But the priestess was right about it being detestable. Zaquel didn't intend to let it continue for much longer. The chief priestess deserved to know this little secret, for there was much wisdom in the woman's idea. And now that Zaquel considered it, she decided that the chief priestess would need to reach a minimal level of acceptance with the holy men in order to do what was going to be required of her.

"They offer girls because they value them above all else. It is indeed detestable, but also understandable for the time being."

The priestess kept her eyes forward and simply bowed her head in acknowledgment.

"However, the men are ultimately loyal to me," Zaquel added. "They will help us in this matter, and in the years to come their practice will be abolished."

"My goddess?"

"In the underworld, I made … other arrangements."

"You are truly magnificent and worthy of praise," the chief priestess said, dropping to her knees. "May you also become the goddess of the underworld."

"Soon, priestess," Zaquel replied with a smile.

"Mwangu Rana!" came the shout of hundreds in unison.

Zaquel looked up to see that they were now drifting through the channel between two contingents of her soldiers, who were all on their knees with their arms spread out to their sides. One of her captains was at the front of the formation. "Where is your general?"

"My goddess, he had an urgent matter to address at the mines. He sent me in his stead with his deepest apologies and to ask your forgiveness." The captain's head never came up from the ground.

"It is granted, though I will speak with him in the temple at sundown."

"Yes, Goddess!"

* * * *

SARIEL'S CAMP

The scroll that Ebnisha had been using to record Sariel's story was becoming full. In just a few weeks he'd have to start a second one. Never in his life did Ebnisha imagine that Sariel, the very angel and protector of mankind from his people's history, would reveal himself here and now. And not just reveal himself, but sit down and talk. There was so much wisdom and insight that Sariel brought to the stories of Enoch and his descendants. Details were confirmed. Gaps were filled in. And strange occurrences that had gone unexplained for thousands of years were finally clarified.

Ebnisha looked up from the parchment and out through the open door of Sariel's dwelling. Most of the children were running through the meadow with sticks in their hands, waving and yelling to each other. The youngest one was on the ground, chewing on something he'd just picked up. Ebnisha cringed before he realized it was just a blade of grass.

This was the most exciting time in Ebnisha's life, and he had thought Sariel felt the same until recently. In the distance, the angel could be seen pacing along the edge of the stream. His arms were crossed and he was talking to himself.

Ebnisha set down his writing stalk and got up from the table. The air outside was mild, the cool of the night still fighting against the midmorning sun. He made his way across the meadow, stopping several times to keep from being run over by the children. When he entered the shade of the trees near the water, Ebnisha caught the last few words of Sariel's mumbling.

"... an option, but I'd have to wait. Who knows how long it might—?" Sariel stopped, suddenly aware of Ebnisha's presence.

"I'm sorry to interrupt."

"No. That's quite alright. Conversations are better with two people anyway."

Ebnisha smiled as he came alongside Sariel and looked out over the water. "Is it from remembering too much?"

"Is what ...?"

"Your sadness."

This only seemed to make Sariel more downcast. "No, of course not. I enjoy the things we talk about. It is just that ... something has been taken from me."

Ebnisha nodded, though he really didn't understand. "Is this the thing you lost?"

"No. Something else ... also very valuable."

"I wish I could take it back for you," Ebnisha offered, "whatever it is."

Sariel reached up and laid his hand on Ebnisha's shoulder. "Thank you."

They were both quiet for a few minutes, watching the stream and listening to the birds in the trees. The laughter of the children behind them drew Sariel's attention, and he looked back over his shoulder. "Does your elder approve of you being here? All of you?"

"Yes."

"You aren't needed for gathering food or building dwellings?"

"No. There is plenty of food. And everyone has a dwelling."

Sariel nodded.

"Would you like us to leave?"

"Oh! I didn't mean it like that. I just don't want to cause any problems."

Ebnisha was relieved. "No, there is not much for us to do in the village. I talk with our elder every time I go back, and he's never expressed any concerns."

"Good," Sariel replied, turning back to the water. After a few seconds of silence, he added, "I was thinking of building a few other dwellings, so your brothers and sisters wouldn't have to go back as often with the children."

Ebnisha couldn't contain the smile on his face. "They would like that very much."

"It's settled then," Sariel replied, crossing his arms. The sadness seemed to have gone away for now.

Ebnisha was curious about something, but he wasn't sure if he wanted to bring it up and ruin the mood. Instead, he contented himself with watching the water.

"What is it?" Sariel asked, now looking directly at Ebnisha.

"Well ... I was wondering. Your dwelling is different from the ones we build. Where did you learn this way?"

Sariel turned around and looked across the meadow. "I learned much by observing the Chatsiyram men, but I didn't build my own dwelling until Sheyir and I lived with the Aleydam. The wood was very different so high up, of course—solid. We had to cut many different pieces and fit them together because they didn't have long grasses for tying. And it didn't rain back then, so the roofs only needed to keep the cold air out. I was able to use what I learned there when Enoch and I founded El-Betakh. I taught him, and he taught me how the people in Sedekiyr built their dwellings and other structures."

Ebnisha was distracted by the fact that he didn't have his writing stalk and parchment.

"Do you want to go back inside?"

"If you don't mind," Ebnisha admitted.

*   *   *   *

IDORANA

Zaquel could see the general's spirit approaching before she heard his hurried footsteps coming from the hall outside the throne room.

"Mwangu Rana!" he exclaimed as soon as he entered the room. He kept his head down as he crossed the polished stone floor, then knelt as he approached the steps.

"What could be so important at the mines that it would prevent you from receiving me?"

"My deepest apologies, Goddess. The miners claimed to have found another vein of gold and requested additional resources to pursue it. I know this is a priority for you, so I went immediately to assess their claims."

"What did you find?"

"All was just as they said, my goddess. Your gold exports will increase greatly over the coming year."

Zaquel didn't bother thanking the general, or responding to his words at all. He was only a man and received sufficient encouragement and motivation through the honor of serving the

Goddess of the Sun. "Your chief priestess will be sailing west to Nijambu. From there she will travel by land to meet with the holy men. You and one hundred of your best warriors will accompany her every step of the way. You will purchase horses and wagons for her as soon as you go ashore. You will serve her in whatever she asks of you. And if any harm comes to her, I will have all of your bodies emptied of blood before my eyes in this very room. Do you understand?"

"Yes, Mwangu Rana! It is my honor to serve you."

"It will also be your honor to serve the chief priestess. Now go and assemble your men."

"Yes, my goddess," he replied, backing away from the throne.

When the general was gone from the room, Zaquel looked down to her chief priestess at the bottom of the stairs. "Find these holy men and accept nothing but their complete obedience. If they have not heard of these stories, make them search until they find what you seek."

"It will be my pleasure to take your name into the west," she replied.

Enoch had slipped through Zaquel's fingers once before—in Sedekiyr, when he was stolen away to the Eternal Realm by the Iryllurym. But that would not happen here. His words would die in this realm. "When you find these blasphemers and make an example of them, have the holy men watch. Afterward, I will hold *them* responsible for any word that seeks to exalt itself above my own."

SA 4228

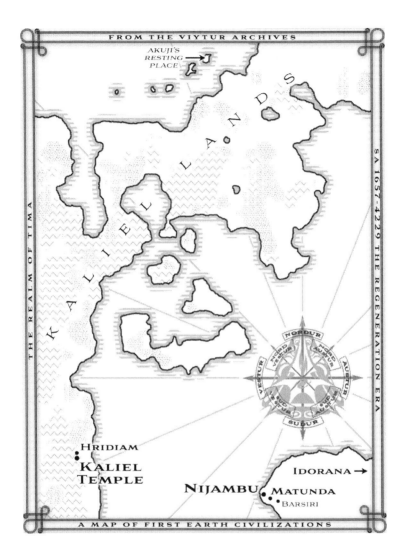

18

SARIEL'S CAMP

The sun was already past its zenith, and Ebnisha was busy packing up his satchel for the day. He was heading back to his village to return some of the scrolls that had amassed in Sariel's dwelling. Everyone else was gathered around the fire pit, though there was no fire. It didn't become cold enough for that until the sun went down, and sometimes not even then. Ebnisha's family still seemed to enjoy coming into Sariel's dwelling to share stories, despite the fact that there were now three other structures that could accommodate them.

Sariel felt as though he'd been talking all morning, which was probably the case. Ebnisha's brothers and sisters were almost as curious as the scribe himself. "I was hoping you could tell *me* a few things ... if you don't mind."

Ebnisha smiled as he put another scroll in his satchel.

Mosi, the oldest of Ebnisha's siblings, looked at the others and shrugged. "What would you like to know?"

"Well, I'm interested to learn more about the other gods of this world."

"You are the teacher ... you do not know these things?"

"No. Ebnisha told me about the Kaliel and the one they worship. Do you know of others?"

"There are many," Mosi replied.

"Female ones," Sariel clarified.

Mosi's wife, Ekua, smiled. "The most powerful is Mwangu Rana of the east."

"Mwangu Rana? What does this mean?"

"Goddess of the Sun," she replied.

"I'm ready to go," Ebnisha announced. "Is anyone else coming?"

Zuberi, Ebnisha's next youngest brother, climbed to his feet. "I will go; I forgot to bring my knife."

"Remember the thread," his wife added.

Zuberi nodded.

Ebnisha looked down at Sariel seated on the ground. "I have a scroll about the goddess of the east that I'll bring you tomorrow. And another about the gods far to the north; many of them are female."

"Thank you," Sariel said, waving as Ebnisha and his brother walked out.

"You may not need it," Mosi said. "Ekua knows much about Mwangu Rana … too much."

Ekua elbowed her husband before she leaned forward. "It is said that the Goddess of the Sun is so beautiful that men can no longer look upon her. In the early days of her reign, her beauty drove men to madness. They worshipped her, but they lusted after her as well. Their devotion was so strong that they lost their desire for their own wives. They could neither eat nor sleep. Her empire became weak, because no children were being born. But the goddess is also wise and full of grace. She knew that for her empire to multiply, she had to protect men from her beauty, so she forbade them to look upon her. The first ones who violated this decree fell dead in the streets, and very few have ever made the same mistake since that time. Afterward, she took the women into her temple and taught them her ways. They learned to make themselves beautiful and to imitate the goddess in the way she moved and the way she spoke. She imparted her wisdom to them, and they became powerful through this knowledge. The desire of men was restored, and children began multiplying again."

Sariel was hearing something familiar in this story. "What does this goddess look like?"

"She is very tall ... they say as much as one man standing on another's shoulders."

"And her skin ... is it like mine?" Sariel asked.

"No, dark like us. Some say that the words of her mouth caused all the tribes to come into being."

That certainly sounded like Zaquel, but Sariel didn't want to get ahead of himself. "Are these just stories, or have people actually seen her?"

"People see her," Mosi replied. "Her temple is in the city of Idorana, all the way to the ocean in the east. That is where they dig into the earth and bring up its treasures."

"What kind of treasures?"

"Mostly gold and onyx stone."

"Silver too," Ekua added. "And stones of every color. The women wear them on their bodies like clothing.

Mosi nodded. "They sell them in Nijambu."

"Does the goddess ever come out of her temple?" Sariel wondered, still not entirely convinced that these weren't just myths.

"Oh yes," Ekua said quickly. "She walks the streets of Idorana, and everyone puts their heads to the ground in reverence."

Mosi was watching his wife's face very closely, which had been glowing since the moment this subject came up.

Ekua glared at her husband before looking back at Sariel. "They say she moves so quietly that no one hears her footsteps even when they bow at her feet."

"She is not graceful," Mosi argued, leaning forward. "She is dangerous. Her explorers once found gold on the shore of a lake, two weeks' journey to the southwest of Idorana. They brought soldiers and claimed it for their own, but it was sacred to the tribe there. When the people resisted, the soldiers fought them. Mwangu Rana heard of the fighting and went to the lake herself. When she arrived, she called her soldiers away so that she could face the tribe alone."

"What did she do to them?" Sariel asked.

"They say that she only stared at them. The tribespeople, men and women, went mad and tore their own skin from their bodies. And the children drowned themselves in the lake."

Sariel remembered the things they said of Zaquel while she served under Baraquijal. She was able to read the thoughts of humans and to control their minds. This goddess certainly sounded like Zaquel.

"The men of her empire are not allowed to learn from the goddess," Mosi continued. "They are forced to be her soldiers and workers. Only the women are permitted to make decisions in the city."

Ekua was looking away at the ceiling, trying not to smile.

"It is not right," Mosi declared, turning to look directly at his wife.

"Why?" she asked, turning suddenly to face him. "Do you think I am not as smart as you?"

"Alright," Sariel announced, climbing to his feet. "I don't want any arguments. Let's talk about something else."

Mosi and Ekua were staring hard at each other, and the other family members were watching them carefully.

"How about ...?" Sariel began, but he couldn't think of a new subject.

Suddenly, Mosi's stern face cracked into a smile. One of Ekua's eyebrows shot upward. Then both of them started laughing.

Sariel glanced at the other siblings, hoping for some clue as to what was happening. But they all began laughing as well. Even the children joined in, laughing so hard that it caused them to roll on the ground. Sariel watched them all in fascination, wondering if perhaps this was some custom of theirs—to assert one's opinion until it became an argument, then start laughing before anyone got their feelings hurt. The laughter died down after a few seconds, and when everyone had gotten control of themselves, they turned to look at Sariel as if nothing had happened.

The complete silence after such an outburst struck Sariel as hilarious, and he suddenly began laughing all by himself.

* * * *

MATUNDA
EBNISHA'S VILLAGE

Voices brought Ebnisha out of a deep sleep. He opened his eyes, but it was still dark inside his dwelling. It felt like the middle of the night. In the distance, he could hear someone screaming. Men were shouting from closer by. Through the small window across the room, the flicker of firelight shone across the ceiling. Ebnisha rubbed at his eyes and sat up on his bed. A man's voice mumbled something right outside his dwelling. Ebnisha turned his head toward the sound.

Suddenly, the blanket over his doorway was thrown to one side, and two men ducked into the dwelling.

Ebnisha flinched.

One man waved his torch from side to side, searching for something. The other noticed Ebnisha and came straight for him.

"Who are you?" Ebnisha yelled, backing against the wall.

The one with the torch raised it above his head and squinted. "Are you Ebnisha?"

"Yes," he answered.

The other man stepped on his bed and grabbed him by the wrist. "Give me your other hand," he ordered, pulling Ebnisha away from the wall.

"Who are you?" Ebnisha repeated.

The man with the torch spun around and began inspecting the inside of Ebnisha's dwelling. He wore only a coarse loincloth that covered him to the middle of his legs. When his torchlight spilled across Ebnisha's collection of scrolls, the man stopped to take a closer look.

The other, dressed the same, was tying Ebnisha's hands together in front of his body with a rope.

"Why are you doing this? Who are you?"

"Come," the man said, pulling hard on the rope after Ebnisha's hands were bound.

Ebnisha was almost dragged across the floor until he got his footing and began to stumble forward.

The man with the torch pulled one of the scrolls from its cubbyhole on the wall before turning to join the other.

Ebnisha was led outside into the cool of night. A handful of villagers were kneeling in the dirt outside Ebnisha's dwelling next to a foreign man holding a sword. Dozens of other men were walking through the village with torches, leading or pushing Ebnisha's people toward the others who were kneeling. Those without torches carried spears and swords. Shouting and crying came from all directions.

Ebnisha looked around in confusion before noticing a cluster of torchlight and a large group of men in tunics approaching from the center of the village. He stared for a few seconds before realizing that some were the holy men. But Ebnisha's people had recently given them a virgin girl; there was no reason for them to be here.

"What is going on here?" he shouted.

As more of the villagers were forced to kneel outside Ebnisha's dwelling, the holy men came forward. There were about twenty of them, many more than were usually seen in one place. They were flanked by an equal number of foreign men in loincloths. The whole group spread out to one side as they reached Ebnisha's dwelling, and a woman stepped out from their midst. She was clothed from her neck to her ankles in loose robes of the finest white linen. With each step, the gold bands around her wrists and ankles clanked together. Gold was even woven into the long braids of hair that were pulled back from her face. In the torchlight, her perfect skin appeared to glisten like water. Her beauty was striking, and it seemed that the very air around her radiated with her authority. When she made eye contact with Ebnisha, he felt as though she were staring into his soul.

"Are you Ebnisha?"

"Why? What is going on here?"

One of the men with spears lunged forward and struck Ebnisha across the face with his fist. The scribe's legs went weak, and the force of the blow sent him backward to the dirt.

"You will answer the chief priestess when she asks you a question!" the man yelled.

Ebnisha's head was ringing, and his nose and jaw suddenly felt cold. His arms were grabbed by several strong hands and he was wrenched to his feet once again.

"We found these in his dwelling."

Ebnisha opened his eyes to see one of the soldiers handing a scroll to the woman. As she unrolled it, Ebnisha glanced to his left to see that the villagers were still being brought before his dwelling and forced to kneel. There were almost fifty of them now, but Zuberi wasn't among them. Ebnisha hoped that his brother had escaped into the night.

The chief priestess had the scroll open and was scanning the page with her piercing eyes. The more she stared at the symbols, the smaller her eyes became. All of a sudden, she brought her hands together and crumpled the scroll. Then she handed it back to the soldier before turning to survey the area around her. She glanced from one place to another, as if searching for something. Then her eyes went up to the large tree whose branches were spread out over them all.

"This will do. String him up there, and pile all of these at his feet," she said, pointing at the damaged scroll.

"Why are you doing this?" Ebnisha shouted.

The priestess didn't answer, or even look at him.

No one struck him this time; the soldiers simply went to work obeying their master. One threw a rope over a thick branch. Another caught the end of it and began tying it to the rope around Ebnisha's wrists.

"You are servants of Mwangu Rana?"

The priestess didn't answer.

Five soldiers gathered at the rope on the other side of the branch. They each grabbed hold of it and began to pull.

Ebnisha's arms were drawn upward. Then his body was dragged a few feet across the ground until his toes left the dirt. He began swinging as the soldiers heaved him up into the air in lurches.

"That's enough," the priestess said, holding up her hand.

The soldiers stopped pulling and tied off the rope on a lower branch.

Ebnisha's body swung and twisted in the air. He could hear crying. The faces of his people spun past his vision, and he tried to look at each of them individually. When his movements slowed, he made eye contact with them. Most averted their eyes. A few stared back with tears. The faces of the children were the most steady, their innocence allowing them to look on without understanding what was happening. Some of the people just kept their heads down, hoping that this punishment would pass quickly. Ebnisha could see now that Zuberi was in the third row. There was a deep gash running across his cheek and mouth, bleeding profusely. There were tears glistening on his face, but also a defiant look in his eyes. He stared at Ebnisha and raised his head slightly. Then he bit his lip and nodded.

Ebnisha nodded back, knowing that this was goodbye.

The pile of scrolls was growing beneath Ebnisha's feet as the soldiers emptied his dwelling of his life's work. They dropped the rolls of parchment in the dirt and went back for more, while others kicked at the errant ones to keep the pile from spreading out.

Ebnisha looked down upon the pages where he had recorded thousands of years of human history among numerous cultures. Descriptions of wedding customs. Birthing ceremonies. Styles of dress. The stories of gods and drawings of their graven images. Details about their cities and how they were built. Stories of war and conquering nations. All of it was there, everything he'd ever heard in Nijambu as well as the stories of his own people. The founding of Matunda was there, the lineage of the families in the village. Everything from the present all the way back through Kham's experiences after the flood, the visions of Enoch that he'd shared with his son, and the knowledge of the Holy One.

"*This* is why?" he asked, gasping for breath as the weight of his own body constricted his throat.

The entire population of Matunda was now on their knees, watching.

The priestess stepped forward and turned to address the holy men. "This village has blasphemed Mwangu Rana." Then she turned to the kneeling people. "You have kept lies in your hearts and have taught your children to do the same." Finally, she turned and looked up into Ebnisha's eyes. "You, Ebnisha, chief among all blasphemers, have made these lies into symbols and have marked them upon the flesh of trees so they may be spread into the world. Your body and blood will be consumed by fire as a sacrifice unto Mwangu Rana."

The priestess reached up to the collar of gold and onyx around her neck. She felt for the thin, gold chain there and slipped it over her head. When it came free, a small glass vial slid out from her robes and dangled in the torchlight. She walked slowly forward until she was standing beside the pile of scrolls.

Ebnisha thought of kicking her as hard as he could, or trying to grab her around the neck with his legs. He doubted he could hurt her significantly before he was run through with a spear, but it wasn't his own pain or death that stayed him. The people of Matunda would certainly be punished for anything he did to the priestess, and so he kept still.

The priestess removed the lid of the vial and began to drip its liquid over the pile of scrolls. She walked around Ebnisha, taking care to be thorough. When she circled back, she began to drizzle the remaining liquid on Ebnisha's feet and legs. By the time she reached his chest and neck, the vial was empty. She shook the last of its contents on Ebnisha's face and dropped the vial on the ground beside the scrolls.

The man who had struck Ebnisha grabbed a torch from the soldier next to him and stepped forward.

The priestess suddenly put out her hand to keep him back. "Give me your knife."

The man immediately removed a small blade from the sheath attached to his belt and flipped it over, offering the handle to the priestess.

"Stay back," she said, taking the knife from him. Then she turned back to Ebnisha and raised the blade.

Ebnisha winced, even before anything happened. The priestess dragged the sharpened edge of the blade down Ebnisha's leg. He tried not to cry, but a yelp escaped his lips. There was a burning sensation on his skin that faded to a cold, wet feeling. She kept cutting, walking around him as she made multiple, long strokes down his bare legs. After the third one, Ebnisha couldn't feel them anymore, but the sound of his own blood dripping on the scrolls made his stomach turn.

The priestess swiped the flat of the blade across Ebnisha's tunic to remove the excess blood. Then she handed it back to the soldier before kneeling to the ground. The noises that came from her mouth were deep and quiet. Her breath could be heard wheezing in and out between the syllables of some foreign language. Then her voice became louder and louder, her utterances becoming a harsh, repeated phrase.

Ebnisha looked down below his feet and saw that the scrolls were moving as if blown by a light breeze.

The priestess continued getting louder, rising from the ground as she did so. When she was standing fully upright, her voice was shrill, screaming into the night. Her hands went out to both sides and she began to move her feet, shuffling them across the dirt in some unknown pattern. Her gold bands clanked against each other, and her whole body began to tremble as if with rage.

Ebnisha looked down on the priestess and felt pity for her. She was a slave, and the goddess she served was a cruel master. The Holy One was the only true God, and one day He would raise up His servant to bring these false gods to justice. Mwangu Rana would not always sit upon her throne, and when she was brought down from it, how great would be her fall. But all these things Ebnisha kept inside for the sake of his people.

The priestess' voice came to an abrupt silence.

The eyes of the holy men, the soldiers, and all of the villagers suddenly went down to the orange light that had appeared below Ebnisha.

The scribe craned his neck and looked down to see that flames were coming out from the pile of scrolls.

The priestess backed away while the holy men gasped in surprise.

The numbness in Ebnisha's legs was replaced by a burning sensation. He pulled his legs upward, but flames were already licking up his feet and calves. He kicked at the air, but the flames only spread. The burning sensation increased to an unbearable pain and he couldn't help but scream out. This time, the pain didn't result in numbness. Instead it kept escalating, revealing new levels of torture. Ebnisha couldn't control the horrible sounds that were coming from his own mouth.

The holy men turned their heads in revulsion.

"You will watch, or I will have your eyes taken out!" the priestess yelled.

Zuberi was weeping, but he wouldn't look away.

Ebnisha bit down on his own tongue to stop the noise. The flames were on his face now, and he'd never felt so much pain in his whole life. Every muscle in his body was flexing uncontrollably, shaking, but there was nowhere to go. No escape.

The flames became so bright that it was all Ebnisha could see. Whiteness in every direction. Like staring into the sun. The pain began to drift away. He felt himself rising, but his body was falling. His spirit was separating itself. The world—just a dream that he was waking from.

* * * *

Sariel stood in the middle of the meadow outside his dwelling. The midmorning sun was warm on his face, but there was a cold feeling in his heart. He looked over to the stream where Mosi had been rinsing his hands, and saw that Ebnisha's oldest brother was looking at the sky above the mountain ridge, in the direction of his village.

Sariel walked across the meadow and came to a stop beside Mosi. "Something is not right."

He nodded. "Ebnisha and Zuberi should have been back by now."

Sariel looked toward the mountain ridge again before he replied. "I'm going to Matunda."

"I'm coming with you."

"No, please. It might be dangerous."

"I'm coming with you," Mosi repeated. "Just let me tell Ekua." He began walking across the meadow toward the dwellings.

Sariel called after him. "Have her keep everyone out of sight."

Mosi nodded.

Sariel waited with his arms crossed, glancing every few seconds at the sun and noting how high it was getting in the sky. With every passing moment, he felt more certain that Ebnisha wasn't coming back. And that thought was so deeply troubling that he couldn't even acknowledge the emotions that came with it. He had to push them aside until he knew whether or not they could be allowed to take over. For they certainly would if his fears turned out to be warranted.

Mosi came out of his dwelling with Ekua and the other siblings following. Sariel couldn't hear the words Ekua was saying to her husband, but he could see the look on her face. She was grabbing at Mosi's arm as he pulled away from her.

"Can you run?" Sariel asked as soon as Mosi was close enough to hear him.

"Can you?"

"Try to keep up," Sariel replied before setting out across the meadow at a rapid pace.

~

It usually took over an hour to make the trip to Matunda. Sariel and Mosi made it in less than half that time. As soon as they began descending from the ridge overlooking the village, it was obvious that something was wrong. There was no movement, no one visible between the dwellings and other huts.

Sariel sped down through the trees, leaping in bursts over brush and other obstacles until the land flattened out. Then he took off at a full sprint, leaving Mosi behind. From the Eternal, he could see that there were no spirits in the village. It was deserted. He ran between the dwellings, heading for the north side of the village where Ebnisha had said his hut was located.

In the Temporal, he suddenly caught sight of something dark covering the ground between the dwellings. He stumbled and slowed to a walk. It caught him by surprise, but he knew what it was before he could even close his eyes and look away. Dark bodies lying on the ground. Blood. Flies buzzing. Sariel opened his eyes again, forcing himself to look ahead once more and keep moving.

As the gruesome sight spread out before him, Sariel came to a stop behind the bodies. All of them were lying facedown in the same direction. Well over a hundred men, women, and children. Their throats had obviously been cut, the dirt underneath them dark with their blood. As if in worship, they lay prostrate before a charred body hanging by a rope from a large tree. If Sariel hadn't already known that it was Ebnisha, he would have been able to figure it out from the pile of ashes and parchment scraps beneath him.

"NO!" Mosi yelled from behind. "NO!"

Sariel kept his eyes forward, absorbing the reality of what was before him. There were no tears yet, for if he let them fall, he was afraid that they might never reach their end. He started moving, walking around the bodies, looking at the soil. To the left side, there was a gathering of footprints where a crowd had watched Ebnisha burn.

Somewhere in the back of Sariel's mind, he knew that Mosi was on the ground, weeping into his hands. But Sariel wouldn't let himself grieve for Ebnisha yet. There was work to be done first. He moved away from the footprints and came to Ebnisha's body. The fire had been set below him, apparently started with his scrolls, but the extent of Ebnisha's injuries couldn't have been caused with only a pile of parchment. Sariel kicked the cold ashes aside until his foot knocked against something hard. He bent down and picked up a small glass vial. It was discolored on the outside and charred on the inside. He sniffed it. Whatever it had contained had burned off and now just smelled like smoke. But the partially melted gold chain attached to it was unique. Gold only came from one place in these lands, and no one who had purchased such an item would have left it here.

"Who would do this?" Mosi whispered.

As the question finally broke through to his conscious mind, Sariel realized it wasn't the first time Ebnisha's brother had asked the question. "The servants of Zaquel."

"Who?"

"The Goddess of the Sun," Sariel replied, turning around.

Mosi was standing amidst the bodies, bending over next to one that looked like Zuberi.

Sariel walked over and handed the vial to him. "This was used to start the fire. It came from someone who has so much gold that this could be discarded without care."

Mosi inspected the vial before looking back to Sariel with a furrowed brow.

"And those wounds are from long, straight blades," Sariel added, pointing down at the bodies.

"How do you know?"

"I just know," Sariel replied. "Who else carries swords in these lands?"

"No one but the soldiers of Mwangu Rana."

Sariel nodded his agreement before turning and walking back to Ebnisha's body.

"But why would the goddess do this?"

"Because of me."

Mosi frowned. "I don't understand."

"I made a mistake; all of this is because of me. But my eyes are open now. I know the Myndarym will never stop. I have been awakened to the mysteries hidden from men since the foundations of the world."

Mosi's forehead suddenly became smooth.

"My feet will tread upon the paths of destruction, and my hands will make war," Sariel added, turning to face Ebnisha's body. With a wave of his hand, Sariel severed the rope. Ebnisha's body should have dropped to the ground, but an invisible force caught it and gently laid it upon the earth.

Mosi stood up to his full height, his eyebrows now raised.

"Bring Zuberi over here," Sariel instructed. "We only have time to bury your brothers and then we must get back to the rest of your family."

~

When Sariel and Mosi arrived at the camp in the afternoon, the family came out to greet them. Mosi ran forward and embraced his wife. Sariel didn't know what to say. "I'm sorry" seemed so insufficient as to be worthless. He headed straight for his own dwelling without a word, and by the time he entered the dark interior of his home, he heard crying outside.

On the table were two scrolls. The largest was a collection of Sariel's stories that Ebnisha had recorded in his own words, and in his poetic way. It covered all the major events from the time of his coming to the Temporal Realm until the destruction of Sedekiyr. The other was one that Ebnisha had just started, containing Sariel's many years of wandering after his merge with Vand-ra. But it was far from complete. Although they had discussed more recent events, Ebnisha liked to work in chronological order, and that was as far as the two of them had gotten.

Sariel put the smaller one inside the larger and tucked them both into Ebnisha's leather satchel that he had carried back from Matunda. Then he took a moment to look around his dwelling. There was nothing else here that he needed to take with him except for the memories, and there were many good ones in this place. Sariel had known when he was building this dwelling that it was probably a temporary one, but he had no idea how temporary. With one last deep breath, he turned and walked out into the sun.

The family was still gathered in the meadow, embracing. Their heads were down and they were whispering comforting words to each other and the children. Zuberi's wife looked weak in the knees, leaning heavily on Ekua.

"Mosi?" Sariel whispered.

The man lifted his head.

Sariel showed him the last remnants of Ebnisha's writing. "We need to hide this."

He nodded.

"Is there somewhere we can go? It's not safe for your family here."

Mosi exhaled and looked up at the sky.

"The old burial grounds," Ekua suggested, raising her head.

"Where is that?"

"A few days from here," Mosi replied.

"Are there other tribes near it?"

"No. It is very difficult to reach."

"Good," Sariel said. "As soon as you're ready ..."

19

The terrain was steep and covered in dense foliage that blocked out much of the sunlight. Mosi led the way, hacking at the vegetation with his makeshift spear. He and his brothers had found suitable branches along the stream shortly after leaving Sariel's camp and thought it would be a good idea to have something with which to protect the women and children. Sariel took up the second position, scanning their ascent for any sign of approaching spirits. Imamu, the second oldest brother, and Wekesa had decided to wait at the lake below, where the waterfall spilled into it. They wanted to stay close to the rest of the family, and only one person was really needed to show Sariel to the burial grounds.

Although it was just a short distance below them, the lake could no longer be seen through the trees. Ekua had been right about this location—it wouldn't be found unless someone knew where to look. Just getting to the lake had been a challenge, with one narrow gorge after another to climb.

The sound of rushing water was becoming louder on their left, and the two began angling across the steep incline toward it. All of a sudden, the tree line ended. They were on a precipice with a narrow gap separating the cliff on which they stood from a wall of vegetation a dozen paces away. The land had been eroded by the force of water pouring down from the heights, creating a narrow cleft that ran deep into the mountains. On either side were sheer cliffs covered by moss and vines that thrived in the misty environment. The side on which they stood had a narrow path that followed the cliff face upward and to the right.

Mosi began climbing the path without pausing to look at the scenery. Sariel followed, and after several minutes they came upon a thick rope of woven vines extending across the gap between the cliffs. On this side of the gorge, someone had tied the rope to the branch of a small tree growing from a crack in the rocks. On the other side of the gorge, the rope angled upward until it disappeared into the middle of the waterfall.

"There is a large cave on the other side of the water, behind the fall," Mosi explained. "If you swing from this ledge here, you will enter at the right height. Follow the first chamber into the mountain and it will lead to the burial place."

"Are you coming inside?"

"I cannot. Only elders are allowed to enter."

Sariel certainly qualified for that designation, though Mosi and his family didn't know the truth about how old he really was.

"You can let go of the rope when you are through. I will gather it up again later from the top of the other cliff."

"What about light?" Sariel asked as he tucked Ebnisha's satchel beneath his tunic.

"There is a torch and a flint on the wall of the first chamber."

Sariel untied the rope and pulled on it, looking up as he assessed its strength.

"It's not as scary as it looks ... I'm told."

Sariel smiled. "And when I'm done?"

"Come back to the first chamber and jump into the flow. There is a deep pool where you will land. The force of the water will push you out of this gorge and you will come up in the lake below. Don't forget to take a deep breath."

Sariel wondered how this place had ever been discovered. The first person to try jumping out wouldn't have known that it was safe.

"I'll be waiting for you at the lake."

"Thank you, Mosi."

The knowledge that there was a deep pool at the bottom of the waterfall was of little comfort when standing before the roar of such power. Sariel knew that if he hesitated, it would only make this task worse. So he gripped the rope firmly with both hands, took a deep breath, and pushed himself away from the cliff. The weightlessness of the swing brought memories of flight to mind, but that exhilaration was stolen the moment his body entered the water. The flow was shockingly cold, and the force of that much water pushing down on him threatened to overpower his grip on the rope.

The sensation passed quickly and he was suddenly on the other side of the water. On instinct, he loosened his grip on the rope and began to slide downward. The drop took longer than he expected, but when his feet touched solid earth with his balance intact, Sariel was relieved that his body hadn't forgotten how to land after flight.

He let go of the rope and stood up from his crouched position. The deafening water at the mouth of the cave gave a shimmering glow to the surroundings, providing much more light than he would have expected. But as the cave narrowed toward the back, heading farther into the mountain, the glittering light was quickly lost. As Mosi had said, there were several torches and a flint lying on a ledge nearby. Sariel struck the flint against the stone wall of the chamber and caught the sparks with one of the torches. The damp bundle must have been oiled, for the sparks caught immediately and grew into a steady flame.

This first chamber narrowed significantly as it went farther into the mountain. At the back, the ceiling dropped so low that Sariel had to crawl on his hands and knees for a moment. But when he was through the natural doorway, he stood up to find another chamber, much larger than the first. The sound of his footsteps no longer echoed, and the light of his torch wasn't sufficient to light the whole space at once. Sariel went forward, pushing back the darkness to inspect the burial place.

In the middle of the chamber, slabs of rock had been piled to form a row of burial sites. There was no soil to dig up, but there were other large mounds of loosely piled stones. The jagged walls around the lower perimeter of the chamber suggested that the burial materials were mined from the chamber itself as needed. What Sariel had to bury was different, and he didn't want to interfere with the pattern of mounds that already existed. Instead, he went to the back wall and set down his torch. He found smaller slabs of rock among the loose piles and brought them over, arranging them to form a smaller box. It took several trips, but within minutes he had a resting place for the last of Ebnisha's written words.

Sariel knelt on the ground and removed Ebnisha's leather satchel. Pulling out the scrolls, he unrolled them on the floor of the burial chamber. Their edges were ragged from the crudeness of Ebnisha's construction, and Sariel knew that these materials wouldn't last long in this humid environment. Shifting his perspective toward the Eternal, Sariel began to sing softly. The melodies drifted from his lips and spread out over the pages like smoke. It was a simple Song of Preservation that helped to keep the natural forces of deterioration at bay—something he'd used in many of his construction efforts in El-Betakh. He'd never told anyone the reason for his singing, and the citizens assumed it was just something he did while working. Then he rolled the smaller scroll within the larger and wrapped them in the oiled cloths that Ebnisha had kept in his dwelling to prevent his writing fluid from drying out. Then he placed the scrolls in the satchel and tied it closed.

As he held the leather bundle, it felt as though something needed to be said. This was an occasion, even if no one else was here to witness it. "Ebnisha," he whispered. "These are only a few of your many words, but they will survive. Your efforts were not wasted. You kept the words of the Holy One. And the memory of you will live on in my heart and in the hearts of your family. You brought me back from utter loneliness. And though we only had a short time together, I will treasure your friendship above all others. Rest now, and know that the words you have written will come to pass."

Sariel had tears in his eyes by the time he finished speaking. They were only a small portion of the emotions he held inside, but their presence was still a surprise; his grief had been set aside for the time being, as there was a more important task that lay ahead. Sariel reached down and placed the bundle inside the arrangement of stones before sliding a heavy slab over the top. He wiped the tears from his eyes, grabbed the torch, and left the words of Ebnisha for another time.

Making his way quickly back to the first chamber, he smothered the flames of the torch and placed it back on the ledge. Then, as Mosi had suggested, Sariel ran to the mouth of the cave and sucked in a deep breath before jumping into the flow.

The cold of the water tried to steal his breath away. The roar in his ears reminded him of what it sounded like when entering the In-Between. He felt the weightlessness of falling. Suddenly, the coldness was more intense, not just pushing down on him but enveloping his whole being. The roar was gone, replaced by a muffled cacophony. And he wasn't falling as much as drifting. He let the water take him, for he knew that it was pointless to fight against such power. The sound lessened. The drifting became slower and more peaceful. And through his eyelids, he sensed the presence of light.

Sariel kicked his legs and pulled with his arms. His head broke through the surface, and he let out his breath and accepted another. He found himself being pushed away from the base of the waterfall and farther into the lake. The sunlight felt warm on his face. All around, the dense trees protected this secluded place. Mosi, Imamu, and Wekesa were standing on the opposite shore, now only a short distance away. As Sariel began to swim in their direction, Mosi waved to him. In less than a minute, Sariel had crossed the narrow lake and found his feet digging into soft sand. He stood up in the shallows and looked back on what he'd just done. From this perspective, no one would ever suspect what lay hidden behind the white cascade falling down from the heights above.

"It is a good hiding place, yes?" Mosi asked.

"I can think of none better. How are the women doing?"

Mosi looked over at Wekesa, the youngest, who just nodded.

"I think they are enjoying their rest," Imamu said.

The trip had been exhausting, mainly due to the terrain they had crossed. "Mosi, you can't go back to Matunda or my camp. I think this would be a good place for you to stay. Make a new village here."

"Yes, I was thinking about that as we waited for you."

"No other tribes will think to come here. It is a safe place for you to reestablish your people."

Mosi nodded.

Imamu smiled. "He can't make any decisions without Ekua."

"Do you think she will agree?" Sariel asked.

"Why?" Mosi replied, now frowning.

"I would like to know where you will be when I come back."

"Where are you going?" Wekesa asked.

Sariel smiled at the boy, then took his time looking at each one of Ebnisha's brothers before responding. "I am going to Idorana."

Imamu's eyes went wide.

"That is all the way to the other ocean," Wekesa replied.

"I have traveled much farther than that in my time."

Mosi's eyes narrowed. "They won't let you just walk into the temple."

"They cannot stop me. I don't know which of her servants she used ... to ..." Sariel couldn't finish the sentence, so he moved on. "But Mwangu Rana will pay for what she did to Ebnisha. She will pay with her life."

Mosi's face softened and he took a deep breath as he nodded his agreement.

"But she is too powerful," Wekesa said. The look on the boy's face made it clear that he didn't want Sariel to leave.

"Yes, she is powerful. But I promise you that if I don't return, it will be because I have given my life to take hers from this world."

Wekesa's eyes began to glisten. Imamu looked at the ground. Mosi straightened his posture. "We will make our new village here. Ekua will agree that this is a safe place for our people."

Sariel placed his hand on Mosi's shoulder. "Good. I hope I am able to come back, so we can mourn Ebnisha together."

20

"Mwangu Rana, there is someone on the river ahead," the chief priestess announced.

Zaquel sat up from her bed and looked beyond the prow, but all she could see were her own boats. Their white sails were full of the breeze, blocking her view upriver. "Some*one*, or some*thing*?"

"Some*one*, Goddess."

Zaquel stood and carried her scepter as she left the shaded area and walked down to the main deck. The sun was bright and hot on this clear day, and the breeze did little to cool the air. They were sailing to her largest mine, which had a shipment ready for transport. She preferred to personally oversee the largest shipments, bringing additional soldiers along for security and to make the spectacle more grandiose for her citizens upon her return to Idorana.

The priestess jogged ahead and up the steps to the foredeck. Zaquel could already see more of the River Njiawaye from this vantage. Her vessel was accompanied by six others—one following, two flanking, and three staggered in front. But the flanking and following ships were pulling ahead of hers, while the ones to the fore were changing their positions into a defense formation.

When Zaquel ascended to the foredeck, she could see their cause for alarm. Upriver, in the middle of the wide expanse of slow-moving water, a man appeared to be standing. There were no sandbars in this area, and there wasn't a boat beneath his feet. She only saw him and the small wake created by the flow of water moving past his feet. Zaquel squinted, seeing white hair and a beard, pale skin and a long tunic. The man certainly wasn't from this part of the world.

"He must be standing on something," the priestess mumbled.

The only one whom Zaquel could imagine fitting the oddity of this stranger's appearance and his method of presentation had been killed by Arakiba in another world.

The accompanying ships were now in position, forming a barricade of rows in a reverse triangle formation—three ships in the first row, two in the second, and the general's ship sitting directly ahead of the royal vessel. The general, positioned on the aft deck of his ship, turned and shouted, "Mwangu Rana, shall we attack?"

Zaquel glanced upriver again.

The man in the distance began walking across the water toward the ships. Then his steps sped to a jog. The possibility of him standing on something suddenly evaporated. No human was capable of such a thing, leaving Zaquel with only one explanation. "Yes. Attack him!"

The general turned and yelled to his soldiers, "Battle positions!"

The decks of the ships were suddenly alive with activity. Soldiers came up from the lower levels and assembled into orderly ranks on the main surfaces of each ship.

"Archers, nock arrows!"

The soldiers on the raised foredecks set arrows to string and waited for their next order.

The man upriver was now sprinting. Each footstep left a small disturbance on the surface of the water, indicating that he was barely making contact with it. His long, white hair flowed behind him as he ran.

"Draw!"

The archers raised their bows and drew them taut, taking aim.

"Fire!"

The first volley of arrows went up like a coordinated flock of birds, condensing as it came down again in a long arc. The arrows glanced off the stranger without doing any harm, splashing in the river like a sudden burst of rain.

The man running across the water didn't even break his stride.

Zaquel could feel the general's confusion, which left him dumbfounded for two full seconds afterward. Then he came to his senses and yelled, "Fire at will!" As the archers responded by setting more arrows to their strings, the general called for shields and spears. The other soldiers on the main decks brought their shields forward and into an interlocked barrier. The spears which had been facing up to the sky were now pointed forward over the top edges of their shields. The first row of boats had turned sideways, their captains trying to use the ships' broadsides as a barrier.

But they weren't fast enough.

The man had already closed the distance, slipping through the gap beneath two curved prows.

The soldiers who had tried running up to the foredeck to reach the enemy with their spears suddenly found their weapons ripped from their hands and sent spinning through the air. The others who tried casting their weapons after the enemy found that they were too late to hit their marks.

Zaquel reached out through the air and took control of the next row, bringing the boats together in an overlapping barrier. She lost sight of the enemy as the ships blocked her view of him, but she could see the soldiers bracing for impact. All of a sudden, the hulls of both ships exploded where they were overlapped. Chunks of wood flew in every direction, skipping across the river. A spray of water went up into the air, carrying soldiers and weapons with it.

The pale man came running through the debris, still moving at a sprinting pace over the surface.

The general's ship floated between Zaquel and the enemy, but the chief priestess standing beside her didn't have any confidence that the men would be able to protect her goddess. She removed a gold chain from around her neck and began swinging it like a sling. The vial of flammable liquid at the end of it flashed in the sunlight.

The general unsheathed his sword and ran down from the aft deck to join his soldiers, who already had their long blades drawn.

* * * *

Sariel spotted a small gap in their ranks and jumped from the water. He dove through the air in a roll, using an Iryllur ramming technique for breaking through enemy formations. It took the men by surprise and they weren't able to react in time. Sariel forced his way between two men at the railing, stripping their weapons as he knocked them over. When he came down on the wide deck of the ship, he rolled across the wooden planks to absorb his momentum. Then he planted his feet and came up inside the enemy ranks, with two swords held in a reverse grip. They weren't as elegant as vaepkir, but they would suffice.

The soldiers were staring, mouths agape.

Sariel took advantage of their shock and lunged into motion, spinning and slashing. He knocked blades aside with one weapon and cut flesh with the other. Swords dropped to the deck with arms still attached. Soldiers fell backward with throats cut. Others tripped on their own feet when their legs suddenly lost feeling. Sariel moved deep into their ranks and attacked so quickly that by the time each soldier could even reach his enemy through the crowd, he'd already received his death blow. In less than a minute, the soldiers had been cut down, and the general was backing away across the deck, leaving footprints of his soldiers' blood.

Sariel rushed forward.

The general swung his sword in a panicked forehand slash.

Sariel ducked beneath it, spinning in the same direction as the blade with one sword blocking and the other attacking. He severed the tendons at the back of the general's legs, and came up behind him.

The general fell to his knees and cried out in pain, his sword clattering across the deck.

Sariel wasted no time. He grabbed the man by the hair and yanked his head backward before running one of his swords across the man's throat. "For Matunda," he whispered into the dying man's ear. Then he pushed the general forward onto his face and let him think about the connection between that village and this day with the last frantic seconds of his life.

In the lull that followed, Sariel realized that the general's choking was not the only sound. Someone was screaming in a language that sounded like a Marotru Song of Unshaping that had been stripped of all its discordant melodies. Sariel looked to the prow of the royal vessel just in time to see a woman, dressed in linen and gold, cast something in his direction. She barked, and the thing she'd thrown shattered in the air.

Sariel reacted, throwing up his hands in defense.

Bits of glass and liquid suddenly changed direction, thrown back at the woman. Tiny flames appeared within the debris, and when it splashed against her body, it suddenly ignited into a ball of fire. The woman grabbed at her face and bent over, screaming in pain. The prow of the ship caught fire and began to burn around her as well. Only then did Sariel understand what she had been trying to do to him. The woman was screaming at the top of her lungs and flailing around like a human torch. Sariel might have taken pity on her had he not realized that this was likely how Ebnisha had died. Instead of pity, he looked on with a feeling of satisfaction. The woman finally crawled to the railing and jumped overboard, the river spitting and hissing as if it were reluctant to accept her.

Sariel watched the bubbles and steam on the surface where she'd gone under. It was a pity that her pain hadn't lasted longer; Ebnisha had received no such relief for his suffering.

Sariel could still see the scribe's blackened body, red beneath the cracks in his charred flesh, hanging from that tree. He imagined what it had been like for the people of Matunda, made to bow in the dirt before the flames. He could hear them screaming. He imagined a blade being dragged across his throat, his skin burning as it sliced open. He could feel the warm blood spilling down his chest and the tired, almost euphoric feeling that would come over him. He suddenly felt exhausted. So much energy had already been expended—this battle, crossing the south lands from Matunda, even his wandering before meeting Ebnisha. It all seemed so exhausting. He could feel his arm moving upward, the sword in his grasp. The sharpened metal edge that would bring relief. He wanted that euphoria. He wanted this struggle to be over. He wanted to rest, and to feel something other than pain. All he had to do was …

All of a sudden, Sariel realized how quickly his attention had been diverted. It seemed so odd in the middle of this battle. He looked up and saw Zaquel standing on the main deck of her ship, a smile on her face. He remembered the power she had exerted over the minds of men in Gongur. He remembered the story that Mosi had told him, and he knew that his thoughts were being manipulated.

Something hit Sariel from behind, followed immediately by dozens of impact noises on the deck around him. He looked down to see feathered shafts embedded in the wooden planks around his feet. Then he noticed a protrusion in his tunic on the right side of his chest and another one lower down at his stomach. He reached up, slowly fingering the hard objects inside of the fabric. His tunic began turning red, and there was pain when he touched the protrusions. But it all seemed so distant, as if he were alone in a field, fingering a species of grass he hadn't come across before. He looked up again, slowly making eye contact with Zaquel.

The Mwangu Rana had her hand extended. She flicked her fingers in a dismissive gesture.

The boat beneath Sariel's feet suddenly rolled. The deck rose into the air, and Sariel tumbled backward. His head smashed into something hard, then the waters of the Njiawaye were all around him. The sky and sun and ships disappeared behind a murky brown haze. Thin shafts of sunlight tried to pierce the water, but Sariel sank into the darkness, watching the world above drift further and further away. Tendrils of red billowed upward like smoke from a volcano in the early days after the flood. Long seconds passed before Sariel realized that it was his own blood. Something about this realization jarred him from his stupor. He realized he was dying, and the opportunity to avenge Ebnisha would soon pass. It seemed unthinkable to let that happen. He couldn't accept it, and yet, he also knew his thoughts weren't entirely his own. But where did his thoughts really come from? Did they originate within his temporal body, or his eternal one?

* * * *

When Zaquel could no longer see Sariel's body, she watched from an eternal perspective as his spirit slowly drifted to the riverbed below. Now that she had read his thoughts, she knew it was indeed Sariel. He must have been multiplied along with the worlds of the Temporal Realm during the Fracturing. The assumption that he had been close enough to attack Baraquijal, and therefore had been pulled into the In-Between like all the other Myndarym, had been an incorrect one. Ezekiyel would find this information both fascinating and disappointing. But the ones who would be most concerned would be Armaros, Satarel, and Kokabiel; it now seemed that Sariel had one self in each world, which meant that one had yet to be revealed.

The swirling coagulation of lights below the water began to rise, and Zaquel now detected other thoughts. Sariel had apparently known Ebnisha personally, and it was this thirst for revenge that gave Sariel the motivation to keep trying. It was admirable, really—almost charming—to see the way Sariel loved this weaker species. Sheyir had drawn him into this realm. Then Enoch's cause had evoked his sense of protection. Now

Ebnisha's memory had drawn him all the way across a continent to do battle with Zaquel and her armies.

Sariel's spirit swam beneath her boat, and Zaquel watched through the layers of wood as he rose to the surface beside the starboard hull and tried to find something on which to cling. He was gasping for breath, choking on the river water, but it was his loss of blood that was killing him. His thoughts were circling around this idea of the Awakened One, the prophecy that Ebnisha had died for. Sariel believed it, believed it passionately. She could feel his intentions. He was going to kill every one of the Myndarym, but how could that be when he was already on the threshold of death?

Zaquel extended her hands and brought her two remaining ships closer to the prow of her own vessel. She could feel that the archers and spearmen aboard were anxious to follow up with their earlier attack. They wanted to kill this intruder, to rescue their goddess, to make her proud.

"Finish him," she ordered, pointing with her scepter at the fragile being who clung to her boat, lacking the strength to even climb aboard.

The other ships moved past her prow and came to her starboard side. The soldiers leaned over the railing, eyes scanning the waterline. "Where is he, Goddess?"

"Right there, you fools!" Zaquel shouted, pointing with her scepter.

The swirling colors in the form of a man, visible through the decking and hull of her ship, began to fade. Zaquel frowned, knowing that one's spirit didn't fade when they died; it persisted beyond the physical body. She marched toward the starboard railing, ready to look upon this enigma with the sight of her temporal body. But the sound of clanking metal behind her caused a jolt of panic.

* * * *

Sariel's temporal body, injured as it was, still had enough strength to climb up to the aft deck behind Zaquel. When he came quietly over the railing, he took his consciousness back from his eternal body. The two male slaves, chained by their necks at the bottom of the stairs, noticed his movement from the corner of their vision. They flinched and cowered at the sudden appearance of the powerful stranger. Sariel waved his hand, and the metal collars around their necks dropped to the deck.

Zaquel was moving toward the starboard railing when she heard the sound. She stopped and spun.

"Attack," Sariel commanded the slaves.

The two men glanced at their goddess and then back to Sariel. One turned and ran to the port railing, jumping overboard. The other turned back to Zaquel with rage in his eyes. He began to growl like a wild animal and run toward her, bounding over the deck on all fours.

Zaquel came on at a run and bent down, bashing the slave aside with a backhanded stroke of her crystalline scepter. The man's bones were crushed before he hit the port railing and flipped over the side. And Zaquel was still coming.

The momentary distraction had allowed Sariel to take hold of the slaves' chains. He ran toward the goddess with one in each hand, swinging them to meet her forehand attack. As the scepter came down at his head, he ducked beneath it and flung the chains upward. One hit the scepter and its links shattered into fragments like glass. The other hit her forearm and wrapped around it.

Zaquel's blow came down through the air where Sariel's head had been, but when it failed to meet its target, the scepter smashed into the deck just below the mast. The wooden planks buckled inward, with a loud crack, and the mast vibrated from the blow.

Behind Zaquel, the remaining soldiers were climbing from their boats onto the foredeck of the royal vessel.

Sariel rolled to his feet and heaved on the chain, yanking Zaquel's arm and immobilizing her weapon.

She quickly moved into his restraining force, stepping forward and swinging with a backhanded stroke.

Sariel only had time to react, losing his opportunity to turn it into a counterattack. He leaped backward and felt the strength of Zaquel's arm rip the iron chain from his grasp.

Her blow hit the support column of her sunshade, smashing through it in a shower of splinters.

The shade tipped forward, and Sariel scrambled up the steps to the aft deck just as it crashed down around him with a great moaning sound. Sariel crawled through the fabric and found an opening, climbing to his feet once again in the open air. But the groaning sound could still be heard, and now the deck of the ship was vibrating. Zaquel was still coming toward him, unaware that the noise was actually the main mast continuing to lean aft without the solid decking beneath to support it.

Sariel backed away.

Zaquel came up the steps toward the stern.

The mast and mainsail came down just behind her, slamming into the deck and breaking through the railing. The sail hit the water with a great splash, and the whole ship jolted, rolling to its port side.

Zaquel and Sariel were both thrown off their feet. The soldiers at the bow tumbled into each other as if a wave had hit the boat. But Sariel hadn't wasted the opportunity; he'd pulled his eternal body toward himself.

When Zaquel came up to her knees, there was a presence behind her, pulling backward on her wide necklace and collar of gold and onyx. She quickly reached up to her neck and grabbed at it, raking her own skin with her fingernails in an attempt to get her fingers behind it. But the decoration was cutting into her skin, choking her. She dropped her scepter and added her other hand to the effort, clawing at her own neck. Finally, she found a fingerhold and pulled with all her might. The collar tore, scattering gold and dark jewels in every direction. Zaquel fell forward to her hands and gasped for breath before looking up with panic in her eyes.

Sariel had her scepter, and plunged the end of it into her skull just above her eyes. The crystalline material, denser and stronger than any other in the Temporal Realm, easily punctured flesh, bone, muscle, and any other bodily structure that stood in its way.

Zaquel's body went limp immediately and dropped to the deck.

Sariel wrenched the symbol of power from Mwangu Rana's dead body.

The soldiers, now on their feet at the prow with swords drawn, were enraged at what they'd just witnessed. They began yelling at the top of their lungs, shouting promises to their goddess. They beat their own chests with clenched fists, and they stabbed at the air with their swords. Then they began running down the steps of the foredeck with bloodlust in their eyes.

But Sariel also saw fear, and that was what he planned to exploit as he twirled his new weapon through the air and ran toward the soldiers.

* * * *

A REMOTE ISLAND
NORTH-NORTHEAST OF THE TREE

Torches lined a steep, narrow tunnel, revealing newly carved steps of stone. Waves crashed far below, where the natural tunnel opened into a chamber at the base of the cliffs. All of these tunnels and hollows were remnants of an older time, when the water below the earth's crust came violently upward and magma had taken its place. Still others had been created when the heat of the magma had vaporized the water, breaking apart the land. Then the magma cooled, and the water tried to find its way back down into the bowels of the earth. There were some places where the water had found its home again, but most of those places had disappeared; the world had changed dramatically. So the water gathered into vast oceans that covered the lowest of the earth's terrain. When its waves crashed now against the land, Rameel imagined that it was the continuing battle of two great forces. The oceans refused to accept their current state, battering continuously at the land until it gave in. These cliffs were the result of a battle being won. Part of the land had just dropped away, its foundations yielding to the relentless seas. But what remained was stable, providing a safe place where Akuji could be allowed to sleep away from the eyes of men.

The passage through which Rameel ascended was cramped, but only for someone of Rameel's size. When his masons were finished carving the stairs, the ceiling would be heightened, allowing someone of a much taller stature to come out when it was time. None of them knew, of course, what it was they were building. Nor did they know who would sleep here. All they knew was that their god had given them a task, and they were working diligently to please him.

Rameel reached the top of where the masons had mined thus far, turning to look sideways into a chamber that was being hollowed out. He watched the men for a moment, pleased with how well they were able to concentrate on their work in his presence. They were a stout breed, with pale skin and dark hair. Their muscular build was the result of generations of battling against the stone. In that way, they were like the ocean. In all other ways, they were like the stone they shaped—hard and unyielding. Even their language was suited for this work. It was full of guttural moans and harsh syllables that retained its meaning after bouncing off numerous stone surfaces.

When the piercing noise of metal upon stone became agitating, Rameel backed away from the chamber. His gaze went instinctively upward, following the tunnel that had yet to be enlarged. It snaked all the way to the top of the cliffs, where another band of masons was building a structure from stacked stones. It would serve as a home for the priests that Rameel would later station here. Like the masons, the priests would also be ignorant of the purpose for which they were truly here. Rameel would tell them that this was to be a new place of worship, like the temple in the southwest region of the mainland. But while they lived here, carrying out their priestly duties, Rameel would have many eyes and ears that could become his at a moment's notice. He would be able to guard his son from afar until he understood the nature of the sickness that threatened him.

Rameel turned and began descending through the passage. As he shifted his perspective toward the Eternal to let the light of the red sky illuminate his steps, he suddenly felt a sense of relief. There was an easiness to the world, as if it were now open and accepting of him. And he was only aware of it because of how drastically different it was from the oppressive challenge it had always been. Something significant had just taken place. That oppressive challenge had been removed.

Zaquel?

Rameel reached out, feeling for her. He'd never been able to communicate with her as Baraquijal had done with all of them in the old world. Yet there was still a connection, or there would have been if someone had been out there to connect with.

There isn't, he realized.

As exciting as this was, it also begged another question.

Why not?

SA 4229

(AĐ 1)

21

Sariel stumbled out from the edge of the jungle and began moving along the rocky shore of a lake. He could see from the Eternal that there was a gathering of spirits in the trees to the south, but he couldn't see them yet with his temporal vision. The lake looked familiar, but the opposite shore had many coves, and he couldn't see the waterfall that would prove he had returned to the right place. Although the sound of distant rushing water gave him hope.

"Saba! He's here! He's here!" someone yelled.

Sariel looked again at the shoreline. The people who had been hidden in the trees were now assembling on the beach. The shortest one of the group was waving, and Sariel finally recognized Wekesa. He waved back, and the boy started running toward him. The others, both male and female, quickly followed Wekesa's lead. The sight of Ebnisha's family running along the shore left little doubt as to their feelings for him. The warmth of their reception brought tears to Sariel's eyes and he hadn't even reached them yet.

Within seconds, the group surrounded him, throwing their arms around him and pulling him into their circle. Tears streamed down their faces, and Sariel finally let his own flow, weary from holding them back for so long. As was their custom,

Ebnisha's family locked arms and leaned toward the center, touching their foreheads to each other. This time, Sariel was eager to join in without the distraction of revenge weighing on his mind. He pressed his face into the group, allowing the awkwardness of such close proximity to melt the coldness in his heart. He'd never shown this much affection to anyone since Sheyir, not even in El-Betakh.

It felt good.

Ebnisha's family knew him as Saba, and he saw no reason to correct them. He felt as though he was a different man from the one who had set out from this shoreline months ago. He closed his eyes and accepted the embrace of a family, while prayers of thanksgiving were shared. They took turns whispering their gratefulness to the Holy One, and after several minutes, the whispers faded and the tears dried.

"Your skin is very hot," Mosi said, pulling his head back to look more carefully at Sariel. "You don't look well."

"Don't be rude," Ekua told her husband. "He's come all the way from the ocean."

"It's alright," Sariel replied. "I don't *feel* well."

"Come and rest then," Mosi offered.

As they began moving along the shore, Ekua reached up and touched Sariel's forehead with the back of her hand. "You have a fever."

"Come. Set him down here in the shade," Imamu suggested, pointing to a sandy area between their camp and the water's edge. When they were beneath the overhanging foliage of the jungle again, they eased Sariel down onto the cool sand. Everyone remained standing except for Wekesa, who sat down next to Sariel with wide eyes.

Sariel took a few deep breaths before unslinging the long bundle from across his back.

"What is that?" Wekesa asked.

Sariel untied a thong and handed a large pouch to the boy, who had grown substantially taller in the time that Sariel had been gone. It was probably more appropriate to think of Wekesa as a young man now.

Wekesa opened the pouch and smiled before plunging his hand inside. When he brought it out again, coins of gold were spilling out from between his clenched fingers.

The whole group inhaled at once.

"Where did you get these?" Ekua asked.

Sariel looked up. "Idorana. I thought you could use them in Nijambu to buy supplies. Help reestablish your people. Seeds. Tools. There's enough gold there to purchase whatever you need."

"This is dangerous. The goddess will come looking—"

"No. She won't," Sariel interrupted. He looked down and began unwrapping the other part of his bundle. "She's dead ... along with her chief priestess, her general, and dozens of her top soldiers." When he was finished removing the dirty linen cloth from the scepter, he reached up and handed the dark object to Mosi. Though it had only been a scepter to Zaquel, it was large enough to serve as a staff or a walking stick for a human being. But there was no mistaking it for a tool of such ordinary usage. This thing, which felt like glass and shimmered more than any jewel, was clearly something fit for a goddess.

Mosi accepted it with reverence, his mouth hanging open. He turned it over in his hands, marveling at it while his siblings stared.

Sariel waited for a long moment before breaking the silence. "Ebnisha, Zuberi, and everyone in Matunda have been avenged."

Mosi's eyes were tearing up again, and this time his lips were quivering also. He looked Sariel in the eyes and nodded slowly.

"Saba, you're bleeding," Imamu announced.

Sariel looked down at his tunic, seeing new blood beside the old stains.

"Were you wounded?" Ekua asked.

"Yes."

"Have you not tended to your wounds?"

"I have, but they keep opening up again. I haven't stayed in one place long enough to let them heal."

"Here, get this tunic off him," Ekua said, pulling at Sariel's clothing. Wekesa and Mosi helped. When the tunic was finally peeled away from his body, almost everyone cringed.

"What are those from?" Wekesa asked, pointing at Sariel's chest.

Mosi reached out and tried to shove Wekesa's head, but the young man ducked out of the way.

Sariel looked down at his own body. "These two are from arrows. They went through my back and came out here. And these," he said, touching multiple places on his abdomen, chest, and shoulders, "are from swords." When he looked up again, Wekesa was the only one who seemed fascinated.

Ekua wiped tears away from her eyes with the back of her hand. "Come to the lake; we must clean your wounds. Wekesa, start a fire. Mosi, get Zuberi's knife."

~

By the time the sun was down and the family was sharing a meal around a fire, Sariel's wounds had been cauterized, treated with salve, and wrapped in fresh cloths. Ekua had torn up several tunics in order to dress Sariel's wounds, and though her patient objected to her wasting such hard work, she refused to listen.

Sariel kept back from the flames, enjoying the cool night air on his flushed skin. The others sat closer, taking turns telling humorous childhood stories about Ebnisha and Zuberi. This was apparently their custom—to focus on the many good memories in order to displace the memory of one bad event.

Sariel closed his eyes, listening to the crackling flames and the laughter. Insects buzzed in the jungle beyond their camp. The occasional cry of a nocturnal animal cut through the other sounds. It was the music of home, and it was comforting. But Sariel couldn't push aside the thoughts that now ran through his mind. He recited the prophecy of The Awakened to himself, thinking through each line again, as he had done hundreds of times on his way back from Idorana. He had believed the prophecy to be about himself, and that was what had given him the confidence to go up against Zaquel. But was it true?

Would this Awakened One have suffered the damage that I received?

If the Holy One had truly raised him up for this task of bringing justice to the Myndarym, it seemed that Sariel would have been more successful. Granted, he had succeeded in killing Zaquel and taking her scepter, but there was nothing left of himself to use against the other Myndarym. He had another self, but that one was trapped in the In-Between. He had a powerful weapon, but so did all the others. He had learned to do things with only his physical body that earlier had required the use of many demonic underlings, but what were the other Myndarym capable of at this point? Zaquel hadn't been the most powerful of the group. What could Sariel hope to achieve against the rest?

If he could make a full recovery, perhaps Sariel would consider himself capable of battling for just one of the three worlds. The logical choice would be this one, as there was only one enemy Myndar left here to confront. But Sariel had been pursued for centuries by Rameel in the old world. He'd seen the dark, winged one set fire to things just by extending his hand. Sariel could move things in this realm by manipulating them from the other realm, but that was the extent of his abilities. Rameel was an even more dangerous enemy, and he didn't feel confident about the next battle waiting for him.

22

The morning sun was low on the horizon, casting long shadows over the lake. Insects hovered above the water, looking white against the dark green surface. Mosi, Imamu, and Wekesa were standing in the shallows with spears, waiting for fish to come near. Sariel sat in the cool shade near the tree line. The women were behind him, working in the camp. He was the only one resting because he didn't have the strength to do much else.

It had been several months since Sariel had returned from Idorana, and though his external wounds were healing well, he still suffered fevers from time to time. His breathing had become coarse and labored. The thought of traveling from here to the eastern ocean and back now seemed impossible, which meant that he had become weaker instead of stronger. The wounds he'd suffered at the hands of Zaquel's army had been severe, but not enough to explain this lingering sickness. Sariel was beginning to think it was the result of Zaquel having been inside his thoughts. Had she launched some other attack that was just now becoming evident? If so, it was an enemy that he didn't even know how to fight. His unconscious mind and his body would have to do battle without his help, and would they win? It didn't appear so.

His third self had been executed. His second self—the only one in any condition to fight—was trapped inside the In-

Between. His only hope was for his first self to find the stump and use Zaquel's scepter to free his second self. If he could accomplish that, Sariel would have two physical bodies and their associated spirits to use against Rameel. He would need that and more to defeat such a powerful enemy. Even with all of Sariel's battle experience, he knew that he was at a great disadvantage. Like Zaquel, Rameel was almost twice his height. Whereas the so-called Goddess of the Sun had been ignorant of how to properly use such an advantage, the demon god understood it well. And he had the ability to fly. If anyone knew how advantageous wings could be in a conflict, it was Sariel. He'd been regretting the forsaking of his Iryllur form since the moment of Sheyir's death.

Defeating Rameel already seemed like an impossible task, but waiting would only put Sariel at a further disadvantage. And it was possible that he might die from this mysterious sickness and lose the opportunity altogether. Time was running out.

"I have to leave again," he announced.

Imamu and Wekesa turned their heads. Mosi kept his eyes on the water, but whispered, "Why?"

"Rameel."

Mosi didn't respond with words; he just turned his head and stared hard at Sariel.

"You're going to fight the demon god?" Wekesa asked with a grin.

Sariel slowly turned his attention to the youngest brother. "Well ... he's not actually a demon or a god."

"Neither are you," Mosi finally replied.

"True. But you also know I'm not human."

While Mosi and Imamu didn't appear to be shocked at all by this statement, Wekesa's eyes opened to their fullest extent. "What?" he asked, his eyes now open to their fullest extent.

"I am a Myndar, just like Zaquel and Rameel. The reason I know the stories of your ancestors is because I have been in this realm since the beginning. Ebnisha never told you because he didn't want to frighten you."

"Why does this matter?" Imamu asked, coming out of the water and onto the shore.

"Because you should believe me when I tell you that we don't belong here."

"You are not like them," Imamu protested.

Wekesa suddenly pointed. "That's why your hair is white … you're Sariel, the defender of mankind!" The water clouded with silt as the young man's excited movements stirred up the water and ruined any possibility of catching a meal.

Mosi left the shallows and dropped his spear on the sand.

Sariel ignored Wekesa's statement and looked to the older brothers. "This realm is for humans, not angels. As long as we Myndarym are here, you will become our servants. We will rule over you and corrupt everything. See what is already happening with the Kaliel? That is the influence of a Myndar, and it reaches all the way into your lands as well. He takes your virgins. What will he take next?"

Sariel suddenly realized that Rameel could try to expand his kingdom across the ocean and into these lands now that Zaquel wasn't present to stand in his way. In killing the goddess, he might have only made things worse for the people here. This was a frustrating thought, but it only reinforced his belief that humans wouldn't be free until the Myndarym were gone.

"We have brought these things upon you by coming into your realm, and they cannot be repaired unless we are made to leave."

"You believe this is your responsibility?" Mosi asked.

"Who else can do it?"

"You are sick, *Saba*," he replied, emphasizing the name that Ebnisha had chosen.

"And I'm not getting any better."

Imamu and Wekesa looked at each other with scrunched eyebrows.

Mosi's stern face slowly relaxed. "Very well. I will go with you."

"Go where?" Ekua called from behind.

Sariel turned and saw that the women had stopped their tasks and were paying close attention to what the men were discussing. He quickly turned back and lowered his voice. "No. I will go alone."

"What are you talking about?" Ekua asked, stepping away from the camp.

Mosi looked up to his wife and the other women who were now approaching. "Saba is leaving to fight the demon god across the sea."

"You cannot go," she replied. "You are too sick."

Sariel hung his head and closed his eyes; this discussion was spiraling out of control. Footsteps could be heard all around him now, and as he opened his eyes again and looked up, he could tell by the sudden increase in the number of stern faces that they weren't prepared to let him go without a fight of their own.

Surprisingly, it was Mosi who came to his defense. "Saba is getting weaker every day. If he waits any longer, he will have no chance of defeating the demon god."

Ekua looked back and forth from Sariel to her husband, but didn't reply.

"Even now," Mosi added, "he is too weak to make the journey on his own. This is why I will go with him."

"No!" Sariel protested, louder and with more force than he intended.

Everyone suddenly turned to look at him with wide eyes.

"I'm sorry, but ... Mosi, I won't be taking anyone with me. This is not a journey from which I expect to return."

A long moment of silence passed before Ekua turned to Mosi. "We have lost our tribe. I will not lose my husband as well."

"She's right," Imamu said.

Wekesa straightened his posture. "I'll go."

"No, you won't," Mosi replied dismissively.

"I'm the only one left without a wife," Wekesa argued. Then he added with a smile, "Ebnisha used to tease me about that. If I die, it will not hurt the growth of our tribe. All of you will live to carry on our people's lineage."

"It will hurt our family," Imamu pointed out.

Ekua nodded.

"This is not your fight," Sariel tried to interject, but it seemed that the family wasn't interested in his input.

Mosi and Wekesa were staring at each other as if they were the only two people in the world. Finally, Mosi turned his gaze toward Sariel. "Very well, you may take my brother with you."

Sariel threw up his hands. "I don't need anyone to accompany me, so this discussion is irrelevant."

"Oh? How will you get there? It is across the ocean; you cannot walk there as you did to Idorana."

"I ... don't know yet. Maybe I'll sail from Nijambu."

The women snickered at this comment, and Sariel didn't understand why this was such a humorous proposition.

Mosi knelt down in the sand before Sariel. "You are not well, my friend. You won't even reach Nijambu without help. And I can assure you that no one will take you across the sea to the Kaliel lands."

Sariel didn't know how to reply. He just looked around at the faces arrayed against him and was moved by the compassion and confidence in their eyes.

"I can see that you will not be persuaded to leave the demon god alone," Mosi added, "but you are part of our family now. If you will not stay here with us, then I want you to be successful in your task. Wekesa can help you. He is smart and strong."

Sariel felt out of breath, and the sweat on his forehead suddenly felt prominent. "Let's say I agree ... and he helps me reach Nijambu. What then? You just said no one will take me across the ocean."

Mosi's face made such an abrupt transition to a smile that it was surprising. "I have a plan."

"What is it?"

Mosi's eyes narrowed. "If you agree to let my brother help you, then I will tell *him* my plan."

Sariel couldn't help the grin that came to his face. He turned to look at Wekesa and received a confident stare from the young man in return. "Alright," he replied, turning back to Mosi. "He can come with me."

* * * *

Rameel's army of masons had completed their work. The tunnel that stretched from the top of the cliffs all the way down to the cavern at the ocean below had been enlarged to create a tall passage with hundreds of stairs. The opening at the top was concealed by a stone fireplace set into the walls of a circular structure that would become the home of the priests being relocated here. Tomorrow, these robed servants of Rameel would arrive by ship with tools to cut down trees from the forest in order to build the roof and other wooden parts of their new home and place of worship. The masons would have a few days with the priests to discuss the construction details before being put on a ship and sent back to the mainland. But for now, Rameel had sent them away to the nearby forests to hunt for their evening meal. He wanted privacy for the most critical part of this effort.

Rameel stood now inside a chamber, twelve human paces wide and twelve tall, forming a perfect cube. On the wall of the narrow passage outside, a torch flickered, casting just enough light into the small room to make everything visible. He looked down upon Akuji, his forbidden son, resting peacefully within his stone sarcophagus. Though his heart was no longer beating, and his chest didn't rise and fall, the Nephiyl's skin was still warm to the touch. Rameel had spoken an incantation over his son during the journey to this place, preserving him in eternal sleep. The features of the Nephiyl's face were graceful, like his mother's had been. But Rameel didn't want to think any longer about the past. The memories were too painful. Instead, he hoped to lay them to rest this night along with his son. Someday he would either possess the knowledge to heal Akuji's sickness himself, or he would have enough leverage over Ezekiyel or Kokabiel to force them to do it. Either way, the future was where he needed to concentrate his efforts. Though he already controlled legions of devoted worshippers, Zaquel's empire was now available for the taking. The stage was set for Rameel's rise to uncontested power in this world, and he would pursue it with all the aggression and cunning he possessed. It would take nothing less if he ever hoped to compete with Ezekiyel.

"Rest, my son," he said quietly. "I go now to prepare this world for your return. When you wake, may it be in health. You will be a prince in my kingdom, and your kind will thrive once again as your ancestors of old."

Rameel backed away and extended both of his hands with palms upturned.

A long, rectangular slab of rock rose from the floor and settled into place atop the sarcophagus. When it was shut, Rameel breathed a sigh, not of relief, but of satisfaction. The box of stone that the masons had created for Akuji was beautiful. They weren't told exactly what it would contain, but they knew that it would be an object of great significance. And in honor of this idea, the carvings that spread across its sides and lid were intricate, depicting scenes of the world that Rameel had yet to bring into existence. The gray rock was inlaid with all manner of precious stones, strategically placed to enhance the scenes with their polished, gleaming colors. It was a work of great skill, and Rameel was pleased that his son would rest within something befitting his status.

The Myndar held out his hand and began walking around the sarcophagus. A Marotru *song* spilled from his lips, binding the lid in place with a power that no natural force would be able to undo. After completing one revolution around the room, Rameel exited through its only doorway. The sight of the torch burning along the wall of the narrow passage brought to mind the other methods of preservation that had been employed. After the chamber had been completed but before the sarcophagus had been brought in, Rameel had ignited the air inside and caused it to burn so intensely that all of the stone surfaces had melted.

Tiny cracks and anomalies in the density of the rock had been fused to seal out moisture or any creatures that might try to get inside.

Rameel turned to face the door and extended his hand. The sight of the sarcophagus began to waver, as if the room itself were becoming excited. All of a sudden, flames began appearing throughout the room, hovering in the air. They grew in length and width until they combined with each other to fill the space of the chamber. The oxygen was purged from the room, and the resulting vacuum sucked the small iron door shut with a loud *clang*. Rameel waved his hand to extinguish the flames. Akuji was unharmed inside his resting place; only the air outside of his sarcophagus had been scorched. Another gesture moved the door's hidden bolts into place, locking it shut, while an incantation sealed it with an invisible force.

Rameel drew in a deep breath, and when he exhaled, he imagined his memories being pushed out of his body along with the air from his lungs. Then he turned and jumped headfirst down the passage of stairs, opening his wings just wide enough to control his fall. The speed of his movement drew the humid, salty air behind him, creating a gust that extinguished every torch along the length of the tunnel.

23

The most difficult part of the journey to Nijambu had been getting out of the mountainous terrain around Barsiri. Once Sariel and Wekesa reached the lower elevations, they only had to contend with the vines of the jungle and the occasional stream crossing. Within days of reaching flatter terrain, Sariel's lungs seemed to acclimate to traveling, and he wondered if the mild exertion was actually doing them some good. Then his fever returned as if to argue this point, forcing them to stop for several days.

Wekesa had begun the trip with a vast supply of patience, but with each passing day, his reserves seemed to wane just a bit more. Sariel wondered if this was due to the natural expiration of one's excitement at the beginning of a journey, or if there was something deeper taking place. Whatever the cause, Wekesa grew more agitated as they neared the port city.

Nijambu turned out to be a sprawling, unwalled conglomerate of structures that had taken over several coves of the western shores. Some areas were populated by hundreds upon hundreds of primitive shelters made from saplings and palm fronds, while others boasted three-story buildings of stone and wood planking. Other than the docks and the main road that snaked eastward to Idorana, there didn't appear to be much organization to the city's layout. Evidently, the same freedom that had allowed such a port to spring up within Zaquel's lands was also the cause of its chaos. And yet, it seemed to thrive. Seafaring people from all over the world came here to buy, sell, and trade their merchandise. And those who were close enough came by land as well.

Of course, Sariel had to take Wekesa's word for most of this; he had only been able to observe the city at night from a hiding place within the jungle. As he waited on the outskirts, Wekesa went into the city and rented a room at an inn. He came back hours later and led Sariel to a centrally located room on the second story of a building, with a good view of an intersection in front and a maze of alleyways in the back if they needed to make a quick escape. All the while, Sariel kept his head and face covered by a cloak that would have been suspicious if worn in the heat of the day. The soldiers of the Rana Empire were known to patrol the city, and Sariel had assumed that they would be looking for the goddess' scepter as well as her assassin.

That assumption was confirmed on their first full day in Nijambu. Wekesa had gone out alone to set his brother's plan into motion, and when he came back that evening, he told Sariel that he had seen more soldiers than usual.

Three days had transpired since then, and each day had been the same. Wekesa would go out in the morning and come back at sunset. Each time, his mood worsened, but he wouldn't speak of what troubled him or what Mosi had instructed him to do. And so Sariel found himself waiting, passing the time by looking through the gaps in the shutters at the city inhabitants on the streets below.

Men and women of various cultures passed by, carrying baskets and pots on their heads. Sacks were slung over shoulders, and animals pulled loaded carts. There were bushels of fruits and vegetables, skewers of roasted meats, and even piles of animals that had not yet been butchered and cooked. Sariel observed rolls of linen, folds of multicolored woven fabric, and piles of animal pelts. Many wooden crates passed through the streets, either carried or carted, and Sariel could only imagine what they contained. At some point this became a game he played to occupy his mind. He would try to listen for the sound of the contents and guess what was inside before shifting his perspective toward the Eternal. Most of the contents were the same as what was being transported in the open, but there was the occasional crate of coins or load of unforged metal. These gave off a slight metallic sound when they were jostled, but only if Sariel was listening very closely.

The sound of footsteps in the hall startled Sariel and brought his attention to the door on the other side of the room. He watched from the Eternal Realm as Wekesa's spirit drifted closer. Then he listened for two quick knocks before unlatching the door and letting his friend inside.

Wekesa exhaled loudly as he came in and set a bundle of coarse fabric on the table.

Sariel bolted the door shut and then joined his friend, who had already slumped into a chair beside the table. "It must be two hours yet until sunset."

Wekesa nodded.

"I would ask how it went, but it seems obvious."

The young man leaned forward and rested his elbows on his knees before hanging his head.

"Since Mosi's plan is not working, perhaps it couldn't hurt to tell me what you're trying to do?"

Wekesa replied without lifting his head. "To buy us passage across the sea with the gold you brought from Idorana. But no one will go near the Kaliel lands."

"They're too afraid?"

The young man's head bobbed up and down a few times. "I have even told the captains that they can name their price."

"Is that it? That's the extent of Mosi's plan?"

Wekesa raised his head. "No. It will soon be time for the annual offering. He hoped that I would coordinate our landing to occur at the same time as the holy men are delivering the virgin ... but in a different location. This way, the Kaliel would be distracted. Afterward, we could follow them as they take the offering to their demon god."

Though reaching the stump was actually Sariel's first priority, and he was confident that he could locate it based on terrain features alone, there was no guarantee that Rameel would be in that same location. Once he freed his second self, Sariel would then have the challenge of finding Rameel. "That's actually a good plan," he admitted.

"It would have been," Wekesa agreed. "But the time has almost passed."

"Why do you say that?"

"It took us too long to get here. And I didn't expect the captains to refuse me. The holy men are already here in the city with their offering. They set sail the day after tomorrow."

Sariel leaned back in his chair, finally understanding why Wekesa had been growing more impatient each day. Then his gaze settled on the bag of gold coins sitting on the bed across the room. The young man had left it behind each time he went out into the city, and now Sariel realized why. "You didn't tell anyone where you were staying ... did you?"

"No, I'm not stupid," Wekesa answered, finally straightening up. He reached for the bundle on the table and began to unwrap it. "People are robbed in this city every day. Some are even killed in the process."

"And no one followed you?" Sariel asked, just to be sure.

Wekesa had the coarse fabric unwrapped and began dividing the meal of bread and roasted fish. "No. Every day, I leave the city in a different direction and circle back through the jungle."

"Good," Sariel replied.

A long moment of silence passed as both of them ate their evening meal. It had become their custom over the few days they'd been in the city. The next morning, Sariel would eat whatever was left over as his morning meal, and Wekesa would buy what he needed as he went out into the city.

"I don't like the gold being wasted like this," Sariel admitted, breaking the silence. "I wanted it to help reestablish your people."

Wekesa waved his hand. "We can make or gather what we need, but passage across the sea can only be bought. At least ... Mosi thought it could be bought."

"Tell me more about the Kaliel. I know why people are afraid, but has anyone actually seen them before?"

"Other than the holy man who survived the first offering?"

"Yes, of course," Sariel replied with a nod and a smile.

"Only the barbarians of the north. There are stories of giants whose skin is as black as the night. They live in the forests of the Kaliel lands, and they only come out onto the moors to hunt. But they do not come looking for animals; they hunt people. They eat their flesh. No one knows for certain if these are the same demons who also live in the forests across the sea here in the south."

Sariel nodded. The eating of human flesh was similar to the stories of the Kaliel, but the holy man who survived the first offering didn't mention the Kaliel as being giants. Only that they were dark creatures with wings and claws, and pale faces with eyes of blood. The giants, on the other hand, sounded exactly like Nephiylim. If Rameel had fathered a Nephiyl army, then getting across the sea would not be the most difficult of their challenges. Before the Fracturing, Sariel would not have feared to battle even hundreds of Nephiylim. In fact, he had done just that in El-Betakh. But he no longer had demonic underlings to do his bidding, and this human body to which he was now confined seemed too frail to even fight another human.

Wekesa swallowed a bite of fish before mumbling, "I thought we could even swim to the shore if I found someone who was sailing west. All they would have to do is bring us within sight of land, but none of the captains were willing to alter their routes."

Sariel smiled. It was amazing to see this young man—who lived such a primitive life—navigate the customs of the city, avoid criminals, and barter with people from other cultures. "How many times have you been to Nijambu?"

"Once every year since I can remember. We probably won't come as often now that ..."

Sariel grimaced when he thought of how this young man had lost his entire village and two of his own brothers. It was probably best to move the conversation away from that memory. "And you're able to speak with all these people from different lands?"

"Yes," Wekesa replied, his face brightening. "Many of them have their own languages, but the one we are speaking now, Shayeth, is known as Common to everyone. It is the language of trade."

"I have to admit I underestimated you."

Wekesa's eyebrows scrunched together. "What do you mean?"

"Though you are young, you are very mature. And wise for your age."

Wekesa grinned. "Not wise enough, I suppose."

"Perhaps I can go with you tomorrow ... to help?"

"No," Wekesa answered quickly. "There are too many of the goddess' soldiers. Twice the usual number. They are looking for a man with white hair and beard. I have seen them harassing the Syvaku because they too have pale skin and hair."

Sariel looked over to the scepter lying on the ground beside the bed, wrapped tightly in linen. "Yes, I'm sure they would like to have their revenge." Then Sariel noticed the knife hanging in its sheath from the back of Wekesa's chair—the same knife that Zuberi had gone back to his village to retrieve. Wekesa had taken his brother's blade with him each time he went out into the city. "If you bring me some water, I will make sure no such man is found."

~

The following morning, Sariel accompanied Wekesa to the docks. His head and beard were shaven as cleanly as possible, given the disappointingly dull edge of Zuberi's knife. The tunic of plant fibers that Sariel was accustomed to wearing had been left behind in favor of a tanned leather one. Because his skin was paler than the native population, dressing like them would only invite attention. Though the Syvaku were closer to Sariel's skin color, dressing in furred animal skins as they did would only draw attention to his lack of hair. The Syvaku typically wore their hair long or in braids. Wekesa decided that Sariel's sand-colored skin looked most like the plains people of the south, and had purchased one of their tunics and a pair of their thin, leather sandals.

The sight of two men from different cultures walking together through the city would not have been rare, but would have been uncommon enough to warrant a second look by the goddess' soldiers. So Sariel followed at a distance and waited as Wekesa went from one captain to another. The young man was persistent, but each of his conversations ended up looking the same—hands and arms waving in various gestures. Wekesa would point to the west. The captain would wave both hands. Wekesa would point at the man's boat. The captain would wave one of his crew members over, and that man would point up at the sail or extend his fingers as if they were claws.

By midmorning, Wekesa was wandering through the docks with his head pivoting back and forth in all directions. It was obvious to Sariel that the young man had exhausted his options. Finally, after half an hour without any attempted bartering, Wekesa's pace quickened. He went to the end of the southernmost dock and approached a short man dressed in brightly colored clothing that looked as though it had been made for a man twice his size. When the arms began waving, Sariel moved a bit closer so he could hear the conversation.

"... on the horizon. We will swim the rest of the way."

"I can see that you are a smart boy. I could put you to work on my boat. But I will not do this thing you ask."

"And I can see that your boat needs a new sail," Wekesa pointed out. "You are obviously a man of business, and you have needs. So ... name your price."

The captain laughed heartily. "You will have your own boat someday, I imagine. Then you will be free to sail wherever you wish, boy. But I value my flesh. And if you are as wise as I think you are, you would not be in such a hurry to give yours to the demons."

The skin on Sariel's head was becoming tender from the bright sun. He was growing impatient with what he could already see was a lost cause, and began to scan the dock areas for a shady place to stand.

"How much do you want for your rowboat?" Wekesa pushed.

The captain turned around to look at the dinghy tied to the gunwale of his ship.

"You don't even need to veer from your course. We'll sail west with you as far as you're willing to go, and we'll row ourselves the rest of the way."

The captain shook his head. "I will not send any man to his death, let alone a boy. Now leave me; I have much work to do."

Sariel's visual inspection of the docks failed to turn up any shade, but he noticed something even more interesting. Among various foreign ships tied to a rundown dock were three long boats, each with a raised stern, almost as high as the prow. The curving protrusions of wood had been carved to look like the heads and tails of mighty serpents, or perhaps the reptilian form that Kokabiel so often assumed in the old world. Each had a single, square sail of white, embroidered with a red emblem of the same creature. The crew was working to take in the ships' long oars, and Sariel could tell at a glance that these men had endured harsh conditions in order to reach Nijambu. Their hair and beards were wildly unkempt. They were much taller than the native population, and despite their obvious lack of regular meals, they still retained more muscle on their frames than most of the city's inhabitants. They carried no weapons, but Sariel could see that these men had a warrior's determination in their eyes.

"... even for thirty pieces? Or fifty? Do you want some other captain to get what could be yours?"

"Please, boy! Go now before I lose my temper."

"Wekesa!" Sariel called.

The young man turned suddenly, as if startled.

Sariel waved him over.

"I'll give you one last chance," he said, turning back to the captain. "Sixty pieces?"

The captain smiled and walked away without another word.

Wekesa put both hands atop his head with interlocked fingers before turning around. Then he came back toward Sariel with a meandering pace. "He wouldn't listen."

Sariel nodded. "None of them will. That's because we're talking to the wrong people."

Wekesa let his hands drop limply to his sides. "No, these are the right men."

"What about them?" Sariel asked, pointing.

"The Syvaku? No. They are not for sale. They have only come here to purchase provisions for their journey."

"Where are they going?"

Wekesa stared at the foreign crew for a moment before answering. "Their country is not too far from here, but they look like they've come a long way. I think they are heading back to their home."

"You are very observant, Wekesa. I would bet that you know something about all the people here."

The young man smiled.

"How many different cultures are represented here in this city?"

Wekesa wrinkled his eyebrows and looked up at the sky. "Over twenty, I think."

"Are they friendly with each other?"

"Some are. Most hate anyone who is not of their ... kind ... their tribe. But everyone who comes to Nijambu accepts that he will have to interact with other peoples. Sometimes they will even work together if the money is enough."

Sariel nodded. "Can you show me these different peoples and tell me why they've each come to Nijambu?"

Wekesa's forehead became furrowed, and he suddenly looked very much like Ebnisha. "Of course. Why?"

Sariel held up his finger. "Because I have a plan ... as Mosi would say."

24

Renting out a tavern would certainly have stirred up rumors among patrons suddenly prevented from entering their favorite establishment. Rumors had a way of spreading quickly, and Sariel didn't want to alert the Rana soldiers. Instead, a single gold coin was all that it took to secure the use of a warehouse near the docks for the evening. With the day's work complete, it wouldn't be used again until the morning, and the owner was happy to accept payment for something that required no work on his part.

It was quiet inside, and with towering piles of fabric and other goods arranged in rows all around, it wasn't difficult to find a private meeting place. Sariel stood on a dirt floor at the intersection of two aisles. A single lamp hung from a nearby support column, casting a soft, wavering light. Sariel waited patiently for Wekesa to bring their guests inside.

"Yes, come in," he heard Wekesa say. "This aisle, here." Then the sound of a door closing could be heard a few seconds later.

When three strangers stepped into view at the end of the aisle, Sariel could see—even in the dim light—that their suspicions weren't eased by the amount they had been paid just to come here.

"It's alright," Sariel assured them. "There's no one here but us. Please gather around." He tried to keep his hands visible to the guests so they would have no other reasons for alarm. "Thank you for coming. I know this meeting is a bit unusual, but you will understand the need for secrecy when I'm done explaining."

"The boy said you would pay more gold if I listen to your words." The man who spoke had ruddy skin and straight black hair, worn long. Aside from his thin leather clothing, he would have fit in perfectly with Sheyir's tribe.

"Yes, that's correct. I have a proposal for all of you, and if you would be so kind as to hear me out, you will receive payment for your time."

Wekesa smiled and gestured to the man. "This is ..."

"Shikoba," the man said.

"... of the Tasunke plains people in the south," Wekesa finished.

Sariel nodded.

"This is captain Unnrik of the Syvaku."

Sariel was quite tall compared to most of the men in the city, but he had to look up slightly to meet Unnrik's fierce gaze. This was one of the fair-haired explorers that Sariel had seen at the docks earlier in the morning. His blond hair was also worn long, with a beard to match. Both had a coarse texture to them, as if they had seen much wind over the years. The captain's clothing was constructed of animal pelts that looked far too warm for this part of the world. Sariel nodded to him as well before turning to the last man.

"And Dochin of the Odt peoples far to the northwest," Wekesa said, finishing the introductions.

This man was the shortest of the group. His hair was also black and sleek, but worn short. His face was cleanly shaven, revealing skin that was just a bit lighter and yellower than Shikoba's. His clothing was thin and fit loosely, reflecting the lamplight more so than the others'. Though he wasn't physically intimidating, Sariel could tell just by the way this man stood that he knew how to handle himself in a fight. And the sword hanging at his hip only reinforced the observation.

Sariel nodded at Dochin, keeping his face friendly and calm. But inwardly, he was smiling as large as Ebnisha would have. How wonderful it was to see the variety of people who had descended by natural means from the inhabitants of the old world. There was no Myndar influence displayed here—nothing like the human creatures being bred in Ezekiyel's city in Third Earth.

"Who are you?" Dochin asked.

Sariel opened his mouth to answer, but Wekesa spoke first. "My people call him Old Man."

"You don't look old," Dochin replied.

Sariel just shrugged. He could tell already that Dochin was very direct and would be difficult to win over. "Thank you again for coming," he said, breaking eye contact to look at the others. "I asked you to leave your crews behind because such a large and ... diverse group would catch the eyes of the Rana soldiers. And none of us wish to—"

"You want us to do something illegal for you?" Unnrik asked.

"No. It's nothing like that."

"Then what do you want of us?" Dochin asked.

Sariel allowed himself a grin before he looked the warrior in the eyes. "I want you to help me get to the demon god across the sea so I can kill him."

A full second of silence passed before Dochin's slack face bunched into dozens of wrinkles. When he looked at the others and started laughing, Unnrik and Shikoba joined in immediately. A short while passed before the men realized that Sariel wasn't joking. His serious demeanor ruined their joyous moment and caused their laughter to die out.

"You have been hit too many times on your bald head," Unnrik said.

Sariel ignored the comment and tried a different approach. "I understand there are more of the goddess' soldiers than usual in Nijambu these days?"

"Yes," Shikoba answered.

"And why is that?"

"They are looking for a man with white..." he began, but trailed off as his eyes seemed to notice something different about Sariel's head all of a sudden.

"Do you know why they are looking for this man?"

"No," Shikoba replied.

Dochin answered, "It probably has something to do with what people are saying about the goddess' scepter."

"Oh, I didn't realize anyone knew about the scepter," Sariel admitted. "What is it that people are saying?"

Dochin looked at the other two before he answered. "The goddess traveled from Idorana across the sea to the underworld with an offering. She went ashore by herself. When she came back, her offering had been accepted; the demon god had given her a scepter in exchange. It was as dark as the night sky and sparkled like the stars. It was a token of peace. But the underworld must not have been satisfied with this exchange. A demon was later discovered in Idorana. It attacked her and stole back the scepter. They say that the underworld has turned against the goddess now. She has gone into her temple and will not come out anymore."

Sariel nodded as he looked from one man to the next. "It is certainly an entertaining story, but not entirely accurate. It was not a demon in Idorana; it was a man with white hair. And the goddess will not ever come out of her temple again because she is dead. You see, they are not just looking for me because I stole her scepter; they are looking for me because I killed her with it."

Dochin frowned at this and looked to the others to see if this was another joke. Unnrik muttered something under his breath in his native language. Shikoba just stared straight ahead.

Sariel remained steady to show that he was quite serious.

"Why shouldn't we just report you to her soldiers right now?" Unnrik asked.

"A fair question," Sariel admitted before reaching between two stacks of piled fabric.

Unnrik and Shikoba took a step back.

Dochin grabbed the hilt of the sword at his waist.

Sariel removed the scepter from its hiding place and dropped it onto the floor at the men's feet.

A long moment of silence passed as everyone stared down at the object that had clearly not been made by human hands. It sparkled in the dim lamplight, just as it had been described.

Dochin slowly let go of his sword hilt and bent down, reaching out toward the scepter.

"Because the man who fought through Mwangu Rana's soldiers, killed her chief priestess, and then shoved this thing through her skull is not someone you want as an enemy," Sariel finally answered.

Dochin's hand came to a stop before touching the scepter.

Unnrik nodded.

Shikoba's gaze came up from the scepter. "Why do you need our help if you can do such things?"

"I have to cross the sea to reach the demon god, and Unnrik's people are the only ones brave enough to take me there. When all of us reach the shore, we will need to travel many days by land. Your people are the best horsemen in the known world," Sariel answered, looking briefly at Wekesa to acknowledge where this information had come from. "We will need your horses and your skills to travel quickly."

"And you need my blade?" Dochin guessed, rising from his crouched position.

Sariel took a deep breath before responding. "I am weakened from fighting with the goddess and her army. I am not yet strong enough to face the demon god, but there is a place across the sea where my healing will be made complete. Getting there may involve confronting the Kaliel, and your warriors are the most fierce and skilled that anyone knows of."

Dochin grunted and nodded his agreement. Then his eyes slowly lowered, inspecting. "You were injured?"

Sariel knew when he was being sized up. He reached out his hand and the scepter leaped up from the floor and came to rest in his grip.

All three men took a step backward this time.

"I can't face the demon god yet, but no man will stand in my way," Sariel clarified.

The warehouse fell silent again as Sariel returned the scepter to its hiding place. Then he straightened his posture and pointed at Unnrik. "You sail across vast oceans to explore the world. You are only in Nijambu to gather what's needed to sustain your journey."

It was the truth, and not phrased as a question, so it came as no surprise when Unnrik didn't respond.

"You," Sariel continued, pointing to Shikoba, "have come across plains and over mountain ranges on horseback. This is no simple task, but the pelts and skins you bring are traded for things that your people do not really need."

Dochin was the last to receive Sariel's address. "And you have come across the sea on someone else's boat to protect cargo that you care nothing for. The payment you receive for this is nothing compared to the value of your own life."

Dochin's eyes narrowed, but he kept silent.

"Each of you has come to Nijambu looking for something more than just money or trade. You are looking for adventure. A challenge. A fight. Glory for your people, perhaps?" Sariel said, turning up his hands. "I'm offering you all of these things and much more. Think of what people will say of the first men who went across the sea and discovered that the underworld was just another part of *this* world—a piece of land. Think of the influence that you will have among your people and others when you teach them that the Kaliel are not demons ... just men who hide in the forest."

The Kaliel were either animals, men, or Nephiylim. Sariel had given it thorough consideration and those were the only possibilities he could come up with. He doubted they were Nephiylim, because the only tribes of humans available for them to hunt were evidently the nomadic barbarians of the north. And he doubted the Kaliel were animals, because the story of the holy man who survived the first offering indicated that the Kaliel had come out from the trees and attacked as a group. Wolves might be compelled to do such a thing, but they didn't have wings, and it seemed unlikely that they would come out into the water to attack men aboard a ship. Sariel was confident that the Kaliel would prove to be nothing more than humans. Perhaps their clothing would account for the description of their appearance.

"People will speak of your bravery," Sariel added.

"You talk as if you are sure about the Kaliel. How can you know these things?" Shikoba asked.

"Words will not be enough to convince you, but I will prove it to you when we get there. You will see with your own eyes that these myths have only been spread so that people will be too afraid to cross over to their lands."

"You only need my ship and crew for the passage, yes?" Unnrik asked.

"I am asking all three of you, as well as your men, to accompany me for the entire trip. After I kill the demon god, you will be free to do whatever you wish. Though I suspect that after you see the truth for yourselves, some of you might wish to stay and claim the Kaliel lands for your own."

"What if you are wrong?" Shikoba said. "What if the stories are true? All of us could become food for the demons."

Sariel put his hands out to either side. "Adventure. Glory. Truth. Such things cannot be won without the greatest of risks, but I know that you would not have it any other way. That is why I invited you here tonight."

Silence returned as each man considered Sariel's offer. In the absence of a conversation to draw their attention, the men inspected each other or the ground in front of their feet. They looked up to the ceiling of the warehouse and then again at the stacks of merchandise around them.

"*I'm* going," Wekesa announced.

Sariel turned to the young man, but held his tongue. He had expected to send Wekesa back to his family when passage had been secured, but arguing that point with him in front of the men would only undermine the logic of Sariel's proposal. There was nothing he could do.

"You aren't afraid, boy?" Unnrik asked.

"No, because my friend speaks the truth and I trust him."

"Ah ... he is hungry for adventure," Dochin said.

"No. I am going because I promised my brother that I would help until the task was complete."

Sariel watched the eyes of the men carefully. It appeared that Wekesa's bravery in spite of his age was having a deeper impact on them than anything Sariel had said. He waited a long moment before addressing the next item of discussion.

"I promised that I would pay you just to listen, and you have all done that, so ..." Retrieving the pouch from the floor near the scepter, Sariel dug out coins and handed five to each man.

None of them seemed eager to put the money away. They just held it in their palms and stared at it.

Unnrik wiggled his fingers and made the coins clank together. "If we agree to this ... how soon?"

"We'll have until tomorrow afternoon to discuss the details and make preparations. Then we sail."

The Syvak captain smoothed his beard before looking to the other men. Dochin and Shikoba seemed to have already made up their minds. Both of them nodded with just the slightest movement. Unnrik looked back to Sariel, his eyes a bit brighter than before. "Very well. Tomorrow afternoon."

25

On its western and northern sides, the boundary of the Rana Empire was defined by the ocean. All ships sailing through the waters in this region had to do so within sight of its shores. Being several days out from Nijambu, with no land visible on any horizon, meant that Sariel and his rented fleet were in violation of the law. Fortunately, the empire no longer needed to patrol the waters between its boundaries and the Kaliel lands; fear of the underworld had become the most effective deterrent.

Sariel sat on the aft deck of the lead boat, next to Wekesa. The young man, who had never been aboard a ship, had been struggling with the constant rocking motion since they'd left Nijambu. He'd lived his whole short life with solid ground beneath his feet, and now there was only the hollow, creaking deck of timbers being thrown in every direction. Sariel had advised him to stay back in Nijambu or return to his family, but the young man had been adamant that he would keep his promise to Mosi. Now he was paying the price for that decision. As miserable as Wekesa looked, Sariel hoped that sickness would turn out to be his only sacrifice.

Wekesa closed his eyes and leaned his head back against the inside of the gunwale.

"It's better if you keep your eyes on the ocean," Sariel told him.

"I tried that already."

Sariel patted the young man's leg. "You'll get used to it eventually."

Wekesa just moaned in response.

Sariel glanced up at the clouds that were becoming thicker and darker with each hour. If it started raining, Wekesa's voyage would become even more unpleasant than it already was. Fortunately, they were aboard the most stable ships that anyone could hope for. The Syvak boats were similar to the ones used by the Rana Empire, but were designed for longer voyages and more varied conditions. Their hulls were wider and shallower, making them less prone to tipping and allowing them to plow through weeds and other obstructions common in shallower waters. Their sails were taller and square, instead of the wide rectangles used on the goddess' ships. And though the Syvak boats appeared less bulky, there was more contact between their hulls and the water. The goddess' ships ran deeper, with the bow and stern sections raised out of the water. They weren't as nimble, which was probably why they needed two rudders to control their movements, whereas the Syvak ships required only one. The deck on which Sariel sat ran the length of the boat, with only the center portion lowered around the mast to create a hold for provisions. He remembered Zaquel's boat curved so much at the ends that it had required raised fore and aft decks in addition to the main deck.

Sariel climbed to his feet and stretched his legs. As he looked out over the waters behind, he could see that the other two Syvak ships were maintaining a close, staggered formation. Each had a crew of eight sailors, with one navigator at the bow, a rudder man at the stern, and six others who managed the sail or rowed when needed. The disproportionate size of the small crew for such a large ship was a testament to how maneuverable these boats really were.

Sariel let his gaze swing northward to the only other object on the ocean—the large ship of the holy men. Unnrik had been keeping it just barely visible on the horizon, paralleling its course and matching its much slower speed. Sariel wondered how the captain planned to reach the Kaliel lands without being spotted by Rameel's subjects. He thought it was worth a discussion and began moving toward the bow. As he passed over the hold, he looked down and saw Shikoba speaking softly to one of the horses. His tone was soothing, almost like a song, and the man was petting the animal's face, just above its nostrils. There were five horses on each ship, totaling fifteen, which was just enough to carry Sariel, Wekesa, Dochin and his five warriors, Shikoba and four of his tribesmen, and Unnrik along with his rudder man. Sariel had wanted to take all of Unnrik's men ashore, but Shikoba didn't want to commit his entire herd to this task. And the Syvak ships wouldn't have been able to carry that many horses anyway. As it was, five of the animals and their supplies took up every bit of space that wasn't occupied by other cargo; Unnrik's fleet was carrying everything it possibly could.

"How is our progress?" Sariel asked as he reached Unnrik at the bow.

The captain was standing beside the serpentine prow, looking out upon the open ocean. His long hair and beard were waving in the breeze. "Slow," he replied, without taking his eyes off the water.

Sariel glanced again at the sail of the holy men far to the north. "How will we keep from being spotted by the Kaliel?"

Unnrik looked north. "The holy men have made this voyage many times. They have kept a steady course and speed since we left. When we are nearing Kaliel lands, I will head south until their sail cannot be seen."

"If we spot land, the Kaliel will be able to see us as well."

Unnrik turned his face into the wind and glared down at Sariel from the corner of his vision. "By that time we will be away from the holy men."

"But ... how will you know in advance—?"

"Trust me, Old Man," the captain replied.

"I've sailed with many different peoples," Dochin said, walking up from behind. "Some use the size and direction of the waves. Others look for birds and if they have food in their beaks."

His comment was meant to satisfy Sariel's questions, but Unnrik was the one who grunted, "Unreliable."

Sariel looked to Dochin, but the man's face was steady, unreadable.

"The smell of the air, then?" Dochin wondered.

Unnrik looked down with lopsided eyebrows at the warrior. "Winds shift."

"You don't know where we are, do you?"

Unnrik stroked his beard as if he were deciding whether or not to be offended. Then his eyes lowered to the sword at Dochin's waist. "This is the secret wisdom of my people. I would not share it unless I received something of equal value."

Dochin followed Unnrik's gaze, realizing what he meant. "Ah! You wish to learn the way of war? It would take years."

Unnrik turned his face back to the sea. "And sailing ... a lifetime."

Dochin grinned. "I would not want you to start learning in the rain. The wisdom of my people is difficult enough."

"The rain will pass after two days' time," Unnrik replied, his head raised to the clouds.

Dochin looked up at the gray sky and squinted.

Sariel had to turn away to keep from laughing at the men's friendly competition. He walked aft and when he reached the hold again, he could see that Wekesa was standing up. The young man had his head over the side of the ship as a precaution. Down in the hold, Shikoba was soothing another horse. The man appeared as comfortable as anyone.

"Have you been to sea before?" Sariel asked him.

"No."

"The rocking doesn't make you sick?"

Shikoba whispered something to the horse and patted its flank before moving on to another one. "This ship is just another horse to me. And the ocean ... a very wide valley."

Sariel smiled. He'd never thought of it like that before, but the horseman's analogy made sense. When he looked again, he could see that Wekesa was relieving his stomach of what little he'd eaten for breakfast. Unfortunately, the young man had never traveled across a valley such as this, and the horse he had chosen to ride was more spirited than any other.

~

When the rains arrived, Dochin became even more interested in how Unnrik was able to navigate. He promised to teach the captain how to fight, and in exchange, Unnrik began revealing the wisdom of his people. The rains passed after two days, just like the captain had said they would. And when the skies cleared, the sail of the holy men's ship was still visible on the northern horizon. Unnrik and his crew were the only ones not surprised by this. Wekesa's stomach seemed to enjoy the sunshine, finally accepting its owner's new life on the sea.

When the puddles on the deck timbers had sufficiently dried, it was time for Dochin to keep his promise. Unnrik had one of his sail men take over navigating, and another take over for his rudder man, Molke, who would be coming ashore with the group. Both men were very interested in learning to defend themselves against flesh-eating demons. While Sariel understood their concerns, he told the warrior to assume that their enemies would be human and to teach with this assumption in mind.

"The first principle of battle is to find your advantage or your enemy's disadvantage," Dochin said as he paced back and forth in front of the sailors. "All other men are smaller than you, so your advantage is your size and strength."

Unnrik and Molke both straightened their posture, drawing smiles from everyone else aboard the ship.

Dochin held up a Syvak spear in his hand. "You are most comfortable with your fishing tools, so we will begin with these. The ropes that you attach will not be needed, because in war, one must never throw away his weapon. It must be kept close. And you will not hold it above your shoulder for throwing; you must keep it in front of you, like this," he said, holding it diagonally across his body with two hands.

Unnrik and Molke imitated Dochin's grip.

"That's right," the warrior said. "Now, from this position, the spear can be used for many different defenses or attacks. The bottom will guard your legs. The center ... your chest and stomach. And the tip will protect your face. At any time, one may attack from here," Dochin said, demonstrating various two-handed thrusts to the front, sides, and back. "And when the opportunity comes—"

All of a sudden, he let go of his front grip and performed a lunging stab with his back hand, stopping the barbed tip of the spear just inches from Unnrik's face.

The bearded man flinched a full second after the weapon would have killed him if the attack had been real. He cursed in his native tongue.

"Always be ready to move," Dochin said. "Another principle of battle."

Sariel watched the faces of both men carefully, ready to intervene if necessary. But to Unnrik's credit, he regained his composure. He had likely done the equivalent to Dochin while teaching him about navigation, so this was Dochin's opportunity to bring their relationship back into balance.

"This weapon has a long reach. With your size, you will be able to control a very large area of the battlefield. If there are crowds of enemies who come in close, you will need a shorter weapon. But for now, this will work. Let's begin with basic defense."

Sariel watched the instruction, wanting very much to take part. Battle was something he understood better than anything in this world. But as soon as the desire rose in his heart, words came to mind from another age—the judgment of the Holy One spoken against the Myndarym.

... all mysteries were not revealed to you. You know only the insignificant ones, and these, in the hardness of your hearts,

you have made known to the children of men. Through these they work great evil upon the earth.

Sariel cringed at the thought. He believed that he was The Awakened spoken of in the prophecy, but for some reason he couldn't escape the nagging feeling that he was also one of the Myndarym being judged. Was it possible for him to be both? Did the Myndarym despise themselves as much as they loved power, and was Sariel the expression of that contradiction?

They have asked for peace but will make war and teach the children of men to do likewise.

Sariel looked up as Dochin made a few slow, mock attacks with the butt of his spear. Unnrik defended them, clumsily at first but with increasing confidence. Then it was Molke's turn. After several iterations of defenses, moving faster with each, Dochin moved on to basic attacks.

"When you pierce a creature of the sea, how do you handle your spear afterward?"

Unnrik looked confused before he realized that the warrior wasn't speaking of casting the spear, but stabbing with it. He extended the weapon then bent his arm and wrist. "We lift," he answered.

"Yes. That is because you don't want to lose your prey," Dochin pointed out. "But in battle ... you do."

Unnrik tilted his head and frowned.

"Here, I will show you. Try to pierce me with your spear."

The captain grinned. "Are you sure?"

"Yes. Try to pierce me."

Unnrik crouched down and narrowed his eyes. Then he swayed back and forth for a few seconds before suddenly jabbing his spear at Dochin.

The warrior dodged to the side and brought his hand up, catching the shaft of the spear behind its barbed point.

Unnrik pulled, but his weapon was captured.

Dochin suddenly lunged forward and knocked the large man's chest with the butt of his spear.

Unnrik let go of his weapon and stumbled backward a few steps.

"While your spear is inside of an enemy, it cannot be used to defend you," Dochin added. "This is why attacks must be swift, and pulled back immediately."

"Will you teach them to fight from horseback?" Shikoba asked, interrupting the instruction.

Dochin turned around with a stern look on his face. "No. Horses are for pulling carts, or traveling. Not for war!"

Shikoba, who had been sitting on the deck, suddenly rose to his feet. The words that came from his mouth weren't in Common, but it was obvious that he took great offense to the warrior's statement.

"What? Speak Common," Dochin said, turning away from the students.

Shikoba walked forward until he was standing just one pace away from the warrior. He took a deep breath and then looked down on the shorter man. "All of you will have to ride when we reach land. What will you do when the Kaliel come for us?"

"I'll jump down and fight them on the ground."

"You would abandon the horse?"

"As I said, they only get me to the battle."

Shikoba grinned. "I will stay on my horse and shoot them with my bow. Then we will see whose people have greater wisdom."

"You mean fear?" Dochin replied.

A long moment of tense silence passed as the two men stared hard at each other.

Sariel remembered the hunting tool that Methu had invented in Sedekiyr. It made for a deadly weapon after it was properly refined, which was something that Sariel now regretted in light of the prophecy. Wekesa had told him that the Tasunke plains people were almost as well known for their use of the bow as they were for their horsemanship skills. Sariel had no doubt that Shikoba would prove useful in more ways than one, but the horseman would need to stop provoking the others if this mission was going to be successful.

"The truth is—you'll need to know both. You may not have the time to climb down from your horse," he told Dochin. "And what if the Kaliel pull you off yours, or cut its legs out from under you?" he asked Shikoba.

Both men were now looking at Sariel, and neither one seemed pleased by his words.

"All we know about how the Kaliel fight is the story of the first offering. And that was many years ago. None of us know what to expect, so I would advise you to prepare for both situations."

The memory of Methu and his bow had already stirred up feelings of guilt, and now Sariel had just explained to these men how to be more effective in battle. He'd said too much already. He turned and began walking aft without another word. His role in this conflict with the Myndarym was becoming more confusing each time he thought about it. Was he The Awakened, raised up to defeat the Myndarym? Or was he one of them, corrupting humans just by his presence? Rameel needed to be removed from this world if these humans were to set their own course for the future. But for Sariel to free his second self from the In-Between, he needed the help of humans, and their lives would only be at greater risk if they were unprepared to fight. It seemed that no matter what he did, someone was going to suffer the consequences.

~

Thirteen days after setting out from Nijambu, Sariel woke in the middle of the night to find Unnrik's men untying the sail ropes from their various positions along the gunwales. The sky was clear and the stars bright. The horses were snorting their uneasiness, and Shikoba had climbed down in the central hold to comfort them. Sariel removed his thick, wool blanket and climbed to his feet. Wekesa was still sleeping. Dochin looked as though he'd woken just a few minutes ago. Sariel walked toward the bow and approached Unnrik.

"What's happening?" he whispered.

"We will reach land in the morning," Unnrik explained. "If our sail is still up, it will be easier for the Kaliel to spot us."

Sariel watched the crew for a few seconds before asking, "How can you tell where we are?"

Unnrik grinned, but didn't answer the question. He walked past Sariel and joined his crew in taking down the sail.

26

Sariel had wanted to go ashore during the night, but Unnrik and the others had been afraid to set foot on land in the darkness, when the Kaliel were said to roam free. Using a weighted rope to measure the depth, the captain had found a suitable holding location before dropping anchor. When the first blinding rays of sun came up over the waters behind them, the small fleet was only a short rowing distance from the shoreline. It was too far out for them to have been attacked by land during the night, but close enough to reach their destination in just a few minutes. It was Unnrik's way of balancing their competing needs for secrecy and safety.

"There," he whispered, pointing to a wide sandy area that would allow them to go ashore. "Six degrees starboard."

The quiet instruction was relayed from crew member to crew member until it reached the man at the stern. As Molke leaned on his rudder, the other six men rowed. The ship turned and began heading for the shore, while the other two followed closely behind. Soon the waves took over propelling the boats toward the sand in lurches.

"Brace," Unnrik whispered.

Sariel and Wekesa, now at the foredeck, grabbed hold of the gunwale.

The warning was repeated from man to man, reaching Molke at the rudder just as the hull hit the sand, vibrating as it came to a stop. The crew immediately took in their oars and jumped overboard, landing with a splash in the shallows. As they hauled on their ropes to stabilize the boat, the other two ships ground to a halt in the sand. Within seconds, Dochin and his warriors were off the ships and spreading out along the beach with swords drawn. They watched the tree line closely, looking for any sign of movement.

The ramp that led up from the hold was already in place, and as soon as the descending ramp was attached to the gunwale, Shikoba led his five horses out of the hold and down into the shallow water. He rode the first animal, and the rest followed without any hesitation. Each carried a set of leather bags stocked with the supplies that would be needed for the second leg of their journey. When the horses from the other ships reached dry sand, Dochin's warriors advanced into the trees, leading the horses as they maintained a perimeter of protection.

When the ramps were clear, Sariel and Wekesa went ashore, followed by Unnrik and Molke. They ran to catch up to the larger group, and by the time they were in the trees and out of sight, the three Syvak ships were already being rowed back out to sea. The landing plan had gone smoothly, but no one besides Sariel knew that it had also gone unnoticed. He'd been watching from the Eternal Realm for the presence of any spirits, human or otherwise.

"I hope the Kaliel didn't see us," Wekesa said, eyes scanning the forest.

Dochin echoed the young man's fear. "We shouldn't be here in the shadows. This is *their* domain."

"We're safe," Sariel assured them before stepping to the center of the group. "Alright. The Kaliel should have received the offering from the holy men last night. We'll ride north along the shore until we pick up their trail." Then he gestured to Shikoba.

The horsemen were on foot now. They already had their animals lined up and waiting. There were five without saddles, implying which ones were meant for whom. Shikoba would be taking the lead position, and the rest of his men were spread throughout the procession to even out the responsibility for their untrained companions.

"Your horses have saddles," Shikoba said. "To mount, hold the saddle here. Put your foot in and pull yourself up, then swing this leg over the top." He repeated the instructions that he had given them while at sea. Now he demonstrated the technique, making it look simple before he climbed down and motioned for everyone to step forward and try for themselves.

Sariel went to the horse in the second position and did as Shikoba instructed. When he was in the saddle, he looked behind to see Wekesa smiling. The young man was good at climbing and didn't seem to have had any trouble mounting the horse. Only Molke struggled to get up at first, but he was successful on his second attempt. The warriors were all quite agile. Surprisingly, the unexperienced group was mounted and ready to go in just a few seconds.

"You only need to hold on to the saddle," Shikoba announced. "All of your horses will follow mine, so there is no need to try and steer the animals yet. Just hold loosely with your legs and hands, but save most of your energy for keeping balanced. Is everyone ready?"

Nods of affirmation were seen all along the procession.

Shikoba pulled on the reins and turned his horse toward the sandy beach. At once, Sariel's horse began following. It moved in a rhythmic lurch, not unlike when Sariel used to ride the largest of his underlings. But there had been no saddle for his demon in the old world, and it had been much taller than this horse. Sariel felt confident that he would quickly learn how to ride. He looked back and noted that Wekesa's smile was even larger than before.

The sun had risen fully above the horizon by the time the procession was clear of the trees. Shikoba held up his hand, and his horse picked up its knees and sped to a trot. Sariel's horse did the same, its lurching motion changing to a fast bounce. He pushed his feet into the stirrups and lifted some of his weight from the saddle. When he turned his head again, Wekesa was no longer smiling.

Shikoba led them along the beach until the terrain became rocky and steep. Then he headed into the trees, hardly slowing at all, as if he knew by instinct which path to take. Each time they came back out to the beach, the Syvak ships were farther away, emphasizing that there would be no rescue if anything went wrong at the beginning of their land journey. The plan was for Unnrik's crew to row east beyond sight and maintain that position until the expected time of their captain's return. Then they would raise their sails at night and come closer to shore, looking for the signal of a torch. If they spotted the light, waving in a predetermined pattern, they would come ashore and retrieve the group. Otherwise, Unnrik had instructed them to sail out of sight and drop their sails before sunrise. The primary reason Sariel had insisted that Unnrik and Molke come along was to ensure that the Syvaku didn't leave them stranded here. It also didn't hurt to have two men of their size along for the journey.

Shikoba wound through the trees and over the sand, looking back at regular intervals to his men who communicated with him by hand signals. When he was confident that everyone had grown accustomed to the trotting pace, he sped to a canter. By midmorning, the group was moving as fast as they were able, galloping anytime there was a stretch of open beach. Before the sun reached its peak, they came upon a small wooden dinghy, overturned on the sand. If there had been any footprints around the boat before, the tide had washed them away. Shikoba went inland, finding a worn path that led away from the beach and northwest into the forest. He held up his hand to stop the procession and then jumped down off his horse. Moving forward in a crouch, he inspected the darker inland soil. When he stood and turned back to the group, there was a smile on his face.

"Humans," he said quietly. "They're on foot."

Sariel could still see the faint remnants of human spirits lingering in the Eternal. He nodded at the horseman before turning around to see how Wekesa was doing.

"Can we get down and stretch our legs?" the young man asked.

"Yes. A good idea," Shikoba replied, signaling his men.

Everyone climbed down from their horses, stumbling as they reached the ground. Sariel took a few seconds to stretch his sore legs before walking toward Shikoba. "How many Kaliel?"

"Forty or fifty," Shikoba answered.

"Good," he replied with a cough. Though Sariel hadn't had a fever in several days, his lungs seemed to tire easily anytime they were asked to accommodate some quick movement from his body. Just climbing down from the horse had agitated them. "They outnumber us, but I doubt they know how to fight."

"Why do you say that?"

"They have no need. Everyone is afraid to come into their lands." He coughed again.

Shikoba raised his head and squinted. "Should we stop and eat?"

"No," Sariel answered quickly. "We can ride a bit farther."

"As you wish," Shikoba replied. Then he raised his arm and moved his hand in a large circle through the air.

Sariel turned to watch the group come back toward their horses, shaking their feet and legs as they walked.

"Already?" Wekesa asked.

Sariel laughed under his breath before another cough came out. "It's faster than walking."

"I won't be able to walk after this," the young man replied, putting his foot in the stirrup and grabbing hold of the saddle.

~

The terrain became more varied as they followed the faint, narrow trail inland. Shikoba moved as quickly as was safe, which was a trot most of the time. They stopped once for a midday meal, and then again when the sun was halfway to the western horizon. The land became a series of rolling hills, and each time they reached the top of a rise, they could see that the terrain to the west was becoming taller. A mountain range was rising above the forest canopy.

After killing Baraquijal, Sariel had never returned to the stump in this world. But he would never forget the range of dark, conical mountains that had risen up from the land in Aden after the flood. He remembered the way they belched smoke and ash into the air as rivers of molten rock flowed down their sides. The group was getting closer to the Tree, and Sariel was more conscious of the scepter across his back.

The trail turned due north and paralleled the mountains. Shikoba took every opportunity to move quickly through the trees, and Sariel was pleased with the progress they were making. By late afternoon, they came to the top of a hill that offered an unobstructed view to the north. Sariel had kept his perspective split between the realms, and he quickly spotted a large group of dull spirits among the barren landscape of the Borderlands.

"The Kaliel," he said quietly to Shikoba.

The horseman turned his head and held up his hand to stop the procession. "Where?"

Sariel pointed ahead. "Do you see where the mountain face comes down into that darker stand of trees there?"

Shikoba looked north and squinted. "Yes."

"They're just to the right of the trees."

"How do you know?" he asked, turning to look at Sariel again.

"I just know."

Shikoba's forehead creased, but he didn't question Sariel's statement. Instead, he asked, "Are they moving?"

"No."

The horseman nodded, then looked to the sky. "It is daytime, when they sleep. We should rest now. They'll start moving again when the sun goes down."

~

Though the group was tired, no one was able to sleep in the light of day. They ate from the rations they had brought, and they rested in the shade while Sariel periodically checked on the Kaliel. Just as Shikoba said, the enemy began moving a couple hours after sunset, when the sky was fully dark. If this was the pattern of their activity, Sariel and his companions would have to adjust their own schedule to match, moving at night and sleeping during the day. It was important to stay with them in case Rameel resided somewhere other than near the stump.

Progress was much slower in the dark, with the light of the moon and stars mostly obstructed by the trees. Shikoba continued leading the procession, and even with an interrupted walking pace, their horses were able to keep up with the Kaliel moving on foot.

Tracking his enemies had become simple now that Sariel's group had caught up to them, but a different challenge now faced them all. The Kaliel never stopped during the night, so there were no periods of rest. Sariel's group couldn't talk with each other for fear of being heard. And the silence, combined with the inability to sleep when exhausted, created a unique kind of suffering that made the nighttime hours seem to stretch out twice as long. Sariel eventually became grateful for the pain that came with riding a horse, as it kept him awake.

Throughout the night, the spirits of the Kaliel disappeared and reappeared. Sariel assumed this was due to the terrain in the Borderlands. Even though both groups were moving through the Temporal Realm, their spirits existed in another. And when a hill or mountain in the Eternal Realm blocked his view of the Kaliel, Sariel would lose track of his enemies. It was a continual test of his alertness to anticipate where the Kaliel would reappear and how long it would take.

When dawn approached, the Kaliel stopped and everyone was grateful. They made their camp on a hill where Sariel could maintain his sight of the enemy. Dochin and his warriors offered to set up a perimeter, but Sariel insisted that he would take the first watch. Everyone went immediately to sleep, and Sariel had yet another hour of silence. But the light of the rising sun was a welcome distraction to his tired body. He was able to get a good look at his surroundings and see how the earth had repaired itself after the flooding. His thoughts wandered to his second self, drifting through the In-Between. Alone. Trapped. Nothing was being shared between the worlds. The flow of light that used to exist had become little more than a faint feeling of pressure. No sights. No sounds. No tastes or smells. Just a barely recognizable feeling detected by a bodiless existence. If not for the experiences of his first self, damaged as it was, Sariel would have found sanity difficult to keep hold of.

Finally, it was time for Dochin's watch, and Sariel woke the warrior carefully. He showed him the best vantage point before asking, "Will you be able to stay awake?"

Dochin rubbed his eyes and nodded.

"Good. The Kaliel are camped in the trees at the base of that bare slope," he whispered, pointing. "They probably won't move, but if they realize we're here and decide to come for us, you'll see movement among the tree trunks there ... or beside that clearing there."

Dochin nodded again. "You've done this before?"

"More times than I can count."

"Get some sleep," the warrior whispered.

~

Sariel awoke with a start. His breath was ragged, and his heart racing. Through the leaves above, he could see that the sun was more than an hour past its zenith.

I overslept!

He pushed himself up to a seated position and glanced around the camp. The horses were grazing on tufts of grass. The bags of provisions were still lying near the base of a tree, but everyone was gone. Sariel quickly jumped to his feet and ran up to the top of the hill.

Unnrik turned his head quickly, startled by Sariel's arrival. "Oh, it's you." The captain was apparently keeping watch, standing beside the tree where Sariel had left Dochin.

"Where is everyone?" Sariel asked, trying to hold back a coughing fit.

"Down by the creek, getting water."

Sariel's lungs burned, beginning to tremble as he looked out across the forest to the north and verified that the Kaliel were still camped for the day. Then a cough spilled out, and one led to another, soon becoming many. When it was over, Sariel was hunched forward with his hands on his knees.

"You are still very sick. Where is this healing place you mentioned?"

Sariel kept his head down. His eyes were watering and he kept them closed until he had taken several deep breaths without incident. Then he stood up straight. "To the north. One of those mountains is taller than the rest."

Unnrik turned to look along the ridge of black that stretched into the distance. "How will this mountain help you?"

Sariel wiped the moisture from his eyes. "It's difficult to explain."

Unnrik stared, stroking his beard.

"Is it my turn to take watch?"

"Not yet," Unnrik answered. "I just started. You should rest more."

Sariel considered the suggestion, but his current alertness told him that he wouldn't be able to fall asleep again. The healing he needed would only be obtained by reaching the stump. After excusing himself, he left the captain at his lookout point and walked down to the creek that ran near their camp. He found the rest of the group gathered in a flat area where there was no undergrowth.

Wekesa was standing near the water with a spear balanced over his shoulder.

Dochin and his warriors were watching carefully, their weapons lying out behind them on a patch of bare soil.

"It is the elbow that you aim with," the young man said. "Not the spear. The spear will go where the elbow leads." Then he reached back and threw his spear into the creek, where it stuck in the sandy bed. "Of course, this only works for short distances. To throw it far is a very different motion."

As Wekesa ran to retrieve his spear, Sariel sat down on a rock to watch. He noticed that Shikoba and his men also had their bows out and strung. It appeared that his traveling party was learning from one another. Though the focus of their efforts was obviously hunting and battle, Sariel could see that other things were being learned along the way—these men of various cultures were learning to respect one another. And this brought a smile to his face.

27

The stars were bright overhead. The moon was low on the western horizon, its silver crescent just visible between the crags of the mountains. Sariel and his companions were on their eighth night of travel by land, and they had become accustomed to it. Shikoba no longer needed to look back at the strangers riding his horses; they were competent enough and they weren't strangers anymore. Sariel kept his eyes forward, tracking the spirits of the Kaliel that were brighter than the landscape of the Borderlands. No one knew exactly how he was able to see them, but they didn't question it. When they were gaining on the Kaliel and needed to slow down, Sariel informed Shikoba. When they were falling behind, he needed only to whisper. But even those adjustments were becoming unnecessary; Shikoba had learned the pace of their enemies and knew how to match it with his horse even though he couldn't see them.

In the early morning hours, Sariel lost sight of the Kaliel, which had happened many times in the past week. As he watched the space between two hills where they would reappear, he counted in his head. But this time, the dull glow of spirits never reappeared.

"I don't see them," he whispered.

Shikoba looked back over his shoulder.

Sariel pointed. "They should have come out of the valley between those two hills."

Shikoba looked north for a moment before responding. "Are you sure?"

"Yes."

"Perhaps they turned. You'll be able to see when we reach the start of the valley."

Sariel didn't reply. He kept his vision focused on the far side of the valley where the terrain of the Borderlands matched that of this world. He shifted his perspective fully to the Eternal, but there was nothing to see. The gradual rises and depressions of the land created many hiding places.

"Should we speed up?"

"No," Sariel answered. "I don't want to ride into a trap. Let's keep this pace for now."

They walked the horses another third of an hour, crossing a meadow and winding through another stand of trees until the terrain began descending. With each passing second, the valley became more visible from the Eternal. After a moment, they had moved beyond the immediate obstructions, but the Kaliel were gone. Shikoba looked back and Sariel shook his head.

"No matter. I can track their footprints," the horseman whispered, pulling his animal to a stop.

Sariel's horse stopped as well. "Something is wrong," he replied. He looked down at the ground, seeing just the faintest hint of illumination drifting across the land in the Eternal. It was like the smoke of a tiny flame, barely visible unless one knew where to look.

"What's wrong?" Wekesa whispered from behind.

Sariel climbed down from his horse. "I can't see them anymore."

"What does that mean? Are we lost?"

Sariel held up his finger as he looked closely along the ground. He picked up the faint trail of their passage again and followed it forward until he passed Shikoba, who had also dismounted.

"What do you see?" the horseman asked.

"They've come through here, but I'll need to stay on the ground if we're going to track them."

Shikoba nodded, then signaled to his men that everyone else should stay on their horses.

As Sariel walked down into the shallow valley, Shikoba moved silently behind him. The horses followed their master without him pulling on their reins.

Sariel watched the drifting spiritual residue lead straight down into the valley, slowly dissipating with each moment. He followed, periodically glancing in all directions to make sure that the enemy didn't suddenly reappear where they were least expected. When they reached the bottom of the valley, Sariel stopped.

"What is it?"

"Their trail diverges into three."

Shikoba bent down to inspect the soil in the faint light of the stars. "You're right. That one goes northwest. This one straight west, and ..."

"That one to the southwest," Sariel added.

"So they *did* turn."

"Yes, but why would they split up?"

"Perhaps they delivered the offering to their demon god and went their separate ways."

It was possible, but Sariel hadn't sighted Rameel's spirit. Instinct told him it was for some other reason. He turned around and walked back to Dochin, who was still mounted. "Have your blades ready," he said.

"Why? What's happening?" Unnrik asked.

"The Kaliel split into three groups when they reached this valley. We need to be ready in case they double back on us."

"What do you suggest?" Shikoba asked, walking up from behind.

Sariel turned and looked over the clumps of shrubbery that dotted the valley. Then he looked to the mountains in the west. They were still a few days south of the Tree, which was Sariel's first priority. It was possible that Rameel would be found to the west or southwest where the other trails led, but Sariel didn't want to verify it with this frail body as his only resource. "Let's follow the one to the northwest."

Shikoba nodded. "You lead the way."

Sariel looked back to the rest of the men on their horses. "Keep your eyes moving and listen for anything that sounds unnatural. If you spot anything, tell me. But do it quietly."

Without waiting for a response, Sariel turned and began following the trail to the northwest. As he stepped cautiously around bushes and wove through a thin stand of trees, he realized that this was what Rameel and Arakiba had done for centuries when tracking him in the old world.

The trail led up the other slope of the valley at an angle, turning west to parallel the lip before finally veering due north and disappearing over the edge. As Sariel came up through the bushes, he got down on his hands and knees and crawled.

Shikoba held up his hand to halt the procession below him in the valley.

Sariel came up to higher ground, scanning the terrain in all directions. But the land continued rising through a dense forest. He stood and waved Shikoba forward before continuing. Another hundred paces brought him to the top of a hill and a clearing. As Sariel walked up the last few paces, taking the highest vantage possible, the rest of the procession was just coming out of the trees.

There was a dull glow on the horizon to the northwest, and Sariel breathed a sigh of relief. But before he said anything to Shikoba, he saw the group was splitting into two. One half moved northwest while the other stayed in place. It was far too early for the Kaliel to be stopping for the day. Perhaps they had reached their destination. But why then would the other half still be moving? As Shikoba came up beside him, Sariel noticed another glow from the corner of his vision. He turned his head to the west and saw that there was another group of Kaliel at the foothills of the mountains.

"What do you see?" Shikoba asked.

The horses came into the center of the clearing, but no one else dismounted yet. They were all watching Sariel closely.

"Some are there, to the northwest. And another group is there," he answered, pointing due west. As soon as the words left his mouth, he spotted the third group. "The remainder are over there, against the mountains."

"Good," Unnrik replied.

"What is this look on your face?" Shikoba asked.

Sariel kept glancing from one group of enemies to another. "They're not moving."

"Isn't it still two hours yet until sunrise?" Wekesa asked.

Sariel nodded. All of a sudden, the areas of darkness between the groups began twinkling with other dull points of light. "Oh no!"

"What?" Shikoba asked.

Sariel kept watching, now seeing the concentrated groups beginning to spread out.

"What are you seeing?" Wekesa asked.

The fear in the young man's voice emphasized his innocence, and Sariel felt himself moving out of an observation mindset and into one of defense. "There are more than just the three groups now. And they're spreading out."

"How many Kaliel?" Dochin asked.

"It looks like ... perhaps sixty or seventy in all."

"Do they know we're here?" Wekesa asked.

"Yes. They've spread out into a line and they're coming this way. We all need to get ready."

"That's so many!" Unnrik replied.

One of Shikoba's men tossed him his bow. As soon as the horseman caught it, he began unwinding the cord that was wrapped around its length. Within seconds, he had the weapon strung.

Dochin and his men already had their swords unsheathed, and they were talking rapidly to each other in their native tongue.

"What should I do?" Wekesa asked.

Dochin suddenly removed the narrow, double-bladed ax slung across his back. "Unnrik. You will need this if they come in close."

"What should I do?" Wekesa asked again, panic rising in his voice.

"Hold on," Sariel said, patting the young man's leg. "Unnrik, you and Molke give your spears to the horsemen. Dochin, have your warriors give axes to the rest. Shikoba, you and your men will need something to swing when your arrows are gone."

The horseman nodded, then glanced at Wekesa. "The boy speaks for all of us. What should we do?"

Sariel glanced at the Kaliel again, noting the pace with which they were closing in. Then he looked to the sky. He hadn't seen any sign of Rameel for the duration of this journey, and to his knowledge, only Rameel was capable of seeing from the Eternal. The Kaliel must have somehow realized they were being followed, but there was no way for them to have determined the size and configuration of Sariel's group. He would have spotted them if they had come close enough to gather that information. This meant that a diversion might work.

"Gather some wood. We need to make a fire," he answered.

"What?" Unnrik asked.

"Won't a fire make us more visible?" Wekesa asked.

"Yes," Sariel answered, reaching up to the saddle of his own horse. "It will draw their attention."

"Why would we want to do that?" Dochin asked.

Sariel removed the scepter from his saddle and began unwrapping it. "I'll explain after the fire is going. Now, please, someone gather wood."

Unnrik jumped down off his horse and jogged over to the trees at the east side of the clearing. Shikoba ran after him. When they came back, each had an armful of branches and downed timber.

"Pile it there," Sariel said, pointing to the center of the clearing.

"We're going to need more," Unnrik said to Dochin, who was already running toward the tree line.

"I'll get it started," Wekesa offered, climbing down from his horse. He removed something from his saddle that Sariel assumed was the flint and steel he'd purchased in Nijambu. He hadn't yet had the opportunity to use it.

Sariel kept looking back and forth across the western horizon. The Kaliel were moving slowly, as if they were cautious of whoever had entered their lands. And their caution was warranted; any intruders who set foot inside the boundaries of the underworld had done so intentionally, and were therefore likely to have the means of protecting themselves.

When Dochin came back with an armful of branches and dried grasses, Wekesa waved him over to where he had already begun stacking the materials in order of size, leaving plenty of space for the air to flow through it. It was clear that the young man had lit many fires in his short life.

Sariel removed a blanket from his saddle as he explained his intentions. "There aren't any Kaliel to the east. Perhaps they intend to drive us toward the ocean ... I can't be certain. But after the fire is lit, I want all of you to take the horses and wait in the trees over there. Stay mounted, and keep the animals quiet. You cannot let the Kaliel know you are here. I will stay by the fire and draw their attention to me. They're moving now in a thin line that stretches from there to there," he said, pointing along the foothills to the west. "As they come in closer, they'll have to close their ranks."

Dochin was the only one who nodded at this.

"They'll start to move in toward each other and become one large group."

Now everyone was nodding.

"Shikoba, when you see the fire flare up, have your men start shooting at the ones on the perimeter. When you're out of arrows, have everyone ride out of the trees and move around this hilltop in a circle. If you can, spread out and keep the Kaliel inside the clearing." Sariel turned his attention now to the whole group. "Cut down anyone in your way and anyone who tries to leave. Do all of you understand?"

"What about you?" Wekesa asked, pausing between breaths as he blew on a few glowing embers.

"Don't worry about me. Just hold onto your spear and don't fall off your saddle. Remember what Dochin said? Quick strikes. And don't let your spear get stuck in one of them."

Wekesa nodded as he sat back from the pile of wood, the embers now tiny flames licking up the sides of the branches.

"What if you ...?" Shikoba started to ask before trailing off.

"If I die," Sariel answered the unfinished question, "there's no reason for any of you to be here. You should ride as fast as possible back to where we came ashore. If you can obscure your trail along the way, do it. You'll only have to survive long enough to signal Unnrik's men. They'll sail in and pick you up."

"Are you sure you want to face them alone?" Unnrik asked.

"I won't be alone. All of you will be nearby."

The big man just stroked his beard without responding.

"Alright. The fire is going. All of you mount up and hide yourselves in the trees. Shikoba?"

"Yes?" the horseman replied.

"It's important that the horses don't make any noise," Sariel instructed.

"The Kaliel won't hear anything."

Each person climbed back onto their horse and Shikoba led them into the trees on the east side of the clearing. Within a couple minutes, Sariel was by himself on the hilltop. He turned to see that the Kaliel were steadily closing in, still coming at a cautious pace. He guessed that it would take half an hour for them to arrive. He set the scepter down on the ground and unrolled his blanket. Then he slung it over himself as if it were a cloak. As he moved around to the east side of the growing fire, he pulled the blanket over his head and arms, hiding the scepter as well as himself. Positioned with the fire between himself and the largest concentration of enemies, Sariel waited and watched them close in.

When the Kaliel finally arrived, coming in staggered clusters, they kept inside the tree line. Sariel assumed that they were waiting until all of their brethren were present. And just as he suspected, when they had all come up into the trees around the hilltop, they began making noises like animals. Screeches.

Barks. Howling. It was a fear-inducing tactic, but Sariel wasn't bothered in the least. He just waited, keeping an eye on their spirits and where they were positioned.

The ones on the north and south extremities of their ranks began moving sideways, slowly encircling the hilltop, moving closer to the trees on the east side.

Sariel lowered his head.

The Kaliel stopped their flanking motions. Their howling became louder.

Sariel began to shake his head.

The movement elicited another response from the Kaliel, whose noises now included grunting as well.

Sariel still couldn't see them with his temporal vision, but he was more convinced than ever that the Kaliel were human. Their spirits were duller than most, but there was no mistaking the way the drab colors swirled around each other. The longer he let this go on, the greater the chance that the horses would become frightened. It was time to draw the enemy out of the trees.

"Be gone, you demons!" he yelled in Common, staying hidden beneath his makeshift cloak. "Go back to the underworld! I claim these lands in the name of Mwangu Rana!"

The Kaliel shouted in rage and spilled out from the tree line. All that held them back was the fear that this intruder might be something inhuman. But when Sariel yelled to them in human words, they came from their place of hiding with murder in their hearts. In the reflected firelight, their pale faces were stretched into masks of death, punctuated by glaring eyes of red. Some hobbled on all fours, while others ran upright. The swarming mass of black bodies flailed with claws and wings, moving toward Sariel like a wave of nightmares.

When the first ones were only a dozen paces away, Sariel threw off his cloak and stabbed at the air with his scepter. The campfire exploded, sending sparks to the sky as tongues of flame shot out toward the creatures.

The front lines of the Kaliel were suddenly engulfed, and their advance faltered.

"I claim this land!" Sariel shouted, jabbing his scepter at the crowd. With each thrust, another flame shot out from the fire. When the center of the opposing force had been halted, he began sending flames to both flanks, but only toward the front of their lines. And each time, he yelled a challenge that would stir up their anger. He wanted to keep their ranks contained and pinned down, without making himself seem like too great an adversary. As one creature after another was ignited like a torch, Sariel could see others among them dropping to the ground, pierced by arrows.

Seconds later, the sound of horses' hooves could be heard beating against the soil. Shikoba was the first to ride into view. He came from the left, riding along the tree line at the back of the Kaliel forces. He had a Syvak spear in his grip and was stabbing at the Kaliel on the ground beside his horse. One of Dochin's men followed, slashing down with his sword. One after another, they appeared, with Wekesa in the rear position.

Sariel began swinging the scepter from side to side, scattering embers and flames in all directions.

The middle ranks of the Kaliel weren't even aware of the horses moving behind them. They just kept pushing forward, eager to slay the man who dared to face them in their own territory.

Sariel attacked just enough to keep them from rushing in, giving his companions on horseback time to spread out from each other. When Shikoba came out from behind the right flank, Sariel pulled his eternal body back to himself, allowing the fire to return to its normal state. With most of the fuel used up, the flames nearly died out.

The hilltop suddenly plummeted into darkness.

A crowd of spirits glowed like embers before Sariel, and he rushed forward into the chaos, swinging the scepter like a sword. The crystalline material smashed easily through his enemies. He thought of Ebnisha's scorched body, hanging from the tree in front of his dwelling, and the memory powered his attack. He struck and dodged, spinning under and between his enemies as they fell dead at his feet. He heard the sound of a horse cry out in pain, but there was no time to stop. Enemies came at him, clawing for his face. He shattered their bones and severed their limbs. Mouths were opened wide with sharpened teeth to tear his flesh. He broke their jaws and sent their heads rolling across the meadow. With each death, spirits dissipated into the sky like smoke. The Kaliel reacted like animals, moving toward the sound of commotion and the glitter of starlight that shone within their midst. But Sariel's instincts were precise, forged in the fires of an ageless existence and honed through countless battles. He moved deep into their undisciplined ranks, smashing everything around him as he drew their attention.

His heart raced, pounding heavier than it should.

Sariel caved in someone's skull with a downward strike.

His lungs ached, unable to draw what they needed from the cool night air.

Sariel broke someone's legs and watched them fall.

His skin burned as if he'd been set on fire.

Sariel plunged the jagged end of the scepter into someone's stomach.

The glow of the spirits began to dim.

Sariel caught his foot on something and stumbled backward.

A spirit moved in from the left.

He turned and swiped with the hand of his eternal body.

The glow broke apart and dissipated.

Something slammed into his body from the side, but it wasn't illuminated from the Eternal Realm. It was the ground; he'd fallen over. Sariel tried pushing against it, but gravity held him in place, crushing him into the musty soil and grass.

The glowing colors above him looked like trees waving in the wind. Their trunks drifted across the ground. Their branches swayed forward and back again. Limbs and leaves broke free, turning to smoke as they swirled into the sky. Then everything was dark.

28

Is this the In-Between?

Sounds were muffled. Sariel couldn't feel his body.

Only one self left?

The smell of dirt lingered. He heard shouting.

Not dead.

"There he is!"

Can't see anything.

"He's over here!"

"Old Man? Are you hurt?"

Why can't I see anything?

"Turn him over!"

"Old Man?"

Sariel couldn't make sense of what he heard, but he knew they were voices. The odor in his nostrils was familiar, but he couldn't remember exactly what it was. Suddenly, the darkness left him and he saw silhouettes against a starry sky.

"There's no blood!"

"Old Man?"

"Let me see!" shouted the voice of Wekesa.

Sariel turned his head toward the familiar sound, and one of the silhouettes began to make sense to his eyes.

"Saba. Can you hear me?"

"Yes," he managed to say.

"Are you injured?"

Sariel could feel the burning in his lungs, but the rest of his body still hadn't returned to his control. "I ... don't know."

"Sit him up," Wekesa ordered.

Sariel felt his body being lifted. "Are they dead?"

"The Kaliel are gone," Wekesa answered. "Don't worry about that now."

"All of them?"

"All of them," answered Dochin from somewhere out of sight. "We did it."

"Did we lose anyone?"

"Molke is dead," Unnrik answered.

Shikoba suddenly appeared in front of Sariel's face. "I lost Eyota as well."

"And two of the horses," Dochin said.

"Another horse has cuts on its legs, but it will heal," Shikoba added.

Unnrik stepped forward and looked down at Sariel. "You don't look well. I'll get you some water."

"No," Sariel protested.

"Food?"

"No, we have to leave."

"You're not going anywhere right now," Unnrik replied.

Sariel shook his head and was surprised by his ability to do so. "The other half of the north group is still moving away from here."

"Let them go," Unnrik replied. "You are in no condition to face the demon god anyway."

"That's why we need to catch up with them. They're heading toward the healing place. It's nearby, and if Rameel is there, they'll warn him about us."

"Who?" Unnrik asked.

"The demon god."

"You are not well, Old Man." Dochin said. "You will die if we move you."

Sariel could see everyone around him now. And he was starting to regain a bit of his strength. "I'll make it."

"Haven't you had enough of these demons?" Shikoba asked. The horseman's face was faintly illuminated by the light of a single flame still burning under one of the stacked logs. The flame was small, but it could be made bigger.

"Bring me one of the Kaliel," Sariel told him.

"What?" Shikoba asked.

Sariel looked up to Unnrik. "Drag one of their bodies over here by the fire."

Unnrik tapped Dochin on the shoulder and the two men went out into the darkness.

"What are you doing, Saba?" Wekesa asked.

"Just wait."

Unnrik and Dochin came back, dragging the body of a demon across the ground. When they reached the pile of scorched wood, they dropped it beside Sariel and wiped their hands on their clothing before stepping away.

Sariel reached toward the flame, and it grew to engulf the other logs. Orange light spilled outward, revealing the clearing and the surrounding trees.

Everyone stepped back.

Sariel leaned forward, away from one of Dochin's men who had been holding him upright. He looked down on the still face of Rameel's follower. The skin of its face was pale, like hot ash, but there were also clumps of white material stuck in its hairline. The area around its eyes was red, but it was clearly not the skin itself—it was painted. Sariel reached over and smudged the red color into the white. "You see? He's human."

Wekesa leaned forward to take a closer look.

Sariel's hand went down to the man's chest where pale bones had been sewn onto the outside of a black, leather tunic. "And this is just clothing."

Unnrik, Shikoba, and Dochin all stepped forward and leaned down to the body.

"These are the claws that you feared would tear away your flesh," Sariel said, lifting the man's arm. Each finger of the man's leather glove had been fitted with long, curving bones that were sharpened at the ends.

Dochin reached out. "Wings," he said, taking hold of a long, thin bone lying on the ground beneath the man. As he pulled, other bones became visible, pivoting at their ends like joints. All of the pieces were attached to others with strips of leather, expanding into a lattice-like structure. And between them were thin, translucent folds of some material that looked like the stomach lining of an animal.

Sariel nodded. "Behold … your demon of the underworld—a creature so terrible that men will not even sail within sight of its domain."

Unnrik smiled before smoothing the hair below his chin.

"As I promised … just another piece of land. And the demons are nothing more than men in disguise. If you noticed, the Kaliel weren't even carrying any weapons besides these claws."

Shikoba straightened up and smiled.

Dochin grunted, whether out of shame for his previous fears or simple agreement, Sariel couldn't tell.

"Put me on a horse," Sariel added. "We have to catch them."

~

Sariel's body jolted uncontrollably. It was all he could do to simply hold on to the saddle as his horse galloped after the rest of its team. The sun was a handbreadth above the horizon, casting long shadows through sparse forests and across open fields. Sariel ignored the barrage of bright colors and shadows, concentrating only on the dull embers that bounced before a dark landscape in his eternal vision. The Kaliel were out there, but he didn't have the strength to tell anyone.

"There!" Shikoba shouted, still in the lead position.

The remainder of his men called out their acknowledgments with whistling noises. Then they set reclaimed arrows to their bowstrings.

Sariel looked to his right and found Wekesa, paralleling him with a short spear clutched in one hand.

Dochin's men pulled their swords free of their scabbards, sending reflected sunlight across Sariel's vision.

"They see us!" Unnrik yelled from Sariel's left side, pointing with his long spear.

Sariel looked ahead and saw a small band of dark figures running into the trees at the end of a clearing. He shifted his sight toward the Eternal and watched their spirits break away from each other and head in multiple directions. One fell and rolled along the ground, but the others didn't notice.

Shikoba's horsemen somehow made their horses to gallop faster than before, pulling away from the group to speed across the clearing. Dochin's men tried to keep up. Within seconds, the horsemen entered the trees and split up, each following a different enemy. Dochin's men were close behind, veering left to track the ones who had gone in that direction. Sariel watched the convergence of spirits as the Kaliel were hunted down. One by one, each dull apparition dissolved into the red sky of the Borderlands.

The horsemen whistled to each other. The warriors shouted in their native tongue. Unnrik, Wekesa, and Sariel entered the forest at the same time and their horses slowed to a trot without any detectable reason. The distant ring of steel could be heard. Someone cried out in pain before the noise was silenced. The horses came to a stop.

"Is that all of them?" someone shouted.

"These two are dead," someone replied.

The trees were thick, and it was difficult to tell where the voices were coming from.

"This one's down," another answered.

"Old Man? Where are you?"

"Over here!" Sariel yelled, exerting himself just to make the sound.

"Are they all dead?" the voice asked. It was Shikoba, but it sounded as though he were quite far away.

Sariel scanned the area and found a glow at the base of a tree a few dozen paces away. But he didn't have the strength to yell again.

Wekesa was staring intently at Sariel. "Do you see anything?"

"There," he mumbled, raising a feeble hand.

Unnrik nudged his horse, but it wouldn't turn around.

Wekesa jumped off his animal and ran in the direction that Sariel had pointed. His short, nimble frame disappeared almost immediately from temporal sight into the trees.

Shikoba suddenly rode into view through the trees from the opposite direction. "Are there more?"

"Over there," Unnrik replied, tilting his head.

As more of the horsemen and warriors reappeared, Shikoba rode past and went in the direction that Wekesa had gone. Unnrik's horse turned and began following, taking the sailor by surprise and throwing off his balance. He quickly grabbed hold of the saddle to steady himself. Sariel's horse also turned and started following Unnrik's.

When they caught up with the others a moment later, the group had come to a stop. Most had dismounted, and their horses were grazing. Sariel leaned his head to one side in order to see through the small crowd.

Wekesa was kneeling on the ground before a dark-skinned girl in a long, white, linen tunic. She cowered in his presence, clinging to the bark of a tree as she cried.

"It's alright. You're safe now," Wekesa said to her in Common.

The girl's eyes were closed, and Sariel could see the circular brand of the Kaliel that had been burned into her forehead. The flesh was pink and raised, indicating that it had been done recently.

"The Kaliel won't hurt you anymore," Wekesa said, his voice softer than Sariel had heard before. "You don't need to cry."

The girl opened her eyes.

"They weren't demons. They were just men, and they're all gone now."

The girl wiped at her eyes, but stayed hunched against the tree.

"You're safe now," Wekesa assured her.

The girl was no longer crying, but her eyes were moving quickly from face to face, evaluating this group of strangers.

"I am from Matunda," Wekesa said. "It is a few days south and east of Nijambu. Have you heard of Matunda?"

The girl looked back to Wekesa and shook her head.

"Where are you from?"

She inspected a few more faces before looking at Wekesa again. "Dagjani."

"Oh, yes! That is on the northern coast," Wekesa replied.

The girl's face softened just a bit.

"Are you hurt?"

She thought carefully before shaking her head.

"Are you hungry? We have food."

She nodded.

"Forgive me," Wekesa said, putting his hand against his chest. "I am Wekesa. What is your name?"

"Ualiyo," she replied, her voice barely above a whisper.

Wekesa smiled and extended his hand. "Come, Ualiyo, you're safe now."

Ualiyo looked around at the strange men once more before she reached out and took hold of Wekesa's hand.

29

The mountain range of black stone that paralleled the coastline had been the group's directional reference for most of their journey across the land. Hours after the rescue of Ualiyo, the range's tallest peak had become visible over the trees to the north, and the directional reference had become a specific objective. They traveled by day and camped during the night. The normal schedule had given Sariel many hours of undisturbed sleep, helping him recover to the point that he felt as strong as the day they had come ashore. They traversed meadows and forests that looked the same as all the other terrain they'd encountered, but with each new day, the mountain was a bit larger and more ominous than the previous.

It had taken three days to reach it, and now Sariel and his companions sat atop their horses in a thick stand of trees near the base of the mountain. The morning air was cool, with only a few clouds blocking the slanting rays of light. Sariel's objective rose from the surrounding environment in a conical shape, with long, flat slopes that converged at a narrow peak. Everyone stared at the unusual sight through a gap in the forest canopy. Sariel was the only one who knew what it contained, and he couldn't help but feel anxious about it. His second self was already in place, waiting just beyond the closed vortex in the In-Between—a body without injury. Sariel's rebirth awaited him.

Or my death, he was forced to admit.

He hadn't seen the glow of Rameel's spirit anywhere along the way. He had expected to find at least a hint of his old adversary moving through the skies at night. Perhaps catch a glimpse above the horizon, like a distant star. But there had been nothing, which was in some ways more unsettling. Where else would the Myndar be if not here among his followers? Did he have another civilization somewhere that he ruled? Some other important mission that kept him away? Or was he waiting, hiding inside the mountain?

The faint trail they had run across after rescuing Ualiyo had led them here. It had become more defined along the way, growing into a worn footpath and then a wider dirt road that led directly west to the mountain. Before leaving the road to hide among the trees, Sariel had spotted another road that split off from the first and led north. Sariel wanted to hope, based on the obvious regularity of its use, that this other road led to another important location. He wanted to hope that Rameel's dwelling was not in the same place as the tree stump. But hope could be a dangerous thing, causing one to expect something that could later get one killed.

"I've seen mountains like this before," Unnrik said quietly. "In the cold oceans to the north, there are mountains of ice with this shape. At the bottom, the soil and rocks are black."

"You have sailed that far?" Dochin asked with a furrowed brow.

Unnrik nodded.

"My country is far to the north," Dochin continued, "and my people know of these mountains of ice. They are so far away that few have ever been there and lived to speak of it."

Unnrik stroked his beard before looking away. It appeared that he was uncomfortable with Dochin's open admiration. And now even Shikoba was looking at the captain with respect.

Sariel had never seen these mountains of ice during his wandering of the earth. He'd kept away from Earth's poles, assuming that, if there were any human or animal survivors of the flooding, he would find them in more habitable places. How strange to think that Dochin's people were out there, along with so many other civilizations, and Sariel had managed to miss them all. Until he found the women from Ebnisha's village walking along the creek, Sariel had thought he was alone. The earth was truly a vast and wondrous place.

"It is said that the depths of the earth are so hot that even the rocks are melted," Sariel explained, speaking to them as Ebnisha would have. "In some places, this liquid fire comes to the surface and erupts into the air. Smoke darkens everything like clouds. Ashes and embers fall down like rain. And when the rivers of fire cool, they harden into mountains of black, like this one."

Wekesa smiled.

"Who says these things?" Shikoba asked.

"All of the peoples of the earth have stories," Wekesa replied. "Saba knows more stories than anyone."

Sariel smiled at the young man. He couldn't have said it better himself.

"Is this where the demon god lives?" Dochin asked, getting to the point of their journey.

"I don't know," Sariel admitted. "If he *is* here, I can't see him. But this is where I will be healed."

"Tell me something, Old Man," Dochin continued. "Are you from this underworld of fire?"

"That's what I was going to say," Shikoba said. "You are going back to your home where your people will heal you. That is how you were able to send the fire against the Kaliel ... it obeys you like my horses obey me."

"Is this why you were able to kill so many Kaliel by yourself, and why you can see them in the dark?" Dochin asked.

Unnrik was leaning forward in his saddle, but he didn't add to the questions that had already been asked.

Wekesa had a knowing smile on his face. Ualiyo sat behind him, her arms wrapped tightly around the young man's chest. Her eyes held a mixture of wonder and fear.

"It is a very long story that I will tell all of you someday," Sariel explained. "We don't have the time right now, but I will admit that I am not from this world. You have guessed that much already. However ... I am no demon. You have nothing to fear from me."

"Why do you want to attack this demon god?" Unnrik said, finally speaking what was on his mind.

"Because he doesn't belong in your world. As long as he's here, your kind will suffer," Sariel replied, his eyes quickly turning to Wekesa.

Dochin pulled his sword from its scabbard, and the steel rang loud over the sounds of the forest. "Then we are ready to send him back to the underworld where he belongs. How many Kaliel are we facing?"

"No," Sariel replied with a shake of his head. "My healing is something that I must do on my own. I want all of you to stay here and wait for me."

"But you need our protection. What if you are attacked along the way?" Dochin replied.

"I have enough strength to get where I'm going. If there are any Kaliel, I won't stop to battle with them. I'll be quiet and go around them."

"What if the demon god is here?" Unnrik asked.

"If he is, you won't be able to stop him or save me anyway. He's too strong. Only in my healed state will I be able to face him. Please ... let me do this. When it is finished, I will come back to you. Then we will track him down together."

Unnrik nodded.

"What if we are attacked while we wait?" Wekesa asked. It looked as though the force of Ualiyo's grip around his body is what had inspired the question.

Sariel stood in his stirrups and leaned from side to side until he found what he was looking for—a spur of the mountain that stuck out to the southeast like a finger. "You see that forested hill, there?"

Everyone turned to look except Wekesa.

"It will allow you to see the land in every direction. Hide yourselves in the trees and make no sounds to reveal that you are there. If you are discovered, that will be the best place to defend yourselves."

"How long should we wait?" Shikoba asked.

Sariel glanced up at the mountain, trying to estimate the distance. The Kaliel apparently didn't move around in the daylight unless they were being chased, so everyone would hopefully be safe as long as the sun was up. "Wait until nightfall. If I haven't returned by then, ride hard to the east until you reach the shore, then go south for Unnrik's ships. All of you know how to ride now, and you also know that the Kaliel are not to be feared above any other men."

The group was silent, likely considering the realities of having to make such a hasty retreat.

Sariel climbed down from his horse and pulled the scepter out from behind his saddle. As he began unwrapping the coverings that kept it hidden, he noticed Wekesa climbing down as well.

The young man walked over to Sariel and spread his arms.

Sariel smiled and embraced his friend, stooping to put his forehead against Wekesa's.

"I will tell Mosi what you have done for us if ..."

"Don't worry; I'll come back," Sariel whispered, hoping that it wasn't a lie. From the corner of his eyes, he could feel Ualiyo's stare. "And you'll be fine either way."

Wekesa let go and stepped back, his eyes glossy with tears.

"Stay in the trees and keep your weapons ready," Sariel told them all. Then he removed the last bit of the scepter's covering and laid it over his saddle. "I'll see you before nightfall."

He turned away without another word and disappeared into the forest. Keeping inside the trees and hidden from any Kaliel scouts, Sariel paralleled the road. It began veering northwest as it ascended the slopes of the volcano, leaving the dense forests for more sparse terrain. As concealment became harder to find, Sariel was forced to move in quick bursts. He paid close attention to the strain that it put on his body, allowing himself plenty of recovery time between each movement. The caution that it required stole away the morning quicker than expected, and by the time Sariel had followed the road to its destination on the northern face of the mountain, the sun was at its peak.

He crouched behind a gathering of shrubbery, taking deep breaths as he inspected the place where he had climbed out of the mountain over twenty-five hundred years ago. It was downslope from his position and no longer simply a wide crack in the dark earth only large enough for a man to crawl through. It was a cavern, opening into the side of the mountain like the burrow of some massive creature. But it was clearly not made by any animal. What Sariel could see of it was a perfectly flat, smooth floor that met vertical walls arching to a rounded ceiling. There was movement inside, but Sariel had to watch for a long while before he saw anything meaningful. Finally, he recognized the bone clothing of dozens of Kaliel when they came out of the shadows near the mouth of the cavern. There were also two robed individuals whose faces were hidden by the cowls of their cloaks. They moved with more confidence than the others and appeared to be in charge of whatever was happening inside the cavern.

It quickly became apparent that Sariel wouldn't get inside the mountain through this route without having to fight or create a distraction that would attract everyone's attention away from him. Neither option was quiet, which was how he intended to keep this mission. He had already passed a similar cavern on the eastern face of the mountain, but it too had been occupied. The only other way that he knew of to reach the remains of the Tree of Wisdom was the large hole that ran straight through the cavern ceiling above it. Sariel remembered clinging to the stump, submerged in floodwaters, looking up through the hole at a cloudy sky. The thought of climbing down into that place from such a great height seemed impossible, given his current weakness, but what other option did he have?

Sariel left his hiding place and traversed the eastern face of the mountain, circling away from the mouth of the cavern before venturing upslope. As he climbed, the soil became thinner and vegetation nonexistent. Long slabs of rock were exposed to the sky, covered in areas by scree. Finding decent footing became the biggest challenge, as slipping and falling would only draw attention, and he didn't have any excess strength to recover from such a mistake.

When the sun was past its zenith, Sariel took the last few steps to the crest of the mountain. But it was nothing like what he imagined. Instead of a jagged opening of sharp and broken rock, crumbling at the perimeter, he found a smooth, flat ring of polished stone. Someone had carved away the stone until a level rim was exposed. And the hole itself no longer seemed like the void created by an explosion of molten rock. It was perfectly cylindrical; someone had hollowed it out. Sariel walked forward, peering cautiously over the inside of the rim.

Steps had been carved into the inside walls—a single staircase with no railing that spiraled hundreds of times downward until it was lost to the shadows. At once, Sariel was both frightened by the realization that this path could lead him to people he wanted to avoid and relieved that there *was* a path. There was no other way to reach the stump, but committing to this would leave him trapped if he were discovered. A body of full health and strength waited for him in the shadows of this pit, so there was only one decision to make.

Sariel walked around to the west side of the opening where the first stairs were located. Without stopping or letting his fears convince him to do otherwise, he began descending into the pit one step at a time. He circled from areas of shade to sunlight and back to shade again, the air growing steadily colder as he went down. Eventually, there was only shade, and later darkness. He lost track of time without being able to see the sun. His legs began to shake from weariness, and a burning sensation grew in his lungs. Sariel knew he should stop and rest, but he felt too exposed on the open staircase. He wanted this descent to be over as quickly as possible. And so he went on, hurrying as fast as he could without slipping and falling to his death. When it became almost too dark to see, he kept one hand sliding over the cold stone of the inside wall as a physical reference.

All of a sudden, the stairs came to an end at a doorway. Sariel could tell just by the way the ambient sound had changed that a large void was open below him—he had reached the ceiling of the cavernous chamber that held the portal. Stopping only long enough to catch his breath, Sariel went through the doorway, feeling the walls of the passage with both hands now that light was completely gone. He went on for a long while before he realized that the path was curving to the right. Then his heart lurched when he stepped into open air. His foot dropped a handbreadth before making contact with the stone again. He stumbled and almost tripped, clawing the stone walls for balance. It took several minutes for his heart to return to a normal pace, and then he continued with more confidence, realizing that he had reached another staircase. Down he went, farther into the earth, curving always to the right.

Finally, the wall on the right side of the passage opened into a spherical cavern that was so large he would not have been able to see the other side without the faint light of torches. The spherical ceiling was still there as he remembered it, a great hole boring straight up through its tallest point. The daylight visible through the hole seemed bright now, whereas it had been almost too dark to see when he stood before the doorway above the ceiling. The water, which had filled the cavern level with the top of the stump, was gone. Now it truly was a sphere—the ceiling curved to become the walls, which became the floor. All of it was smooth and dark, with long lines that created a spiraled pattern as they came down from the ceiling and converged at the base of the stump. Only now, the stump looked more like a column sticking up from the floor to the exact center of the spherical void. The molten lava that had flowed through this chamber after the Fracturing had solidified around the base of the Tree, covering the roots that Sariel had witnessed in Aden.

But what Sariel found even more fascinating were the gigantic statues carved into the walls. The black stone had been cut back in areas, and where it had been left, the raised image of nine Iryllurym had been revealed. They stood with their hands and wings outstretched. Their legs pointed straight down, ending at feet that were level with the top of the stump. As Sariel walked down the last few steps between two burning torches and onto a raised platform of wood, he turned and looked up at the wall behind him. The statue above had the form of an Iryllur without battle armor, and yet the body and face of a female Myndar. It took several seconds before Sariel recognized Danel's likeness. And when he did, he immediately turned to look at the next. It was Turel. One after another, he turned and recognized each of his fellow Myndarym. On the opposite side of the cavern was a likeness larger than the others. It was too far away to make out the facial features, but Sariel could see enough of it to know that its wings were of skin and bones—not feathers. Rameel had made himself out to be the most powerful of the temporal gods. Sariel was standing in the middle of a three-dimensional depiction of the Kaliel symbol—the very same one that had been drawn in ink on Ebnisha's scroll and burned into Ualiyo's forehead. This was no longer just a cavern; it was a temple.

Sariel shook his head as a physical way of refocusing his thoughts. He hadn't come here to marvel at the skill of masons or the crafting of a building. He had something far more important to do.

The platform on which he stood grew narrow as it left the wall, becoming a bridge that spanned the lower hemisphere of the cavern. It was wide, but had no railings, making it treacherous like the spiraling stairs above. Sariel took a few bouncing steps to test the strength of the wooden columns that supported it. When he was satisfied that it would hold him, he began walking out into the cavern. His steps quickened, and he began to jog, paying attention to the strength of his lungs. As he neared the center, he saw that the bridge split into two paths, encircling the lip of the stump. Another bridge extended from there to the opposite side of the cavern. Sariel came to a stop just two paces from the edge of the stump. Its black surface glittered like moonlight where the shattered rings of the Tree were visible.

Sariel looked down at the scepter in his hands—a missing piece being returned to its home. He suddenly realized that he didn't know how to use this key. There were no keyholes or features that he could see carved into the stump. Perhaps it didn't work that way. He thought of his time in Third Earth, when Ezekiyel and the other spirits gathered around the stump in that world's portal chamber. Except for Danel, Turel, and Arakiba, the rest had disappeared in a matter of seconds. When Sariel had finally managed to sneak into the chamber, the fragment of the Tree was also gone. And there were none of these keys lying around or stuck into the stump as they might have with a crude lock built by human hands. Ezekiyel had gone from world to world, closing each vortex as he crafted these keys. In order for him to get back through the sealed vortex of his own world, he must have carried his key with him.

Sariel held out the scepter and walked forward, watching the surface of the Tree for any signs of change. All the other times he'd entered the In-Between, there had been an aura of blue light and the sensation of an immense pressure upon all sides of his body. As his foot left the wooden platform, his senses were straining, anticipating what was about to take place.

The faint sound of wind reached his ears. It was sudden and unexpected, causing him to flinch. The moment he realized the sound was coming from behind him was the same moment he felt something slam into his body. The force of it knocked the air from his lungs and the scepter from his hand. As his body pitched forward and tumbled through the air, he heard a clattering sound like glass that couldn't be broken. Then his body hit another hard surface and he felt a cracking sensation. He hoped it was the wooden planks of the bridge and not his bones.

30

Wekesa sat beside Ualiyo, both of them leaning back against the clustered trunks of an unknown sapling species. Ualiyo had just finished telling him about her village, but she'd hardly made eye contact with him the whole time. Now her head was down and turned slightly away.

Wekesa took out his brother's knife and made a cut in the bottom of his tunic. Then he used his hands to rip the fabric.

"What are you doing?" Ualiyo asked.

The tear followed the weaving lines, resulting in a strip that was still attached at both ends. Wekesa used the knife again to sever the ends before extending the strip to Ualiyo. "To put around your head."

She frowned.

"I don't mind, but you seem embarrassed by it."

She reached out slowly and took the fabric.

"Your eyes are beautiful. I would like to look at them when we talk," he added.

Now Ualiyo smiled. As she bent forward to wrap the covering around her forehead, Wekesa looked out to see Unnrik pacing among the trees. The large, pale man was whispering to himself and swinging Dochin's ax from side to side in slow strokes. It looked like he was practicing what the warrior had taught him. He took a step, swung the ax, stepped back, then swung it in the opposite direction. The muscles of his thick arms rippled each time he moved. Then he spun around and jabbed with the Syvak spear he had in his other hand.

"Stop moving around so much," Shikoba said in a harsh whisper from farther away.

Unnrik glared at him and shrugged.

Shikoba shook his head and looked away. He and his men were spread out through the trees, their fingers resting on their bowstrings. They hardly moved at all, and when they did it was a slow, crouching movement, as if they were stalking prey. Their eyes searched the trees around the hilltop, the only part of their bodies that was constantly moving. The horseman looked over to the other side of the hilltop and whistled a gentle, warbling sound that Wekesa would have mistaken for the trill of a bird.

Dochin turned and looked at Shikoba before shaking his head. The lead warrior and his men hadn't found any reasons for alarm yet.

Wekesa looked up to the sky. Sunset was just over an hour away, and Saba hadn't come back yet. He hoped that the old man was being healed and that they wouldn't have to leave without him. He wanted to go home as soon as possible, but not without Saba. The thought of going back through the Kaliel lands and across the sea without the old man's wisdom and protection was something he would only face if it were forced upon him. That choice would come at sunset, but until then, he would concentrate on the beautiful distraction sitting next to him.

Ualiyo had the strip of fabric in place now. She turned and noticed Wekesa staring, and her face lit up with a smile.

Wekesa looked away, suddenly embarrassed. Then he smiled too as he realized how quickly their situations had reversed.

* * * *

INSIDE THE TEMPLE OF THE KALIEL

Sariel rolled across the bridge, coming to a stop on his back. From one corner of his vision, he caught just the briefest glimpse of large, black wings before they rose into the shadows near the ceiling. From the other corner of his vision, he saw a faint blue light. Sariel rolled over and tried to push himself up, but something was wrong with his balance. A second after he realized it was due to his right arm, a searing pain shot up from his wrist. Sariel looked down and winced, finding that one of his hands was missing. He was pushing against the wooden planks of the bridge and blood was gushing out from his wrist where his hand used to be. It was a shocking sight, but something he didn't have time to consider properly; death was coming for him. He rose to his feet and tucked the injured limb beneath his other arm, squeezing it as hard as he could to stop the flow of blood.

Movement drew his eyes upward, where he watched Rameel descend from the ceiling and land with outstretched wings on the bridge near the cavern wall.

The landing sent vibrations through the wood, which Sariel felt in his legs.

The Myndar's skin was as black as the walls of the cavern, but the weapon he held in one hand glittered like starlight. It was a dagger, held in a reverse position, with the blade facing upward along his forearm.

Several realizations flashed through Sariel's mind. His hand had just been severed by that weapon. The way Rameel held the dagger reminded Sariel of a vaepkir. Rameel was almost twice as tall as him, and yet he looked less imposing than the Iryllur soldier he was trying to imitate. Sariel was injured, perhaps fatally, but there was still some strength left in this doomed body. All of these thoughts occurred at once, but the last one lingered. It was the response of a warrior. There was no more time left. Attack or die.

Sariel began running across the bridge toward Rameel.

The Myndar squinted as if he couldn't believe his eyes. Then he reached out with one hand.

Sariel felt it before he saw it—the hairs on his body stood up, and his skin began to itch. Then the air before his eyes turned orange. The sight of Rameel wavered before disappearing altogether. It wasn't until he felt the burning sensation that Sariel realized the orange color was fire. He ran straight into it, shifting his perspective toward the Eternal. The bright glow of Rameel's spirit was there, floating above the desolate landscape. The flames poured from his outstretched hand like a torrent of dark water.

Sariel reached out and sent his own spirit forward, separating it from his physical body. His perspective went with it, speeding through the flames toward his enemy. His hands, both intact in this realm, brightened into points of light that grew to include his forearms. He brought them up and crossed them, pushing back the flow of the enemy's attack.

All of a sudden, the flames disappeared from Sariel's temporal vision. He was still running across the bridge, the smell of burned hair and clothing thick in his nostrils. His injured arm was outstretched, the open flesh now charred. The fire that was being pushed aside by his eternal body spread out in all directions, flying toward the ceiling and walls. The flames that were shooting down ignited the bridge. As Sariel caught up to the retreating wall of flames, he jumped, merging with his eternal body again. His whole self flew through Rameel's fiery attack and came out the other side, both legs landing squarely against the Myndar's chest.

The flames evaporated and Rameel stumbled backward, hardly affected.

Sariel's body, having come to an abrupt stop, fell immediately to the bridge. He tried to roll in order to absorb the impact, but he landed awkwardly on his elbow and shoulder, just managing to keep the air from being knocked out of his lungs. From the ground, he quickly spun and lashed out with his eternal body, his kick sweeping low to shatter his enemy's leg bones.

Rameel lifted his leg, letting the attack pass harmlessly through the air below it. Then he bent down and grabbed Sariel by the neck, dragging his limp body into the air.

Sariel could feel the opportunity presenting itself. As he was forcefully drawn toward Rameel's face, he readied his spirit for a death blow to the head. But Rameel never stopped to glare into Sariel's eyes; he spun, heaving his enemy through the air before letting go. Sariel floated as if he had wings. Then his body smacked into the cavern wall. This time, there was no doubt about the crunching sensation. His body immediately went cold, and he hardly felt any pain when he dropped half a dozen paces to the wooden platform in front of the arched passage. It all happened so fast that there hadn't been time to react. And now Sariel lay motionless on the ground.

His mind screamed at him to move, but his body wouldn't obey.

Rameel stared down, his black skin a stark contrast against the yellow flames that were rising from the bridge behind him.

Sariel pushed with his spirit, and his physical body moved. He rolled onto his stomach and pulled his legs and arms underneath him.

Rameel seemed in no hurry now; he must have known he had already won. A smile spread across his face as he watched the suffering taking place.

Sariel moved only by the power of his spirit; his physical body was unresponsive. He pushed against the platform and rose to a crouched posture. Then he hobbled into the dark passage, hoping that the movement would awaken his temporal body. He could hear Rameel's slow, deliberate footsteps behind him, but he pushed them out of his mind. The sound of his own wheezing breaths was more important; it meant that his lungs were working. He kept going, one step after another, seeking out a place from which he could turn and attack.

"We searched for so many years," Rameel said, his growling voice echoing through the stone passage.

Sariel reached an intersection and turned, picking up speed as his temporal legs began to wake from their sleep.

"Centuries, in fact. Arakiba enjoyed the hunt, but I wanted what was waiting for me at the end of it. I promised myself that I would savor the moment when I killed you ... if you ever stopped running. But you just kept going and going ... like a coward. Just like now."

Though his voice growled like an animal, the words came out in a calm manner, as if he were doing nothing more important than talking with a friend.

"That's when I knew we had you beat—the soldier who wouldn't turn and fight. The Iryllur who'd confined himself to a human body. I was going to enjoy your death. But then ... the centuries passed. This realm was multiplied, and a new world began. Learning about Baraquijal's death gave me hope that you might have survived. The Marotru said they'd find you, but they never did. So much time ... and I lost hope."

Sariel's legs were working now, but there was excruciating pain with each step. And his breathing was getting worse. He could see that his abdomen was swelling; he was bleeding internally. And each step made his ribs crunch together.

"Then Ezekiyel apparently found you in his world. Before I was even told about it, he gave Arakiba the honor of taking your head. I'm not ashamed to admit I was disappointed by that."

Sariel turned again, this time to the right. The pain in his leg caused him to stumble and he fell against the wall. There wasn't enough strength in his body to stop himself from sliding to the ground, but he refused to give up. Seeing a doorway ahead, he crawled forward. He promised himself that if he could just reach it, he would wait on the other side and pretend to die while Rameel came closer.

"I'm sure you can imagine my surprise when I felt Zaquel's hold on this world suddenly gone. It was like someone choking you and suddenly letting go. She would never have let go. She had too much ambition to kill herself, and no human is capable of doing such a thing. That's when I knew you hadn't been pulled inside the In-Between like the rest of us. You had been on the outside. You had been multiplied like the Temporal Realm. And that meant that there were two of you left. But what excited me even more was the thought that you were able to kill Zaquel. That meant you still had some fight left in you ... despite your inferior form. Or forms. That's when I knew would come for me. You've always been a traitor—more human than Myndar. Just think of it ... I will have the honor of killing you twice."

Sariel was through the doorway now. His head was pounding as though it would burst. He couldn't catch his breath, and each time he tried, a gurgling sound came out. His fever had returned, or maybe it was his scorched skin, finally regaining feeling. Either way, the stone felt cold and refreshing beneath him. All he wanted to do was stop and lay his head against it, to have a moment of peace. But he kept going, forcing his temporal body to reach out and pull, forcing his spirit to push against the ground. He slid, bones grinding against each other, charred flesh scraping across the floor. And then a wall was before him. He had come to the end of the room. There was no point trying to go left or right; his body wasn't capable of it. He stared at the wall for a moment before setting his head down. As the dark and cold stone eased the burning feeling on his face, he noticed a trail of blood stretching away from his mouth. It ran across the floor and curved out through the doorway where Rameel had just stepped into view.

"Tell me ... where is your other body? If you would like, I'll wait until you bring it here to rescue this one?"

Now was the time for Sariel to make his last stand. Rameel was close enough for an attack, and his guard was down. He summoned all the strength left in his body and pushed away from the ground with his spirit. His body rose from the floor, shaking from the exertion. He could imagine what his attack would do, what would happen when the fingers of his spirit ripped through Rameel's legs. He shoved himself away from the floor and tried to pivot, but it didn't happen the way he imagined it. His body lost all feeling and crumpled to the ground, too much of a burden for his spirit.

"Ah ... you want to have it out one body at a time? Very well. Have it your way. I'll just track the other one down. I'm patient ... and persistent. But you already know that about me." Rameel adjusted his grip on the dagger, turning it so the blade faced forward. Then he knelt down and gently placed the tip of it against the side of Sariel's ribcage.

Sariel could only watch as the crystalline blade, with only a slight amount of pressure, eased into his flesh. His heart, beating much too quickly, faltered before coming to a stop.

* * * *

OUTSIDE THE TEMPLE OF THE KALIEL

A distant howl brought Wekesa's attention back to the present. He'd been thinking about the first time Ebnisha had showed him the characters of their language in written form. Now he thought the sky looked paler than the last time he'd looked up. Sunset was fast approaching. Ualiyo had been napping, and now she sat upright with a puzzled look on her face. Shikoba also looked concerned. He kept glancing from side to side with a scowl on his face.

Another howl came through the trees, closer than the last one but from the east this time.

Dochin and his men turned their heads in that direction, before one of them slowly changed his position.

"What's happening?" Ualiyo whispered.

A barking noise sounded to the north, only a stone's throw away.

Unnrik pivoted and took a few steps in that direction.

Wekesa grabbed his spear and got to his feet.

Ualiyo crawled into the cluster of saplings she'd been leaning against and shrank down.

Another barking noise sounded to the south, at the bottom of the hill on which they were camped.

Shikoba and his men raised their bows, and lowered themselves into crouched positions.

Wekesa looked down at Ualiyo, who was shaking from fear. He felt it too, but there was something stronger than fear coursing through his body. Ualiyo had never looked so innocent as she did right now, so fragile. If anyone tried to harm her, he would put his spear through them without a moment's hesitation.

31

Rameel wiped the blood from his dagger on Sariel's tunic before standing. Then he looked down on the pathetic body that his adversary had died in. It was a disgusting sight—bloated, oozing fluids, lacking structure in certain places. It almost made him want to vomit. Then he noticed what his fire had done—the burned clothing, the charred skin, the hair and beard that were now just dark, bubbled splotches. This grotesque sight was an abomination, a defilement of his temple. But fire could purge the contamination and make the temple clean once again.

Rameel walked out of the room, stepping over the trail of blood. Then he caused the air inside the room to ignite. Waves of heat spilled out, distorting the light in the hallway. It burned like a furnace, glowing with red and orange light. Flames licked up the sides of the doorway to its arched top. Rameel backed away from the heat but stayed in the hall for a long moment, scorching the room longer than was necessary. When it was finished, he turned and walked away without bothering to look inside. He knew what he would find—fused stone and perhaps some ashes. It was no longer worth his attention.

When he got back to the portal chamber, he saw that the fire on the bridge had spread. Fortunately, the timbers were thick, and the damage was only superficial. He reached out his hand and quieted the flames, choking them until they were only thin whispers of smoke. Then he stepped over the charred wood and walked along the bridge toward the portal. With the eyes of his eternal body, he scanned the entire cavern, verifying that he was alone. He had hoped to find Sariel's remaining self, perhaps lying in wait for him, but now he considered the possibility that his last adversary wasn't even in this world. Arakiba had killed one in the throne room of Ezekiyel's city. Perhaps Sariel had one body in each world and was, at this very moment, hiding in the jungles near Armaros' village. Or spying on Kokabiel, thinking of some way to kill a Myndar who could still *shape* himself. Perhaps posing as one of the citizens of Satarel's city. There were a million possibilities, but all of them disappointing because they wouldn't end with Rameel doing the killing.

Zaquel's scepter was lying on the circular platform, just beyond the edge of the Tree. There was no sign of Sariel's severed hand, nor was there any blood. But the dagger had cut so easily through Sariel's wrist that the blood wouldn't have started flowing for several seconds afterward. Rameel came to a stop in front of the scepter. He looked down on it, trying to remember if this was where it landed. He'd heard it clatter against the surface of the portal. And he remembered seeing blue light, but after ascending to the ceiling and banking into a turn, his attention had been focused on Sariel. He looked around the cavern again, failing to see the glow of Sariel's spirit.

Perhaps the scepter hadn't been moved. Perhaps this was where it had landed after opening the portal for just a moment. Perhaps the idea that Sariel's remaining self had put it here was just false hope.

* * * *

Sariel clung to the underside of the platform encircling the stump. This feat would have been impossible with his other weakened body, but his second self had no such limitations. Rameel stood on the opposite side, with the stump itself blocking him from view. Sariel couldn't see him from his eternal perspective, because the stump existed in the Eternal Realm as well, making it the only viable concealment in the whole cavern. Hopefully, the winged Myndar was staring at the scepter. Though it had landed on the stump, it might just as easily have been thrown off the bridge to the bottom of the cavern by the momentum of Rameel's attack. After coming out of the In-Between, Sariel had placed the scepter on the platform in the same direction as it had fallen. With any luck, Rameel was thinking through the probability of where it had landed, which required at least some amount of his attention.

The disembodied spirit from Sariel's first self hadn't been pulled across the void and into the place of holding as one might expect. There was still a physical body in the Temporal to which it was attached. As Sariel clung to the wooden timbers supporting the platform, he drew this spirit toward himself. It was no different from when he had demonic underlings at his disposal in the old world. At any time, he had been able to see through their eyes and take control of their bodies if needed. Now, he simply led his other spirit from the room of his death and into the halls, retracing the path of his retreat from Rameel in just a few seconds. Through the eyes of this other spirit, he saw Rameel's eternal body come into view. The Myndar was floating above the desolate landscape of the Borderlands, but Sariel could tell by his enemy's posture that he was getting ready to bend down and pick up the scepter. This was the moment of distraction he had been waiting for. He rushed forward, rapidly closing in on Rameel from behind.

In his physical body, Sariel began climbing out from under the platform. He grabbed hold of the outer edge and prepared to pull himself up and send his second spirit forward.

With his first spirit, he rushed at Rameel's back, stirring up the air as he moved.

Rameel was crouching down to grab the scepter when he sensed that something was wrong. At the last moment, he spun around.

Sariel's second spirit was already in motion, moving over the edge of the platform and across the stump. Both sprits converged upon Rameel, with one pushing while the other pulled.

Rameel fell over and slid to the middle of the stump. The scepter remained on the bridge behind him, but the dagger was clutched in his hand.

Blue light began emanating from the surface of the stump.

Rameel started to squirm, realizing what was happening to him.

Sariel's spirits held his limbs down so he couldn't move.

Sariel's temporal body was over the edge of the platform and rising to his feet. With his temporal sight, he watched the image of the cavern waver and draw inward.

Rameel began to thrash, trying desperately to throw off the spirits that clung to him. He overpowered them enough to flip over on his stomach, but then the gravity of the portal had its grip. It began pulling him away from the Temporal Realm toward another.

Sariel released his spirits from Rameel and converged upon the dagger, wrenching it from the Myndar's grip. But the power of the portal drew them away as well. From Sariel's temporal perspective, he watched Rameel's body dissolve into the blue light that was shooting outward in all directions. The key was being pulled after him, and Sariel's spirits with it. But he refused to let go. If it ended up in the In-Between, Rameel would find it and escape. Sariel pulled with all his might, willing both of his spirits back to himself.

The cavern flashed with a blinding light, and then everything went dark.

Sariel felt the pull of the portal suddenly gone, and his physical body fell backward from the release of it. He stumbled, and then regained his footing.

The cavern was silent.

The torches had gone out, but there was a faint light coming from the hole in the ceiling.

Sariel flexed his grip and was relieved by the satisfying feeling of a solid object in his hand. He raised it, watching the dagger sparkle as it amplified what little light was available.

Only, it wasn't a dagger to his human body; it was large enough to be a sword. He glanced across the surface of the portal and found the scepter lying where he had left it. Reaching out with his other hand, he drew it around the outside of the stump until it came to him like an obedient pet. When both hands of his remaining body held the keys of his enemies, he allowed a smile to spread across his face.

What had just taken place was profound on many levels. There were hard truths to be accepted and conclusions to be drawn. Sariel knew that it required careful and considerable reflection to understand his own actions, but he was also aware of a more pressing matter. It was nearly sundown, and his friends were vulnerable outside. Just because Rameel was no longer a threat didn't mean that the Kaliel weren't. Turning away from the Tree of Wisdom, Sariel began running along the bridge. With two spirits at his disposal, his steps became light and fast. His body moved with an unnatural speed and agility. Within seconds, he was bounding up the stairs and entering the tunnel that led to the peak of the mountain. This temporal body, free of the injuries that the other one had suffered, found the physical demand of the climb to be almost imperceptible.

* * * *

OUTSIDE THE TEMPLE OF THE KALIEL

The animal noises were all around the hilltop now. Howls, barks, whistles. There seemed to be hundreds of the Kaliel, though none had yet revealed themselves. Ualiyo was covering her ears and crying. The warriors and the horsemen were steady, holding their weapons and waiting for the inevitable. Unnrik paced around Wekesa, swinging his borrowed ax slowly from side to side, anxious to make use of it. There was something about Ualiyo's terror in contrast with the readiness of the men that caused Wekesa's heart to calm. There was no way to change what was happening. No way to hide from the Kaliel. They had been discovered, and whatever was going to happen couldn't be changed. Crying wouldn't make it go away. Fear would only draw out the occasion, lengthening it with emotions that he'd rather not feel. Better to face death with something other than fear, like Ebnisha would have. Wekesa felt his heart swell with confidence, and then a righteous anger.

"YOU THINK WE ARE AFRAID OF YOU?" he yelled.

Unnrik turned his head.

Wekesa was shaking, knuckles pale around the shaft of his spear. "MEN WHO DRESS LIKE ANIMALS? SCREAM LIKE ANIMALS?"

Unnrik smiled.

Dochin turned his head and nodded.

Wekesa was pacing now, his body tense. He had such an abundance of energy that he didn't know what to do with it except to move and yell. "YOU ARE WEAK, AND WE WILL SLAUGHTER YOU LIKE THE ANIMALS YOU MIMIC!"

Dochin began banging the flat of his blade against a tree, and yelling at the top of his lungs. His warriors quickly followed his lead. The banging sound of metal rang out as a clear indication that they were armed.

The horses, who had been grazing at the center of the hilltop, were stomping their front hoofs against the ground. Their tails swished from side to side, and their ears flicked back and forth. Shikoba saw what his animals were doing and then lifted his head to the sky. He yelled with a deep-throated sound that was quickly echoed by his horsemen.

Unnrik now had a toothy grin on his face. He banged his spear and ax together, adding to the metallic warning sound.

"WE ARE NOT AFRAID OF YOU!" Wekesa yelled. He was jumping up and down as he paced, his arms ready to force his spear through someone's heart. "LET US SHOW YOU WHAT OUR BLADES CAN DO!"

The sky was growing dark, but the trees became darker still, filled with shadows. The Kaliel had the hilltop surrounded and began closing in. The twang of bowstrings sounded in response and a few of the shadows fell forward. Others stepped over the bodies and moved closer, only to fall when the next volley of arrows was loosed.

The blades of the warriors went into motion, and Wekesa watched in awe. Dochin lunged from one place to the next, his movements precise and calculated. Each time he came to a stop, several Kaliel fell to the ground. His men were spread out through the trees, and the Kaliel advance on the southern and eastern sides came to a halt. Shikoba and his men were covering the north and west. The forest on those two sides was littered with dark bodies. The horsemen had already gone through the arrows they had reclaimed from the last confrontation, and now they were swinging their axes. Unnrik was advancing north with both weapons, but the Kaliel seemed afraid of his size. They backed away before he could reach anyone.

Footsteps sounded from the east and Wekesa spun around.

Two Kaliel were running straight at him, their clawed gloves reaching.

Ualiyo screamed when she saw them.

Wekesa planted his foot and thrust his spear into the chest of the first. The painted man came to a sudden stop, and the one behind crashed into him. Wekesa was thrown backward to the ground as both men collided with him and tumbled over the top. Wekesa pushed them off and rolled as quickly as he could to his feet. When he came up, he saw that the second man was trying to crawl toward Ualiyo. Wekesa pulled his brother's knife from its sheath and pounced on the man's back, driving the blade into him again and again until he collapsed to the ground. Wekesa wrenched the knife free and spun back to the trees, ready for more. But when he turned, the battlefield had changed.

The Kaliel were yelling, not like animals, but like dying men. They were looking around in terror as something pale flew among them. It moved around the hilltop in circles, weaving through the trees with incredible speed. In its wake, the dark forms of the Kaliel dropped by the dozens. White flashes of light pulsed, and Wekesa thought he saw a Kaliel man torn in two pieces. He watched, unable to comprehend what was happening.

The Kaliel began retreating from this deadly apparition, backing down the hill. When the pale blur pursued them, moving in ever widening circles, the Kaliel turned and ran. Seconds later, the hilltop was quiet. The distant sound of running footsteps and breaking branches faded away. Wekesa looked around at the hundreds of dark shapes littering the forest. Unnrik stood among several, his weapons covered in blood. Shikoba was kneeling next to another of his fallen horsemen. Dochin was still alive, but there were only three of his warriors standing on the south slope. Where the others were, Wekesa didn't know. To his surprise, the horses hadn't run off. There were several dead Kaliel on the ground beneath them; it looked as though they had been stomped to death.

Saba came walking up through the trees on the west slope. He was breathing heavily, and his tunic was stained with blood. "Is everyone alright?" he asked, but no one responded.

The sight of him was so different from when Wekesa had seen him last, that he didn't know what to say. He just stared at the man whose head and face were no longer covered with short white hairs. This one had long hair that fell to his shoulders, and a beard that went to the middle of his chest. His tunic was a different color, made from some other material than the one Ekua had given him. His skin was no longer reddened from the sun. And his body was thicker with muscle. He looked years younger and far healthier than before.

"Saba?" Wekesa called out.

"I'm sorry I couldn't get here sooner," the old man replied as he came up to the peak of the hill.

Unnrik turned away from the trees and walked toward him.

Shikoba stood up and waved for his two remaining horsemen to come near.

Dochin came up from the south with his three warriors. As they climbed, their steps were laden with more than just fatigue.

Wekesa held Ualiyo's hand as she climbed out from the thicket where she had hidden herself. Then the two of them walked over and stopped in front of Saba.

The old man surveyed the battlefield before looking to Shikoba and Dochin with heavy eyes. "I'm so sorry. I came as fast as I could."

Both men just looked at the ground and kept silent.

"You are healed, and you have a new weapon," Unnrik said.

Saba looked down at the sword in his right hand as if he had just realized it was there. Then he slowly raised it, together with the scepter, for everyone to see. "The fighting is over. The Goddess of the Sun is dead ... and the demon god will no longer interfere with this world."

Wekesa's mouth fell open. It was almost too good to be true. "He's gone?"

"Yes," Saba replied.

"He was in the mountain?"

"It's done," Saba assured him.

Wekesa wanted to shout for joy, but he could see that Dochin and Shikoba were in no mood to celebrate.

Saba turned his attention to them. "If you want to bury your friends, or whatever custom you follow, we can stay. I'm strong now. I can protect us if the Kaliel come back."

Dochin wiped the sweat from his forehead, but didn't answer.

"He was my brother," Shikoba replied.

Saba's eyes welled with tears and he quickly shut them.

"They all died bravely," Unnrik said.

Everyone nodded.

Dochin finally looked up. "When the spirit leaves the body, the warrior is gone. We can go."

Shikoba glanced at his remaining horsemen and received nods of agreement. Then he turned to Saba. "We will take my brother's body back to the plains where his spirit can be set free."

32

It was midday, but clouds had rolled in throughout the night. There was a cool breeze, and the air smelled wet, as if it might rain at any moment. Shikoba was in the lead position again, taking the group due east toward the coast. They hadn't run into any other armies of Kaliel, and with Sariel at full strength, the ride was both faster and more enjoyable. Shikoba expected to reach the ocean by sunset, and then their progress south along the beach would become even more efficient.

As Sariel's horse galloped beside Wekesa's near the back of the group, Sariel noted how the land beneath them was fraught with deep cracks that weren't visible to temporal sight. He could see how the plates of land had overlapped one another when they were forced into each other by the strength of the floodwaters. One had gone up and the other down, allowing the lower molten regions of the earth to rise to the surface. The mountains behind them were the result of this violent collision and the subsequent eruptions. But all of this was just a distraction from the thoughts that had been running through his mind since yesterday.

The most obvious was that he was not the Awakened One spoken of in Enoch's prophecy. He suspected as much after suffering his injuries during the battle with Zaquel and her soldiers. But now it was confirmed in his mind. Rameel had killed his first self, and had exhibited such superior power in the process that Sariel knew he couldn't win. Not even with his second self at full strength. It was something that would have been hard to explain to anyone—something his Amatru superiors in the Eternal Realm would never have accepted. But Sariel knew it to be true. When he attacked Rameel and failed to even injure the Myndar, he knew he was outmatched. The frustrating thing about it was that it was only due to the physical form he'd chosen. With his training and experience, Sariel could have easily defeated Rameel had their forms been similar. He'd only been able to defeat Zaquel because she'd spent her life strengthening a different ability. She didn't know how to fight a physical battle.

The fact that Sariel had lost his first self, and the absence of confidence that came shortly after, were two proofs that he couldn't be The Awakened. And so he trapped Rameel—it was his only remaining option. The other worlds were ruled by the Myndarym, and they would surely be corrupted in time, but at least this world was now without their influence.

Or is it?

Sariel was still here. Would his influence corrupt this world? Perhaps it would be best for him to sail as far away from any human civilization as he could and live there alone. But as soon as the thought came to his mind, he dismissed it as impossible. He'd already lived alone for centuries.

No. Millennia, he corrected himself. *And how did that turn out?*

He had suffered, had become nearly unrecognizable to himself. Little more than an animal. And when the first opportunity presented itself, he couldn't resist human contact. Would it turn out any different if he were to isolate himself intentionally?

Probably not.

Now the portal was just sitting there, without any significant deterrent to keep people away. When other cultures learned that the Kaliel weren't demons, and that their god didn't exist, they would spread into these lands. Someone would eventually find the temple and the stump. Of course, it was closed. No one could let Rameel out without a key. And Sariel controlled both of them. But would he always? How could he know what the future would bring? Both keys were potential problems waiting to happen. What if he somehow lost them? What if they were taken from him? What if there was something in the future that he couldn't account for? What might this world become in another thousand or two thousand years? The portal and the keys both looked the same. It would be a logical conclusion for someone to bring them together. Perhaps Sariel could hide them. He wondered if he should take them to the same place where he had hidden the scroll. But would that place still exist a thousand years from now? There was no way to see into the future and plan for all contingencies.

Sariel could smell the ocean now, even though he couldn't see it yet. The smell reminded him of the days after the floodwaters receded. Aside from rotting corpses and decaying vegetation, the other predominant smell had been that of the ocean. And when he thought of all that water, he remembered seeing it as light, moving through the In-Between.

What if someone enters the In-Between from the other worlds?

He nearly fell off his horse when the thought occurred to him. After regaining his balance, he considered the possibility carefully. And the more he thought about it, the greater the risk seemed. If Ezekiyel or one of the other Myndarym entered the In-Between, they might find Rameel. Or Rameel might find them. Either way, there would be a key present to allow Rameel to return. And if he did come back, how might his approach to controlling this world change? Rameel would be more aware of his weaknesses. His approach would likely be far more aggressive. The only way to prevent that from happening was …

To hide the temple instead of the keys!

"I need to turn around!" he yelled to Wekesa, suddenly pulling back on the reins.

The young man turned and leaned forward to see beyond Ualiyo, who still rode with him even though there was a spare horse for her to ride.

Sariel's horse came to a stop.

Wekesa yelled something to the group before peeling away and slowing his horse.

Several heads turned, but it took a long while before the whole group stopped riding.

Everything seemed quiet now as Sariel looked back over the fields they had just crossed. There was a gentle breeze against his face. His horse shifted its weight, moving sideways. The terrain descended toward the west in a gradual slope. Sariel looked through the land with his eternal sight before he found what he was looking for. Then he pulled the reins to the side and turned his horse west before nudging the animal with his hips.

The horse started moving, but without the conviction that it usually displayed when following Shikoba. Sariel nudged it again and the walk became a trot. After several minutes, Sariel had reached one of the places where there were cracks below the soil—weaknesses in the earth's crust. He pulled his horse to a stop and climbed down.

"What are you doing?" Wekesa called to him. Somehow, the young man had gotten his horse to gallop and had caught up to Sariel quickly.

Behind him, to the east, the rest of the group was scattered across the plains. Shikoba had gone the farthest and was coming back toward the others.

"Why are we turning around?" Wekesa asked, pulling up alongside.

Sariel looked up to him. "I just realized there's something I need to do first. Will you take my horse back to Shikoba and ask everyone to wait there?"

Wekesa nodded, but his eyebrows were scrunched together.

Sariel handed him the reins. "It may take a while."

Wekesa took the reins and then nudged his horse into a walk. They circled around Sariel before heading east again toward the others, who were now gathered around each other.

As the sound of hooves receded into the distance, Sariel looked down into the earth again. The fracture in the land below his feet stretched as far as he could see to the north and south. It paralleled the mountain range still visible on the western horizon. And it was only one of hundreds. Where the group had gathered, the land was solid, but Sariel decided to get some distance from them just in case. He walked for a few minutes to the west until he found another fracture line that zigzagged through the depths like a bolt of lightning frozen in time.

The only way to prevent Rameel's return for certain was to block the surface of the stump. But piling rocks on top of it, or some other similar idea, wouldn't be sufficient. If Sariel were able to collapse the mountain on top of it, that might work. But he wasn't capable of that. Perhaps the inherent weaknesses in the earth's crust could be agitated to do the work. Sariel wasn't sure he was capable of that either, but something had to be done.

He shifted toward the Eternal just enough to see his spirits. Then he sent them down into the earth. He spread them out along the crack and tried to push against the western side. It was this portion of the land that ran beneath the temple, and if he could cause it to split apart just a little, the inherent tension between the two sides might accomplish the rest of the work. He closed his eyes and pushed, holding his breath as he strained. But there was no movement.

Perhaps another spot?

He walked farther to the south and found an area where the fissure was more defined. But when he sent his spirits down, they could only go as far as the land in the Eternal Realm. He continued south to another spot were the terrain in the Eternal left the temporal terrain exposed. He pushed there with all his might, but to no avail.

When he lifted his head to catch his breath, the saw that the dull light of the sun behind the clouds had already moved a handbreadth through the sky. He had no idea he had been at this for so long already. He looked east and found his traveling companions sitting in a circle on the ground. The horses were a short distance away with their heads down.

Sariel took a deep breath and wiped his forehead before scanning the ground again.

~

Hours passed by without any success. The group had started a small fire, and it smelled as though they were cooking something. A fire would have been considered an enormous risk only days ago; their confidence in Sariel's ability to protect them was heartwarming. Sariel only wished that his abilities would translate to a different use at the moment. He was on his hands and knees, trying to push both sides of the fissure away from each other. He thought that even his insufficient strength, if he applied it as he moved along, might be enough to set something in motion. But this wasn't working either. He had considered using the scepter and sword as tools that he could drive down into the earth, but it seemed ridiculous—like trying to split a tree with a pine needle.

Sariel finally came to a stop, staring at his hands in the dirt.

No ... definitely not The Awakened.

He breathed a sigh before sitting back.

Holy One, please help me!

It would have been Enoch's first instinct to ask, but the idea had only just occurred to Sariel. He felt ashamed to even try speaking with the Holy One, but who else was strong enough to do this? He closed his eyes and took a deep breath.

Holy One. I know I don't deserve to hear from You. I don't deserve to even ask for anything. But I'm asking anyway. Send this temple into the sea. Bring the mountains down around it. Please! I ask not for my own benefit or safety. I ask for these people ... these descendants of Adam. I know You have a plan for them; the Viytur made it a point to tell me that. I can't imagine that Your plan would include Rameel ruling over them. Please!

Sariel ran out of words to say, but he'd asked for what was needed. What else was there? He kept quiet, his eyes closed, listening for some response. He thought of what it must have been like for Enoch—to actually hear the voice of the Holy One. All he heard now was the breeze swishing the grasses around him. He was about to open his eyes, when he suddenly felt like there was more to say.

Holy One. I'm sorry for what I've done. I never should have come here; I know that now. Sometimes I wonder if Sheyir would have lived a long life if I hadn't interfered. I know I can't shift myself into the Eternal anymore, but if it were still possible, I would come back. I would present myself to Your Amatru and face whatever judgment You have for me.

Sariel breathed a heavy sigh. Even if the Holy One wasn't hearing his words, it still felt good to let them out.

I wanted Sheyir for myself. I loved her. After she was gone, I wanted revenge. I thought You had abandoned this realm. Then I thought that perhaps my rebellion was part of Your plan. I wanted to help these humans. So many motivations over the years … I can't remember them all now. I just know that I have failed. I kept trying to make things better and everything kept getting worse. Like Ebnisha …

Sariel began to cry. He thought of his friend being burned alive because of what Sariel told the Myndarym. Then he remembered Ebnisha's smile and his innocence, and it made him feel worse.

I'm sorry. I'm so sorry.

It was all he could think to say, over and over again. Every other word became jumbled in his head as if there was too much to say, and his apology was all that came out.

When he finally opened his eyes again, the clouds seemed to have cleared away. The fields were brighter than before, even though the sun was low on the horizon. He wiped at his eyes and looked to the east. His friends were now on their feet. Wekesa was pointing, and there was something about the way the others were standing that put Sariel on alert. He turned suddenly, glancing to the west.

But there was no army of Kaliel, or any such enemy approaching as he suspected. Instead, it appeared that the sun had come down from the sky to stand just a few paces behind him. The light was so intense that he couldn't look at it directly. It towered above him, and when it moved, Sariel fell backward and scrambled across the dirt.

"Do not be afraid, Sariel," said a voice out of the light.

Whether from fear or disbelief, it took several seconds before Sariel realized that it had used his name. He stopped crawling, but his heart was still surging within his chest.

The brightness dimmed and began to take on form.

"I'm sorry. I'm sorry," Sariel repeated.

"I know," said the light, now dim enough that the form of an angel could be made out.

Sariel watched the brightness continue fading until an Iryllur stood before him—one with mottled plumage of red, brown, and tan. His chestnut-colored hair was the first thing Sariel recognized, but it was the large golden eyes that brought his name to Sariel's lips.

"Tarsaeel?"

"Hello, Sariel." His voice was clear and deep, yet quiet, as though its natural power were being restrained.

"What are you doing here?"

"The Holy One has sent me to answer your prayer."

Sariel climbed to his feet and wiped his hands on his tunic before looking up again. "He heard me?"

"Nothing goes unheard from His ears."

Sariel didn't know what to say.

Tarsaeel turned to look east, where the others were still standing. They seemed frozen with fear. "Your friends are far enough away that they will be safe."

Sariel nodded, but wasn't sure what the angel meant.

Tarsaeel looked west toward the dark mountains along the horizon. "Let it be as you have asked," he said with a wave of his hand.

The ground began to vibrate, faint at first, growing to a rumble. Then the sound of thunder rolled across the plains, but not from above. It came from below. Sariel felt it in his feet, getting closer with every second. It seemed to build in intensity, then suddenly jolted, throwing him off his feet. Sariel stumbled, taking numerous steps before falling to his side on the dirt and grass. All of a sudden, the ground stopped shaking, while the sound of thunder continued. Sariel climbed to his feet and followed Tarsaeel's gaze to the west. All along the horizon, the mountains were moving. The temple mountain rose, and then the others followed it. Then it reversed direction and sank from view, dragging the others down as well. They fell in succession as a swell moves across the sea. One swell headed north and another south, crumbling the mountains as they moved. Then the field several hundred paces away split from north to south, and a great crack opened in the earth. A horrendous crashing sound filled the air, jolting the land with each sharp increase of volume. As far as the eye could see to the north and south horizons, the land west of Sariel began to break apart and drop from sight. The earth moved in swells and waves like water, with trees falling over on their sides. The rippling went in all directions, shattering everything into pieces.

The process seemed to move in a long, drawn-out moment, allowing plenty of time for Sariel to be amazed at Tarsaeel's demonstration of power. At some point, Sariel realized that the rippling fields and forests were actually liquid. The sea was swallowing up the land, breaking it apart and liquefying it.

The quaking of the earth slowly calmed. The thunderous crashing sounds gradually diminished. And when Sariel realized that it was over, the sun was close to the western horizon. It reflected off the muddy sea in a line of bright orange that cast shadows wherever chunks of land and floating debris were found. The waters still churned as they swallowed the last remains of the mountains, but the earth was now completely still.

Tarsaeel turned away from the new coastline and looked down at Sariel with a calm expression.

"How were you able to do that?" Sariel asked.

Tarsaeel's eyes narrowed. "Everything is different now ... since the Fracturing. I wish you would have stayed in the Eternal Realm."

Sariel wished that too, and he couldn't help but hang his head. After everything that had occurred, from Semjaza all the way to Rameel, human suffering had been the common thread between it all. Sheyir. Enoch. Ebnisha. All meaningful relationships; all fraught with suffering.

"Sariel, look at me."

Sariel lifted his eyes as he was told.

"All of this time in the Temporal, it has been your guilt driving you. What you intended for good always led to more problems, which in turn drove you to overcome them. And the cycle continued."

Sariel nodded. It was exactly how he felt.

"But I want you to know something ... your first instincts were correct."

"What do you mean?" Sariel asked.

"Do you remember Pri-Rada Himel?"

"Of course I do. He was one of the reasons I decided to leave the Eternal."

Tarsaeel came down on one knee as if he were speaking to a child. "He was inhabited."

Sariel stared into his friend's golden eyes, wondering if he was using the term correctly. "By a demon?"

"Yes."

"While I served under him?"

"Yes. All those times you struggled with his authority ... All those decisions that you disagreed with ..."

Sariel's hands came up to his face, but stopped short. He didn't know what to do with his own body while his mind raced with implications. He tried to recall all of the missions that he knew ahead of time would fail and the angels he'd watched die as a result.

"You were feeling the strain of serving under a demon."

"Did you know at the time?" Sariel asked, feeling anger beginning to rise inside his chest like fire.

"No, but others did. They couldn't tell you; it was an ongoing operation. They were feeding him information knowing that it would make its way to the Idnan."

Sariel suddenly realized something. "That day, when you came to me outside Bahyith ... you said I had no idea what I was getting myself into."

Tarsaeel nodded.

"You knew then, didn't you?"

"Yes."

"Why didn't you try harder to convince me?"

Tarsaeel's head tilted slowly to one side. "As I recall, we were practically yelling at each other. I *did* try harder. Why didn't you just trust me?"

He was right, of course. The words they'd exchanged that day revolved around Sheyir, and there was nothing that Tarsaeel could have said that would have made Sariel let go of her.

"As you can see," Tarsaeel continued, "we have been given more power. The war is changing dramatically, and the Holy One has reorganized the Amatru as a result. He has plans for this realm."

Sariel nodded. That fact had become increasingly obvious over the time he'd been here. If he had known it from the beginning, he wouldn't have felt the need to leave the Eternal Realm and help the people in the Temporal. But now that he looked back on it, Sariel could see that humans had been at the center of everything—the Amatru's attack against Semjaza, the Viytur's desire to save Lemek. Everything.

Humans were indeed important to the Holy One. And the most recent event that seemed to accentuate that point was Sariel's realization that he wasn't The Awakened. It was a human that would be raised up ... it seemed so obvious now. The Holy One would empower a human to defend humans. A human to battle the Myndarym. A human to bring angels to justice. With all of Sariel's training, experience, and cunning, he hadn't been able to end the reign of the Myndarym. They were too powerful, and he had stepped away from the challenge. In the eyes of humans, Sariel had the power of a god, and yet he had failed. Whoever this human warrior was, or would be, his power would have to be equal to the task. What a sight that would be to witness.

"I thought you'd like to know something else," Tarsaeel added.

Sariel realized he'd been lost in his own thoughts. "Yes?"

"The Holy One has invaded the Temporal Realm."

"He has? Where?"

"Second Earth ... as you would think of it."

"The one with Armaros?"

"And Satarel. And Kokabiel. Yes."

Sariel glanced to the east, watching his friends for a few seconds. Tarsaeel's appearance must have been frightening for them. They'd never seen an angel in natural form before. It had been frightening enough for Sariel. The thought that the Temporal Realm would now be getting support from the Eternal was comforting. "I'm glad the Amatru have finally been given authorization. How many soldiers?"

"No, it's not that kind of invasion. The Amatru didn't come. Just the Holy One ... by Himself."[7]

"I don't understand."

Tarsaeel smiled. "I know. And I can't explain any further. It's an active operation. What I've told you the Marotru already know. That's the only reason I'm authorized to disclose it to you now. All other details are classified."

"Of course they are," Sariel replied. There was always something he wasn't allowed to know. "So, what happens now?" he asked, looking back to his friends.

Tarsaeel took a deep breath that sounded ominous. "You took a human form. You were almost killed by a Nephiyl. Then you allowed yourself to be inhabited by a demon. And if that weren't enough, your body and spirit were multiplied."

Sariel nodded. "Yes, and now two thirds of me is dead. Why does this matter?"

"You are not well, my friend."

"I'm not what I used to be, but I feel fine enough."

"We made an agreement a long time ago. You would help the Viytur, and in return we would heal you. I'm here to honor that agreement. Vand-ra's presence is still intertwined with yours."

"I suppose it is," Sariel admitted.

"You will sleep for a time, and when you wake, your body and spirit will be healed. I do not know exactly how the changes will feel to you, but I know they will be significant."

"For a time? How long?"

"As long as it takes for you to recover."

"And then what? Will you take me back to face judgment?"

Tarsaeel's eyes narrowed. "You have sacrificed much ... in this realm and the other. Your decision to live as a human cannot be undone. It was by your own will that it happened. But the Holy One knows your desire for justice. You will be allowed to participate in His plans for this realm."

Sariel smiled, but tears came to his eyes as well. It felt like he was on the verge of something, the magnitude of which he couldn't understand. And by instinct, he knew this healing would take a very long time. He looked across the fields. Wekesa was looking back. The others were talking among themselves. "I need to say goodbye."

"Wekesa knows how you feel about him. As does his family. What can be said that hasn't already been spoken?"

Nothing, Sariel realized. But he didn't answer.

"They have their roles as well," Tarsaeel added.

It wasn't a promise, and yet it felt comforting to Sariel. "Very well."

"Lie down and close your eyes."

Sariel did as he was told, watching Wekesa's confused face disappear behind the stalks of grass as he lowered himself to the ground.

"First, you will sleep. Then I will sing over you."

"Tarsaeel," Sariel said, looking up into the golden eyes of his friend. "I'm sorry ... for everything."

Tarsaeel's smile was a sad one. "I know."

* * * *

When Tarsaeel finished singing over his friend, he picked up his limp body from the ground and stood. The humans waiting nearby looked more confused and frightened than ever. It was time.

Tarsaeel began walking toward them with calm steps. With the length of his stride, it took less than a minute to cross the field to where they were standing. As he approached, they shrank back.

"Don't be afraid," he told them. "I will not harm you."

They didn't look convinced.

"Shikoba, come forward."

The horseman of the plains appeared surprised that Tarsaeel knew his name. He was hesitant to move, but there was a great deal of courage within him. After several seconds, he let go of the reins he was holding and stepped forward.

Tarsaeel bent down and held out Sariel's limp body. "Shikoba of the Tasunke, I charge you to take my friend back to your people. Feed him and care for him. Protect him at all costs. Instruct your people to do the same until the day he wakes."

Shikoba nodded as he reached out and accepted Sariel's body.

Tarsaeel stayed in a kneeling posture so as not to intimidate the humans any more than they already were. "Wekesa. Bring me the scepter and the dagger."

The young man looked around nervously at his companions before walking to Sariel's horse and removing the items from the saddle. As instructed, he brought them over and handed them to Tarsaeel.

Tarsaeel separated the items and handed one back. "The scepter I give to you with the charge of keeping it hidden. Take Ualiyo back to your family. Pledge yourselves to one another. After a time, you will take your wife and children to another place. Wherever you go, take the scepter with you."

Wekesa accepted it with a nod and a furrowed brow.

"Dochin of the Odt."

The warrior came forward immediately, kneeling before Tarsaeel.

"This dagger I give to you with the charge of keeping it hidden. Take it back to your country, but do not let your people see it. Guard it with your very life, and instruct your children to do the same."

Dochin bowed his head before reaching up to take the weapon that was as large as a sword in his hands.

"Unnrik of the Syvaku."

The captain stepped forward.

"The land where your crew was to come ashore has been swallowed up by the sea. Even now they are sailing north to find their captain. All of you are to remain here. In three days' time your crew will arrive at this shore," Tarsaeel said, pointing south to the fields that now descended into the ocean nearby. "You will sail your companions back to Nijambu so they may go their separate ways."

Unnrik nodded before stepping back.

"And to all of you, I give the charge of revealing the truth. Tell your peoples that these lands are not the underworld. There are no demons here. There is no demon god to prevent them from settling this land. To anyone who will listen, tell them to drive the Kaliel out from wherever they are found. The followers of Rameel must not be given a home in any country. Do you understand these charges I've given to you?"

Everyone nodded.

"I must hear your agreement."

"Yes," they all said. "We understand."

Tarsaeel stood and surveyed the group that Sariel had assembled. Various cultures, each with their own practices and skills. Strengths and weaknesses. Their interactions would shape this world in the coming years and centuries. All was ready for the coming of the next age.

Tarsaeel extended his wings and took to the sky, warping the Temporal Realm around his body as he shifted into the Eternal.

EPILOGUE

Unnrik's crew witnessed the sinking of the land, and they braved the waves and swells that came after it. They knew Unnrik and the others had ridden north of where they went ashore, so they continued sailing due north from where the coastline had been. When they finally sighted land, it was a large peninsula with one coastline leading north and another heading to the northwest. The land to the northwest was steep and jagged, with cliffs of mud and rock where the other land had broken off from it. They sailed up this coastline for a few hours to survey the damage before turning south again, expecting to sail back to Nijambu without their captain. When they reached the tip of the peninsula, they were surprised to find Unnrik and most of the others waiting for them.

After returning everyone to Nijambu, Unnrik bid farewell to his traveling companions and sailed back to his homelands in the southwest without his rudder man, Molke. But what he brought back to his people would greatly affect their way of life. Dochin had let Unnrik keep the ax he had used in battle against the Kaliel. The combat instruction the captain had received from the warrior along the way, which had kept him alive in the face of so many enemies, had become the most prized of all his possessions. Though Unnrik had only just learned these skills, and had only a simple understanding of them, he began to teach what he knew to his people. He told them that the underworld was just another land, and the inhabitants were only men who dressed like demons to scare others away. Being a seafaring people of exploration, the Syvaku decided to send more explorers to this new land and test what Unnrik had taught them. One after another, they crossed the sea and established colonies. When they encountered bands of Kaliel, they fought them with their spears and axes, pushing the Kaliel farther inland. By the time Unnrik died, his people had a significant presence in this new land and had acquired a taste for conquest. Over the centuries that followed, the Syvaku became known for their raiding of coastlines all over the world.

When Dochin and his warriors returned to their own lands in the northwest, they too had been changed. But instead of passing on their knowledge to their people, they isolated themselves. Dochin feared that, if these new secrets were shared with the Odt peoples, he and the ideas would be challenged and rejected. Having seen a winged creature of the spirit world, and witnessing what the old man had been able to do against the Kaliel, it seemed to Dochin that there was much his people didn't understand.

He and his warriors had been entrusted with a sword of such beauty and perfection that it required deep contemplation. Its blade was curved just enough that each strike landed with the perfect combination of chopping and slicing actions. This maximized how deep each cut would penetrate into an enemy. The length of the handle required two hands to wield it, and yet it was light and balanced enough to be wielded with one. The tiniest of details, if observed with careful reverence, spoke volumes to these warriors. Over time, their weapons and methods evolved to accommodate this wisdom.

During all their years of travel, when they had been hired to protect shipments of precious cargo, Dochin and his warriors met thousands of people from dozens of other cultures. But no one impressed them more than the young man they had met in Nijambu. Wekesa had been quiet and introspective, possessing wisdom far beyond his years. While at sea, he had often been observed staring out over the ocean, his lips moving as he quietly recited something that he had memorized. On land, it seemed that he had conversations with the trees, laying his hands against their trunks as he spoke. When Dochin asked him what he was doing, the young man would answer with very few words, but somehow those words held layers of meaning that unfolded over the hours that followed. At the time, Dochin had thought that Wekesa's weakness was the price he had paid for achieving this wisdom. Yet when they all faced the Kaliel in their final battle, the young man had been so ferocious as to inspire everyone around him. As Dochin and his warriors later isolated themselves from their own people, Wekesa's practice of deep contemplation blended well with their study of combat, evolving into a new way of life for them. When their families grew over the decades that followed, the wisdom of these warriors became both a threat and a prize to others. By the time Dochin passed away, he left behind a new culture of the world's most secretive and feared warriors who lived within a walled fortress, forbidden and inaccessible to others, sitting high atop cliffs of sheer stone.

Wekesa took Ualiyo back to his family's new village near the burial grounds of Barsiri. Despite the Kaliel symbol burned into the girl's forehead, Wekesa's family welcomed her with open arms. They asked immediately about Saba and were saddened to learn that he wouldn't be coming back. During their evening meals, with everyone gathered around the fire, Wekesa told them everything that had transpired since he and Saba left for Nijambu. It took several evenings to tell the whole story, due to Wekesa's considerable memory. But when he had finished, his family seemed satisfied with what had been accomplished, making the loss of Saba more bearable.

Wekesa tried to give Zuberi's knife back to Mosi, but his oldest brother told him to keep it. And Mosi never teased Wekesa again, about finding a wife or anything else. Wekesa had left as a boy and come back a man. Over the following years, Ualiyo and Wekesa had many children. And though Wekesa was happy with his growing family and their place within the village, the scepter began to weigh on his mind. Having it so close to the hidden scroll seemed to be a great liability, and he feared that the Rana soldiers would find one or both and slaughter everyone as they had done before. And so Wekesa eventually took his wife and children, and they struck out on their own. There were several uninhabited islands off the southern coast of the Kaliel lands, where the Rana peoples were still afraid to venture. Wekesa's family flourished there for many generations.

As years passed by, and Mwangu Rana failed to come out of her temple, her empire began to change. The men, who had been so thoroughly oppressed by her power, found that their bitterness could be acted upon without repercussions. Being uneducated laborers and soldiers, they acted out in the only way they knew—with physical violence. The women, in turn, fought back with the skills they had learned from their goddess, using their beauty and their cunning words to inspire others to their defense. This only fueled the conflict, causing the men to fight back in order to maintain what little progress they had made. The conflict spiraled out of control, and the effects of it spread outward from Idorana to engulf the entire empire. The tribes that comprised the empire chose sides and warred against one another, and what had been the most powerful nation in the world eventually tore itself apart. In the aftermath of this prolonged civil war, the infrastructure that Zaquel had built for mining, trade, and agriculture was largely destroyed. Those who survived formed new tribes that reverted to their old ways in the absence of an overarching authority. In the following centuries, the southern lands became known as a densely populated region of primitive and superstitious people. Idorana was seen as a cursed place and fell into ruins after being abandoned. Nijambu kept operating as a trade port, but shrank drastically without the export of precious metals and other products for which the Rana Empire had become known.

It wasn't until many centuries later that Nijambu came back to life but for an entirely new type of export. With such a large population of people who had abandoned the long-term and large-scale thinking of previous generations, the southern lands became the hunting grounds for slave traders. Thousands of tribes, each with their own languages and beliefs, realized that they could profit from those whom they conquered. Without a unifying concept of identity, the tribes had no reservations about selling each other to the foreigners who still sailed to Nijambu from countries around the world.

After returning to Nijambu, Shikoba rejoined his other horsemen waiting there and all of them rode back to the plains of the south. They took Saba with them and cared for him just as the winged spirit had instructed them to do. The old man required no food or water, nor did he need to relieve himself. He just lay still, breathing steadily as if he were sleeping. But morning after morning, he failed to wake. Eventually, Shikoba taught others to care for the old man and gave responsibility for him to his son before passing away.

The Tasunke had always been a nomadic people. They followed the herds of mammals that kept them fed and clothed, continuing to breed and train their horses wherever they went. They had few enemies, and for many centuries, their way of life remained unchanged. Perhaps this is why the winged spirit, in his eternal wisdom, had given them the old man to care for. His white hair and beard grew and had to be trimmed every year, but beyond this no age came to the pale man. Saba became like a token to them, an unchanging object to represent their unchanging ways. Due to the expansion of other cultures, the Tasunke migrated away from the southern plains and settled again in the east. But their culture remained intact, and they kept their promise to care for the old man.

Sariel slept for almost two thousand years, and when he woke, he had no memory of the past or even his own identity. The nomadic people who cared for him as a prized possession called him Saba, which simply meant Old Man. He understood their language, but nothing else. And so he questioned them about how he had come to be among them, and how long he had slept. But the Tasunke gave little attention to years past or the years to come. They understood the cycles of the sun, but as their lives revolved around the present they could not recall the things Saba wished to know. Saba left them and wandered on his own for a time. He traveled the world and lived among various cultures, quickly discovering that he had a deep love for people and knowledge—both in learning it and in sharing it. He seemed to know, by instinct, things that these cultures had acquired over long periods of time. He was fascinated to see the subtle, and sometimes drastic, differences between the peoples of the earth. This fascination was strong enough to keep him from settling in one place for more than a few years. It seemed that there was something missing from his life.

In his dreams, a vision kept returning to him again and again. He stood on a peninsula, looking west across the ocean. The setting sun was reflected in the waters, a dazzling display of orange light that danced before him as if it were alive. Saba felt that if he could only find this place, his soul would be at rest. So he searched the world until the terrain around him looked like the one in his dreams. It took many years, but his journeys eventually brought him back to the lands of the Kaliel, though he had no memory of the battles or the friendships that he had experienced there.

By the time he arrived, a new nation had been established; the Orudan Empire was already thriving. Its people had come from a different part of the world, bringing with them everything they had learned through the myths about the gods of old. Their ideas about how various parts of a nation should function were unique among humans, and they brought with them a highly skilled and disciplined military. Both were put to the test as they encountered what they believed to be the native barbarians of the land. They fought with the Syvaku, destroying their villages and steadily pushing the tall, pale savages back into the ocean where their boats could take them across the sea. The Orudan also battled the Korgan barbarians, forcing these nomads to retreat to the mist-laden moors of the northeast from where they had come. And when these dark-haired, pale primitives had been driven beyond where the Orudan cared to live, the empire erected a stone wall along its northeastern boundary to keep them out. But if truth be told, the Orudan hated neither the Syvaku nor the Korgan. They simply had to make room for themselves if their empire was to flourish.

Their hatred had been saved for the Kaliel—the dark, filthy creatures who wore the bones of animals in order to frighten others. They called themselves demons, and lurked in the forests at night. They stole children from their mothers and anyone else who ventured too far away from their village or city. It was said that the Kaliel ate human flesh, and that their demon god gave them power when they did so. The Orudan pursued the Kaliel with all their might, following them into the forests and caves where they hid. The last of the Kaliel strongholds was discovered on an island far to the north, where priests of their sickening order had written down the knowledge of their god and had kept their own history. The Orudan sacked their village on the cliffs, but the Kaliel priests escaped with their writings. For decades afterward, stories about the demon god circulated, much to the anger of the Orudan. It was said that the god of the Kaliel, who had been more powerful than any other, left the world and its inhabitants so they might understand life without him. When the peoples of the earth understood the mistake of their waning devotion, and repented of their unfaithfulness, their true god would return to claim the world as his own once again.

After he left, ocean levels all across the world dropped and eventually stabilized. The only one who could have understood the cause of it was asleep. It was the portal, hidden deep within a mountain of black stone, which pulled the ocean water into itself. The key that had opened the portal had been removed before its owner had completed his passage. And since the portal had no limit to its capacity, it continued drawing in the oceans until the top of the mountain was exposed and all the water inside was emptied. Being the tallest peak of the mountain range, it was the only one exposed to the open air. The other mountains lurked just beneath the surface, creating shallows where coral thrived. The reef prevented humans from sailing through the area, and so the portal remained hidden from men. It wasn't until the final decades of the Orudan Empire that a man, seeking ancient and forbidden knowledge, reestablished the Kaliel and rebuilt their temple in secret. His devotion was so strong that he found himself able to hear the voice of the demon god and receive his wisdom. Among the goals given him by his god were two of the utmost importance. The first was to locate an object of great power that would usher in the return of his god. The second was to find and imprison a certain old man with white hair and beard.

It was under these circumstances that Saba found himself settling down in Bastul, the southernmost port of the Orudan Empire. The city had been built around the bay on the tip of a peninsula, and was known as the southern jewel for its spectacular view of sunrises and sunsets over the ocean. The sandy finger of land had come into existence ages before, and no one remembered how. As Saba was accustomed to doing, he began making friends and integrating himself into the culture there. After a time, his wisdom had earned him a reputation and caught the ear of the governor, who was in need of a tutor for his son.

It was a simple twist of fate that later caused a merchant sailor to wander from his intended route along the western coast near Bastul. When he disappeared, the governor went looking for him and accidentally stumbled upon secrets that had been hidden for millennia. Unknown to him at the time, this man's actions would trigger a series of events that would set into motion the resolution of an ancient struggle. These events marked the beginning of the next great epoch of this saga—the time of The Awakened. But that ... is a different story.

THE END

OTHER BOOKS
BY JASON TESAR

THE AWAKENED SERIES

Over five thousand years ago, a renegade faction of angels abandoned the spiritual realm and began their inhabitation of earth. Worshiped as gods for their wisdom and power, they corrupted the realm of the physical and forever altered the course of history.

Amidst the chaos of a dying world, a lone voice foretold the awakening of a warrior who would bring an end to this evil perpetrated against all of creation. But with the cataclysmic destruction of earth and rebirth of humanity, the prophecy went unfulfilled and eventually faded from the memory of our kind—until now!

In his debut series, Jason Tesar delves into the heart of an ancient legend, embarking on an epic saga that will journey from earth's mythological past to its post-apocalyptic future, blending the genres of fantasy, sci-fi, and military/political suspense.

AWAKEN HIS EYES | BOOK 1

The physical dimension is fractured. What remain now are numerous fragmented worlds moving simultaneously through time, sharing a common history, connected only by a guarded portal. On a parallel earth, in the city of Bastul, Colonel Adair Lorus disappears while investigating the death of an informant, triggering a series of events which will tear his family apart and set in motion the resolution of an ancient struggle. Kael, sentenced to death after rising up against the cruel leadership of his new step-father, is rescued from prison and trained in the arts of war by a mystical order of clerics. Excelling in every aspect of his training, Kael inwardly struggles to give himself fully to the methods of his new family, or the god they worship. Maeryn, bitter over the disappearance of her husband and supposed execution of her son, fears for her life at the hands of her newly appointed husband. Finding comfort and purpose in her unborn child, she determines to undermine his authority by reaching out to an underground social movement known as the Resistance. After being forced from his home, Kael's former mentor, Saba, uncovers a clue to Adair's disappearance. Sensing a connection to his own forgotten past, Saba begins an investigation which leads to the discovery of a secret military organization operating within the Orudan Empire.

PATHS OF DESTRUCTION | BOOK 2

Returning to his home city of Bastul, Kael finds the Southern Territory of the Orudan Empire under invasion. As he races to unravel the secrecy of the enemy's identity, he becomes entangled in a brutal conspiracy to gain control of the government. After years of collaboration with the Resistance, Maeryn coordinates the covert exodus of the entire slave population of Bastul. Along their treacherous journey to the capital city of Orud, she is faced with the pressures of leadership as she attempts to protect her daughter and ensure the survival of her companions. Saba, held captive by a mysterious military force, escapes after years of solitary confinement. Propelled by an elusive memory, he chases after the hope of rediscovering his past and learns that everyone's future is in jeopardy.

HANDS TO MAKE WAR | BOOK 3

After fighting his way back from a paralyzing defeat, Kael resolves to bring an end to the enemies of the Orudan Empire. Enlisting the help of his family and most-trusted friends, he faces off against an ancient evil and embraces his destiny. As Maeryn rises through the ranks to attain a command position within the Resistance, she learns of a conspiracy in her organization and realizes the enormous resources at her disposal. Determined to set things right, she seizes control and sets a new course for the movement. Reacquainting with his closest friends, Saba pieces together the identity and motive of the enemy. Bringing his vast knowledge to bear, he collaborates with Orud's High Council to force the enemy into the open, while waiting to reveal a secret of his own.

SEEDS OF CORRUPTION | BOOK 4

The All Powerful is dead, but the scars of his influence remain, haunting Kael's memories and discoloring his outlook. Seeking closure, Kael retraces the steps of his past. When he discovers that his father may still be alive, the course of his life once again takes an unexpected turn. Determined to answer the most profound questions of his childhood, Kael ventures across the fractured physical dimension. What awaits him is an advanced civilization of private armies and foreign weaponry, and only one path leads to his goal. Entering a covert war of intelligence and paramilitary operations, Kael must adapt to this new world and confront the possibility that his own destiny is just beginning. The seeds of corruption have taken root, but the Awakened has come.

HIDDEN FROM MEN | BOOK 5

A powerful adversary is surfacing and Null's covert battle is on the threshold of open war. Reunited with his father after twenty-two years, Kael must find the balance between protecting him and confronting the enemy who stands between them and their home world. The timelessness of the In-Between has stolen the years that separated Kael and Adair by age, leaving them as distant equals. Having glimpsed Kael's destiny from the Eternal Realm, Adair struggles to find his role in the life of a son who no longer needs him. Through a global maze of counterintelligence and espionage, a multinational team of operatives has to survive long enough to turn the tide of war. And a father and son will discover how to rebuild what was taken from their lives.

FOUNDATIONS OF THE WORLD | BOOK 6

Kael has seen into the mind of the enemy and witnessed an abomination beyond imagining. Thousands of years of collaboration have allowed the Myndarym to construct a vast and complex system for exploiting the earth and its inhabitants. It is an ancient legacy of evil, and for the remnants of Null to destroy it, they must capture the system's last surviving creator. Kael has only one advantage against this ruthless warrior, but leveraging it will take him through a battlefield of the world's most advanced weaponry and expose his greatest weaknesses—patience and trust. The journey will bring them all together in ways they never thought possible, leading to a startling revelation that will shake the very foundations of the world.

BOOK 7 AND BEYOND...

Watch Kael's destiny unfold with the continuation of the *Awakened* series. Visit www.jasontesar.com for behind-the-scenes information and release dates for future books.

ABOUT THE AUTHOR

The third of four children and an introvert from the start, Jason Tesar grew up as an imaginative "middle child" who enjoyed the make-believe world as much as the real one, possibly more. From adolescence to adulthood, his imagination fed itself on a diet of books, movies, and art, all the while growing and maturing—waiting for its opportunity. Then, during a procession of monotonous, physically laborious day-jobs, his imagination leaped into motion, bringing together characters and locations of a world that would someday come to life on the pages of a book.

In late 1998, Jason made his first attempt at writing, managing to complete a whole scene before returning once again to reality. A year and a half later, a spontaneous night-time conversation with his wife encouraged him to take his writing seriously and to keep on dreaming. Over the next seven years, Jason carved time out of the real world to live in an imaginary one of epic fantasy, science-fiction, and military/political conflict. The fruits of this labor became the first three books of the bestselling AWAKENED series.

Due to the amazing support from readers around the world, Jason has continued his trajectory into make-believe, recently jumping from stable employment in the micro-electronics industry into the mysterious abyss of full-time writing.

Living in Colorado with his beautiful wife and two children, Jason now spends the majority of his time fusing the best parts of his favorite genres into stories of internal struggle and triumph, friendship, betrayal, political alliances, and military conflict. His fast-paced stories span ancient and future worlds, weaving together threads of stirring drama and intense action that provoke reader comments such as, "I couldn't put it down," and "I'll read anything he writes."

GLOSSARY
AND PRONUNCIATION GUIDE

The following is a glossary of names, titles, terms, places, and characters that are used throughout this book.

The *vowels* section below contains characters, or arrangements of characters, which are used in the pronunciation section of glossary entries. Each vowel sound is followed by an example of common words using the same sound.

The *additional consonants* section also contains characters, or arrangements of characters, which are used in the pronunciation section of glossary entries. These sounds are not used in the English language, but examples are found in other languages and are listed for reference.

Glossary entries contain the word or phrase, its correct pronunciation (including syllables and emphasis), the translation of the word or phrase, its culture of derivation, and a description. The format for each entry is as follows:

Word or phrase \proh-**nuhn**-see-ey-shuhn\ *Translation* [Derivation] Description

Vowels

[a]	apple, sad
[ey]	hate, day
[ah]	arm, father
[air]	dare, careful
[e]	empty, get
[ee]	eat, see
[eer]	ear, hero
[er]	early, word
[i]	it, finish
[ahy]	sight, blind
[o]	odd, frost
[oh]	open, road

[ew]	f<u>oo</u>d, shr<u>ew</u>d
[oo]	g<u>oo</u>d, b<u>oo</u>k
[oi]	<u>oi</u>l, ch<u>oi</u>ce
[ou]	l<u>ou</u>d, h<u>ow</u>
[uh]	<u>u</u>nder, t<u>ug</u>

Additional Consonants

[r]	<u>r</u>oho (Spanish)
[zh]	<u>j</u>oie de vivre (French)
[kh]	lo<u>ch</u> (Scots)

Glossary

<u>Adam</u> \ah-**dahm**\ *Man* [Shayeth] The first human, created rather than born. Husband of Eve. Father of Kahyin, Hevel, Shayeth, and Yahsad. See Genesis 2:19.

<u>Aden</u> **ey**-den\ *Pleasure* [Shayeth] The first place of human habitation on earth. See Genesis 2:8.

<u>Akuji</u> \ah-**kew**-jee\ *Dead But Awake* [Kham] Rameel's favorite Nephiyl son.

<u>Amatru</u> **ah**-mah-trew\ *Faithful* [Angelic] The combined military forces of the Eternal Realm who have remained faithful to the Holy One. The angelic military.

<u>Aleydam</u> \al-**eyd**-em\ *People Above The Mist* [Shayeth] The mountain tribe that accepted Sariel and Sheyir into their village after the war against Semjaza.

<u>Aleydiyr</u> \al-**eyd**-eer\ *City Above The Mist* [Shayeth] The city of the Aleydam.

<u>Ananel</u> **a**-nah-nel\ *Unknown* [Angelic] The first angel to befriend Enoch, whom he encountered after the Kahyin took the Prophet captive. See The Book of Enoch 6:8.

<u>Anduar</u> **an**-dew-ahr\ *Land Force* [Angelic] The singular name for a member of the land force of the Amatru. Angel of the land.

Anduarym **an**-dew-ah*r* im\\ *Land Forces* [Angelic] The plural name for members of the land force of the Amatru. Angels of the land.

Aniyl \\an-**eel**\\ *Fallen of Land* [Angelic, Kahyin] Singular name for a Nephiyl of Anduar and human origin.

Aragatsiyr **ah**-*r*ah-gaht-see*r*\\ *Woven Trees* [Shayeth] The name that Enoch gave to the city of the Myndarym, which they established after their rebellion from Semjaza. See also Senvidar.

Atah \\ah-**tah**\\ *Destroy* [Demonic] An Unshaper of the Marotru. The demonic name for a Nin-Myndar.

Aytsam **eyt**-sahm\\ *People of the Trees* [Chatsiyr] A human tribe, descended from the Kahyin, which attacked the Chatsiyram and took Sheyir prisoner.

Azael **a**-zey-el\\ *Unknown* [Angelic] Former Fim-Rada of Semjaza's Iryllurym and one of Semjaza's personal guards. See The Book of Enoch 6:8.

Baerlagid \\bey-air-**lah**-gid\\ *Songs of Creation* [Angelic] The comprehensive, musical language used by the Holy One to bring all things into existence out of nothing. A small subset of Baerlagid was taught to the Myndarym for the purpose of *reshaping* the Temporal Realm to make it self-sustaining after its separation from the Eternal Realm.

Bahyith \\bah-**yith**\\ *House, Dwelling* [Chatsiyr] The village of the Chatsiyram, situated between the mountains of Bokhar and Ehrevhar.

Barsiri \\bah*r*-**si**-ree\\ *Hidden Sleep* [Kham] The ancient burial grounds of Ebnisha's people.

Chatsiyr **kat**-see*r*\\ *Grass* [Chatsiyr] The singular name for a member of the small human tribe, descended from the Shayetham, which used to occupy the valley between Bokhar and Ehrevhar. The people of Sheyir. The residents of Bahyith.

Chatsiyram **kat**-see*r*-am\\ *People of the Grass* [Chatsiyr] The plural name for the members of the small human tribe, descended from the Shayetham, which used to occupy the valley between Bokhar and Ehrevhar. The people of Sheyir. The residents of Bahyith.

Dagjani \dahg-**jah**-nee\ *Long Leaf* [Kham] The name of Ualiyo's village.

Dochin **doh**-chin\ *Unknown* [Shem] The leader of the Odt warriors that Sariel met in Nijambu.

Ebnisha **eb**-ni-shuh\ *Unknown* [Kham] Friend and scribe of Sariel. Brother of Mosi, Imamu, Zuberi, and Wekesa.

Eili **ey**-i-lee\ *Eternal* [Angelic] The Eternal Realm. The portion of the creation spectrum that is eternal, in contrast to the portion that is temporal.

Ekua \e-**kew**-uh\ *Wednesday Born* [Kham] Wife of Mosi. Sister-in-law to Ebnisha.

El-Betakh \el-be-**tahk**\ *God's Safety, God's Protection* [Shayeth] The city founded by Enoch, so named because the Holy One showed Enoch where his people would be safe from destruction.

Enoch **ee**-nahk\ *Dedicated* [Shayeth] Friend of Sariel. Husband of Zacol. Father of Methushelak. Prophet of the Shayetham. See Genesis 5:18.

Eve **eev**\ *Living* [Shayeth] The first human female, formed rather than born. See Genesis 3:20.

Eyota \ey-oh-**tah**\ *Great* [Shem] One of Shikoba's horsemen.

Ezekiyel \e-ze-kee-el\ *Unknown* [Angelic] A master *Shifter* and *Shaper* of the Myndarym who taught others how to move beings from the Eternal Realm to the Temporal Realm. See The Book of Enoch 6:7.

Galah \gah-**lah**\ *Exile* [Shayeth] The city of Adam, so named because the earth outside of Aden was the place of his exile.

Gebhuza **geb**-ew-zuh\ *Butcher, Slasher* [Kham, Yefeth] One of Rameel's Nephiyl sons. Akuji's younger brother.

Hridiam **hrid**-ee-uhm\ *Cliffs of Darkness* [Yefeth] Rameel's cliff city, north of the temple.

Idnan **id**-nahn\\ *Knowledge* [Demonic] The Marotru intelligence organization. The counterpart to the Amatru's Viytur.

Idorana **i**-doh-*r*ah-nah\\ *Eye of the Sun* [Kham] The capital city of the Rana Empire and home of Zaquel.

Imamu \\i-**mah**-mew\\ *Spiritual Leader* [Kham] Ebnisha's second oldest brother. Birth order is Mosi, Imamu, Ebnisha, Zuberi, and Wekesa.

Iryllur **eer**-i-lewr\\ *Air Force* [Angelic] The singular name for a member of the air force of the Amatru. Angel of the sky.

Iryllurym **eer**-i-lewr-im\\ *Air Forces* [Angelic] The plural name for the air forces of the Amatru. Angels of the sky.

Kahyin **kah**-yin\\ *Possession* [Kahyin] The firstborn son of Adam, who killed his younger brother Hevel. Also, the singular and plural name of the largest human tribe, descended from Kahyin. See Genesis 4:1.

Kham **kham**\\ *Hot/Heated* [Shayeth] Middle son of Noah and Beyahn. Brother of Shem and Yefeth. See Genesis 5:32.

Khanok **kan**-ahk\\ *Dedicated* [Shayeth] The Shayeth name for the home city of the Kahyin tribe. See Genesis 4:17.

Lemek \\le-**mek**\\ *Powerful* [Shayeth] The firstborn son of Methushelak and Jurishel. See Genesis 5:25.

Marotru **mah**-*r*oh-trew\\ *Unfaithful* [Angelic] The combined military forces of the Eternal Realm who rebelled against the Holy One to follow the Evil One. The demonic military.

Matunda \\mah-**tuhn**-duh\\ *Fruitful* [Kham] The name of Ebnisha's village.

Methushelak \\me-**thew**-she-lak\\ *Man of the Dart* [Shayeth] The firstborn son of Enoch and Zacol. Father of Lemek. Also called Methu. See Genesis 5:21.

Molke **mohl**-key\\ *Gull* [Yefeth] The rudder man of Unnrik's ship.

Mosi **moh**-see\ *Firstborn Child* [Kham] Ebnisha's oldest brother. Birth order is Mosi, Imamu, Ebnisha, Zuberi, and Wekesa.

Mwangu Rana \mwahn-**gew** *r*ah-**nah**\ *Goddess of the Sun* [Kham] Goddess of the Rana Empire. Zaquel's title.

Myndar **min**-dahr\ *Shaper* [Angelic] The singular name of a member of the Myndarym.

Myndarym **min**-dah*r*-im\ *Shapers* [Angelic] The plural name of the angelic race that was entrusted with a small subset of the Songs of Creation for the purpose of *reshaping* the Temporal Realm to make it self-sustaining after its separation from the Eternal Realm.

Nephiyl \nef-**eel**\ *Fallen* [Kahyin, Shayeth] The generic singular name for any child of angelic and human—or animal—origin. See Genesis 6:4.

Nephiylim \nef-**eel**-im\ *Fallen People* [Kahyin, Shayeth] The generic plural name for any children of angelic and human—or animal—origins. See Genesis 6:4.

Nijambu \ni-**jam**-bew\ *Unknown* [Kham] The largest port city of the Rana Empire, located on its western shore.

Njiawaye **njahy**-ah-wey\ *Path of Tears* [Kham] The great river that flows east through Idorana and into the eastern ocean.

Noah **noh**-uh\ *Rest* [Shayeth] Son of Lemek and Elah. Husband of Beyahn. Father of Shem, Kham, and Yefeth. See Genesis 5:29.

Nyaden **nahy**-ah-den\ *New Pleasure* [Angelic, Shayeth] New Aden. Ezekiyel's city in Third Earth, built around the stump of the Tree of Wisdom where Aden used to be.

Odt **oht**\ *Star Flower* [Shem] The name of Dochin's people, who live in the north.

Pri-Rada **pree**-rah-dah\ *Third Rule* [Angelic] The third position of rank among the Amatru.

Rada **rah**-dah\ *Rule* [Angelic] A title of respect among the Amatru, used to signify one's superior.

<u>Reshaping</u>   The period in creation's history, immediately following *The Great Turning Away*, when the Myndarym used the *Songs of Creation* to *shape* the Temporal Realm so that it could become self-sustaining after it began separating from the Eternal Realm. Also called Omynd.

<u>Sariel</u> **sah**-ree-el\ *Minister Appointed by God* [Angelic] Formerly a Myndar, who became a soldier of the Iryllurym and was later confined to a human form. See The Book of Enoch 6:8.

<u>Sedekiyr</u> \sed-e-**keer**\ *City of Justice, Righteousness* [Shayeth] The city founded by Yered, so named for its location on the level plains or flatlands, and not as an indication of morality.

<u>Semjaza</u> \sem-**jah**-zah\ *Unknown* [Angelic] Formerly a Pri-Rada of the Amatru until his invasion of the Temporal Realm. See The Book of Enoch 6:7.

<u>Senvidar</u> **sen**-vi-dahr\ *Twisted Trees* [Angelic] The city of the Myndarym, which they established after their rebellion from Semjaza. See also Aragatsiyr.

<u>Seraph</u> **sair**-ahf\ *To Burn* [Angelic] The singular name for the angelic creatures who surround the throne of the Holy One. Each one has six wings (two that cover the face, two that cover the feet, and two that are used for flying). Each has a human-like body with arms and legs. See Isaiah 6.

<u>Seraphym</u> \sair-ahf-**im**\ *To Burn* [Angelic] The plural name for the angelic creatures who surround the throne of the Holy One.

<u>Shalakh Akhar</u> \shah-**lahk** ahk-**ahr**\ *After Exile* [Shayeth] A reference point for measurement of time; also abbreviated *SA*. The first humans were immortal prior to their exile from Aden, therefore, the passage of time was irrelevant to them. The practice of referring to events and objects in the past-tense only came into being when there was a noticeable difference between their past and present states. This occurred during the time of their banishment and the translated phrase *after exile* came into use.

<u>Shape</u> The ability of a Myndar to alter its form or the form of another being or object.

<u>Shayeth</u> **shey**-eth\\ *Compensation* [Shayeth] The thirdborn son of Adam and Eve. Also, the singular name for a member of the Shayetham. See Genesis 4:25.

<u>Shayetham</u> **shey**-eth-em\\ *People of Compensation* [Shayeth] The plural name for the second-largest of the human tribes, descended from Shayeth. See Genesis 4:25.

<u>Shem</u> **shem**\\ *Name* [Shayeth] Oldest son of Noah and Beyahn. Brother of Kham and Yefeth. See Genesis 5:32.

<u>Sheyir</u> **shey**-eer\\ *Song* [Chatsiyr] The youngest daughter of Yeduah. Wife of Sariel.

<u>Shift</u> The ability of a Myndar to move its body, consciousness, or another object from one point to another along the spectrum of creation.

<u>Shikoba</u> **shee**-koh-bah\\ *Feather* [Shem] The leader of the Tasunke horsemen than Sariel met in Nijambu.

<u>Tarsaeel</u> **tahr**-sey-el\\ *Unknown* [Angelic] Sariel's friend in the Viytur. Formerly a Myndar who became a soldier.

<u>Tasunke</u> \\tah-**sewn**-kahy\\ *Horse* [Shem] The name of Shikoba's nomadic people, who live on the southern plains.

<u>Tima</u> **tee**-mah\\ *Temporal* [Angelic] The Temporal Realm. The portion of the creation Spectrum that separated from the Eternal Realm and became temporal.

<u>Ualiyo</u> \\ew-**al**-i-yoh\\ *Floating Flower* [Kham] The girl who was given as an annual sacrifice by the holy men to the Kaliel and later rescued by Wekesa.

<u>Unnrik</u> **ewn**-rik\\ *Wave* [Yefeth] Captain of the Syvak explorers that Sariel met in Nijambu.

<u>Unshape</u> The ability of a Nin-Myndar to destroy the form of another being or object.

<u>Vaepkir</u> **veyp**-keer\\ *Arm Blade* [Angelic] The singular and plural name for the arm-blade weaponry used by the Iryllurym. When held in the standard position, it functions as a ramming

weapon during air-based attacks. When held in a reverse position, it functions as a stabbing weapon during ground-based, or hand-to-hand combat.

<u>Vand-ra</u> \vahnd-**ra**\ *Evil* [Demonic] The Atah or Nin-Myndar who was Sariel's greatest adversary in the Eternal Realm.

<u>Vidir</u> \vi-**deer**\ *Sea Force* [Angelic] The singular name for a member of the sea force of the Amatru.

<u>Vidirym</u> \vi-**deer**-im\ *Sea Forces* [Angelic] The plural name for members of the sea forces of the Amatru.

<u>Viytur</u> **vee**-tew*r*\ *Wisdom* [Angelic] The Amatru intelligence organization. The Viytur is a cross-branch force, specializing in the gathering and analysis of information and controlled implementation of its conclusions.

<u>Wekesa</u> \wey-**kes**-uh\ *Harvest Child* [Kham] Ebnisha's youngest brother. Birth order is Mosi, Imamu, Ebnisha, Zuberi, and Wekesa.

<u>Yefeth</u> \ye-**feth**\ *Opened* [Shayeth] Youngest son of Noah and Beyahn. Brother of Shem and Kham. See Genesis 5:32.

<u>Zuberi</u> \zew-**be**-ree\ *Powerful* [Kham] One of Ebnisha's younger brothers. Birth order is Mosi, Imamu, Ebnisha, Zuberi, and Wekesa.

REFERENCES

1. ... the angels which kept not their first estate, but left their own habitation, he hath reserved in everlasting chains under darkness unto the judgment of the great day ... **wandering stars**, to whom is reserved the blackness of darkness forever (Jude 1:6, 13, KJV).

2. ... for the Lord God had not caused it to rain upon the earth ... But there went up a mist from the earth, and watered the whole face of the ground (Genesis 2:5-6, KJV).

3. And the ark rested in the seventh month, on the seventeenth day of the month, upon the mountains of Ararat (Genesis 8:4, KJV).

4. And God said unto Noah, The end of all flesh is come before me; for the earth is filled with violence through them ... (Genesis 6:13, KJV).

5. And it came to pass in the six hundredth and first year, in the first month, the first day of the month, the waters were dried up from off the earth: and Noah removed the covering of the ark, and looked, and, behold, the face of the ground was dry (Genesis 8:13, KJV).

6. And the Lord said, My spirit shall not always strive with man, for that he also is flesh: yet his days shall be an hundred and twenty years (Genesis 6:3, KJV).

7. Behold, a virgin shall be with child, and shall bring forth a son, and they shall call his name Emmanuel, which being interpreted is, God with us (Matthew 1:23, KJV). And the angel said unto her, Fear not, Mary: for thou hast found favour with God. And, behold, thou shalt conceive in thy womb, and bring forth a son, and shalt call his name Jesus. He shall be great, and shall be called the Son of the Highest: and the Lord God shall give unto him the throne of his father David: And he shall reign over the house of Jacob forever; and of his kingdom there shall

be no end (Luke 1:30-33, KJV). And the Word was made flesh, and dwelt among us, and we beheld his glory, the glory as of the only begotten of the Father, full of grace and truth (John 1:14, KJV).

ACKNOWLEDGEMENTS

I would like to thank Mike Heath for creating some of the most awesome fantasy covers I've seen. There is a great deal of symbolism in each piece, and when the whole collection is viewed as one, it captures the essence of what I have been trying to accomplish through writing. This has been a fun project on which to collaborate.

I would also like to thank Marcia Fry, Ronda Swolley, Claudette Cruz, and Nicholas Cowan for their editing inputs. It's easy to miss the forest for the trees, so I'm thankful to have a team of people looking at the details to find the things I've missed.

Made in the USA
Columbia, SC
18 August 2020